Also available from Ruby Lang

Acute Reactions
Hard Knocks
Clean Breaks

Practice Perfect: The Complete Series

THE UPTOWN COLLECTION

RUBY LANG

carina
press

carina press®

Recycling programs
for this product may
not exist in your area.

ISBN-13: 978-1-335-00854-1

The Uptown Collection

Copyright © 2020 by Mindy Hung

Playing House
First published in 2019. This edition published in 2020.
Copyright © 2019 by Mindy Hung

Open House
First published in 2019. This edition published in 2020.
Copyright © 2019 by Mindy Hung

House Rules
First published in 2020. This edition published in 2020.
Copyright © 2020 by Mindy Hung

This edition published by arrangement with Harlequin Books S.A.

For questions and comments about the quality of this book, please contact us at CustomerService@Harlequin.com.

Carina Press
22 Adelaide St. West, 40th Floor
Toronto, Ontario M5H 4E3, Canada
www.CarinaPress.com

Printed in U.S.A.

CONTENTS

PLAYING HOUSE

Chapter One

Sunday

In all their years as wary mutual acquaintances, Oliver Huang never expected Fay Liu to be so happy to see him. But here she was, in this showcase home on the Mount Morris Park historic house tour, flashing Oliver a huge, almost desperate smile. She stepped right up to kiss him heartily on the lips, and in the process knocked his glasses askew, smudging them.

Then as he reached up to adjust them, she commandeered his arm and linked hers through his.

Fay was a fellow urban planner and, most importantly, she was a partner at Milieu. They had mutual friends. He'd even sent her firm a CV, and had finally received a follow-up from one of her partners expressing interest just that morning. For a fuzzy moment, he wondered if she was here, had sought him out directly, to arrange the interview. Still, he hadn't expected Fay to be quite so warm and, well, *handsy? lipsy?—was that a word?*—about greeting a potential employee.

And wasn't she married?

But she gripped him more tightly and snuggled into his side. She felt *good* tucked into him. So, he allowed himself to relax, to enjoy touching another human body again, to almost hug someone, to feel needed, and wanted, and seen.

It was such a fleeting, wonderful connection. Fleeting, because in less than a minute, he understood what this was.

A man clomped up to them and scowled at the picture Oliver and Fay presented, standing in the upper hallway of the brownstone, looking for all the world like a pair of proud new homeowners.

Such a lovely illusion.

"Oh, so this is the boyfriend you were talking about," Clompy Man said.

Fay tipped her head back, her glossy hair catching the light, and gazed up at Oliver adoringly. "Oliver, Brent here was offering to take me to the rest of the stops on the tour. But I said I was waiting for you to arrive, because I know you're such an architecture hound that you wouldn't want to miss it."

"I'm sorry I was late. I got held up at the, uh, boxing gym."

To her credit, she did not roll her eyes. *Boxing gym.* Oliver had never been inside a boxing gym if that's what they were called. Fay said, "That's all right, honey. I know how much you enjoy sparring. You're so strong and quick on your feet."

She gave his biceps a squeeze, two, as if the first weren't enough, and he almost laughed aloud.

She felt it, too. Even if their improvised dialog was stilted and terrible—or maybe *because* it was—they shared genuinely amused grins.

Brent the Clomper didn't appear quite as delighted with their acting skills.

He stood there, looking at them, breathing heavily. Eying Brent's heavily muscled torso, Oliver wondered if he was about to get into a fight for the first time in his adult life. It was unlikely—very unlikely. And yet, Oliver found himself considering what would happen if he had to take the bigger, younger man. Oliver *was* actually quick on his feet—but Brent was taller and much heavier. But Oliver also knew—he *knew* this for a fact—that if Brent swung, Fay would join in angrily and enthusiastically. Both of them together could definitely defeat one Clompy Brent, although they'd probably break Oliver's glasses, not to mention scuff the dark wood floors of this brownstone, knock over the antique side table that held a collection of candles and pictures, and possibly damage the expensively restored newel posts of the gorgeous staircase in the process. That would be a damn shame.

Nonetheless, Oliver tightened his fists. So did Fay. For a moment, they stood tense, frozen, the smile on Fay's face becoming slightly wider and more ominous, although the scariest thing about it was how attractive Oliver found it.

The old floor creaked. The sounds of greetings came from downstairs. A small group of people was likely bounding up the porch steps, eager to ooh and aah over Harlem real estate.

Clompy Brent flicked his eyes down toward where the sound emerged and he grunted. Evidently deciding that historic preservation was the better part of valor, he gave Fay a curt nod and went ponderously down the stairs.

Oliver sagged in relief—and a little disappointment. When the crowd passed beneath them through the front hall, he turned to Fay and she turned to him and they said, simultaneously, "Are you okay?"

A pause.

Fay started again. "He was so persistent. Sorry to involve you."

Then, as if realizing they were still standing close, Fay slipped her arm out from his and they stepped away from each other.

"Don't apologize. It's messed up that you felt like you needed a cover."

Fay shook her head as if to clear it. "That was tense, wasn't it? He started pestering me one house back on the tour. I said I wasn't interested, and he didn't listen. When we got to this house, I told him I had a boyfriend and then I started trying to edge back downstairs to find the greeter when you arrived. But really it was nothing. It was fine."

Oliver was quiet for a bit, trying to process what she'd said. She was slightly embarrassed judging from her abrupt manner—not that she had anything to be ashamed of at all. But the other thing that stood out was that she'd made up a fake boyfriend instead of referring to her husband. Which meant… He glanced at her hand. No ring. Maybe she wasn't married anymore. *So* not the point here. But why did he suddenly feel so— not happy, not relieved, but…alert? Interested.

He hadn't felt interested in anything for a long time.

She added grudgingly, "I'm really glad I ran into you."

"An architect friend had a ticket that he couldn't use. I wasn't about to pass up a chance to scope out people's houses."

She laughed at that—maybe a little too hard. So, he

asked gently, "Would you like a cup of coffee or some water, or something? Or if you don't mind, would you show me around? It's the first time I've ever been on the Mount Morris Park house tour."

"Are you kidding me? The restorations are gorgeous, but the tour also really highlights this area's community-led revitalization. Have you seen all the businesses that have opened up on Malcolm X Boulevard lately? Plus, what New Yorker doesn't love ogling real estate?"

The fact that she relaxed instantly told him he'd done the right thing in giving her a project: namely, him. But of course, *he* couldn't quite feel at ease around her because her firm had his CV. If he didn't want to live with his brother forever he was going to have to get that job. She still hadn't said anything about it—in fact, she seemed oblivious—but Fay could potentially be his next boss. His sexy, non-ring-wearing-and-therefore-possibly-available boss. It was the worst kind of in-between space to be in with her: not closely acquainted enough to be friends, not quite coworkers, not quite flirting.

Instead of thinking about jobs or how he'd always liked her, he concentrated very hard on the leaded glass skylight that she was pointing out and tried to ignore the tingle that crept up his spine when her insistent hands pushed him toward the next set of stairs in order to show him the pitted, stained brick of an old fireplace that hadn't yet been restored. They chatted with the greeter, Ms. Gloria Hernández, who was oblivious to the drama that had taken place upstairs.

"Oh, we get all sorts of people here who want to know about the history of the area. And then there are the ones who think they're on some kind of house shopping spree and say things like, *I'm gonna rip out that*

*tile over there and put in a chandelier made of dia-
monds and hundred dollar bills up here.* And some
people who just want to poke through their neighbor's
medicine cabinets."

Ms. Hernández peered at them as if to decide which
of the three categories they belonged in and Oliver tried
not to look like a rich asshole or a person with too much
curiosity about other people's meds.

Fay said hastily, "We love the neighborhood. Also,
we both have a professional interest."

"Are you historians?"

"No, we're urban planners."

"What's that all about?"

"Well, we work with city government and developers and community groups to look at how land is used
to figure out how to grow and accommodate a community's needs. We look at zoning and infrastructure.
We talk to the residents and community leaders and
try to help all these groups figure out what kinds of
businesses they need, or if they need more schools, or
more bike lanes—"

"No bike lanes. Hard enough for my sister to park
already. Every Tuesday and Thursday she has to sit in
her car for a half-hour to wait out the street cleaners.
She's read everything by Toni Morrison twice already.
Although I suppose it doesn't sound so bad when you
put it that way."

"We also make recommendations for more affordable housing."

"Well, I know all about that. I've lived in my building since 1969, and if I hadn't bought early, I wouldn't
be able afford five square feet to myself anymore. A
young couple like you, if you want to start a family in

this neighborhood, if you aren't the CEO of something, you can forget about it," she said. "Urban planner, that's a real job, huh?"

Fay laughed. "Oh, it's very real."

But Oliver noticed that Fay didn't bother to say that what wasn't real was Ms. Hernández's assumption that he and Fay were a couple.

When they were safely out of the house and on their way to the next stop, Fay explained, "There was a lot to unpack in what she was telling us about the neighborhood. It seemed harmless to let that one thing go. Plus, you could have jumped in at any time."

"I like letting you take the lead."

She gave him a slow smile that he felt down to his feet. "I like that you let me take the lead."

She walked off and it was a few seconds before he managed to catch up to her.

A few other people at the next stops made the same assumption, too, and neither bothered to correct them. It was easier to concentrate on other matters: to pause to look up the history of the neighborhood on their phones, to hold up before and after pictures of houses that had been burned-out shells, to hope that more houses had stayed in the hands of Black residents, to pause to argue lightly about the Whole Foods that had sprung up on 125th Street. "I'd forgotten how slowly I move when I'm with another urban planner," Fay said suddenly, laughing. "But that's how we earn those billable hours, isn't it?"

It wasn't a bad thing; in fact it was a small inside joke. But thinking about his billable hours—his career, his current lack of a job, the fact that her firm had been so slow to respond, the fact that he was living with his brother, well, it put a damper on Oliver's mood. He could have asked for her number right then. He could have said something about meeting again next weekend to walk through Marcus Garvey Park, which they hadn't had nearly enough time to explore. But he had no business asking out anyone right now, not when he was a mess, and especially not when he felt that slight thread of unease around the fact that he was in the running for a job with her firm.

But she obviously didn't remember or care, otherwise, she would have mentioned it.

There was a lot they hadn't said to each other.

She was still smiling at him. But he didn't ask for her number. He didn't ask if he could see her again.

So, when she paused, almost expectantly, he said, "I'll walk you down to your platform."

And he watched her get on her train.

Fay was still smiling that evening as she pulled a pot out of the moving boxes in order to make dinner.

On the way home, she'd bought the *fancy* instant ramen, a bunch of green onions, and a single grilled chicken breast. She shredded some of the chicken and the scallions with her hands and dumped them in with the noodles. Then she found a pair of disposable chopsticks from a takeout bag she'd left on her counter and sat down on the floor cross-legged to eat from the pot. Her mother wouldn't quite approve of her methods, but at least Ma Liu would be happy that Fay used only half the seasoning packet.

She should have taken that Saturday afternoon to unpack, but she just couldn't stomach it. She'd moved twice in the last year: once into a sublet when she'd asked her husband for a divorce (he could keep the apartment and its expensive lease), and then into this old, pre-war one bedroom with worn floors and tall windows that rattled when it stormed. But it was hers. She'd bought it with her own money.

It was probably a mistake.

She hadn't had time to brood about it, though. Her marriage unraveled at the same time that the firm that she'd started with two college classmates had been going through growing pains. But while the extra work had been a welcome distraction, she and her partners were clearly shorthanded and needed desperately to hire someone. She'd thrown herself into putting out fires at work and her partners had been left to hire HR consultants, go through CVs, and interview people.

This was the first weekend she'd taken off in a long time. And now that she had a chance to glance around, the apartment was in rougher shape than she remembered. She had a lot of furniture to buy—she didn't even have a bed. Her mattress sat on the floor. It seemed too difficult to summon the depth of will she needed to start a new project, to whip it into shape. She wanted something polished, finished. She wanted just one thing— one thing—in her life to be ready for her.

But this was no time to wallow. She was going to hold on to the good mood that Oliver had helped her earn for as long as she could. She tapped on FaceTime and propped her phone up on a box.

"Not wallowing for a change," Renata said approvingly. "What happened to you today?"

Renata was on the patio of her house in Seattle, sipping something from a tall glass while her kids screamed in the background.

"I had a good time. But I see you've started drinking."

"It's four in the afternoon on a Saturday, and I've already shuttled to and from two kid birthday parties, and my wife's been on a business trip for the last week. The drinking started hours ago."

Fay held up her ramen bowl. *"Cin-cin."*

She slurped her soup, which earned her an outraged squeal all the way from Seattle.

"You're as gross as my children."

"I'm sitting on the floor eating ramen and scraps of chicken and onion that I've rended with my own hands, Renata. You don't know the half of it."

"And you still haven't made any progress with the unpacking, I see. You're usually right on top of projects."

Well, this conversation was not helping Fay maintain her buoyant mood. "Stop mom-ing me, Renata. I already have one, and she's enough. Maybe I'm turning over a new leaf, trying to be more relaxed about everything. Maybe I'm tired. Besides, you'll be happy to know that the reason I was happy was because I went out—and not to the office."

"Good! Where?"

"The Mount Morris Park house tour!"

"That sounds like planner work."

"It was fun! The houses are beautiful. I love looking at real estate, and I wanted to learn more about how Central Harlem has changed in the space of ten years—"

Renata made a warning noise.

"—And Renata, you yourself were telling me that I should look around for ideas for my apartment."

"I meant in magazines or on, like, Pinterest. God, did

I just recommend Pinterest? Maybe I am mom-ing you. Not that there's anything wrong with moms."

"Well, this was a really great self-guided tour, and I got to see some beautiful things…except there was a guy who got way too aggressive about asking me out. Like, following me around and talking to me for a while, especially when there was no one else around—" Renata opened her mouth to say something, and Fay cut her off quickly. "But that turned out okay, too."

"What, did you give him a right hook and send him backward off the porch? You did, didn't you? That's why you look happy. Is he dead? I knew this day would come, I have just the person to represent you. Let me get—"

From seemingly out of nowhere Renata hauled up her briefcase and set it next to her wineglass.

"No. No. No one's dead—or hurt."

"There's a story here."

"Not much."

Renata lowered the briefcase out of sight again. Fay didn't know why she was suddenly reluctant to share. Nothing had really happened, after all. "Oliver Huang showed up. I pretended he was my boyfriend and the dude backed off."

"Oliver Huang?"

She cleared her throat. "Yep."

"The one with the cheekbones." Her friend was now peering hard at the phone, trying to read Fay's face. Luckily the light was bad enough in her apartment that Renata probably couldn't see Fay's blush.

Renata said slowly, "Oh yes, I do remember him. He went to grad school with that colleague of yours when you worked at the city—what's her name."

"I've been racking my brains trying to think of it."

"Funny you know him but you can't recall her."

"Hilarious. I'm sure I'm friends with her on Facebook or something. I should check."

Not to be diverted, Renata said, "He's a very good-looking man."

"Yeah."

"And nice. Remember Sofia's wedding? Good dancer."

"I get the idea—"

"He's the one who rescued you from the bugs that other time."

Fay shuddered. "*Aided*, not rescued. I don't want to talk about that."

"But you've reconnected."

"It wasn't a date." And apparently it never would be. Fay turned red again. "He helped me out of a jam— that I could've gotten out of myself. But I was glad he was there."

"Did you ask him out?"

Reluctantly Fay said, "No-o."

"Well then, did he ask you out?"

There it was. "No."

Fay had been sure he would. And she'd been prepared to say—what? *Yes.* She had been prepared to hesitate and then say yes. But now she was only embarrassed. "It's not like that between us. We're casual acquaintances. Friends," she amended, "now that we've spent an afternoon together."

"An afternoon in which you pretended to be boyfriend and girlfriend."

"Just for a few minutes."

Well, it was longer than that if she counted the other times through the rest of the tour when they hadn't contradicted other people who had assumed they were a couple—when she'd managed to fool herself that they were a couple. It felt *good* to be with Oliver. It felt easy to just let the mistakes pass without correction, to stand a little too close, to brush up against his solid, warm arm, and to pretend that it was all real.

Renata smirked at Fay's silence and Fay found her irritation growing.

"I'm not interested in starting anything with Oliver Huang anyway. It would be awkward. I know too many people that he knows, and we're in the same small professional circle. We have the same urban planner friends, and the same urban planner jokes and interests. People introduce and reintroduce us to one another all the time. To change that, that's the definition of awkward."

"You said that word *awkward* a lot."

"I repeated it because I was afraid you weren't understanding my important point. He isn't what I need. I need someone who isn't playing around, like Jeremy was—"

Renata snorted. "Jeremy was lazy. All talk, no action."

Lazy wasn't exactly correct. It wasn't that she had been more ambitious than her ex. If anything, judging by all the high-flown ideas he'd had, his imaginings for what he could do and how much money he'd make, or what ideals he'd uphold, his aspirations went wide and far. Jeremy was the one who was sure of himself. He was the one who thought he could make things happen. He was the one who'd tried a handful of different careers, always putting in minimal effort and expecting success to fall into his lap, and when it didn't, heading off in search of greener pastures.

But Fay was the one who had focused on one thing that she wanted to do and was doing it.

She continued as if she'd been uninterrupted. "I need someone who understands my perspective. Someone driven, who doesn't just let me talk the whole time, or have me lead him around from house to house showing him things." Although, that wasn't entirely true, was it? She'd liked that Oliver let her take the lead, and she'd told him so. Maybe he'd been waiting for her to take the next step, too? "Besides, the moment is gone."

"You could easily get his number from any one of your many mutual acquaintances in your small professional circle. You need to go out with someone."

"I've gone out on dates." She had dated since the split with Jeremy was finalized nine months ago. She'd been very diligent about fitting it in, going out on at least twelve coffee dates with twelve people, all in accordance with the protocols of getting over a divorce.

"Not in months. And I know you. You only did it because you felt like you had to prove something. You need to go out with someone you *like*, on a date with real stakes. Otherwise you're going to stay in this holding pattern."

"A date is not the answer. And I'm not in a holding pattern. I'm keeping it together just fine. My job's busier than ever. We're supposed to hire someone soon, if Teddy can get it sorted. I'm even—" she waved her empty noodle pot at the screen "—feeding myself."

"Isn't *keeping it together* the very definition of a holding pattern?"

She set the pot down with a clang. "Why have you been pushing me this entire call?"

"Because it always works on you." More quietly. "Because I'm worried about you, and I'm not there."

Fay's shoulders relaxed a little but her pride still felt bruised, and her words were pricklier than she intended. "Well, you're the last person I'd expect to send me toward a man just to solve my problems."

"But he's the first person—first anything—to give you any sort of spark in months. Look around you at all these boxes on the floor, all the unfinished projects, your low energy. Is this normal for you?'"

Fay closed her eyes. "Nothing this year has been normal for me, all right, Renata?"

A pause.

"Fay, I want—"

"I have to go."

Fay pushed End.

Then after a couple of moments, she sent a text with a kissy face—and received a blue heart back.

It was possible that she and Renata were better friends now that they lived on opposite coasts. Now that she could just hang up when Renata became too *much*—or was it too insightful? Fay could take a break and retreat to her corner—like now. They were a lot alike and their intensity had worked for them when they were both young, professional women in their late twenties. Fay missed her friend, of course, and sometimes Fay wished that she could go over and flop on Renata's couch—she always had the most comfortable couches—and yell and eat Renata's mom's *conconetes*. But mostly, it was better now.

Fay was at peace with her bigger choices; she knew that she shouldn't be married to Jeremy, and she was very glad she didn't have kids with him—but it was still hard to take it when Renata mothered her, especially when her friend acted like she had more experience, more knowledge about life.

Fay had her own kind of knowledge.

For instance, the truth was that this afternoon, she hadn't had to take the subway to get home. Her new apartment was only about fifteen blocks from the last house she and Oliver had toured.

She could've asked him to walk home with her, maybe invited him up, messy and unfurnished as the place was. He was a planner. He'd love the neighborhood. He would see the possibilities of the place that she'd seen—and needed to be reminded of. She'd read up on the history and architecture of this part of Manhattan. Maybe she would have taken pleasure in showing him the slot in the bathroom for razor blades, the old penny tile, a stove that came straight from the seventies, an ugly slab of a fridge from the early 2000s. The apartment was like an old Gothic cathedral that had changed styles midway through building because the construction had outlasted the lives of the people putting it together. But instead of a place of spiritual worship, it was a place of common living, every decade of its existence evidenced by an outdated appliance, or a piece of cabinetry or wallpaper.

And maybe, while she and Oliver were exploring the apartment together, she would have gotten him to sleep with her. Peeled off his jeans, pushed him down on the mattress, and watched him watch her lower herself onto him. But she hadn't done any of that because, well, she was scared.

She sighed. The truth was, she *did* want to be with someone again. She wanted sex and kissing and a pair of solid, warm arms to hold on to. She did want to find a person she was compatible with—and the only way to do it was to date more. As Renata had pointed out, Fay *liked* Oliver. He wasn't a complete stranger from the internet like her other dozen post-divorce dates had been. But because she liked him and knew him and he knew her, he could reject her and it wouldn't just be awkward, as she kept repeating. It would hurt.

That was damn scary.

She picked herself up off the floor and rinsed her pot out in the sink. She could do this. She could call him—but later. She didn't have to always be that woman who did everything *now*. Later was fine.

Chapter Two

Monday

The text message from Fay came at just past eleven at night, and it was brief. This is Fay Liu. Call me when you get a chance.

Oliver wasn't sure what to make of it.

He'd thought about Fay a lot over the last twenty-four hours. He'd thought about her hair, which had briefly brushed his cheek after their hurried surprise kiss, about her tense strength beside him when Clompy Brent had been sizing them up. Her laughter filled his mind when he woke up, and he summoned her spirit when he needed to confront his inbox.

He did have freelance work, so it wasn't like he was unemployed and with nothing to do. But aside from attending the occasional meetings with his client, he was working from home these days—well, not *his* home. He was living with his younger brother, Nathaniel, in Nat's Upper West Side apartment. It was spacious by New York standards, with a good view of the Hudson River. But Oliver spent most of his time tapping away on the smallest laptop on the smallest desk in the small guest room or alone at the breakfast bar. There were no watercooler breaks or innocuous chitchats with co-workers to break up the monotony.

He read the message and reread it. *Call me*, it said. Not *Text me*. But it was too late for work calls, and late for personal ones unless they were *very personal*, and he was not getting that from the message. He wasn't getting much of anything from the message, honestly.

He thought about it and was playing a video game about it when Nat got home.

"It's 2 a.m.? What are you still doing up?" Nat yawned.

"Waiting for you."

Nat smiled lazily. "I had the most magical evening."

He sank down into the couch with his eyes closed.

"In love again?" Oliver asked.

"Of course. The boy of my dreams. He's got dimples. And a cleft chin. He's just bulges and depressions in all the right places."

"Is he a man or is he a topographical map?"

"He's the valleys and the mountains, and I'm going on a long hike along the trails—all the trails, baby."

Oliver glanced back at his little brother again. Nat could take care of himself—more than that. He was taking care of Oliver. Letting Oliver live in the guest room, even though having his older brother there had to be cramping his style. Making sure Oliver ate. Tying his ties and lending him shoes for job interviews.

Wow, it had come to this.

Oliver pressed his mouth into a thin line and continued his game. Badly.

"Have you left the house in the last few days?" Nat asked.

Oliver tried not to sound defensive. "Yeah. Yes. I did.

An architect buddy gave me a ticket to the Mount Morris Park house tour on Sunday. Ran into an old friend, as a matter of fact."

"Oh-ho. Anyone I know?"

"Probably not. Fay Liu."

"Did we go to school with her?"

"No, she's from California originally. She's a planner, too. Worked at the city with one of my grad school classmates."

Clearly, Nat scented blood in the water. All Oliver could do was try not to swirl it around.

"Which one?"

"Her name is at the tip of my tongue."

"But you can't quite recall. Funny how you remember this Fay Liu but not your classmate."

Oliver tried to sound nonchalant. "I see her around. My friends know her friends. I've seen her at conferences, parties. I may have taken a day trip with her and a couple of people—"

"May have."

"It was all very casual."

Oliver snuck a glance at Nat. He was grinning. The fucker.

"If you say so," his brother said.

"Anyway, Fay wasn't the one to email me, but someone from her firm is supposedly looking at my CV—they've had it awhile now."

Nat blinked sleepily. But Oliver knew better. Nat might seem careless, he might seem to not be listening, but pretty soon he'd throw out a question—or five—that would force Oliver to think. This was probably why his brother made big bucks as a risk analyst.

"So you've noticed her a lot over the years."

Yes. "Maybe."

"Have you slept with her before?"

"No, asshole. Not that it's any of your business."

"But you like her."

"She told me to call her."

"And you haven't."

"Did I mention she's one of the principals?"

Oliver abandoned the game. He watched his character stand stock-still. The locusts descended upon him. Presently a funeral director came out and put him in a tiny coffin and lowered him into the ground.

He shut off the console. "I should go to bed. Lots of…desk-sitting to do tomorrow."

"You aren't working with her yet."

"But I don't have a regular job. In addition to the fact that she might become my boss, I don't have a steady gig. What do I have to offer anyone right now? You're making money hand over fist. You can stay up late and look fresh in the morning and make sense of large datasets. I'm almost forty, Nat. I have some consulting work and nowhere to live."

"Sure, you do. You're with me."

"I can't stay here forever."

"I wouldn't mind."

His brother meant it, too. Oliver got up from the floor and hugged him.

"You don't have to be perfect to go out on one tiny date, Oliver," Nat called after him.

Well, he damn well knew that. It had never bothered Oliver before. But his last relationship had ended a while ago. Then six months ago, the consulting firm he worked for had gone bust, dragged down when their big client had itself gone out of business. He wasn't broke. He had savings, and the smaller contract jobs paid fine. But it felt precarious enough that he'd given up his Brooklyn apartment when the landlord issued a rent increase. Oliver was a planner, yet everything felt up in the air. He was thirty-six, single—never married—and he lived with his younger brother. "Shiftless, just like your father," his mom had said in a mixture of Mandarin and English when he told her he'd lost his job. He sure didn't look like a great bet for someone who probably wanted more, and Fay was surely a woman who wanted more.

Well, now Fay wanted to talk to him.

He'd spent the past day remembering all the things he'd heard about her—things he already knew either by experience or from their mutual friends. She had moved out here for college. She was generous, both with money and with her time as a volunteer. She didn't like bugs, he recalled, from one very memorable incident (although neither did most of their mutual acquaintances, it seemed).

And she was driven. Fay had started her own shop after stints with the city and at two global planning firms. Keeping in touch with her was good for his career; the problem with him was that he wanted to ask her out more than he cared about work—and wasn't that confirmation of how shiftless he was?

Given the curtness of her message, maybe it was about the interview. She'd been thinking about him, yes, and perhaps in asking around, she'd remembered that she had his CV. Or her partners had asked her to set it up.

He couldn't believe he felt disappointed at the possibility of a job interview.

Oliver tossed the video controller on the couch and turned off the screen. He'd go to bed and call her tomorrow at a more reasonable hour, like a functioning human.

She didn't need to know he was only pretending to be one.

Saturday

"I was thinking we could walk up to see the old Harlem Fire Tower first," Fay said. "It's the oldest remaining watchtower in the city. And we'd get a fantastic view of the ground we want to cover today, too."

She flicked a glance at him to gauge his reaction but found him watching her.

He smiled slowly. "You've been doing research."

Maybe he was flirting with that reply, maybe he wasn't. It was funny how *research* sounded affectionate, like teasing, like some sort of subtle caress when it came out of his mouth.

Then he asked, "Do you ever stop working?"

So much for enjoying what he had to say. "This isn't work; this is pleasure."

But *pleasure* seemed awkward the way she choked it out. She covered by standing up. "No job talk," she declared. She was supposed to be having fun with him so she'd kept reminding herself of that rule since he'd called her back on Tuesday and they'd made plans to meet today.

She tried to smile and signal that she was relaxed as they walked briskly through Marcus Garvey Park and toward the destination she'd chosen for them. *Stroll don't stride. This is supposed to be fun.*

Oliver seemed unbothered, though. He had his usual chunky, black-framed glasses and was dressed in crisp trousers and a light button-down shirt with his sleeves rolled up. She tried not to stare at his wrists, strong slashes of tendon and muscle even when his hands were relaxed. She remembered one time one of her friends had joked that for a planner he dressed like an architect and that impression remained in the sharp lines and stark blacks and whites of his clothing.

They didn't talk much as they walked past the blue-and-yellow play structures, past a teenage boy playing the saxophone on the paved hexagonal stone path. Under the shade, a man was frantically doing crunches while his baby slept in a nearby stroller. Joggers swept by, serious and sweaty. It was early afternoon and the sun was strong that day, enough that, after some hesitation, Fay took off her canary-bright cardigan and revealed her floaty top, her bare arms.

She saw the flash in Oliver's eye, but he didn't say anything. She remembered she'd always found him quiet and reassuring, but he noticed a lot. She had always liked that about him. Maybe back when she was married, she'd thought vaguely to herself that it might be good to work with someone like him. Perhaps she'd even mentioned to her partners that they might try to lure him to their firm. But now she wondered at that version of memory. She had felt very aware of him—maybe she had been interested this whole time.

At the top of the sweeping stone staircase, they gazed at the fire tower in all its restored cast-iron glory and began to play a game of building-nerd I-Spy where they tried to identify landmarks and streets, points for obscurity and oddball facts. And then eventually they just watched, companionably taking in the view.

"Spot any fires, chief?" Oliver asked after a while, putting his hands in his pockets.

"Not even a whiff of smoke."

Well, *she* was feeling warm. Oliver wasn't standing that close to her. Sometimes, he moved in to point at something and she'd imagine she felt his breath on her cheek. And sometimes she would do the same, and it seemed almost as if he turned, he leaned toward her, his touch a phantom hovering just above her skin. She sighed and he heard it, judging by the tilt of his head, the inquiry in his eyes. By unspoken agreement, they picked their way down the stairs. And paused.

It really was a beautiful park.

"I know you probably have a whole itinerary we're supposed to be marching steadily through or something," Oliver said, "but it's really tempting to suggest we just laze in the grass in the shade for a bit."

She nodded. Shade. That sounded…cooling. And surely, she wasn't so uptight that she had to *do* something every minute. Was that how he saw her? Fay frowned.

They found a patch of grass and she sat down, drawing her knees up to her chest, and Oliver lay down with his arms behind his head. He gave a blissful grunt and closed his eyes, again, allowing her another chance to look at him, his long, lean form like an exclamation mark in the grass, his shirt drawn tight against his flat belly, the outline of his thighs and knees. What would it be like to have that shape punctuating her moans, her cries?

He opened one eye. "Is this okay for you?" he asked quietly.

"Yes, it's good."

She blushed remembering the direction of her thoughts. This was the problem with sitting still. She'd never been able to do it for long. And when she did, she had *thoughts*. Like the ones she was currently entertaining about Oliver Huang.

"Ants on you," she said.

Oliver sat up slowly. It was nice to watch. He inspected his arms, his pant legs. He gave her a questioning look.

It was an invitation to touch.

"Here," she said. And she brushed a few away gently.

He was again very still while her fingers were on him.

"Remember that time a group of us were at a site in New Jersey, and you waded into the grass and got all those insects on you?" he asked her.

"Oh, you aren't going to bring that up! That was embarrassing."

He laughed. "It wasn't. And I like that memory. You waded into some tall grass, and when you came out your ankle socks were covered in bugs, little gnats or green flies or something. Someone—I don't remember who it was so long ago—started shrieking about ticks."

"Don't remind me." But it was too late.

"You were so calm! You got behind the car and took off your shoes and some of your clothing and asked for help to be inspected—just in case."

"And you stepped up. No one else would. Everyone was too busy freaking out the minute I said the t-word."

"Yeah."

"And you were not gross about it." She smiled at him.

"High praise. I try." He grinned back, his cheeks reddened as their eyes locked for a beat longer than necessary. Flashes of memory came—his hands, confident and cool with long tapered fingers closing around her ankle. Her blood stirred, but he looked away first.

She cleared her throat, "So is this a story about how great you are or about how great I am?"

He laughed. "Luckily you were fine. And someone did have a change of clothes. But you insisted that we go to a store and get you new ones."

"I remember. Rob. He'd been at the city with me, too, and Linda."

"Linda! My classmate. That was her name."

"Yes. So, Rob—it was his car—didn't really want to stop. I think he was worried you hadn't done a good job and that he'd have to industrial-strength clean his precious Acura." She wrinkled her nose. "Can you blame him?"

"Yeah, I can. He was being a jerk. Did he think he should leave you stranded? You were his colleague. It wasn't like you were spilling an entire colony of ticks onto his upholstery." He shook his head. "And then he wanted to go to a big box store."

"Against all of our community planning principles." She snickered, and Oliver started laughing, too.

"You managed it so well! You said, no, let's stop in this other nice town. And you arranged to get the car vacuumed out!"

"It wasn't thorough."

"It was something. You bought all new clothing in five minutes. And you got all of us milkshakes and got the diner owner to give you the very unfiltered scoop on how townspeople felt about all the redevelopment going on in the area. And then we were all chummy again."

"Yeah, but I don't think Rob ever let me in his car again after that. In fact, I suspect he moved to Virginia just to save his precious upholstery from me."

"His loss," Oliver said, so easily and quickly that it nearly took her breath away. Fay shifted closer. His eyes were bright with life, and she thought very seriously for thirty seconds about leaning in, bringing her mouth to his. But she couldn't quite bring herself to do it. This time, she looked away first.

"Besides," Oliver continued, "it's not like I've always had wonderful experiences with the great outdoors, being a city boy myself."

"That's right. You grew up here."

"Yep, born and raised in Queens, the best, most diverse borough in the world. I say this both as a New Yorker and as an expert on how cities are supposed to work."

"Is most of your family still here?"

"My brother and sister, and my mom. My dad, well, I have no idea where he is. I guess I don't care."

She didn't probe. Instead, she said, lightly, "Maybe you could show me around there sometime."

He watched her. "If you'd like that, I could."

Why did she keep blushing? "I would really like that."

It was all a little too much. So, she sprang up to start moving again, and Oliver followed her, a little more slowly. When they got to the West Side they crossed the street to peer more closely at the old brick buildings and perhaps start their walk through the district. Suddenly, Oliver stopped and pointed to a flier taped next to some door buzzers. They went up for a closer look. "There's a couple of open houses taking place here."

"Are you looking to buy?"

"No. No, sadly I'm not. But…"

He raised an eyebrow.

Not quite a house tour, but it *was* an opportunity to see inside. "Let's do it."

They were buzzed up. The fact sheet, bearing the logo of a prominent uptown brokerage, said there were two apartments showing in the building. They decided to go to the higher floor first. They made their way noisily up a set of creaking stairs, pausing at one landing to stare at the skylight. "Do you think it's original to the building?"

"Hard to tell. For sure, it hasn't been cleaned in a long time."

A Black teenage girl was slouched in a chair in the hallway, staring at her phone. "If you and your wife could just sign in," she mumbled, barely glancing up.

Again with the assumption that they were a couple—but they were on a date, after all. Maybe. After a pause, Oliver quirked Fay a smile, and wrote "Oliver and Darling Wife," on the clipboard, along with what seemed like his real email address.

Not that she had looked it up or anything.

She had to laugh at the little heart he put over the *i* in Darling, too. And then she stopped laughing. Because the joke seemed to hit a little too close to home.

It was a pretty teacup of an apartment, with a bright kitchen with a big window that looked right into the branches of the tree that stood on the street. The walls had been painted yellow, and there was no lack of sunshine in the living room. It felt cheerful and modern and altogether without context; she and Oliver could have been standing anywhere. Most of the period details had been plastered over, sanded, and stripped over the years.

She and Oliver glanced at each other at the same time, as if they were really in the market for an apartment, and they both shook their heads.

They stepped into one bedroom—a nursery—where the roof sloped down over the crib. It was tiny. Not much room for anything besides the crib and a chair. But someone had built a clever set of drawers and bookcases around the window.

They went into the bathroom, which was really too small for both of them to be in at once. And yet, it was exciting standing in there with him so close, with him watching her in the mirror, and her watching him. Why was it easier to look him steadily in the eye when it was through a mirror? To notice how his lips seemed so soft compared to the sharp planes of his face? Her own lips parted a little. She was near enough that she could feel his breath quickening, feel the subtle way they turned their bodies toward each other.

A door slammed somewhere in the apartment. Voices.

She ducked her head and left the bathroom. He followed. And they stepped into the last room. The bedroom.

Most of the room was bed.

She devoted a part of her mind to wondering how difficult it had been to wrestle the mattress up the narrow flights of stairs. But the darkest corner of it was wondering how hard it would be to tip Oliver down into the bed, how willing he'd be to fall.

They were still standing close with just a narrow

strip at the foot of the bed to walk around in. He leaned a little closer to her. "Fay," he whispered.

She half turned, and her hand slid up his chest.

"Hellooo," a voice called cheerily from behind them. They both turned.

"Ah, a pair of honeymooners."

The Black woman with chunky jewelry and a blue suit was clearly the actual real estate broker. Fay tugged self-consciously at her top and hoped her face wasn't too shiny.

But the broker beamed at the two of them and neither of them moved or denied a thing.

"Isn't it a great place? A perfect starter apartment with just enough room for a small family."

"It's lovely," Oliver said. "Lots of light."

His hand slid around Fay's waist. She wanted to turn toward him and sigh.

The broker smiled at them widely. "Is this the kind of space you had in mind? Is it in your budget?"

"Oh, well, we wouldn't mind seeing the downstairs," Fay found herself saying.

"Sure. It's a much bigger layout. More room to grow. Maybe more along the lines of what—" she checked her clipboard "—you, Darling and Oliver, are looking for."

As Sharon, the broker, led them downstairs to the ground floor, chattering all the way, Oliver laughed softly into Fay's neck.

"Maybe we should stop doing this," Fay whispered.

Her lips were practically on his ear. If he took a step down she'd be able to nip him.

"Doing what?"

"Pretending that we're together. It's like last week. It's…it's too easy."

Oliver opened his mouth to answer, but Sharon was directing them through the door. And once inside, they both gaped.

It was huge, dramatic, and beautiful.

"Not as much light as the third-floor apartment," Sharon was saying, "but look at those tall windows."

They let go of each other but stepped forward together.

Unlike the upstairs, this apartment was well preserved. Crown molding studded with whorls and curlicues ringed the ceiling, and glossy woodwork framed the windows and the high doorways that separated the living room from the dining room. The walls had been painted a dark forest green, and Sharon had lit lamps that glowed softly in the far corners. Fay shivered as Oliver reached out and traced his finger along one of the frames. "This seems original. When was this built? Late 1800s?"

The broker cocked her head. "Are you two architects?"

"Nooo," they both said.

"We're urban planners," Fay said. "But we're interested in the history of this area, too."

"Oh, that must be how you met. That's so wonderful having a profession in common. I can tell that with you two that the shop talk doesn't get in the way of the love talk."

Fay very deliberately did not look at Oliver as he answered. "I think that it all ends up being part of the same love language no matter what."

The broker beamed at them. "Oh, he's a darling, uh, Darling. You're a lucky one."

Sharon showed them the old nonworking fireplaces,

the pocket doors leading to the study off the kitchen, a set of French doors to a small backyard. She chattered as they went upstairs into the master bedroom. "And here's a great walk-in closet, with built-in shoe shelves on her side, and a tie rack on his. But these things don't have to be gendered, do they? No reason why it can't be for scarves and things." She gave a little wink. "And this middle platform here is built-in storage for accessories. Oh, oh, there's the buzzer."

Sharon scampered out to answer it and the door swung closed, leaving them once again alone together.

"Oliver, she thinks we're in love and that we're going to have perfect credit scores and a preapproved mortgage and two judges and five doctors writing our reference letters for the co-op board and that we're going to close within two months and announce that we're pregnant as she hands over the keys and that we'll live happily ever after. You can practically see the hearts in her eyes when she looks at us. Or dollar signs. A little of both. That woman is already planning on *knitting* something for us."

"That's why she's a successful professional—she has vision. I think I'm kind of enjoying this story she's made up about Oliver and Darling."

"That *we've* made up entirely."

"That has some tiny kernels of truth. Like we're both urban planners and that's how we met. That we genuinely love and admire this neighborhood, and good woodwork—"

"Oliver."

"And that we can't help being fascinated by which details were added and what's original." He took another step toward her. "That we gravitate toward each other in a huge room—or a small one."

Fay found it very hard to breathe suddenly. It was a closet, but they could have made space between them. And they had chosen not to—they'd chosen to be close.

"Fay," he whispered. And then she stepped into him. She rose onto her toes, letting her hands slide over his chest again, she breathed on his neck, admiring the way the cords of his neck tightened, and she nipped her way slowly up his chin, until his lips swooped down on her, his tongue stroking through almost immediately to meet hers, his hands moving up and down her waist.

Another murmur and he backed her to the platform. With one more movement, he could boost her right up so that they would be aligned—his face on the same level as hers, his chest against hers, his stomach, the hardness of him in the right place. She felt everything surge upward for her to meet him. But then he pulled away from the kiss, his arms sliding slowly away from her back and down to his sides. His face was a study in desire and bafflement.

"Fay, what are we doing here?"

Chapter Three

Fay looked as confused as Oliver felt.

Neither of them knew what to do with their hands, their arms, their lips that had just been all over each other. For a moment their interesting and sensitive parts had been pressed close, and it was the best feeling in the world—and now they were not, and Oliver didn't know how to act anymore.

Sharon, because her timing was impeccable, bustled in. "Oh, you newlyweds getting busy in the closet," she twinkled. "I'm just going to make sure you have the fact sheet. The maintenance is very low, and the co-op has a healthy nest egg. Just let me know if you have questions about either apartment. Although to tell you the truth, I think this one suits both of you more. I can just picture you loving it up in here."

If they weren't already both blushing guiltily, then Sharon's last words were more than enough to set Oliver's face aflame.

By silent agreement, they thanked Sharon, who had already moved on to the next adorable and (probably) more real couple that had come to see the apartment. They escaped out onto the stoop and they both took a deep, deep breath.

Fay turned, and with her usual directness said, "We need to talk. Let's go sit down somewhere."

"Coffee? Or something cool to drink."

God knows he could use a moment to think about whether or not he'd just scrapped his chance at another job. Last week's behavior could have been overlooked. Sure, it had involved lips, hipbones bumping, and an intimacy that started off as fake and turned into something real, too. But she'd initiated it. He'd been a convenient bystander.

An all-too-willing one.

Today's hadn't been a simple kiss at all. There was a dark grain of illicitness to their small, private act playing out in a place where anyone could have walked in on them. To the fact that they weren't, in fact, a loving, legally or emotionally bound couple looking for a home to decorate with rugs and beds and 500-thread-count linens. That they hadn't been close before—that even though he was Oliver, she was Fay—she wasn't Darling.

And then there was the kiss itself, in which her lips had opened under his, lush and wet. He had felt himself just—just *sinking* into her, right into that one point where their mouths met as if he tried hard enough, if he focused, his whole body could be immersed in that pleasure and warmth.

But his personal lust ocean had already started walking west. He blinked for a moment in the sunlight and followed. Sitting down right about now would be a good idea—it would probably be a very good idea.

They went into a buzzing cafe on Malcolm X Boulevard and ordered strong coffees that came in tall cups. "What are your intentions toward me?" she said, as they sat down at their table.

"I—I… What?"

The coffee cups flanked her like a pair of henchmen. He wanted to glare at them.

"That came out a bit harsh. But I mean it."

"I can tell."

"If I don't protect myself, no one else will do it for me. I'm not some newly divorced woman wanting a giggle and a cuddle. I don't need a fling. I already did that—sort of. I'm going to be honest with you: I want something serious with someone serious."

He took a breath. This had escalated quickly. And he still hadn't found a way to mention the possible interview at her firm, the potential that they'd be working together. "Well, to be honest, I wasn't thinking about that. I was wondering more about—"

"I know Maria, and Priya, and Liz, and some of the other women you've been out with, for example."

Oliver paused, confused by this turn of the conversation. "Fay, you've known me for more than ten years. I dated Maria for a few months about… I don't know, five years ago? And I went out on one date with Liz when I was barely out of grad school—"

"Two. And one of them was a wedding."

"You kept track?"

That was frightening. Or flattering? Maybe both.

"Well, no. But I was—am—friends with other people, and I have a good memory."

"Okay. I'm not sure what you want me to say here."

"Why didn't you ever get married?"

Oliver opened his mouth, and then closed it again, trying to understand where all of this was coming from. She wanted something serious—and maybe he didn't. He'd never been married. It was never the right time:

he'd always been in school, or just starting out his career, or his partner had been doing the same. And now he hadn't had a serious relationship in a long while, and didn't have a steady job. Did she know that? Had Teddy mentioned he was interviewing with them? Or would be, if they'd ever schedule the damn thing. At the rate they were going, he wasn't sure she was in a position to talk about being slow off the mark.

She didn't think he was a serious person. Serious people had jobs. And yet he was annoyed by her assessment of him. He hadn't met the right woman. The timing was never good. He was cautious. He didn't want to be shiftless and jobless and as unreliable as his father, for fuck's sake.

And none of the people he'd dated had been her.

He opened his mouth again, but at that crystallizing moment, someone came up to their table. "Fay! *Oliver.*"

Sally Chin. He'd gone out on two—no, three—dates with her eight months ago; she was the last person he'd been out with, actually. She had decided they weren't clicking and he'd been somewhat relieved. Although he would feel better right now if it weren't written all over her face that she'd been the one to drop him; she was the picture of contrition and smugness.

Perhaps that was uncharitable. But he was allowed to be a little petty right at this particular unfortunate moment.

She gave Fay a kiss on the cheek while Oliver stood up. She leaned into him and Oliver tried not to be stiff, or friendly, or sad, or studiously nonchalant. For four seconds he held himself *extremely medium*, and afterward, when he saw Fay was very carefully not watching him and Sally, he wondered why he'd bothered.

"Let me get you a chair," he said, needing a few moments away from Sally's orbit as possible.

"No. No, Oliver. It's all right. I don't want to interrupt."

Too damn late.

She continued, "I'm just so glad to see you both. And doing so well. Getting out there, you know."

Fay bristled at that a little, but Sally continued, oblivious. "*So* glad to see you dating again."

He shot a quick glance at Fay, who was frowning. "Well, we're not exactly—"

"I was watching you two for a while before I came up. I recognize that look. And Fay, really, if you're worried that you're violating some sort of girl code by dating someone I went out with—"

Fay turned to Oliver and arched an eyebrow. Whether it meant, *You went out with Sally?* Or, *I told you you'd gone out with everyone I know.* Or, *We aren't that close, so I don't need her permission*—or, all of the above, Oliver wasn't sure. A single eyebrow could convey a lot, but there was a lot to convey at this particular moment.

"But I don't mind," Sally was saying. "It wasn't a significant relationship. A blip, really."

"Gee thanks, Sal."

It was true, though.

"But Oliver, you were such an important step to finding the person I *did* want to be with. I am *so* happy with Doug. I want everyone to feel this way."

She patted Oliver's hand consolingly. For a minute she looked like she wanted to do the same with Fay, but Fay's expression seemed to have finally penetrated Sally's thick marshmallow of happiness.

Fay said, "Oliver and I aren't *together* together, Sally."

Sally rolled her eyes. "*You two.* Listen, I know when to back off—"

Fay may have snorted. Or maybe it was one of the espresso machines.

"It's such a small community we work in," Sally was saying. "So, I can see you probably don't want those rumors *flying.* I mean, we're a gossipy bunch, I'll admit that. But the way you were gazing at each other when I came up, so *intense*, like you'd released this dam of emotion. There's clearly a story here. And if there's a story, that means there's something."

"It's something all right," Fay may have muttered.

But Sally was done sprinkling her fairy-tale glitter over them. She said something about leaving them to *explore each other* and fluttered a goodbye and was soon out the door in a jangle of bells, bracelets, and mixed feelings.

"What the hell was that? I used to think she was okay," Fay grumbled. "I can't believe you went out with her, too."

"I was trying to get to know her."

Instead of jumping straight into "intentions," he didn't say, because it was unkind and perhaps a bit unfair. In fact, he felt a twinge of sympathy for Fay. The way she'd responded so quickly to Sally that they weren't together *together.* His head was so far up his own ass that he hadn't noticed that this, whatever this was, was a big, scary step for her. And that overbearing Sally—and maybe that real estate broker from before—had trampled all over Fay's feelings.

"I am so tired of this," Fay said, suddenly. "I am so

tired of that look people get and of everyone saying they're glad I'm *getting out there*. I have gotten out there. I was out there before. What the hell do these people know about being in there, out there, or anywhere in between? You know what was shitty? Being *in there* with someone who didn't support me, who got jealous when I worked too hard, got restless when I spent time with him but never fucking told me how he felt until it was too late. *In there* wasn't good these last few years. It was a trap. *Out here* is scary, but at least I have hope it can be better."

She was just a woman who'd been with one person for a long time and who was trying to figure out how to date again. She'd called him up. He knew he wasn't very scary, but she didn't. She'd done something brave.

"I'm really sorry about your marriage, Fay. That you ended up feeling that way."

She took a deep breath. "I think that's the first time anyone has said that to me. Oh, you know, people say they're sad about the divorce. Or if they can't bring themselves to ask me about that particular D-word, they ask me very significantly how I'm doing. But no one ever says anything about how I must have felt in order to end my marriage, or that maybe it was good for me, that it will be better for me."

"I think it has been better for you."

"Well, my best friend thinks I'm a mess, that I have no energy left, that I can't finish one single thing anymore."

Oliver raised an eyebrow. "I think you might be the most driven person I know." Then, thinking it sounded cold or off-putting somehow, he hastily added, "That's a compliment, by the way."

Fay snorted. "Isn't it ironic that my husband didn't like how ambitious I was, didn't like how much I did? You know, at first, I thought it would be great to be with someone who was so easygoing. And it was, at first. When we were both toiling away, trying to climb up the proverbial ladder. But after I launched the firm with Teddy and Sulagna, he changed. He started sulking when I talked about work and got snide when I tried to ask about his. When I asked him normal questions about his day, his job, he said it was so much pressure. *Why was I hounding him?* But I wasn't. Even innocent questions about his coworkers—*Does Jenny still bring in baked goods?*—and he'd snap at me. He was the one who ended up being hard on me. By the end, he just didn't like me—or himself. It was difficult to tell."

"Those are pretty normal questions."

She shook her head. "God, this is exactly the trap I wanted to avoid falling into—being that self-unaware person who ends up endlessly rehashing my baggage when I'm trying to move on—no—*when* I'm moving on."

"You don't need to apologize."

"I wasn't really. But that's how women are supposed to be, right? Play it cool, be quiet about what they want, and just hope they get it *somehow*."

She was staring at her coffee cup as if she could incinerate it. Her hair had started to curl from the warmth she was generating, and he wanted to reach over and pull on a stray lock. The thought that it would make her angrier made him want to laugh. Maybe he wanted to lean toward her and kiss her pink cheeks and have her eyes snap at him even more. It was exactly the wrong thought to have right at this particular moment. He didn't want to be drawn to her, he didn't want to find her funny or endearing. He didn't want to have the urge to protect her. He didn't want to worry about Fay at all when he should be worried about protecting himself.

But what he said was, "That's what I've always liked about you. You have this way of sticking up for yourself and making it come out right. It's like that time with the bugs."

"Oh God, not that again."

"Fay, my point is that you did the right thing for yourself and turned the situation around, too. And you're doing that now—with your life. You got divorced because you were unhappy and you needed a change. I could stand to learn from that."

"It doesn't feel like that. It feels like I'm at the bugs-on-my-legs-and-everyone-recoiling-in-horror stage."

"But that just means the chocolate-milkshakes-for-everyone stage is right around the corner."

It coaxed a smile out of her, which was what he intended, but Oliver continued to think about the things Fay had confessed, marveling at her resilience. Here was a clear-eyed woman, who'd seen that her life was stuck in a place she didn't like and changed it.

He'd call Teddy first thing Monday to try to nudge them about an interview. It was time to get serious.

Sunday

In the end, Fay had drunk up that entire giant cup of black coffee from the cafe. And although it hadn't made her jittery, it did keep her awake that night, playing their conversation in her head over and over.

No, not just their conversation—their kisses in the

closet, the firmness of him against her, his shoulders, tense and desperate, his mouth.

She'd tried to get some work done. She'd thought about calling Renata. But in the end, she'd stretched out on her mattress and given herself over to thoughts about Oliver.

The truth was she remembered too well that he'd been the one to help her on that day long ago when she'd waded into a bug-infested field in New Jersey. She remembered emerging, trying not to panic as almost everyone around her squealed and ran away. She'd tucked that afternoon in a back corner of her mind a long time ago. But it was still there, a little blurry around the edges, but the important parts were intact. Maybe she'd kept it hidden away because she'd labeled it a minor bad memory. But now, after Oliver talked about it, her recollection of it had changed. She recalled that she'd enjoyed walking in that field, away from the chatter of her friends. It was sunny, the grass was cooler, and she could feel the humidity rising up. And after she emerged, after the fuss had died down and Oliver was calmly helping her, she remembered thinking that there was something wrong about the fact that she was intensely aware of being scrutinized by him. She'd stood facing the car in a pair of borrowed flip-flops, while he carefully and gently looked her over, and she had *felt* it. She'd been with Jeremy at the time, but of course, she'd been conscious of Oliver's eyes on her, of knowing that she was safe with him, that he would be careful.

Even as she recalled the long-ago scene, the memory changed and blossomed. In her mind, Oliver wasn't the carefree young thing he'd seemed back then. In her new version, the warmth of yesterday's afternoon kisses slipped in. She was free of Jeremy. She could let Oliver look. She could stand outside in the sunlight, let him touch more than her ankle, let him trail his thumb up her calf and along the tensed, grooved muscle of her thigh, then inside, while their friends' voices buzzed in the distance. He would be careful this time, too, but this time all of their care would be about keeping quiet.

She closed her eyes against the image, against the deep, wet pulse down between her legs. Her mattress creaked as she shifted, trying to get comfortable, trying to ignore how her nipples dragged along her T-shirt, under her sheet.

Finally, with an impatient huff, she reached down and pulled off her sleep boxers and placed them neatly on the pillow beside her. She sat up and pulled off her tee. She told herself she was going to do this really quickly—just to take the edge off—and then she was going to stop thinking about Oliver and go to sleep.

But even as she made the sounds indicating her impatience, she could feel her pulse speed up in anticipation. And that irritated her. Because it wasn't as if Oliver were really here, on this mattress on the floor, looking at her as she sat in bed.

She could hear herself panting.

Right. Down to business. She lay back and slipped her hand down, trying to get to the point, *as it were*, as efficiently as possible. But even as she put her fingers right on her clit—no sense in being coy and tender with herself—she couldn't help saying his name. She tried to do it in as normal a voice as possible. It seemed loud in the largely unfurnished room—loud and almost electrifying.

She closed her eyes. *"Oliver."*

His name had seemed so stuffy when she'd first
met him. It made him seem like the kind of person
who might wear a bowtie. And then the name became
him: *Oliver.* In the afternoon, in that townhouse closet,
they'd kissed and she'd felt wild. Even as her mouth had
opened against his, as she'd pushed herself against his
hands, his chest, the stiffening of his cock, she wanted
to claw at him to pull him even closer. But now as she
whispered and murmured his name over to herself, her
fingers working through her own slickness, she spread
her legs wide and opened her mouth to the *O* and licked
her lips to the *L* and the *V*, tossing her head back and
forth to the last syllable as she came.

She remembered this the next morning during her
early Sunday jog through St. Nicholas Park. The summer flowers were already in full bloom, and even
though it was before 8 a.m., people were already stak-
ing out their barbecue spots. She remembered while
she spent a few minutes prying tile from her bathroom
floor. During her phone call with her parents, she'd even
stopped listening to them for a few minutes to imagine
what Oliver was doing. What he could do to her. They
didn't notice that she wasn't speaking. They were arguing with each other on separate landlines, as they usually did, in a mixture of Mandarin and English, with
names of relatives and friends sprinkled in, that made
it hard for her to follow anyway.

They mentioned something about coming to visit,
and she shut that down quickly, saying she had to renovate and didn't have anywhere for them to sleep, and
then after they hung up, she made a new plan.

It was almost noon. Fay was home in her still unpacked apartment with mounds of work she could do.

But she wouldn't be able to concentrate. The worst he could say was no. She called Oliver.

"I know this is last minute. There's this townhouse on Striver's Row. I was talking to the broker about it. She's having an open house. I wondered if you'd like to see it. With me. Like, this afternoon at around four? We could walk around the neighborhood afterward. We could even go to Alexander Hamilton's Grange if there's time, and it's still open, and there aren't hordes of tourists."

"More real estate. I feel like I'm being wooed."

"Well, it's real estate that neither of us can afford. Fantasy real estate. But yes, I want to see you, and uh…"

She stopped. She didn't want to talk to him about her *feelings*.

"I can't stop thinking about you either," he murmured.

She swallowed.

She wished she could see his face right now—or that he could see hers.

Chapter Four

Oliver was at his mother's in Forest Hills when Fay called. He and his brother drove over every Sunday morning to Queens. Last year, they and their sister, Macy, had pitched in to buy the place for his mom. Although, for the past few months, Nat had covered his brother's share of the mortgage. It was a nice enough two-story, still within New York City limits, but in a grassy, house-y section of the borough that may as well have been the suburbs, the kind of genteel place his mom or Macy had probably dreamed about when they were all crammed in that two-bedroom apartment in Elmhurst after their dad had abandoned them. All of Oliver's objections about how isolated Ma would be from her friends had been overruled. Plenty of Asian-American families here, Macy pointed out, as if it was all the same, but Ma alone wasn't exactly a young, Asian-American family.

While Nat lounged around inside and was fed the rice porridge and bits and pieces that his mother kept on the family table, Oliver trimmed the hedges and mowed the grass and probably made the neighbors hate him with all the noise from the various yard-keeping machines he'd had to learn to use. Of course, when Fay called and asked him if he'd meet her, he said yes.

Then he went to tell his mother that he'd be leaving.

Nat was holding one of his loafers in one hand and a damp paper towel in another. Ma was scolding him. "Why do you buy expensive things if you don't know how to take care of them?"

"It's just a little scuff."

"You don't clean shoes with dish soap and a paper towel."

She darted to the kitchen and came back with a gallon container of vegetable oil. She was still grumbling.

Nat was laughing. "What, are you going to deep fry my Guccis?"

"Won't taste worse than that expensive restaurant in Midtown you took me to last month," Ma shot back.

"Maybe better. This is *fine* leather."

Oliver cleared his throat. "I'm taking off."

Ma gave him an accusing glare that traveled from the hairs on his head down to the shoes he'd just put on—sneakers, of course. No buttery cowhides for his feet—he'd had to take care of the yard. Ma gave a huff, no less withering for the fact that she was still hefting a giant-ass bottle of Mazola. "You're not going to stay to see the girls?"

Macy and her kids would be there, like clockwork, for the family dinner at 1 p.m. They had it every Sunday, seemingly for the sole reason of allowing his whole family to cluster around him to tell him that his lack of ambition was a disappointment. Most days it didn't bother him. But ever since he'd lost his job, he'd wondered if they all thought he was turning into Dad. Sometimes, when he was feeling low, he feared it, too.

"Next week."

"What's so important that you don't have time to see your family?"

"I'm meeting someone."

"No work and suddenly you have a fancy meeting on a Sunday."

Oliver bit his tongue. As if suddenly remembering why she was there, Ma grabbed the paper towel from Nat and carefully poured a spot of oil onto it. She handed it back to Nat. "Use."

Nat, bent over at his task, said, "You want a ride back to Manhattan?"

Ma scowled.

Oliver said quickly, "Nah, I'll take my chances with the Sunday subway."

"Let me at least drive you to the station."

Ma suddenly looked anxious. "You're both leaving?"

"No, Ma. I'm just driving Oliver to the subway. It's too far to walk to it in this heat. Plus, Macy and the kids will be here soon. You won't be alone."

His mother said nothing and stalked away. That was all the goodbye he was going to get from her. He'd spoiled her and Nat's moment by interrupting. Then again, if he stuck around, he'd have an entire afternoon of this. Nat could handle it—he never took their mother's comments to heart.

"What was that about?" Oliver asked when they got in the car.

"She doesn't like it when we leave her alone anymore."

"Could've fooled me."

"I think all the peace and quiet of suburban Queens is getting to her."

"It's what she and Macy insisted she wanted."

Well, he'd laid out his arguments long ago, but his informed opinion about a healthy neighborhood for his non-driving mother to live in hadn't counted for much. He didn't feel like rehashing that with Nat.

At the station, Oliver hopped out of the car and onto the E. He tried to read his book. But by the time he had to transfer to an uptown train at Columbus Circle, he'd tucked his phone away and was thinking of Fay.

It took him nearly an hour to get back to Nat's apartment—another reason why that part of the Forest Hills house was so inconvenient—but he still had enough time to clean the subway off himself and change into the outfit of someone who would want to look at a townhouse on Striver's Row. He polished his glasses, picked up his keys, and glanced down at his shoes—the sneakers his mom had huffed at.

He kept them on.

Oliver had agreed to meet Fay at the 137th Street stop. He was already waiting for her when she hurried out to the corner, but there was a pause as she decided how she wanted him to greet her.

Well, when she was back in her apartment and she'd thought of this moment, she'd wanted Imaginary Oliver to grab her by the waist and make out with her quite urgently. But what she wanted from Real Oliver was something different. Not because he wasn't beautiful in his button-down shirt, and with his dark glasses, another slash of handsome across the sharp angles of his face. Real Oliver was so much more potent than Imaginary Oliver. An urgent kiss would be exciting from Imaginary Oliver. From Real Oliver, it would do damage.

Real Oliver, of course, also saw the slight hesitation she gave before she leaned in to peck him on the cheek. And, of course, she closed her eyes and her fingers slipped down to grasp his shirt, and all she could think of was that she'd masturbated while saying his name over and over last night. The light press of his hand made her shiver.

She cleared her throat. "Oliver," she said. "Hey, thanks for coming. Nice to see you."

Nice. Well, it was more than nice to see him. Although maybe he was getting that idea from the fact that she still hadn't let go of his shirt. It would probably be cool of her to release him, but his hand came up and closed around her wrist—gently. "Thanks for asking me," he said in her ear.

They were standing very close and holding on to each other.

"I like your jeans," she said. Because she did. Especially on him.

"I got the memo." He stepped back. "We're wearing our good-but-not-trying-too-hard-to-look-like-a-gazillionaire-who-can-casually-drop-a-few-million-on-a-townhouse clothing."

In truth, she'd worn her skinny capris because they had zippers at the ankles. Somehow she'd thought that made them sexy, although she wasn't sure why.

"I like the zippers," he said.

It was as if he were reading her mind.

"It's not like they unzip anything fun. You already saw my instep and my calves all those years ago."

He darted a quick, hot glance at her. "Fun is where you make it."

It would probably be a good idea to start moving, she thought, lest things get too amusing right at this subway stop.

She cleared her throat and started walking. "So, I should let you know, the broker thinks we're actually interested in buying."

"Together."

"Yes. It's an open house, but only by appointment."

"I don't understand that."

"I don't either. I guess she just wants to cut down on gawkers."

"Like us."

"Like us."

They ambled across 138th Street. She was aware of Oliver looking around at her neighborhood. A woman selling *coco helado* stood at one corner under the umbrella of her cart, fanning herself with a piece of cardboard. Older people sat on lawn chairs on the sidewalk, clustered around stereos or just laughing and talking. The shops near Amsterdam Avenue had gotten more and more expensive—admittedly because of people like her moving into the neighborhood. A fancy panini place that featured complicated coffees had opened on the corner, and there was a gastro-pub going in where a laundromat had stood. Rumor had it that they'd be getting a Citibike stand soon. What was heartening, though, was that some of these businesses were being opened by locals. She'd seen the young men behind the counter coming out to kiss their *abuelas* and setting them up at low tables, the fancier menus in old standbys.

She could observe it all with her professional

eye—she knew Oliver was seeing it, too—and sexual awkwardness aside, she was happy to show the neighborhood to him. She walked down these streets often, of course. But she liked watching how Oliver saw them. The way his head turned curiously just as hers would when they saw the long line for the Dominican bakery, the way he took in the signs for the small hair salons, shuttered now on Sunday afternoon, or how he paused slightly at the entrance of the urban garden bristling with flowers and sun-hatted people. The way his eyes went up and down and everywhere, taking in levels of activity, signs of renewal and growth, the way it all made sense together.

She eyed his jeans again, noting the way his thighs pulled taut, long lines against the material every time he took a step.

"What have you been up to today, then?"

"Helping my mom. Yard work. She lives in Forest Hills."

"In Forest Hills Gardens—?"

They chorused, *"One of the oldest planned communities in the United States."*

It was the first real laugh they'd had together that morning. Oliver had thrown back his head, and he was looking at her with something like affection. Blink and it was gone. "No, not the Gardens area. If she lived there, I'd lead with that. *Hi, I'm Oliver Huang-my-mom-lives-in-Forest-Hills-Gardens-which-was-conceived-by-Olmsted-and-Atterbury.*"

"They're right when they say Asian names are difficult."

"Yeah, I don't think that's going to fit on an official

form. But if it were true that she lived there, I'd change it in a hot minute, if not just to spite ol' Freddy Olmsted."

But speaking of historic communities, they'd hiked across the park and were turning onto 139th Street and before them stood the old townhouses of Striver's Row. "Oh, wow," Oliver said, stopping short.

She took a breath.

Beautiful regular rows of redbrick brownstone buildings stood on the south and the shadows of tall trees dappled the yellow-and-white limestone on the north. A delivery man pedaled his bike slowly down the middle of the street, seemingly taking in the buildings the way she and Oliver were.

"I know. I love all sorts of streets in the city, all the weird old mews and the new steel and glass buildings on the far west side, and the half blocks where you can find a cluster of shops all selling the same things— furs or door accessories. But this, this calls to me." She sighed. "I guess it's why I moved up here. I wanted to be near it."

"*You* live up here?"

"Well not *here* here. If I did, I'd lead with that. *Hi, I'm Fay Liu-I-live-on-Striver's-Row*. But I'm back there, near Amsterdam Avenue."

Something flashed across his face, too quick for her to read.

She took a deep breath. "It's not the ritziest address, but maybe you'd like to come up. Afterward."

Chapter Five

Oliver very much wanted to come up to Fay's afterward. So much so that he almost. *Almost* didn't want to tour this Striver's Row townhouse. Maybe being in an anticipatory sexual state was the only condition in which one should look at houses. It likely made for quick viewing and practical, unsentimental decisions, which was how people were allegedly supposed to look at real estate— *as an investment*. Well, that was one way of figuring out where to live.

Not that he was doing that now. He and Fay weren't buying anything today—they were barely together as a couple. Besides, the only thing Oliver was interested in right now was a bedroom—or maybe a few sturdy walls and a little privacy in which to appreciate Fay's glorious, preferably naked skin.

But he tried to push that thought aside; they were on a public—renowned, at that—street, and it was afternoon, and he was supposed to play a casual, solvent grown-up who was interested in home ownership.

They walked slowly to the house on the north side of the street and up a set of terracotta stairs flanked by elaborate ironwork railings.

Fay turned to him, took a deep breath, and rang the doorbell.

Footsteps sounded. A young Black woman opened the door. She had a professional smile, a suit, and an iPad. "I'm Magda Ferrer. You must be Darling and Olly—is that right?"

Whoosh! As he turned to Fay—*Darling, dammit!*—the air went out of his lungs again.

Fay smiled somewhat sheepishly at Oliver. "Is that how it is?" he mouthed.

She shrugged, but her eyes twinkled. Damn her. She was cute.

He edged closer to her. "Darling and Olly? Are we solving mysteries in a quaint English village?"

"No, in Harlem."

The air-conditioning was cold in the foyer, but Oliver felt hot. He took off his glasses and wiped them so that he'd see better. Magda was checking something off on her tablet and saying something about the weather and the sunlight coming in through the leaded glass of the doors. Fay had moved to examine them and was standing right where the sun glinted on her. She was shiny and beautiful and out of reach, and yet here she was, reaching for him.

"There's so much light—I didn't expect that," she said, taking his hand, just as a Darling Wife really would.

"It's under renovation. I can show you the plans. You'll see that the kitchen has already been beautifully updated—a dream to cook in. Viking range with granite countertops and under-cabinet lighting."

With each feature that the broker listed, Fay squeezed their joined hands, each one pumping blood and excitement to every part of his body. Again, he felt that illicit thrill, the promise that had been in their first—no, *second* kiss. He was being stupid. They were just there to look at a house—a house that under normal circumstances he wouldn't come to see. He should concentrate on that, not on the suggestion that there might be sex afterward. Maybe by the end of the tour, Fay would change her mind. Maybe he would.

Still, his mind worked. Even as he nodded and smiled at the real estate broker, specifically, he began to try to figure out a way that he and Fay could be left alone for, say, fifteen minutes without Agent Eagle-eyes following them—ten minutes, even. Okay, five, if Fay was as keyed up as he was.

Magda showed them the huge entry gallery and rushed them past the coat closet. (It was too small and temporarily lined with paint cans and construction equipment that would hurt if they came tumbling down while he and Fay rocked against the shelves.) The half bathroom had perhaps once been a closet—maybe that would work, but the floor creaked in there. Part of his brain worked out whether he'd be able to get his hands on the original house plans, another part lamented that it would be hard to be quiet. The kitchen was too open, and the deck could be spied upon by a neighbor.

But he wouldn't give up. Because he wasn't Oliver Huang right now. He was *Olly*—urbane, murder-solving, closet seducer, casual provider of luxury townhomes and real estate to *Darling*, who he probably didn't appreciate because he was the kind of careless bastard who always expected his cigarettes to be lit by others and who had a valet to press his not-trying-so-hard jeans. As in response, Darling Fay's fingers were now trailing up his forearm and down his back, and she was now squeezing her curves into his side even as she asked a question about the history of the house.

Magda seemed happy to elaborate, chatting about the architect Stanford White who had designed the set of homes on this street, pointing to the ceiling, and to the millwork—most of it was new—and when Fay tilted her head and arched her back obligingly, he got a glimpse down her shirt, down into the faint glow of skin, the curve of her cleavage in a shadowed bra. The hand that caressed his butt told him that she knew what she'd done.

He cleared his throat and tried to focus. Could he cause a distraction? Start a small fire that wouldn't ruin this spacious home? Surely the floor plan hadn't always been this open. If he recalled correctly—and in his *determined* state, he couldn't quite be sure he would—Stanford White had been a horrendous perv. Well, if he had, you'd think he'd have designed a lot of nooks and crannies to get up to funny business—if ol' Stanford was going to be loathsome, he might have redeemed himself by also being useful.

They followed Magda up the stairs to a formal dining room. The room had been staged, with fresh flowers on an old table and chairs, and two full place settings at opposite ends of the table—two kinds of wine glasses, a gleaming array of forks, knives, spoons, napkins rolled in fancy jeweled rings, plates and those bigger plates that went under them that you weren't supposed to actually eat off of. But glass cabinets shone back at them, empty. Magda pointed out the picture frame molding, the smooth hardware, and the pocket door that led to the living room. Someone had installed a swooping light fixture with a shade in a vivid bordello red. Oliver switched it on and off briefly, and all three of them were a little startled by the sharp electric light. The room was scrupulously clean and smelled faintly of lemon Pledge, and Oliver briefly wondered if the broker had been here herself just before they'd arrived, wiping down the surfaces. Surrounded by all this beautiful, dark, gleaming wood, he was tempted to touch all of that smoothness.

He wasn't alone in that thought. As Magda talked more, spinning a comforting tale about the wonderful dinner parties that he and Darling could have here, Fay wandered off to trail her fingers across the empty surfaces. She paused to swing open the built-in china cabinets with one hand, her other still caressing the smooth surfaces behind her.

He wondered what she was thinking. Maybe she could almost hear the clink of silverware, the soft murmur of wealthy people. Perhaps she was wishing that she could really live here with all this space, with all this sleek polished wood that probably ran like silk under her fingertips. He'd never really cared about money, but security had been another matter. Another worry to thank his dad for, he supposed. But it was his own fault he didn't have a job, and sooner or later he'd have to talk to Fay about her firm. He stared hard at the two place settings and imagined her sitting at one end of the table unfolding a napkin and smiling blankly at the person at the other end.

What did it mean that she'd given the broker fake names? What did it mean that he hadn't corrected Magda about his name? Not that Olly couldn't have been one of his nicknames. But it wasn't. He was Oliver; he'd never had to insist.

But as Oliver was about to say something, Magda's phone sounded and the doorbell rang. She said something about the next interested clients being early, which was likely supposed to be an incentive to spur Olly and Darling to make an offer. She quickly excused herself downstairs, her ear pressed to her phone.

"Let's go up," Fay said abruptly.

That was the line he'd been planning to use, but she delivered it much better. She had already headed out and up to the third floor where the bedrooms were. After a moment of checking the floor plans, just to be sure, Oliver followed her.

She was waiting for him inside one of the still-under-renovation bathrooms, perched on the edge of a claw-foot tub, one shoe dangling precariously from her toes. He admired the long graceful arch of her foot, the strong line of muscle under her jeans up to her knee. He'd like to touch that knee, trace the line of bone and muscle up the inside of her thigh.

Oliver asked, "Should I close the door?"

"Lock it."

He sprang to action. He shut the door quietly and looked for the locking mechanism. It was an old-fashioned knob with a pin that could be twisted. It did not twist. He jiggled the handle, turned it to the right, turned it to the left, and tried again. The door didn't seem to want to cooperate. Oliver silently cursed vintage hardware, slow restoration efforts, and the lack of WD-40. He opened the door. He closed the door, more firmly this time, and twisted. Nothing.

He got down on his knees and jiggled the doorknob and he tried again, once, twice.

The room was getting stuffy and warm. And not

just because Fay was waiting patiently. He got up and opened the door. He tried the lock while the door was open. It didn't budge. He straightened. A thin trickle of sweat had started down his back.

It was a lot cooler downstairs.

"Never mind," Fay said, her voice a little strained. "Just close it."

She was starting to look nervous, too. They'd wasted time. They didn't hear anyone from below, but in some ways, that was worse. Fay moved as if to come off the tub, but her shoe finally slipped off her foot and fell on the floor with a loud *thunk*.

They both jumped. And when Fay twisted to pick it up, she lost her already precarious balance at the lip of the tub and with a yelp, slid in ass first, taking part of the flimsy shower curtain with her with an ominous rattle.

Oliver sprang forward and pulled the plastic off of her. "Are you all right?"

"I'm fine. I'm—fine."

"Let's get you out of here in case that whole curtain track decides to come down."

Fay started giggling, and it only made her legs, which were sticking out of the tub, flail more. Oliver tried not to laugh as he helped pull her out. But Fay was too far gone to notice. "Oh God," she said, wiping her eyes, "I cannot wait to explain this to Magda."

"It's a very boring story," Oliver said, brushing the dust out of her hair. "We came upstairs to take a look at the bedrooms and bathrooms and not at all because we wanted to make out like teenagers—"

"Right. That's all we wanted to do."

"Please do not torture me with what could have been.

We came upstairs, and you backed into the bathroom to take a picture and most certainly did not look extremely alluring just before you took a spill."

"Extremely alluring, is that how I looked?"

Fay shucked her other shoe and hopped up on the ledge of the tub. By tacit agreement, Oliver stood by the tub, letting her steady herself against him as she re-adjusted the track. And when she was ready, he helped her hold up appropriate sections of the curtain. Luckily it was mostly not torn. Mostly.

Oliver grasped her waist while she popped the un-damaged sections into the curtain rings. He helped her down again. It wasn't quite how he'd hoped their tryst would go, but he had at least gotten to touch her knee, her hip.

But as Fay bent to put on her shoes, Oliver noticed a very white streak of dust over the back of her dark capris. Fay twisted around and grimaced. "Serves me right for attempting the luge down the side of a tub in a house that's still being restored."

"Can I help?"

"Yes, I—"

Oliver started to dust her off. And that's how Magda and her new clients found them—urbane, polished, murder-mystery-solving Olly slapping Darling's butt in the third-floor bathroom while Darling bent over laughing, her head turned to watch his progress.

"I thought she was pretty understanding, considering," Fay said when they reached the end of the block.

Magda had not let them out of her sight after that moment. Although she probably didn't suspect that he and Fay had been trying to find a place to tryst and was more likely afraid that Fay—no, *Darling*—would smash a stairway spindle or accidentally cause a collapse of one of the brick fireplaces rather than get up to any naughty business. It was Fay's guilt causing her to turn red. Oliver managed to appear perfectly serious and apologetic as he gave Magda a version of the events that had led to that moment. The broker had also refused the twenty dollars Oliver quietly offered to pay for the shower curtain.

They'd stayed to admire the rest of the house—the bedrooms, the windows, a walk-in closet that had been installed sometime in the 1990s, the washer and dryer. Oliver had asked questions about the boiler and the roof that Magda relished answering—the broker really seemed to want to use all of her knowledge and research—and that had at least restored Olly and Darling in her eyes somewhat in the end.

Fay stopped. She faced him. Might as well be direct. "What are you thinking? Are you interested in coming back to my place? Or have we had enough adventures?"

"I want to see your place," he said simply.

Something about that was so reassuring, that she didn't worry much about the fact that she didn't have a couch and that her apartment was only partly unpacked, and that her bathroom floor was a mess of pried-up tiles. If anyone was likely to see the potential in the confusion of all of it, it was Oliver. Oliver who helped her when she needed it, and who looked at her in a way that made her feel like she could say what she was thinking, who thought she was alluring even when she was sitting on the edge of a tub in a dusty old bathroom.

The day had gotten a lot hotter. And by the time they walked the three stories up Fay's apartment, they were both sweating in their casual-but-upscale house-hunting jeans. "It's a mess. I just moved in. But I can get you some water. Or a beer?"

"Water would be great. Beer, too, if you'll have some."

"I have a fan somewhere, too."

"I see it."

By the time she got back from the kitchen, Oliver had rearranged the fan and some cushions and boxes into some semblance of comfortable order. "You have a lot of cartons of books."

"How do you know they're books?"

"They're heavy. The boxes say 'Books' on them. Let me guess, fifty copies of Jane Jacobs's *The Death and Life of Great American Cities*."

"Yes, that's it. I was planning on leaving one at the door of each of my new neighbors."

"Doing the Lord's work."

"You have that right."

She sat down carefully on one of the low cushions near Oliver. If she wanted to—if he wanted to—she'd be able to slide over beside him and put her face up and pull him down for a kiss—and it wouldn't be a completely uncomfortable position.

But she would have to be patient. Oliver picked up and drained his entire mug of water, and she watched his throat, watched the small bead of moisture that had traveled along one cheekbone and along the clean contour of his jaw.

"How long have you lived here?" he asked, setting down the glass.

"A month. I'm still—" she grimaced "—I'm working on it."

"Let's see what you're doing."

He stood up gracefully from the floor. How did he do that? And he helped her up, too. Their hands meeting, sliding over each other in a firm grip. That was nice. It was also nice that he didn't step back when she was up. That he looked down, a question in his eyes and she nodded, and he leaned over and kissed her.

That was very, very good, too.

She took a deep breath and stepped back, pulling his hand, still in hers. "Come see the hall closet," she said. "It used to be a dumbwaiter shaft."

It was a pleasure showing him the apartment. He didn't ask her why she hadn't gotten furniture, why she hadn't fixed certain things or unpacked others. He didn't expect her life to be complete and perfect, and he didn't complain about sitting on the floor or drinking beer from the same mug that had held his water. What he did do was get as excited as she'd felt when she first saw this place.

She took a deep breath and led him to the hall in front of her bedroom.

He was staring at the doorway. "Look at this. I'll bet there used to be a transom window over this door. You can almost see the outlines of it."

"Oliver."

Her hand slid up his arm.

He glanced down, blinking.

"This is my bedroom," she said.

She was usually a decisive person, used to figuring out a situation quickly and deciding on a path based on what was in front of her. What was in front of her now was Oliver. And she wanted him. She'd been touching him all afternoon, and he'd been touching her. And it had been wonderful and frustrating. She liked kissing him—more than liked it, she craved it. And because her body was as good at decisions as the rest of her, it had mapped out for her across her skin a guide, a flow-chart, detailing every step, every degree of how good it would feel to have his body against hers.

She put her arms around his neck. Oliver caught her and pulled her closer. He lowered his head. He could have kissed her, but he was still searching her face, still hesitating. "Are you sure about this?"

"Yes. I know my own mind."

He gave a short laugh. "I don't know my own half the time."

That caught her up short. "But do you want this, too?"

"Yes."

It was the truth. She could tell by his hands, which moved up and down her back of their own accord, and then stopped abruptly every time he had a doubt, a shadow, a memory. She wanted to tell him how much she liked him, how considerate he was, how fun he was, how much she could already trust him—but she'd always had trouble praising people, especially when she cared. And all of those words seemed so small and cold compared to the warmth behind what she felt. How could she explain to him how important and rare it was to know someone who helped her out of bathtubs, who walked through her neighborhood, her apartment, her everything, and listened to her?

Not that she was getting emotional about this. So instead, she drew him down and tried to kiss his doubt away.

She moved her lips along his jaw and licked the sharp

turn of his cheekbone. She kissed up to his eyes, which were closed, fluttering under his lids. She ached deep down, she was thick with aching, and the sound of it came out in a long moan.

His hands became surer, and then more urgent. In one swipe, he pulled up the back of her shirt, his fingers skimming across the valley of her spine, and up around the front to her breast. They found each other's lips now, their tongues, the heat of their mouths and the desperate clash of their teeth.

She stumbled backward out of the doorway, and pulled him with her, bumping him into the door frame once or twice. Not that he seemed to mind.

In a moment, they were both kneeling on the floor by her mattress. "Kiss me, please keep kissing me," she said, even as she bent her own head out of the way to fumble with the buttons of his shirt.

Her own tee was off and on the ground somewhere. And he was slowly, softly biting her earlobe and breathing into her neck, raking down the straps of her bra. "Like this," he said, nudging her head up to him again and taking her lips once more.

His kiss was lush and soft, and then hard when her tongue met his. He'd succeeded in pulling her bra down and the cotton of his shirt, which she'd been less successful at removing, rubbed against the tips of her breasts.

She could feel herself sinking farther down. But he was trying to pull her melting, uncooperative body onto the mattress. "Help me here," he murmured.

She forced her legs, which didn't want to do much besides open, to lift her. She lay down on the very edge, with Oliver following, with him on top of her. They were both still in their jeans, those stupid, too-hot jeans they both wore because they'd been trying to prove something instead of just getting straight into bed.

He reared up, panting, his hair wild, his glasses smudged, and he looked at her for a moment. Then his head was down again, kissing her, moving to her breasts, lipping her nipples, and then he slid himself lower, between her legs.

His fingers traced the seam of her pants.

She shifted uncomfortably.

"Are you all right? Are you okay with this?"

"I do want it. But it's hot out, and I'm sweaty. I'm not usually shy about stuff like this." She almost laughed. Usually? What did that mean? She'd been in another relationship for the last ten years. She couldn't say that finding Oliver Huang—or anyone else—on her mattress was commonplace.

He pressed her with his thumb, and she whimpered at that. Oh, she wanted him to do it, she wanted him to lick her right there. He raised himself again and said, "I like your soft skin. I like your heat. I like all the scents of you. I would like to see more."

"I want the same things you want—okay, not exactly the same, you get the idea. Are you still with me? Is this still okay?"

"Uh, yes. Definitely."

They both paused to laugh a little uncomfortably. Then Oliver took a deep breath. He undid the button and stroked the small patch of skin revealed. He slid the zipper down slowly, slowly.

She shifted again, this time, impatient. She could feel the warm rush of wetness gathering as he looked at her intently.

He cupped his hand under her ass and slid everything off, his hands, leaving a warm trail to her legs.
He kneeled back and unzipped his own jeans and pulled
his pants down, giving his cock a sure stroke. She enjoyed that. She could have watched him for longer. But
too soon, he took his glasses off, put them on a box,
and settled between her legs again.

"Do you like this?" he asked, pressing his thumb
down on her mound. It was the lightest touch, but she
felt her legs opening wider as he moved. She threw her
head back as his fingers gently traveled down the folds.
She caught a glimpse of him lowering his head and then
the warmth of his breath was on her. The first swipe of
his tongue and she let out a tortured gasp, the grip of
his other hand on her thigh, on her butt.

She dug her heels into the mattress and tossed her
head back and forth, trying not to thrust into him as
he touched her, carefully at first and then with growing assurance. Then, he angled his finger into her and
sucked, and she cried out.

She was getting a crick in her neck from trying to
hold herself up on her elbows, to watch him. But she
had to—she had to see him, to see all of it. With one
hand he was careful and delicate, feeling his way along
her skin, with the other, the other that held her thigh, he
was strong, a brute, his thumb digging into her jumping
inner muscle, causing her to screech and growl.

He looked up at her, catching her eye, and that was
what did it. Her head fell back, her body lifted itself into
him and turned itself up and over and out into the air.

When she could breathe again, she looked down at
him, still low between her legs, watching her, smiling.
"Come up here," she whispered.

The old mattress creaked, dipped hard as he crawled up on his elbows. "This is like being a teenager. And having secret sex in an abandoned house," she said, pulling his shirt off.

She was perhaps a little too brisk with the way she removed his remaining clothing—or maybe it was her tone. Because despite his obvious arousal, he hesitated. He said, "You don't have to. I can finish off if you don't—"

But she wanted to. Maybe not quite with the urgency that she'd felt before—she usually took time to recover her desire—and certainly not with the desperation he felt, if she could judge by his face, the panting escaping his lips. But that was intriguing, too. She liked the way he was watching her as she pulled down his jeans, making sure, as she did, to slide her hands along the firm thighs, tracing the long swoop of muscle, pausing to tug slightly on the hair of his legs and to look at his ankles, his instep, the solid slabs of his feet—and back up, slowly, of course, to his cock. She liked his cock, too—enough that when she put her hand on it—decisively, the way she thought he'd like it, she felt a surprising tingle. But now wasn't the time to dwell on this. "Are you sure you want to?" she asked him.

"I do, I really do."

He was watching her take charge, letting her do what she wanted with him, even though at this point, he was gritting his teeth and muttering as she swung herself off the mattress and found a box of condoms that she'd put in her room just this morning.

"Fuck," he said, once, very clearly, as she smoothed the condom over him.

He rolled up slightly, pulled her head down and

kissed her fiercely, and she was surprised to feel the low flame of excitement start to burn in her again. She carefully straddled him, the mattress dipping fiercely under the two points of her knees, and as she lowered herself down, he rose up to meet her again.

Oliver was cooking in Fay's kitchen. Fay was solidly asleep—so deep under that he'd checked her fridge, decided to leave a note, grabbed her keys. He had time to go out and find a grocery store, dither over ingredients, come back, unpack, and wash a couple of pots. And when he went to check on her, she was still snoozing, openmouthed, under the comforter where he'd left her.

The night had cooled down considerably and Fay's fan had done its work, pushing the night air into the apartment.

Oliver chopped up vegetables and tofu for a stir-fry. When he finished cooking, he looked at it, waiting for a moment, feeling a little foolish. Should he wake her up? Should he just eat in her kitchen without her and leave her a portion? What made him assume that she wanted him to stick around?

The beauty of the stir-fry seemed to mock him. He'd bought two kinds of peppers—red and yellow— for God's sake. He'd impulse purchased a mango on a stick that had been carved in the shape of a rose. Two kinds of peppers for dinner and a mango flower for dessert was probably a sign that he already cared too much. He'd even made rice on a stove top—he could not remember the last time he'd made it in a pot and had to pay attention to it. Even in college, he'd had a tiny rice cooker. The Huang kids had never gotten fancy new sheets and towels when they'd moved into the dorms—they'd always just nabbed them from their beds at home—but Ma Huang had gotten all of them shiny mini rice cookers.

Well, he'd done without, and the meal had turned out well. It was nice to feel like he'd accomplished something. He'd made something beautiful. He was just about to put the lid back on the food when Fay padded into the kitchen. "You cooked!"

And she grabbed him and kissed him and held his face, looking into his eyes; that was enough for Oliver to know that he'd done the right thing.

"I also brought you a mango rose."

Why not just spill everything now?

"What?"

He backed away to go to the fridge, but she clung to him. So they opened it together. Inside, on a paper plate, was a mango flower that he'd bought from a street vendor who'd been packing up to leave. "A rose is a rose," he said. "Unless it's a fruit."

His presentation left something to be desired but she kissed him again more slowly this time, and despite the fact that he was hungry and he'd just spent the last five minutes wondering if he should flee, he didn't want to be anywhere else. Except maybe in the bed again.

His hand slid up under bare thigh and she sighed. "We should eat," she murmured against his mouth.

"Where are the forks?" he said, tightening his hold on her ass.

He kissed her again.

"I don't know. Where did you find the plate?"

They both took a deep breath and let go of each other.

In a few minutes, Fay dug up some bowls and disposable chopsticks. They set up a box in the living room, put the food in the middle, and sat down cross-legged to eat.

"Is this peanut sauce? This is so good," Fay said, groaning.

Oliver, feeling slightly less limber after their mattress athletics, was trying to settle himself into a comfortable position. "My mom's always talking about how men should be useful for a change. It seemed pretty useful for me to learn how to cook."

"Did she teach you this recipe?"

He laughed. "No. Plus, her comments don't usually result in—what do you call it?—constructive criticism or advice. I found some version of it on a blog somewhere and make it all the time."

"Asian moms. The more they criticize, the more they love."

"That's the theory at least. The reality always feels much more complicated. Is yours like that?"

"Yes and no. The reality is complicated. I'm an only child, so both of my parents tend to focus on me a lot even now that I'm in my midthirties. It's intense—and it wasn't always great during the divorce. I needed some time apart from talking about it with them. In a way, it's good that they live across the country."

Oliver huffed a laugh.

She added, "I just realized that I hardly know anything about your family. How can this be? We've been acquainted for years."

"Because we always end up talking about planning. Or our planning friends."

She rolled her eyes. "Well, we are dedicated to our work to a very uncool extent."

Oliver looked down. "Sure."

It may have been a good time to get the fact that her firm had been thinking of interviewing him out in the open. They hadn't responded to his email earlier this week, and Oliver was almost relieved that they didn't seem interested anymore. But maybe it would be the moment to broach the subject of jobs. Fay would most likely have some ideas about where to look, who was hiring people with knowledge of preservation planning, even if her firm clearly wasn't. She'd probably have all sorts of good advice for him, from who to talk with to which commas to take out of his CV.

No, now was a terrible time. He should have brought it up before, but he hadn't been using his brain. And right now, right at this moment, he was with a woman who made him happy. They were eating food. They were comfortable in each other's presence. He didn't want to talk about his personal failings—not this kind, not when she admired him and was pleased with him and the things he could do. Maybe it was selfish, but he didn't want his so-called problem to be the thing they talked about for the rest of the night. Because it could easily become that. He could see how he would slip into the role of one of her projects. Because she was energetic, and she was a natural rescuer of people and places.

He didn't want to become her project. He wanted her just to like him, to like being around him.

He knew, too, that it was a double-edged sword. He couldn't share with her how much he was looking forward to his upcoming gig. How despite the stress of expectations from his family, his upbringing that told him moving from job to job made him unreliable, he was enjoying working for himself. It was even grimly satisfying to have to stay on top of his finances. But she'd said they shouldn't talk about work, which was funny considering that it had drawn them together, that her passion and absorption with it had made him want to listen to her, to know her.

No job talk. Well, now—now they had something else together.

Fay hadn't noticed Oliver's preoccupation. "I just think it's so funny. I mean, I always thought you were handsome. Renata—you remember my friend Renata—talks about your cheekbones a lot."

"Just that particular part?"

"They are striking. But this is a new way of thinking about you. I'm surprised by it."

"Well, I'm the middle child," he said. "With a rheumatologist older sister, and a younger brother who captains the captains of industry for a midtown hedge fund, I'm the underachiever making obscure improvements around the city."

Her smile grew. "My parents don't know how to tell people what my job is so they switch to English. *Our Fay is a PARTNER in a FIRM in NEW YORK MANHATTAN.* And then everyone assumes I'm a lawyer. I don't even bother to try to correct them anymore."

Oliver had to laugh. "There is nothing slower and more painful than trying to explain to your elderly relatives what your job is and why you've decided to do it. I'll say, *No, I don't actually construct bike lanes or low-cost housing. I help communities decide if they put them there*, and they'll stare at me. It's like I have the power to stop time—I just try to define *land-use planner* in Mandarin and everything freezes."

"If only there were some way to turn its time-defying powers into a skincare line."

"We'd make millions."

"We could quit our jobs and never have to explain what we do for a living again."

"I know that would give me a glow."

"You and your cheekbones would become the face of our product. You know, this explains a lot about why you look the way you do."

"Is that why I'm here? Because I'm a pretty face?"

"I like other parts of you, too."

"True, my cheekbones are pretty, but they don't cook."

"You're different than I imagined. I don't know why people don't appreciate you."

Her eyes were soft. And he felt oddly even more vulnerable at that moment because a warm, competent person he cared about—who he was beginning to care about a lot—*appreciated* him. Maybe he should say more. "There's a lot I'm not good at—" he began.

"Shh. Let's concentrate on the positive, shall we?"

She stood up in one fluid movement and flung off her shirt.

To be fair, he didn't forget what he was going to say next. But neither of them were quite in the mood to talk.

Chapter Six

Wednesday

Fay was happy that week.

It wasn't that she'd necessarily been unhappy before. Her life didn't lack for jokes and friends and good conversations and absorbing work. Even when she'd been in the middle of the divorce and seething, or spending hours on FaceTime with Renata, she'd still managed to laugh.

But there was a difference—it was like the difference between breathing when she had a mildly annoying cold and then one day, taking in a big lungful of oxygen and realizing the airways were clear. This was what it meant to feel well.

She took in a breath and enjoyed it.

And she and Oliver weren't texting each other constantly, but she knew he was thinking of her as often as she thought of him. Sometimes, Oliver just sent her a picture with a small comment—yesterday it was a photo of one of the last functioning telephone booths in the city. The other day, it was a photo of the historic church that had been rezoned for condominiums but was now going to be opened as a children's museum. Sometimes, when she felt especially giddy, she'd read the four or five informative words he'd sent as a caption aloud to herself as if he'd been sending her poetry.

It was better than poetry.

She was staring at her screen once more when her coprincipal, Teddy, walked in. "Did you get my email?"

She checked her inbox. "You sent this less than a minute ago."

"Yeah, so I finally have free time to interview for the manager position, and I wanted to see if you'd review these three, give me your opinion on them. We really need someone in place who can hit the ground running."

"Yes, Theodore, I am aware. Save the spiel for the interviewees. I'll look these over."

She opened up the first CV as she spoke and saw the name at the top.

Oliver Huang.

Her Oliver.

She ran her eyes quickly over the document. His phone number, the Columbia degree. Yes, it was definitely him. And of course, he knew she worked there. Her picture was on the website.

She read more closely and saw that he was doing freelance consulting work—the last time he'd held a full-time position was with Greenblatt. She'd known he was at Greenblatt and heard they'd folded, but she'd assumed he'd gotten out, gone somewhere else. Why had she assumed that?

He hadn't mentioned any of this to her.

How had two people so dedicated to work failed to actually discuss work for an entire week? They'd touched on mutual planning friends and abstractly talked about projects they worked on, and she'd surely mentioned the firm. So, how had they not discussed that Oliver was currently job hunting...*at her firm*?

Well, she had deliberately put the brakes on talking about their day-to-day, hadn't she? They'd been too busy pretending to be Olly and Darling.

And now Teddy wanted her opinion.

Fay didn't know what to think. On one hand, she had to admit, just now seeing his name had been exciting—it had made her happy.

On the other, why had he sent the CV to her firm? Did he expect her to give him a job?

She took a deep breath and closed out the screen. Then she got up and paced around her office and tried to think clearly.

She wouldn't be Oliver's direct boss if he got the job, but it was a tiny firm, and she was a partner. How would he feel about essentially working for her? Would he say he was fine with it? Maybe it wasn't even ethical—she certainly would have to excuse herself from hiring if her own boyfriend was among the candidates.

Would he be enthusiastic only to resent her in the future?

Why hadn't he said anything?

She cast her mind over their conversations again and felt almost guilty. Had he mentioned work once? Had she put him off because she had trained herself not to talk about her job? And wasn't that sad to realize that Jeremy could do that to her—was still doing that to her?

The best thing now was to be direct.

She took a deep breath and picked up her phone.

Usually, Oliver liked that Fay got right to the point.

Usually.

"Why didn't you tell me that you were looking for a job?"

Before he could even take a breath to respond, she said, "Your CV appeared on my desk just now."

Oliver was still sweaty after a run in the park. But seeing her name had made him so eager to talk to her. He'd picked up the phone and rested it against his damp face. Now he paused to wipe his forehead with his T-shirt.

It didn't really do much.

"This wasn't a great way to find out," Fay added.

"I'm sorry. I didn't know when to bring it up and if it was still relevant. I sent that CV almost half a year ago and when Teddy finally emailed last Sunday, it was only a vague note that they were starting interviews. I didn't hear anything back and even after a follow-up and... I assumed they weren't really serious."

It was pathetic. He should have tried harder to work it into conversation. The truth was he hadn't wanted to, hadn't wanted anything to interfere with the perfect little world he'd been building with Fay.

"Last Sunday? The day we met on the tour?"

Sweat was now streaming down his forehead, stinging his eyes. But it was more from panic than physical pursuit now.

"How could you not bring it up?"

"I—I didn't want it to be an issue between us—you weren't the one hiring me."

"But it's my firm. I'm one of the partners, Oliver! You must have thought they'd call you in. You must have—maybe you resented me. I thought we talked about everything."

"We didn't really talk about that specifically. And I thought maybe you knew—had seen my résumé."

She was silent at that. He couldn't blame her, it sounded weak even to his own ears.

"At some point, I said something about work and you—well, I thought you didn't want to talk about it. We chatted about friends. We pointed out features of the streets we were on and joked about what we'd do if we could live in the houses we've seen. We had conversations about our field, about city-building—not our actual day-to-day." When she didn't respond again, he said, his voice now stumbling out faster than usual, "You said 'No job talk.'"

Even as he spoke, he knew it seemed like he'd been trying to weasel out of a serious discussion—and since when were they on serious terms? But they were. He knew it, and that serious part of himself hadn't wanted her to find out that he was an unemployed adult living with his younger brother, and that he had been in the running for a job in her firm. And that he really, really wanted a steady position.

He was tired of thinking this way. He got enough of this from his family. Besides, was there something wrong with not having a job—something fundamentally wrong with him? He *was* working, and he *liked* the fact that his work was shorter term, God help him. The feedback was more immediate, his labor was important. He *wasn't* terrible.

But even as he tried to tell himself this, a voice whispered that he'd avoided bringing this up for fear of this very reaction. How many times could he have steered the conversation to the actual realities of their work—and how many times had he stopped short?

He hadn't technically done anything wrong. And yet, he couldn't precisely say that he was blameless either.

"Fay, please, say something."

Nearby a pigeon cooed and a herd of kids swooped by on bikes.

"You're outside?" she asked, almost in a normal tone. It sounded like she was tamping down accusation and anger, but keeping those feelings in check didn't mean they weren't there.

"Yes," he answered cautiously.

She was quiet for a minute. "I have to think about this," she said.

After they'd hung up civilly but not warmly, Oliver sat his sweaty body on a nearby park bench.

He knew that he was hurt and annoyed at Fay's abruptness just then. His response probably did look deceitful, or weak. Maybe he was. That was the problem. He understood where Fay's mistrust was coming from. But where did that leave his own frustration? Only a few days ago, it seemed like she was an oasis: here was someone who had liked his silly mango rose, had liked the fact that she could talk to him about the things that interested her, who could laugh with him, who had known him for a long time.

Someone with whom he could see himself falling in love.

Defeated, he pulled himself off the bench and made his way back to the apartment. Nat was at home, riffling through a pile of unread mail. "On my lunch break— not slacking off, I swear. I just need to grab this—" He held up an envelope triumphantly.

Oliver took off his shoes and aligned them carefully on the floor. "Relax," he said shortly. "I'm not going to accuse you of being lazy. Why is everyone in our family so obsessed with working all the time?"

Instead of turning to leave, Nat put down the envelope and then his phone. "You're in a mood. Did you get turned down for that job?"

"No. Maybe."

His brother crossed his arms. "Does this have anything to do with the fact that you cut out early on Sunday and didn't come back 'til early Monday morning?"

"I didn't mention to Fay that I was up for a job at her firm."

"What? She had no idea this whole time?"

"None."

"Oh, Oliver."

"I just— I was going to say something, but I was enjoying myself for the first time in a long time. She liked me. It was nice to be around someone who wasn't disappointed by me."

"No one is disappointed in you."

"Oh really, have you met our mother?"

"In case you haven't noticed, very little makes our mother happy. It's her natural state to be displeased. It has nothing to do with you."

"Well, I'm tired of all the little digs about how I could've been a lawyer or a doctor. I am never going to make money hand over fist. I am always going to nerd out about cities and communities and all the little ways they work and don't work. I'm always going to be a quiet kind of person who prefers a quieter life—but that doesn't make me a failure or unreliable. I would just like to be accepted for that, *liked* for it." And for a few minutes, with Fay, he'd thought he was.

"Hey, novel idea, but maybe you should tell Mom that?"

"I have in many, many ways."

"Then you need to fix it in yourself and part of that means accepting that she's not going to change—the same way that you're not going to change."

Oliver paused. His brother had been studiously sifting through three pieces of mail for the last five minutes.

Well, standing up to his mother wouldn't fix Oliver's Fay problem.

"Any other words of wisdom you'd like to impart, little brother?"

"Yeah, you need to talk things out with this Fay like a grown-up."

"This from a person who falls in love with a new guy every couple of weeks and dumps him when he turns up with the wrong color shoes. And what if I don't feel like a grown-up right now?"

"All I'm saying is that if Fay's so different—if you feel like she gets you and she does want a chance to talk it out with you—then you have to treat her differently. Or maybe she's terrible. I don't know—you have another chance to find out for sure."

He harrumphed noncommittally at his brother.

"Look, Oliver, I know you worry about turning into Dad—we all do in our own ways, even Macy. Well, the one thing about Dad was that he gave up easily on everyone, including himself. So if you don't want to be like him and don't have at least one more conversation with Fay, then you have to live with that for the rest of your lonely, miserable life."

"Fuck you, Nat."

"Love you, too. And in my humble opinion as a risk analyst, you really do have nothing to lose."

"You're a comfort, bro."

"I try."

Thursday

It turned out to be fairly straightforward for Fay to tell her partners about Oliver, even if the relationship wasn't straightforward in her mind. At around five, she walked into Teddy's office to ask him if he could meet, and Sulagna was already there, sitting on a corner of his desk and directing Teddy on his latest project.

Fay cleared her throat. "So, about Oliver Huang's CV—I have to take myself off of the hiring on this one. I'm…friends with him."

Teddy laughed. "And? We all know each other. It's a small community."

But of course, Sulagna picked up on what Fay was trying to hint at. "Friends—or *friends*?"

"Wait," said Teddy. "You mean you're going out with Oliver Huang?"

Sulagna was already off and running. "You know, I think Oliver's a great candidate. I've met him a couple of times, too—very personable—plus he fills in our gaps in heritage planning and preservation. I think this is exactly who we need in this position."

Teddy said, "But won't it be awkward for Fay?"

"Of course it won't. We'll make sure Oliver's not working with Fay. He's supposed to be supporting your projects anyway, Ted."

This was getting away from her. Everything Sulagna said about Oliver was certainly true and she was glad Sulagna picked up on his talents—she'd thought the same herself just the other day.

But Fay had come in here to take herself out of the hiring process and instead, she'd actually highlighted Oliver's candidacy. Their firm was too small to have a

full-time HR manager and their freelance consultants
had been disasters; Sulagna clearly felt that the need
to hire was so urgent that she was going to jump at the
opening that Fay had created.

But Fay didn't know what she wanted. When con-
fronted with only the possibility of seeing him in their
offices, she was hit with a sudden wave of regret, so
huge and seemingly out of proportion that she had to
put her hand to her chest. What would happen if he
were around every day? How would she deal with it?

This wasn't exactly something she could admit to her
partners right now. If she told them that yes, she would
be uncomfortable working with Oliver, then she'd be
threatening Oliver's chance at the position. She did want
him to have a job; he'd be good at it, and because, if
she could put her stupid feelings aside, his knowledge
would fill in a lot of gaps at Milieu. He ought to have
mentioned it to her, yes, but maybe she had cut off conversation about work. They had talked about planning
without talking about their day-to-day specifically and
part of that had been a deliberate choice for her. After
all, she'd talked about the firm, and the personalities,
and the meetings and clients with Jeremy, and the whole
time it turned out he didn't care about it. It sounded
like such a small thing—a man not paying attention to
his wife as she talked about her day. But apparently, it
was enough to crack her open, to seed a small fissure
in her confidence.

But, of course, none of this was appropriate to tell
Sulagna and Teddy right now—the conversation they
were having was already veering into the inappropri-
ately personal. And she knew, also, that if they hired
Oliver it might be awkward, but not because of anything

on his part. He would be considerate. Because that was how he always was.

Teddy said, "We haven't interviewed him yet."

But unless Fay said something right now, that interview was looking more and more like a formality.

She said nothing.

Later that night, over FaceTime, Renata said, "So he's going to be working with you."

"They haven't interviewed him."

"But he's going to get the job."

Fay sighed. "Yes, and he's exactly what we need, and if I'd been using my brain instead of—well, when I met him on the house tour, I would've tried to steal him from Greenblatt. Except Greenblatt was already gone, and I wasn't thinking about jobs at all when I was with him—maybe he was. Maybe he got close because he thought I'd get him a position."

"No. No insecurity. We talked about this. And one way out of that thinking is to know that he must be genuinely interested. Fay, do you really need me to do that girlfriend thing where I tell you how *fierce* and *awesome* you are—and then you don't believe me? Because you are, and he doesn't deserve you, and no one ever will. But here's what I also know: you're both obsessed with your subject. And I can see how you both probably got busy talking about how much Harlem has changed and wondering aloud whether or not small business ownership went up on 125th Street or whether or not chains have dampened local activity, and all that shit that I have to listen to when I'm around your crew."

Fay shifted uncomfortably. "Are you bored by it?"

"I've learned a lot. It taught me a new way of thinking about cities and towns, from top to bottom. *Zoning.*"

"Oh God, you really are bored by it."

"Sometimes. But I don't make a secret of it. And I do like how much all of you think about your line of work, how much you care about it. I don't care much about estate law half the time. But that's not the point. Speaking as your friend, if he makes you uncomfortable, do not hire him. If you really think he cozied up to you just for a job, do not hire him, especially if it makes you doubt everything he says. If you think that it will make your coworkers and employees wary because they know that you dated him, do not hire him. It doesn't matter if he needs a job. It doesn't matter if he's a perfect fit otherwise."

"But the other partners think it'll be fine."

"The other partners didn't sleep with him."

And that was Renata, cutting right to the heart of it. Would Fay ever truly be able to look at Oliver Huang again and think of him as nothing more than a colleague?

"Honey, you need to ask yourself what you want him to be to you and why exactly you need that."

"I want someone—someone serious, and who works hard, and who makes his opinions and all his wants clear. I mean, this is someone I am supposed to know. All those years and it comes down to nothing. Just like Jeremy. I lived with someone for so long, and it turned out he didn't actually give a shit about me."

"Hey, it's only really been a week you were dating though, right? You don't know him yet. And just because Jeremy pretended to care about things doesn't mean Oliver is."

"No, don't give me that pitying look, Renata. I can see it even over this crappy screen. I *am* over the marriage. But this fear? This is something else entirely. This small niggling insecurity is going to crop up at the worst moments for the rest of my life. And I hate that I have it now." She sighed. "I mean maybe, maybe Oliver didn't have designs on me. His CV *was* in our mailbox for months. When I asked him to come out with me this time—I thought he genuinely enjoyed spending time with me."

"Of course he did."

"How can you know that though? With Jeremy, I didn't see how he lied to me—and to himself. I thought I was finally getting the hang of this, Renata. I thought I was over my slump. I gel penned my *letting go of my feelings* into a bullet journal and even bought the right washi tape for it, like we're supposed to do in the strong woman handbook.

"But it wasn't enough, was it? With Oliver, I started looking forward to things again. It was so playful, what we were doing. How often do I get to do that? Just... pretend and play? But if it turns out he wasn't serious and just wanted a job? I don't know."

"How he feels about you or why he did it can't take away the fact that you had felt good and had fun in the time you've been with him. And the truth is, I guess you'll never really know unless you ask him."

"Oh, I'll ask him, all right."

Just not now.

Chapter Seven

Teddy and Sulagna regarded Oliver across the conference room table with curious bird-bright eyes, hunting for crumbs of information.

Clearly, they knew about him and Fay. Worse, they seemed to want gossip.

Oliver tried not to cough or fidget. How much of his discomfort was due to the fact that he was at a job interview, and how much was due to the fact that the partners knew that he had something with Fay, he wasn't sure. He kept his mouth shut because to open it would have been inappropriate—and because he didn't want to talk about it with them, dammit. But his silence didn't seem to disappoint them. Sulagna volunteered that Fay was out meeting clients today and wouldn't have sat in on this interview anyway.

"Not that you'd be working under her," Sulagna added.

He wasn't sure that they knew that he and Fay had argued—or most likely that it was over. He'd had a longer "relationship" with Sally Chin than with Fay. Oliver hadn't heard from her all week—nor did he try to talk to her. Yet, somehow, he'd expected Fay to give him a final word.

But then, if they hired him, it wouldn't quite be *final*, would it? It was a small firm. And they couldn't guarantee that they wouldn't work together, no matter what Teddy and Sulagna insisted. Even if they both hid in their offices all day or went to see clients, there were all the other ways they come upon one another: at the elevator, at the coffeemaker, passing in the halls. He had worked with people he'd broken up with before. It was almost inevitable given that he ran in such small professional circles. But somehow this was different—maybe because he'd poured more hope into this brief moment they'd had—because hope meant more to him nowadays—and because she had seemed to do so, too.

At least the senior partners didn't seem malicious in their curiosity. If anything, they seemed eager and happy to learn more about him. They were *friendly*.

Fay was lucky to have people who seemed to genuinely care about her. No—he corrected himself—she'd worked hard and surrounded herself with good people whom she could trust in the workplace and as friends.

On Wednesday afternoon, he got the phone call from Teddy with the offer. They tussled amicably over salary, and Teddy hung up, promising that papers would be sent out Friday before the Fourth of July weekend or Tuesday at the latest. They took for granted that Oliver would accept, but even though it was the opportunity that he'd wanted for months, he found himself hesitating.

It would be stupid to say no. If their relationship, brief as it was, meant so little to Fay that she'd not bothered with even a brush-off phone call, then she'd be just fine seeing him all the time.

Yet, he was sure it had meant more to her—it sure as hell had been significant for him. He couldn't find it in himself to breathe it out, to let it roll over him like all the regular disappointments that came from bring a grown up. Being with Fay hadn't simply made him enjoy again—it showed that life *was* enjoyable. And that was also how he knew Fay cared; she didn't do things for no reason—it was something he loved about her, about getting to know her.

Of course, he could call her to end it himself, put them both out of limbo. He had to make a decision, but he figured he had time until those offer papers came.

He plunged himself into his consulting project that night and worked through Saturday—whether or not he accepted the job, he was at least going to wrap up this quick contract. Working was better than brooding. In fact, all that time, he found the job absorbing enough that he could occasionally forget.

Until he remembered that he couldn't talk about it with her.

On Fourth of July Monday, he drove out with Nat to Forest Hills to see their mother and Macy.

Nat suggested they go out to lunch instead of lying around the house. He, of course, came up with the name of a posh spot somewhere back in Manhattan— a prospect that made Oliver groan. They'd just come from there and holiday midday traffic through Queens wouldn't be ideal. But luckily, Ma insisted she wanted to go to Chen's Taiwanese in Elmhurst, their old neighborhood. She bristled at getting in the car—she'd never gotten used to driving around—but once they arrived and got out, she gazed around her with an unreadable expression. "Do you miss it?" he found himself asking.

"Yes."

She said it without her usual snap, and it was so sad and odd that he put his arm around her for a moment.

It didn't last long.

His mother, never able to stand still, moved out from underneath the comfort of his arm. Oliver tried not to take it personally.

Through lunch, old friends and acquaintances kept coming up. Ma gave them tight smiles but she said very little. Maybe she wasn't used to all of this chatter anymore; he could sympathize. He wasn't sure how often she'd left the house this week while Macy was away. He felt a small prick of guilt. He'd been busy, but he should have checked on her. Then again, his mom would have sniped if he'd come along to interrupt her. Or maybe she'd ask him why he wasn't out looking for a job, as if that involved walking the streets, cap in hand. Not that he even owned a cap—she'd probably yell at him for wasting money on one.

"You're quiet, Ma," Nat said. "Maybe we should've gone to someplace in Manhattan instead. Given you something to complain about, at least."

"No," Ma said. "I just miss it here, that's all." She took a deep breath. "Your brother was right all along. That house isn't right for me. I want to move back to Elmhurst."

There was a silence. Well, as much silence as could be obtained with glassware clinking, and the chorus of diners chattering and enjoying their *you tiao* and fresh soy milk.

Macy was the first to recover. "But, Ma, your place is beautiful and the neighborhood is so clean. Is it the neighbors? Are they unkind? Is someone making trouble for you?"

"The neighbors are fine. They are very nice." She spat that word out. "But I'm not fine. I can't do my shopping or see people unless you give me a ride—"

"But the bus—"

"Hardly ever arrives, and I have to wait in the sun all afternoon for it to come. I never talk to my friends anymore."

"You hate your friends," Nat said.

"Yes, but I've known them all so long."

All the adults took a breath right then.

Macy looked...crushed. Nat was amused. His mother seemed defiant? Excited? Whatever it was, it was an expression he had never seen on her face before.

As for him, Oliver wasn't sure what he felt. His mother had said he was *right*, and although he enjoyed it, it was bewildering, confusing. OK, he mostly wanted to say *I told you so*, but this wasn't quite the moment in which his insight would be appreciated.

"Mom, why don't we get you driving lessons? And then we could pitch in for a car," Macy said.

"I'm old. I don't want to spend the rest of my time in Queens traffic. I want to be able to walk around while my legs are still good. I want to be able to get good groceries."

"But you could buy bulk and put the food in a car and bring them back and that would be cheap."

"I live alone, and I'm sixty-seven. Just how much bulk do you think I eat?"

"I just don't want to think of you living here again." Macy sniffed.

"What does that mean? You grew up here. Everyone knows everyone. There, I fall down. No one hears me screaming for two days behind those triple-pane, burglar-proof windows."

"We can get you a—"

"*No.* I heard about an apartment. Mrs. Wu and Mrs. Tsai live in buildings that have places I can look at. I won't be alone."

"But where are the kids going to play when we come to visit?"

"I could go see you."

"But—"

Ma gave Macy a look, and it was as if his sister—and all of them—finally realized that she'd been contradicting her mother for five whole minutes.

Nat piped up. "Or the girls could come to mine and Oliver's place. Or we could go out to brunch sometimes. I could take you all out for something expensive and terrible."

Even his mother laughed at that. And Oliver hugged Nat for being generous and funny in so many ways.

Nat said, "Goes to show, we should've listened to Oliver when he said it wasn't a good fit for you."

"Yes, Oliver was right," Ma said. She flicked a glance at her middle son, "Don't let it go to your head."

"When am I ever allowed to let anything go to my head?"

Nat snickered, and Ma tried to shoot them both stares, but it was hampered by the mischief in Nat's face and the mutiny in Oliver's.

Macy still seemed to be having trouble processing. "I don't get it. I thought you loved that house. I thought this would be a wonderful move."

"I love that house, but I don't like me in it. It wasn't

great for me, but I understand what you were trying to do. All of you. Things were not easy after your dad left that last time. You are trying to make my life better now. But it is stupid for me to pretend that I like living there, that way, by myself. We can resell for a good price, maybe even make some money for all of you. I already talked to a neighbor who was interested if I ever wanted to put the whole thing up for sale. Maybe, Oliver, you can speak with him because you know the most about the condition of the house and the yard."

Macy opened her mouth and shut it.

Ma added, "It's better than all of you paying the mortgage for forty years."

"But you'll still have to *rent*," Macy muttered.

"Homeownership isn't necessarily a good in and of itself," Oliver couldn't resist pointing out.

"I can afford rent. And if I can't, I'll ask you kids for help."

Nat thumped Oliver on the shoulder.

Oliver still wasn't sure what had happened, but it seemed that his mother might have actually been listening to him.

They drove back to the house soon after. Nat was pulling Macy up the walkway, talking to her softly while the kids ran ahead. Ma stayed and wandered around to the backyard. He couldn't remember seeing her out here before, although of course, she must have come out, if only to yell at him.

"It's pretty," she said after a while.

"Don't tell me you'll miss it—not now. We don't want Macy to get her hopes up."

Ma snorted. Then she said, "I thought I would enjoy it. It wasn't just Macy—I thought that this was what I needed out of life. What we were all working for. But it wasn't like I expected."

"Our goals have to change as we adapt to new situations and environments, Ma."

"Sounds like something out of your undergrad thesis."

"Did you really read that?"

"I tried."

Oliver stood quietly, trying to process that. He hadn't thought she'd cared enough to attempt to look through his (in retrospect, embarrassingly naive) paper on fair housing in historic preservation districts.

After a while, she clucked. "You should just say, *I told you so.*" She added, "Soft-hearted."

This time it didn't sound like an insult—not the way it usually did. Maybe it never had been.

She went on, "You could be harder on me for wasting time and money. But instead, you are too nice. When you were four years old, we took you kids to the duck pond, and you wanted to feed the ducks your snack. I told you ducks can get their own food. So the next time we go to the pond, you had a pocket full of rice for the ducks. Cooked rice! You were four years old and you planned and kept it in your pocket for a week! All your smartness goes to helping ducks. Too nice. Just like your father."

Oliver blinked. "My father was too nice to ducks?"

"No. He helped others before he helped us. Always scared of letting other people down. When he couldn't do anything about that, he left."

"Well, I've certainly never been scared of disappointing you."

Unexpectedly, she laughed. "That's true. Maybe you

aren't nice at all. You never did one thing I wanted for you. Everyone says you are my kindest child. But you are quiet but stubborn. It is a slow strength. Sometimes I don't recognize your qualities because they're so different from what I know."

"Ma, are you complimenting me?"

"Tcchhh."

He could have said that he was starting a new position with a new company, he might have given her this. In a lot of ways, telling his family was more official than receiving or putting his name on the paperwork—paperwork that still hadn't arrived. But he kept his mouth shut. He hadn't yet opened his email because he wasn't sure he wanted to see the attached offer documents. And, of course, it didn't help that a wrathful Fay might be waiting at the end of this job.

All of this flitted through his head before he opened his mouth again. And what came out surprised him.

"Ma," he said quietly, "You know, if you think I'm such a failure, then you're going to have to admit that you failed when you raised me. But I don't think you want to because you're strong and just as stubborn as I am, and you taught me to be resilient. Trust me that I know what I can and should do. Trust the work you put into me."

Ma stared at him for one moment, and for that minute, it was like he saw all the annoyance, all the love, all the worry, all the ambition, all the betrayal she'd endured from his shiftless father. All the *everything* shone in her eyes as she gazed at him.

Or maybe it was the glare of the sun reflecting in her eyes. She blinked. It was gone. She turned and motioned him to follow. "Let's go see what trouble your brother is making inside."

Teddy had been out sick for most of the week leading up to the long weekend. Sulagna wanted another set of eyes on Oliver's offer papers before she sent them to their new hire, so now the documents sat on Fay's computer. It didn't bode well that despite the fact she wasn't supposed to be involve in Oliver's hiring, she was overseeing so much of it. She let the file sit there. She let her confusion sit, too.

On Saturday, Fay resisted the urge to go into the office. Instead, she finally unpacked her apartment. She cleaned out the kitchen cabinets and put in her dishes and plates and bowls. She started a new list of furniture she needed to buy—a couple of stools for the counter, a night table, some shelves, a coffee table—and hired someone to retile her bathroom floor. Her genial super, Roberto, helped install an air-conditioning unit in a living room window and told her he liked what she'd done to the place. The bed she ordered arrived, and she managed to put it together by herself. She smoothed clean sheets over it and arranged the pillows. Her bed looked so comfortable and her room so changed, and she was so tired that she cried and then felt silly about it. It was just a room. She should have done this weeks ago.

Why hadn't she done this weeks ago?

Of course, the previous weekend, the mattress on the floor had made her happy in other ways. Correction: Oliver had made her happy in other ways. It seemed another case of not knowing she was sad until she was hit with how she'd been making allowances for everything she did.

She told herself that if she got a nightstand, she could have a drawer full of vibrators. Every shape and size and speed and intensity.

But that wasn't it.

What she'd had with Oliver had not been just about sex. If it had been that, then she could have stayed married and gotten all the vibrators, too.

She sighed and stared at the documents now open again in front of her. Pretty straightforward stuff. She read through the nondisclosure, changed the font, and changed it back. She hated to admit it, but she was *almost* looking forward to having Oliver work there. She wanted to see him. She wanted him to talk with the people she worked with, to understand how proud she was of her firm. After all of this, she wanted to see Oliver succeed—she knew he would.

How had she become this pathetic?

Well, someone had to send these offer papers to the man. And if she didn't get cracking they wouldn't get these out.

She emailed her approval to Sulagna and was relieved to get a reply back almost immediately. She wasn't the only one checking work email on a Saturday. Thank goodness they'd stopped prying about her relationship with Oliver—unless Oliver had said something in the meeting that had satisfied their curiosity. No. She knew him well enough to know that he wouldn't do that.

If she, Teddy, and Sulagna had been more organized, less frantic, Oliver would have been working at the firm before she'd ever run into him at that house tour. She would have felt instant relief at seeing him—strong, sharp, a pillar of Oliver—but she would have hesitated to touch him because she would have been something else to him instead of a friend looking for support.

Maybe there was some way she could fix this.

The weekend went by, though. Teddy's whole household had been felled by rotavirus. Fay and Sulagna scrambled to reschedule his meetings and cancel others, make sure projects were staying on schedule. By the time the dust settled, it was Thursday afternoon. Sulagna came into Fay's office and asked her worriedly, "Have you heard from Oliver?"

Fay had just been thinking of Oliver. Her couch was supposed to be delivered tomorrow—a coffee table, too. He was probably going to start the week after. She had envisioned taking a picture of her room, with flowers and sunlight and the couch and the old wood floors. She was trying to come up with a quip she could send with this imaginary picture when Sulagna had come to the door.

Sulagna expected her to still be in contact with Oliver. Fay was doing plenty of chatting with him—in her mind.

"We sent out the papers a little late," Sulagna added. "Remember that last prospect we signed who then backed out? Does Oliver think we're too disorganized? Is he changing his mind? I really hope not. Can I tell you how much we liked him?"

"When did you send the agreement out?"

A sheepish hum. "Yesterday. Things got mixed up with Teddy out and with the long weekend and all."

"And you haven't heard from him?"

"He emailed to say he'd received them, and he'd send them back as soon as he could."

"That's more than reasonable. Let's wait until Monday. We were late with—well—everything, after all."

She could tell that Sulagna had more questions. Why couldn't Fay pick up the phone and ask Oliver why the delay? Why didn't she already know? It was clear that Sulagna expected her to give Oliver a little nudge.

Fay wanted to see him. She had a whole speech prepared and rehearsed for the next time she saw him. She wanted to ask him herself if what they had had been worth anything or if it was just as fake as Darling and Olly. But the efficiency that had returned when Oliver had put her in charge had disappeared once again. She knew what she wanted to say, but she couldn't say it— not just yet.

Chapter Eight

Friday

Oliver had been up since 4 a.m. reviewing his review of the case study. Spacich Group had appreciated the recommendations he'd made on the project so far. When he finished with this one, they wanted him to start on another. Oliver wouldn't be able to take more work, of course, if he signed the papers that Fay's firm had sent him on Wednesday.

It was a generous offer, but he still couldn't quite pick up the pen and put his name on the dotted line. He was getting used to being in limbo, so another afternoon of silence wasn't going to hurt him or anyone else.

As if reading his thoughts, Bill from Spacich called him. "Oliver, I just wanted to follow up with you again. We have another project that we'd like you to keep in mind. And, just between you and me, with your knowledge of preservation planning, we're hoping that we can depend on you for a little while longer?"

Oliver leaned back in the dining room chair he'd been using at his makeshift desk. Was Bill—was he sounding worried?

"It's always good to have some continuity on these

projects," he was saying, which made it annoying that they couldn't out and out hire Oliver.

But of course, Bill probably wasn't in a position to make all those decisions even though it sounded like they needed someone like Oliver. *Welcome to the new economy.*

He looked at his phone.

"Oliver? Oliver? Are you still with me?" Bill's voice came anxiously across the line.

Oliver laughed a little. He said something sincere yet noncommittal about how he'd enjoyed this project with Bill and how he hoped to continue to have a great working relationship, and something about Oliver's tone of voice or his words made Bill huff out a sigh of relief before they both hung up.

But Oliver sat and stared at his phone for a little while longer.

Granted, he was not the corporate hotshot that his brother was—but could it be that his skills were in demand? He sat back.

He could make a decent living doing what he was doing now.

He *was* making a living.

He leaped up from his chair and started to pace. The thought didn't exactly startle him—the numbers had always been at the top of his head, but he hadn't admitted it to himself until this moment.

Being in business for himself wasn't what he'd been working toward—it wasn't close to what he thought he'd wanted out of life by this point and maybe that was what had him fooled for so long. When he wasn't worried about what he was supposed to want and what other people wanted for him, he liked this. He wanted to know what Bill had in mind for him. He wanted to know what other firms might have for him.

Ideas solidified at the back of his mind. No one could say he'd been lazy. No one could say he hadn't been trying this whole time. He'd been working all along—on projects he'd enjoyed—just not maybe in ways that his family, or say, Fay, understood.

No, that wasn't true. Fay understood him better than anyone, because she knew what mattered to him.

She mattered to him, too, in so many small and big ways. But since he couldn't live in hope or expectation that what they'd had for those brief moments could be salvaged, at least he should figure out the best way for both of them to go forward.

He could fix this one thing, make it better for both of them, even if he couldn't mend the other.

He started to shake his head, laughing occasionally at himself as he grabbed his laptop and started typing, formulating plans about how he could work with other companies or get in on other projects through the city. His notes were in all capitals. Clearly, he really wanted to shout at someone about this. Luckily, his phone rang and he picked up, ready to shout at the next person, not even bothering to see who was calling.

It was Fay.

"I wanted to say," she began hesitantly, "I'm sorry for not calling all week."

He hadn't expected her to contact him at all and he didn't know how to respond.

He asked cautiously, "Are you getting in touch with me because you're sorry about how we left it, or is it because you really need my answer about the job?"

"Sulagna has been asking me to check in."

She'd been told to call him. He'd put her in a terrible position.

Now he had the chance to take her out of it. He steeled himself and put on his most professional voice. "The firm kept me waiting a long while, Fay. I needed to take my time, too. There were a lot of decisions to make and I wanted to make sure I was doing the right thing."

Oliver tried not to wince as her voice became a degree colder, "It's true, we dropped the ball. We've been going through a lot of growing pains as the firm expands and I apologize. But you should have disclosed to me that you were up for a job."

He blew out a breath. He didn't have to be an asshole about it. He just had to fix it. "You're right. I'm sorry, Fay. I didn't mean to deceive you and I really didn't want to make you lose your trust in me. It— Well, that was the worst thing about this, the thought that you were going to look at me differently."

"Oliver—"

"That really is what makes me a bad fit for your firm. That you don't trust me personally and that there's a good reason for it, even if… Well, I shouldn't have tried to shoehorn myself into this slot, especially now that I'm starting to realize that it's wrong for both of us. I don't need this job. I—" He drew a breath. He had to tell the truth, to her, to himself. "*I don't want it.* Not if it makes you and me miserable. And that's not a reflection of how I feel about you, or of what we started with each other. It's not at all. That's what's most painful about this—" He kept his voice steady. "I like what I am now a lot better than what I thought I was supposed to be. I know that sounds cryptic but I'm just starting to work it all out."

"Did you—did you just talk yourself out of working with us while we were on the phone?"

"Yes. Well, no, but yes."

"What does that mean?"

"It means I've decided not to take the job." He let out a whoosh of air, ruthlessly quashing any anguish he felt. He felt good about his decision to strike out on his own, but he was letting the dream of Fay go.

He said more—he couldn't remember what else came out of his mouth—but Fay had gone silent. There was no use prolonging it.

Sometimes *better* didn't mean getting everything he wanted.

It means I've decided not to take the job.

And he'd laughed. The damn man let out a laugh, saying, "I'm so glad to finally get that out. To tell myself, to tell *you* that I'll be happier this way. You're the one I want to share all my news with, and you're the one I shouldn't confide in."

She should be angry, confused, but part of her drank up the words, that joyful sound. It was completely the wrong reaction to have. She ought to have been trying to convince him to change his mind. She ought to have been trying to figure out what she was going to tell Sulagna and Teddy. But all she could do was listen to him and wish that he were in this room with her so that she could see his face.

He was talking again. "I'm sorry again, this time for leaving your firm in the lurch. It's unprofessional—well, this whole thing has been unprofessional, or extra-professional."

She couldn't argue with that.

"Fay." His voice was gentler now. "I can understand if you are disappointed in me, and maybe it's the best for both of us if I just end this conversation here. I'm sorry. The one thing I wish is that it had worked out between us because…well, I'm sorry none of it did."

He waited for an answer. And when she said nothing, he said goodbye and hung up.

What just happened?

She took a deep breath and hugged her arms around her.

He wasn't taking the job. She should be relieved. Another project tabled—not completely satisfactorily but at least she could put the worst of it behind her. But she didn't want that.

He had found something outside of the glossy bubble of imagination they'd created for themselves over the course of a few weekends. His reality was the opposite of everything she'd done with him in all the dreamy temporary spaces they'd shared—even what they'd done in her own transitioning apartment, a space borrowed in time.

So why had it felt so real? If it had been merely an interlude, then why was this so painful?

When they were playing house together, of course, it was pretend. But they'd been moving through neighborhoods and houses, standing in front of brick and mortar fireplaces, kissing in closets. Their bodies were real. They'd sat on the floor of her apartment and since she'd met up with him again, she always pictured Oliver there with her. She could see him so clearly even though he was gone.

Fay sent a terse email to Teddy and Sulagna about

Oliver's decision. Then she switched off her phone and went home—early.

She spent the evening and the next morning finally unpacking the last of her boxes. She put books on bookshelves and started hanging pictures on her walls. She came across the cartons which held personal documents: her birth certificate, expired passports, old tax records.

Her marriage license.

She'd had a serious relationship and life with Jeremy. The marriage had been a done thing—a solid mass like a paperweight on all the contracts and tax forms that came with life—or so she'd thought. She'd treated their relationship like something she had finalized so that she could put it behind her, and go on and do the real work.

But in doing so, making the marriage so—so *done*, she'd stifled herself and probably Jeremy, too. She'd wanted to grow and change. Maybe he had, too, in different directions. She had never bothered to inquire, had she? They'd both treated their commitment like it was *finished. Over.* Maybe that's why Jeremy got bored with her. She'd lost interest in him, too—and he'd known it.

Oliver was still figuring things out. Well, didn't she need to do the same? One thing she knew, he certainly didn't get to have the final word on this. He didn't get to feel regretful—not when she still had plenty to say to him.

Oh yes, she was ready to talk to him now.

She picked up the phone. "Oliver," she snapped, before she lost her nerve, "I'm not done with our conversation. Don't worry, I'm not calling you to ask you to take the job—but you didn't let me talk about us yesterday, and you owe me."

There was a pause in which she thought he might hang up on her. "I do. You're right."

"Oh."

"It so happens that I'm looking at apartments right now—the kinds that I can actually afford. So, uh, for old time's sake, would you care to join me? The real me, that is?"

She took a deep breath and closed her eyes. When she opened them again, she made her voice brisk. "Where should I meet you?"

Chapter Nine

Oliver was waiting for Fay at the top of the 215th step streets in Inwood, the northern tip of Manhattan. With Oliver was another person, who put away his phone as she approached. "Nat Huang," said the man extending his hand. "This guy's brother. And yes, I stayed this far uptown for another half an hour just so I could get a good look at you."

She probably should have laughed. But she was winded and hot from climbing up the long sweep of stairs. Plus, her body had blossomed even more warmly now that she was around Oliver again. A blush prickled her cheeks, and she was very aware of every irregular flit of her pulse. She swallowed and gave Nat a grimace-smile. "I guess it's a good sign that you wanted to look and not yell at me."

"I also wanted to be here in case you decided not to show up, and I had to bring this sad mess home."

That wry turn of voice, the mischief in his face—there was definitely a family resemblance, not that she could quite look at Oliver long enough to compare even as her eyes kept moving toward him. How could she miss him more while he was right in front of her? But he still hadn't said much, and Nat's friendly chatter was an uncanny echo of the ease she'd had with Oliver.

But now, silence. She realized she hadn't spoken for a minute. She swallowed and cleared her throat.

Oliver handed her a bottle of water, and she was too discomfited to thank him. Their fingers touched. She heard his sharp intake of breath. Or was it hers.

Too much.

Nat laughed quietly into the silence. "Well, since you two probably won't get into it until I leave, I'm going to find my way home to the comfort of my air-conditioned apartment."

Nat pushed Oliver on the shoulder and left. And now she and Oliver watched Nat skip down the stairs and turn toward the subway.

She cleared her throat and opened the bottle of water. "Thank you for this."

"It's a hot day. I thought you'd need something."

"Yeah, thank you. It's humid. Thank you."

And now that she *was* talking, she couldn't stop thanking him. Where was all of her bravado? God, this was awful.

"Nat was helping me out this morning when you called. But although he has many excellent qualities, he isn't really much good at apartment hunting. Started pretending he had altitude sickness. I mean, he lives in the fifteenth floor of a building on the UWS. Anyway, I thought this neighborhood looked like a good place to land. I've always loved Inwood."

He was trying to put her at ease even though he didn't have to anymore—not the way they'd left it.

"Should we head over to the apartment?"

She nodded, managed to get down a mouthful of water without choking and coughing, and they walked through a cluster of tall apartment buildings and into a marble-walled lobby, the stone polished and buffed to a high shine.

"Art Deco," Oliver said.

She turned around slowly to catch the way the light glinted on the smooth surfaces. When she'd made a complete revolution, she came to a standstill in front of Oliver.

He was watching her—not looking around at all.

"So bright," she said.

He nodded and they stood there a moment longer before heading into the elevator.

They were greeted at the apartment door by a bored-looking broker who glanced up briefly from his phone. "We're showing another apartment across the hall if you and your wife are interested."

"Oh, we're not married," Oliver said. "This is my... longtime acquaintance. I wanted her opinion on this place, too."

The broker gave a perfunctory nod and gestured as if to shoo them into the rest of the apartment.

"Longtime acquaintance?" Fay hissed as they hustled into the narrow kitchen, finally glad to have something other than yearning and awkwardness to latch on to.

"Well, what was I supposed to say? *My, um, friend?* Helper? Partner in crime solving?"

"No. Partner in crime solving is Olly and Darling."

"So it was."

They looked around the kitchen and at everything but each other. "I like it," Oliver said grudgingly.

"If you take those blinds down, it'll be much brighter in here."

"The appliances are new."

"You'll cut up peppers for another one of your stir fries with peanut sauce right on that butcher block counter."

"I only make those for special people."

Fay looked up. And finally she allowed herself to meet Oliver's eyes.

"I said our conversation wasn't over. Because I want to keep talking with you. I like talking with you, and I know you do with me," she said. "I was planning to call you. I've been making some changes in my life lately, in the week that we haven't really communicated with each other. I wanted to tell you about them. I wanted to see your face to just…share with you."

Oliver picked up where she trailed off. "I'm sorry again that I didn't say anything before. Because I want to share these things with you, too. I care about you. I like being with you. I miss it. I know now that we can't expect to go back to what we had for those couple of weeks. But in the back of my mind, I hoped that you'd call me up one Saturday morning and forgive me and take a chance with me anyway."

"I'm sorry I assumed that you just wanted a job from me."

"I should have said something sooner to keep you from reaching that conclusion. I didn't want you to think of me as that disappointing guy who lives with his brother and doesn't have a job. I didn't think enough about the effect of keeping the truth from you. And now that I've had more time to talk to you more clearly, I want to say, it's not because I wouldn't want to work with you. I think that would be fun—well, our very specialized definition of fun. But I've decided that I want to strike out on my own. I think I really need to, so that I can concentrate on the kind of work I enjoy, make new goals for myself, enjoy figuring out who I am and what I want. But it's not going to be easy being around me while I muddle through this."

They had been talking softly and their steps had led them past the living room, down the hall to a small, light-filled bedroom.

Fay released a breath. "That sounds wonderful, Oliver."

"It does?"

"It really, really does. I've never liked easy. And I'm making changes, too. I feel like I've been starting over for a long time. But with you, for the first time in a while, it felt like I could have fun—*be* fun and be full of hope. So, I've talked to my partners about how we need to distribute the burden more evenly and be a lot more organized. And I made an appointment to see a therapist, and I'm feeling really optimistic about it. That time I was with you made me feel excited about my future again."

Fay couldn't read his expression, so she kept talking. "I'm not saying we should do exactly the same thing— pretend to be other people, fool strangers and ourselves. The afternoons we spent over those couple of weeks was probably the best time I've ever had. But we were playing around, acting, being silly. We're not Olly and Darling showing up to Striver's Row with enough cash to make a deal on a house. I don't necessarily want to do that again. But what I do want is the chance to attempt even silly things, to mess up, to succeed. It mattered that I tried something different and new and that I let myself enjoy it. That was good and real."

Oliver stepped closer, eyes intent on hers. "If you want, this could be real now."

She reached out her hand and slid her palm into his, and he accepted it.

He stared at her for one long moment, and then he was pulling her out, through the sliding doors and onto the terrace and they were kissing. His lips felt so good on hers, his body felt good pushing her back into the worn old stone of the wall outside the apartment. They were there for a long but fleeting moment, learning each other's mouths again, warming and wetting each other, breathing into each other. She wanted to hold on to this, his solidity, the strength in his shoulders and back, this moment. She moved her teeth and tongue over his chin, along the sharp line of cheekbone and over to his ear. His hands stroked up and down her back, pulling her closer and closer with each movement until her entire body was molten and pliant and molded into him.

Someone slid the terrace door closed, and shuffled away again.

They pulled their heads away—just a little. She laughed softly into his neck.

"So, I have an offer to make," he said.

"For this apartment? Or for me?"

"Both. Well, I've already made an offer on this place, and the senior broker is looking it over."

"Not that guy out there."

"No, someone more enthusiastic. But I also have an offer for you."

"Get on with it, then."

"Fay Liu, I like you a lot. I like your smile, your lips,

your energy, your directness, your visible impatience, our mutual sexual frustration right now. I'm pretty sure that one day I could even love you. So I'd like to offer a newer, improved me. I'd like to begin again—again."

His hand stroked up and down her side and she softened against him. "I like it. I like you."

"Okay." He leaned into her ear. "So, how should I start? My name is Oliver Huang. I've just started a new business, and I think I have a new girlfriend."

"A lot going on in your life."

"Yeah, it's an exciting time."

"I'm Fay Liu." She pulled back to survey the view. "Nice place you have here."

* * * * *

Acknowledgments

A long list of marvelous people contributed their talent and energy to help me produce this short book. Deepest gratitude to my agent, Tara Gelsomino, who shepherded me through tough drafts, confusing negotiations, and general messiness.

Thanks and love to Amber Belldene, whose insight and warmth I rely on so much.

A huge debt of gratitude to my longtime friend Kristin Olson, who cast her planner's eye over this manuscript. All mistakes are very much my own.

Much love to my husband and daughter for their warmth and good humor and for their faith in me.

Special thanks to my wonderful editor, Alissa Davis, and to Kerri Buckley, Angela James, and the excellent folks at Carina.

Finally, much of *Playing House* is set in Harlem, a Manhattan neighborhood rich in Black culture and history. Readers interested in Harlem-set romances might enjoy Rochelle Alers's The Best Men series, a contemporary about a trio of friends who co-own a gorgeous brownstone, and Alyssa Cole's luminous *Let Us Dream*, which takes place during the Harlem Renaissance.

Author's Note

The town houses of Strivers' Row on West 138th and West 139th Streets between Adam Clayton Powell Jr. Boulevard and Frederick Douglass Boulevard (officially the St. Nicholas Historic District) are real, as is the account that Magda gives about their conception, construction and history of ownership. (However, I would not advise strenuous activity on the rooftops of these homes—much less during a blackout.)

The 136th Street Garden is not real, although it could be. Many urban gardens—some city sanctioned, some not—thrive in once-empty lots across Manhattan, planted by people who saw the potential of these spaces to become beautiful.

OPEN HOUSE

This place could be beautiful, right?
You could make this place beautiful.

From "Good Bones," by Maggie Smith

Chapter One

This pair was not buying what she had to sell.

Still, they were polite, if somewhat nervous, and they'd made an appointment to see the Strivers' Row brownstone that newly minted real estate associate Magda Ferrer had been trying to move for the last month. Plus, it was no hardship spending this hot June day inside a handsome air-conditioned historical home.

So now she pasted a smile on her face and talked about lintels and linen closets and tried to pay attention to Olly and Darling—the potential buyers—as they moved through the space.

Olly and Darling. They sounded like they were here to solve a mystery. *The Body in the Brownstone.*

Well, if she wasn't careful she'd walk into the materials left after the last round of renovations, and the mystery here would be how could she have been so absentminded as to get herself killed by tripping on a bucket of plaster tucked into this corner. She smiled once more, gestured toward the elaborately staged dining room, and launched into a story about the parties Olly and Darling would have there.

What she was *not* talking about was the fact that this home belonged to her mother's late sister's husband, Byron, and that Uncle Byron had been through five brokers at five different firms over the last four years. She didn't mention that each of those brokers had told him to renovate a little and to lower the price a lot, and that he'd renovated a lot and the price was still stuck right up there. He'd taken the house on and off the market, each time in a fit of pique that his brownstone hadn't managed to sell. Buyers didn't like a property that stayed on the market like a pebble that refused to be shaken free of a shoe; it made them ask what was wrong with it even as more attractive places floated out of their grasp. Other brokers didn't like it because they wanted to show their clients a place that they had a chance of moving.

She did *not* tell Olly and Darling that her uncle's property was earning the reputation among real estate professionals as a white elephant, even though the truth was weighing down every word that came out of her mouth when she showed the townhouse. She kept to her canned history of the building and banished the edge of desperation from her voice. Most of all she tried not to think about how damn much she needed to make this sale.

"Every part of this room has been restored or renovated," she said, touching the statement choker at her throat. "It's just perfect for large family gatherings or intimate dinners. Or even just doing homework with the kids." She glared at the lurid red shade of the overhead light and continued smoothly, "This warm space with this dark wood makes it both welcoming and sophisticated."

Maybe she was laying it on a bit thick, but desperate times called for desperate measures. She was drowning in student debt, and her usual duties of writing up listings, updating the database of her small firm, taking potential clients to see apartments for rent, coordinating staging and photography, and helping her boss, Keith, staff his open houses wasn't going to pay off her loans. When her uncle had, in an uncharacteristic fit of family loyalty, offered her the chance to sell this property, she'd jumped at it even as her misgivings fired when he explained ponderously that he'd decided to take matters *into his own hands*.

Taking matters into his own hands apparently meant putting them in hers. She did make sure he signed a standard agreement, though he tried to argue that she didn't have to take the full broker's fee because he was essentially *giving* her the place to sell. He continued to call her almost every day to fuss about renovations or complain that she wasn't bringing enough prospective buyers in. But he'd given her a chance to make some real money—to put a real dent in her debt—and she had to take it, didn't she? Though so many before her had failed and though she'd been thoroughly burned by taking chances before, though Keith, head of the boutique brokerage that employed her, had discouraged her from taking on the sale, worried that the small brokerage's reputation would be dragged down by an eighteen-foot-wide unsellable Harlem townhouse. Though she'd only passed her licensing test mere months ago and was acutely aware of her inexperience.

So here she was, selling her little heart out. She'd learned the history of the house thoroughly. She could talk about schools in the neighborhood, and the nearest grocery stores and subway lines, all of which she relayed to Olly and Darling.

Darling was trailing her hands along the cabinets and Olly was watching her intently, hands jammed in his pockets. They seemed very much in love.

She hoped they could find room in their hearts for this house.

Magda's phone trilled and the doorbell rang almost at the same time. She muttered something about her other appointment—she hadn't expected people to show up on time—and moved to the door even as she answered the phone.

"Got something for you," boss-man Keith yelled into her ear. "Empty lot, zoned for residential."

She could hear talking in the background. He was probably in a coffee shop. Keith did love to bawl into phones in coffee shops. She said, "I've never tried to sell a vacant lot before. Would I need to test for another license?"

"I'll be the broker on it, and you'll just do the showings and so on. It's a good learning experience for you, a chance to earn some money. Sending you the details. It's up near that big place you're trying to off-load on your own, so that'll be convenient for you."

She grimaced. Keith had been against her accepting her uncle's listing, but now it looked like he'd found one advantage to her being uptown: She'd do all the legwork, and he'd swoop in at closing and take his check. Oh well, that was the way it worked.

Magda reached the door and was about to open it when Keith slipped in one last piece of information. "Only problem is that you'll have to get rid of the people using the lot as a community garden."

She yelped a muffled *What?* but he'd already hung up, and her next potential buyers of the townhouse were right there. There was nothing to do but paste another smile on her face and hold out her hand. "David and Davis? So nice to meet you. I'm Magda."

And I think my boss just screwed me.

The rest of the showing did not improve. David and Davis frowned at the construction materials lying around. "We were hoping it would be in move-in condition," one of them—impossible to tell which—said. They kept talking about how the house was very dark.

David and Davis sounded like an accounting firm. In reality, they were a corporate lawyer and an orthodontist. Still, despite expressing dismay with the ongoing renovations on the building, they bargained the whole time, making remarks about the asking price to test how flexible she'd be.

Meanwhile, Olly and Darling had disappeared, only to be found again in one of the upstairs bathrooms, dusting white streaks from their pert, expensive butts. Magda sincerely hoped that their mess wasn't evidence that they'd wrecked something important, like an entire wall of plumbing.

All four of them left without making an offer. She wouldn't be selling the house today or tomorrow.

She needed to do something that paid off a little more quickly. She sighed and opened up the email Keith had sent her with details on the lot. As he'd noted, she could walk there right now.

She got a dustpan and broom and cleaned up bits of plaster in the bathroom. She had debt from college and graduate school, debt from culinary school, debt from all the things that allowed her to be standing here—a

professional woman in a nice suit she'd found in a con-
signment store—and more invisible debts to her family than she could hope to repay. So she was careful
when she went through the house, turning off the lights,
making sure the taps were closed, the central air was
off. None of this was hers. Everything was borrowed.

When finally she shut the door behind her, she tried
to be optimistic. Because that's what she'd been taught.
Fine, her showings hadn't gone well, but she had a few
scheduled for tomorrow night. And she'd check out this
empty lot and figure out how to sell it—it could certainly take a chunk out of her loans, even if it couldn't
erase her sense of failure over the past careers she hadn't
been able to start.

The air was hot and she took off her suit jacket as
she turned left out onto 136th Street and strode past a
beauty salon. A car drove past, and she could hear a
faint chorus of trumpets playing on a distant stereo—
and she could smell something sweet in the air. Flowers, a fence thick with leaves and morning glories. As
she walked in through the open gate, a cloud of butterflies flitted up. She looked at the sky and groaned.

Empty lot, my ass.

Because as soon as she'd entered, half a dozen tiny
elderly heads had popped up to survey her. This wasn't
going to be an easy sale—this was a nightmare.

She was going to have to kick a bunch of aunties out
of their fucking fairy-tale meadow.

Tyson Yang had not expected to see a woman in a prim
skirt and neat blouse emerge out of a butterfly cloud
at the entrance of the garden. Sure, New York had its
fashionistas and oddballs—sometimes it was difficult

to tell the difference between the two—but even his own workplace was usually business casual, and accountancy was as stuffy as it came. Plus, it was summer.

They were in a *garden*.

She seemed too hot—temperaturewise, at least.

Mrs. Espinosa had already dusted off her knees and hopped up to talk to the stranger, her smooth brown face alight with curiosity. He decided to remain where he was, distributing little trowels of fertilizer to Mrs. Hadley's plants while she was in Atlanta visiting her grandkids. She'd written out a feeding and watering schedule for him to follow. It was the opinion of many in the garden that Mrs. Hadley spoiled those plants, although how anyone could spoil a plant was a question that he had not yet had the courage to pose to the ladies of 136th Street Community Garden.

Plus, he was hardly dressed to impress in his dirt-smeared straw hat, holey T-shirt, old cargo pants with their many, many pockets for gloves, and gear.

Maybe she was trying to sell something to Mrs. Espinosa; Ty somehow doubted it was seed packets.

He stood up and moved closer, in case there was trouble.

Mrs. Espinosa was speaking with the woman in Spanish, Mrs. E rapid-fire, the woman more slowly.

The woman smiled, the corners of her liquid eyes crinkled and her rich brown skin glowed. Ty felt himself go very still inside. Maybe he'd stay kneeling and gaze at her forever. That would be nice. The garden needed a statue.

Sharp-eyed Mrs. Espinosa had spotted him. She waved him over. "Ty! Come over here! This *single* young lady wants to learn more about our community."

Mrs. E wasn't even trying to be subtle.

He brushed himself off, aware that his hands were dirty and his face, too, probably. He took off his hat and resisted the urge to run his hands through his hair.

"Magda, this handsome boy here is Ty. My knees aren't what they used to be or I'd show you around."

She twinkled and then skipped off merrily, bum knees and all.

"So, were you thinking of joining the wait list for a plot, or just general volunteering? Plenty of ways to get in the muck."

Muck. Well, that was extremely suave. He suppressed a wince.

"I was curious about the garden itself, what kinds of things you do, how long it's been around."

"I think it was an empty lot for a long time and Mrs. Espinosa and Mrs. Freeman started planting some herbs and flowers, leaving buckets to collect rainwater, that kind of thing." He glossed over the part where it had been overrun by rats, and the fact that they'd hauled nearly a hundred pounds of broken glass, cans, shoes, underwear, condoms, needles and other choice bits of city waste out. "And now it's the clean, modern operation you see here."

She laughed, glancing around at Mrs. Freeman and Mr. Serra squabbling over seeds, at Mrs. Espinosa, who was avidly watching Magda and Ty. She gave them a thumbs-up.

The laugh seemed to break up some of the tension around the woman's eyes. "Does Mrs., uh…"

"Espinosa, Mrs. E."

"Yes, does she get some sort of prize for setting you up? She seems really determined."

"I'm beginning to wonder what she thinks will happen."

"Maybe you'll have to cart her around forever in a wheelbarrow decorated with flowers culled from the garden."

"That's part of my regular duties here."

Magda laughed again.

Okay, maybe this could be good. Maybe he wouldn't be so averse to making friends if pretty, vivid women with beautiful curls and overly formal suits kept wandering into Mrs. E's clutches. "So, uh, a lot of people like to grow tomatoes here, peppers, squash. We have rainwater barrels, but also we've got an agreement with the co-op next door to use their hose to water the garden. Compost heap over there. That solar panel over there was built by the kids at the Jessie Fauset High School and they maintain their plot over there.

"We have a schedule on Google calendars. Nothing strict but we keep track of the plots now and someone has to lock up the storage shed at night and unlock it in the morning."

"Where's your plot?"

"Oh, well, I'm not an actual member. I just kind of help out with everyone else's stuff sometimes—if I have time. Don't want to be tied down to the land. Gotta keep my on-the-go lifestyle."

On-the-go lifestyle.

Luckily, she hadn't seemed to notice his babbling. "That's funny that you say you're not really a member because Mrs. E described you as important to the whole operation."

"She's trying to talk me up."

"So how *did* you end up working here?"

"I live down the street. And one day, a couple of

years ago, I saw Mrs. E struggling to pull her shopping cart out of here. It looked a lot different back then." That was the understatement of the world. "At some point, there had probably been a fence, but that had been mostly vandalized and torn down 'til it was just raggedy dangerous-looking wire. Mrs. E. had loaded her cart full of trash and she was trying to pull it through even more garbage. So I helped her get it out of here and dispose of all of it and that was how it all started."

"So you're not only a member. You're a founding member."

"I'd hardly call myself that. I like hanging around."

She cocked her head.

But they didn't know each other. She didn't need to hear all of his shit, and explaining it to her implied exactly the kind of intimacy he wanted to avoid.

Maybe she understood that, too, because she changed the subject. "From the sounds of it—and the looks of it, too—this garden has really improved the neighborhood."

"It's always been a great place to live. But an empty lot can become a dumping ground, and dangerous if kids start to get into it at night. I don't think I ever gave much thought to it before I started coming here, but now that I have, I see these spaces like this all around and I think about what they could be. How welcoming and beautiful they could be. But it's not even about that. I've met so many more of my neighbors just by coming here and being here."

"They've kind of adopted you."

She kept watching him as if trying to figure him out, and for some reason her scrutiny made him blush.

He ducked his head. "They certainly keep trying."

Ty had enough to deal with emotionally when it came to his own fractured family—he wasn't about to allow the gardeners to get too close, no matter how many welcoming lures they sent out. Not that this stranger needed to know that. The garden was his place to relax, haul some dirt, make pleasant conversation. That was it.

He said abruptly, "So, I believe we have plots available, volunteer hours if you'd prefer that. What are you most interested in doing here?"

She was definitely not meeting his eyes now. Had he been too curt? She fiddled with the strap of her bag before finally looking him full in the face. "Actually, I'm not really looking to join, per se."

"Oh, okay. That's no problem—" He was blushing again. What the hell?

"It sounds wonderful, but—"

"No, it's okay. It's not like I've really committed—"

"That's not it. It's because I'm here to help sell it. I'm here to try to sell the lot."

Chapter Two

Later That Day

It was a short subway ride up to Magda's mother's apartment in Inwood for Sunday dinner. By the time she let herself in with her key, the place was buzzing with chatter of her older sisters and their families.

"It's Magda, and she's dolled up," Flora yelled as she came to kiss her younger sister on the cheek.

It was funny that Magda was the one who often showed up at dinner wearing her fancy business-lady attire; her sisters Flora and Alma, both in capris, were attorneys and probably had more claim to those tailored suits. Flora headed a nonprofit in Brooklyn and Alma worked in family law in New Jersey. Her older sisters were polished and driven, and they had cute kids. And she, the baby of the family—a full nine years younger than Flora—was single. Her sisters and mother saw that as a problem that needed solving, but she was fine with it. It was harder not to compare herself with her older siblings in other ways; while they'd established themselves, she'd taken a more meandering path, accepting odd jobs, dropping out of grad school, out of culinary school. If she were being honest, after today, she was feeling very much like she wanted to drop out of real estate brokering, too. But she couldn't. All of that student debt wouldn't let her.

She decided to avoid her siblings for now and went into the kitchen to kiss her mother. "It smells good in here, Mamí."

"You're going to have to help me. But go and change out of those good clothes before you start."

"It's fine. I can put on an apron."

Her mother made a face and pushed her firmly out the door.

Magda sighed. It was sensible—her mother was kind but no-nonsense. She was a family doctor, widowed before Magda was born, and she was used to being listened to by everyone. Because really, they should. She was also practical and never threw anything out, so Magda went to one of the old bedrooms and found an old T-shirt from high school and a pair of track pants that had probably belonged to Flora. When she entered the living room and dining room to say hi to the rest of the family, she realized she was now underdressed—or at least that she looked more like one of her nephews, even though she'd be turning thirty soon.

She slipped into the kitchen and took up a position beside her mother, chopping up onions, and after a while, she noticed the kitchen was too quiet and her mother was simply watching her. Never a good sign. A barrage of questions would likely soon follow. Magda said a little self-consciously, "All that culinary training has got to be for something."

"Were you at Byron's house today?"

"I was. No bites."

"You'll sell it," Mamí said with her usual confidence.

She had plenty to be self-assured about. Magda, not so much.

"I'm pretty sure none of the people who saw it today were interested. I don't understand. It shouldn't have been this hard to unload. It's beautiful. It's in a great neighborhood."

"Byron has always been difficult. He insisted on meeting buyers before going into contract like he was some sort of one-man co-op board. He didn't like this buyer because he said he'd block up a fireplace. He didn't like that one because she wanted him to pay for a new washer and dryer. Ariana would've told him to get his head out of his behind."

"He changed all the light fixtures anyway. But if Tía were still alive, she and Uncle Byron would still be living there and he wouldn't be selling at all."

Ariana had died nearly eleven years ago when Magda was still a teen. But Magda remembered how she'd teased her grumpy husband, and how much he'd adored her.

Mamí nodded. Magda knew her mom was sad about her aunt. She'd been close to Ariana the way Flora and Alma were close. "If he gives you any trouble, send him my way."

Magda sighed. "I can handle him."

She couldn't run to her mother or sisters every time something went wrong—which seemed pretty often with her. Easier to change the subject.

"I got a new commission today." Technically Keith had gotten it for her. "It's an empty lot"—not so empty—"near Byron's house."

She careened on. "That area's really coming up these days. It'd be a great opportunity"—or it would have been if it weren't stacked against her—"to put up apartments, or a house. Something really sleek and modern."

Her mother lifted a lid and stirred carefully. "That's wonderful, baby."

"It is."

She did not feel wonderful. Magda could still feel the accusing stares of everyone in the garden as word had spread. She'd intended to be discreet, get the lay of the land, maybe take a few pictures for reference. But she didn't want to deceive old ladies and she didn't want to be a jerk to Tyson, the man who'd shown her around. She'd noted how the tips of his ears had turned red when Mrs. Espinosa had trilled the word *single*; he'd jammed on his hat as if he knew he was showing those colors. Maybe he knew how vulnerable he looked despite the strength and rugged clothing. He'd looked at her with big brown eyes that had absorbed every word she'd said—and she knew she couldn't contaminate the waters with dishonesty. She couldn't lie to someone who was that much of an open book. It didn't help that she also found him distractingly attractive, with his lean body and long fingers dirty from digging in the earth. She'd tried not to notice the taut cording of his forearms as he'd turned to casually help a fellow gardener, but she was all too human.

"Let's hope some of the places they build will still be affordable for people who live there," Mamí said carefully. "It's a great neighborhood. Your uncle's family was there forever and everybody seemed to know everybody else."

Magda thought of the easy chatter of the gardeners. "It still seems that way."

"Well, it would be a pity to lose that kind of community. But of course, that's not really your responsibility."

It could be. But she was never really held responsible for anything, was she?

She didn't say anything more. But Magda knew that later her mother would be relaying everything to her sisters. They all sat down to dinner shortly afterward and for a while, Magda could relax and concentrate on the familiar taste of bistec frito. Soon, too soon, her brothers-in-law were on the couch, and she was sitting with the little ones—of course, they weren't so little anymore. She had pulled the besitos de coco closer to her and was picking them off one by one while watching Seb, her youngest nephew, play "ThinkRolls." He held the game out to her a couple of times because he was a good kid, but she held up her hand and pleaded sticky fingers.

"You can wipe them on my shirt, Tía."

Her sisters were still at the table with her mother laughing together about something, their heads bent together. She heard some names, some words in Spanish, and tried not to eavesdrop on their every word like she had when she was younger. It had always been this way with them. When she was a child, they could stay up later with their mother. When she was a teen, they could come back home and take their mother aside for serious conversations.

She knew that sometimes they talked about her.

She glanced at Seb and then down at her own threadbare old shirt. Then she deliberately swiped her fingers on the hem.

The two shared a smile.

"Sebastian!" Flora hurried over to them with a napkin. She scrubbed her son's face, the iPad screen, and then she turned to her baby sister and scrubbed her.

Then, to add insult to injury, she bustled off with the dessert.

"Hey," Magda exclaimed indignantly. But her sister laughed and said, "You're welcome, Nena," even though Magda had definitely not thanked her.

She knew Flora would take her aside later, and Alma would call her during the week. They'd both be encouraging. They'd both have advice. She had sisters who loved her and told her they supported her no matter what she did, especially when what she did was screw up. She was drowning in their indulgence. And if she was frustrated that their expectations of her were so low, well, that was her own fault for never finishing anything, wasn't it?

"Magda," her mother called as the kids started to troop toward the door yelling their goodbyes and accepting kisses. "Do you want to see if your sisters want some of the flan? And make sure you put your stuff back in the fridge afterward."

Glad to avoid the flurry, she went to the kitchen. A fleet of plastic containers stood ready on the counter, waiting for her sisters to transport leftovers home. Her mother had already portioned everything out and started to clean up, of course. There was little for Magda to do. Mamí assumed Magda would probably be spending the night, judging by the way she'd bundled Magda's smaller bag of leftovers in the fridge. It would be easier to stay. Her apartment was in Brooklyn. At the time it had seemed like a good idea to get some distance from the family, but it was proving to be inconvenient since so much of her business was uptown in Manhattan. She could spend the night, then zip down to her office and get an ad together for the lot. She had her suit and her iPad. It would be less of a hassle to spend the night at her mother's.

In the end, maybe it was easier to give in to expectation.

"I guess I'm just surprised to find out that my older brother, rule-follower extraordinaire, has been helping a bunch of people illegally squat on land," Ty's sister Jenny said, stretching out on Ty's couch.

Ty gestured with his chopsticks. "I am going to protest every single word in that sentence. Starting with you saying you were *surprised*, because you aren't—you're clearly *amused*. Moving onto the part where you called me a rule-follower—"

"You're an accountant. It's your job to make people follow rules and not ordinary ones, either. You work on their *taxes*," Jenny said. "Taxes are the ultimate in rules."

They were eating cheap American-Chinese takeout on Jenny's night off from making "authentic" *haute* Chinese. Whenever it was Jenny's choice, she gravitated toward greasy and fried. Ty had no objections.

"Excuse me, I optimize the taxation experience, while keeping in mind that they do help the greater good," Ty said. "But back to what you said. I also protest the way you said I was abetting squatting. It's occupation by people from this neighborhood who have an interest in keeping it safe and clean. They saw a problem in the community and they took steps to improve it."

"Ri-ight and they don't benefit from it at all. It's all

altruistic and they don't cart off big bunches of herbs and they definitely don't sell them for a profit."

"I doubt they're growing enough cilantro to make a dent in the local economy. Although there is usually a *lot* of zucchini. You can't even give it away."

Jenny waggled her eyebrows. "So you're saying that, like dick, zucchini is abundant and low value."

"I—I'm going to ignore that lesson in supply and demand capitalism."

"Big words."

"And I'm going to add that they don't grow enough to keep themselves fed, much less fuel some sort of underground urban farm economy like you're suggesting."

Jenny pouted. "I was really digging the idea of your running a vegetable cartel."

He knew Jenny was baiting him, but he couldn't seem to stem his earnestness. "We're not trying to do big business. It's small. Tiny. But the gardeners benefit. Everyone gets something. That's the point."

"Everyone except the landowner."

"The person who owns it does well by not owning a rat-infested garbage hole."

"In the end, if they want it to be a rat-infested garbage hole, it's their right." Jenny held up her hand. "You can't protest that. That's a true statement."

"Yeah. But—"

"Here we go."

"Why would the owner want it to be full of junk and rodents, when it isn't? It's worth more money this way. But more important, it's beautiful."

"Dad said we were going to get more conservative as we got older, but somehow I don't think that's happening with you."

Ty grumbled as he got up to help himself to more beef with broccoli. "You are dampening my fire."

He sat down again and started chewing, only to stop when he noticed that Jenny was quiet. "What?"

"I don't mean to, you know. It's fun to make fun of you. But I'm glad that you're so stressed out about this."

"Gee, thanks."

"No, I mean it. The last few years have been hard, with Ma's cancer, and Dad selling the house and moving back to Taiwan, and well, everything in the world the way it is. The garden has been good for you. Making all these new friends has been great."

"We're not really friends. Besides, you teased me for being nice to old ladies. Which they are not, by the way. There are lots of people of different ages and from different backgrounds there all the time. I didn't latch onto the gardeners as a substitute for Mom if that's what you're saying. I'm very detached, very objective."

He sounded a little defensive, even to himself. "This situation has me a little riled, that's all."

"I know. I know. Maybe I'm jealous, even. You have this whole community. All I have is work."

"I don't really."

"Yes, yes, Mr. *I don't get attached anymore*. My point is that I'm glad you're taking an interest. You're not sitting stoically getting it done, like what was happening with us, with Dad, three years ago. You've even got a whole new wardrobe for the garden—like, Henleys and hats and cargo shorts."

"The cargo shorts have lots of pockets. It's practical."

"Practical. Right. You've been dressing up for the ladies. And now you're all *fired up*—as you put it—to defend them. It's like you're undergoing some sort of superhero make-under. It's sort of great."

"Well, I don't feel wonderful about having to do it. I liked it the way it was before. I enjoyed not being angry and worried."

Maybe *enjoyed* was too strong a word, but all the feelings he had now were definitely too much at once. He'd never stopped to think much about the garden having an owner and neither had anyone there, it seemed, until that real estate broker, Magda Ferrer—he'd been sure to find out her full name and which brokerage she worked for from Mrs. E—had shown up with her suit and her smile. He could picture her even now; coming through the gate of the garden, and while recalling the rush of wonder, he could feel the disappointment. She'd seemed so intrigued by the garden, so interested in talking to him; it turned out the whole time she'd been gathering information, *casing the joint*, like some sort of femme fatale.

He was an idiot.

His beef with broccoli was congealing at the bottom of his bowl.

"This is crap," he said.

"You could always cook for me."

He got up and began closing up the takeout containers. "I want you to take some of this home," he said. "You don't eat enough during the week. And okay, it's not the healthiest but—"

Jenny rolled her eyes.

He picked up the dishes and went to the kitchen to wash up.

He chose one feeling to deal with: his worry, and followed that. Mrs. Espinosa's son was supposed to be doing a search to see who the owner was, but even if they turned up that information, what could they do? The gardeners had dispersed quickly after Magda Ferrer had made her announcement, and later that evening, the worried texts started appearing on his phone. They ranged from panicked questions about whether they should dig up their plantings and move them to their stoops and balconies, to suggestions that they form a human barricade against the oncoming bulldozers. Mrs. E had messaged him to say she might go down to Magda Ferrer's office to give her a piece of her mind, and he had convinced her to at least postpone it until they had more information.

Well, at least Mrs. E wasn't trying to set him up with Magda Ferrer anymore.

He agreed to attend a meeting for the next evening to figure out what they could do *even though he wasn't really a member.* It was probably going to be chaos, but Mrs. E asked him and he couldn't say no to her.

"Follow the money," he murmured to himself. "That's what we're going to have to do."

From behind him, Jenny clapped.

"*Yes.* You're even spouting taglines."

It was his turn to roll his eyes at her. But at least she was following his advice and packing up the leftovers to take home.

"I'm just trying to think things through," he said.

He followed her out to the hallway.

"My brother the L.L. Bean superhero," she said, giving him a peck on the cheek.

"Oh my God, get out of here, please."

She laughed as she disappeared into the elevator. "Even when he's kicking me out, he says please."

Chapter Three

When Magda peeked through the monitor that morning, she recognized Tyson Yang on her doorstep.

Well, technically it was Uncle Byron's doorstep. But still.

She tugged at her suit jacket, smoothing it down self-consciously. Then she remembered herself. She didn't need to primp for him. She took a breath and opened the door. Or rather, she tried. It wouldn't release. Damn it. Uncle Byron had ordered electronic locks installed during the week, and either they were malfunctioning or she had used the wrong setting. Either way, she hated them and she secretly wondered if engaging real estate brokers was Byron's way of getting people to supervise the improvements he was making on the house while he stayed in his primary residence in Miami.

She fumbled for her phone as Tyson rang the doorbell again.

"One minute," she yelled. "I'm coming."

Well, she was already there but—

A few taps on her phone and luckily she heard the

beep telling her that the security system was going to let her get away with opening the drawbridge.

"Really? You've taken to locking out the rabble?" Ty asked.

She'd been ready to be civil to him, she'd even been glad to see him. So much for the fluttering in her stomach when she'd peeked at the screen and saw his dark flop of hair, his wide eyes.

The fluttering had probably been the dregs of bodega coffee curdling in her stomach.

At the same time, it was a relief that she didn't have to be polite to him. "Do you have an appointment, Mr. Yang?"

He frowned. "No. But isn't this an open house?"

"Are you interested in buying?"

She gave him a saccharine smile. She was being an asshole. She could see his hesitation. But even now, he was honest. "I wouldn't be able to afford it."

"I'm afraid I'm busy with serious buyers only."

"Are you?"

He peered inside. "I'm the only person here." His tone softened. "And I promise not to take up much of your time. You wouldn't return Mrs. E's calls."

"You'll have to make an appointment."

"For an open house? I just—"

"Ap-point-ment."

She pointed at her phone.

He really looked puzzled now. "Look, English isn't quite my first language, but it is a pretty close second, and I'm pretty sure I know what *open house* means."

She grimaced. "It means what you think it means, but this is to cut down on gawkers and to help keep track of potential buyers."

"You mean it's open for rich people."

"No, it's for won't-waste-my-time people."

She'd finally snapped and, of course, that was the thing that made him laugh. But almost immediately he sobered.

"Okay, I apologize. I showed up here instead of making an appointment. I promise I'm not trying to be obnoxious or intimidating. I'll leave if you tell me again. Again, I know you're not the owner of the garden—just the representative. And I wanted to ask questions and you're the only one who can help me."

He held his palms out and she couldn't help looking down at them. His hands were clean, his fingers slightly curled, the lines etched deeply in them. Her eyes traced the curve of his thumb down to his wrists, over the bony joint to where the dark hairs of his arms started. She was alarmed to discover she liked looking at them. His wrists were a lot like the rest of him: strong, stark, beautiful.

She raised her gaze to his and tried to dispel her wandering thoughts with a huff. "You can come in."

She stepped back and held the door open wider. "But when one of my real appointments shows up you have to be quiet."

Magda tried to tell herself it would be better to have him here. Sometimes seeing people in this vast, empty house did spook her. Tyson Yang did many things to her that she didn't feel like analyzing, but he didn't creep her out.

He stepped inside carefully and wiped his feet on the mat, which made her want to smile. He wasn't muddy today. He was wearing khakis and a blue button-down shirt and part of her wondered if he'd dressed up for her.

His eyes were traveling all over the entrance gallery, clearly somewhat overwhelmed. "Wow, this staircase, and all the light. This is incredible. I'm not used to this much space and I'm only in the lobby, or whatever this is called. Okay, I really have the overwhelming urge to take off my shoes so I don't get everything dirty."

She did have to laugh at that, especially because he clearly was restraining himself from coming further off the rug, even as he twisted his body around to look at everything around him.

"I've already invited you in," she said. "So come."

It was funny. She wouldn't say she was quite used to the place after a month spent getting the rooms staged, and photographing and showing it. She would never be able to pass the china cabinets in the dining room without touching them, for instance, which is why she also spent a lot of time polishing them. And there were signs of renovation all over—ladders leaning in the hallways, buckets of plaster, paint and drop cloths at random and inconvenient intervals throughout the house. But some people made her gaze around anew, made her admire it. Annoying Tyson, with his clear delight, was one of them.

She couldn't help a rush of pride over the fact that she was the one showing it—even if she was the last resort.

"When was this built?" he was asking.

"Early 1890s. They had great views of City College, plus they had all the conveniences of 1891, I guess. Those gates at 138th and 139th that say *Private Road, Walk Your Horses*? You could have delivery out back. They got Bruce Price, and Clarence Luce's firm to work on the other houses along the row. They were notable architects at the time. Stanford White's firm designed the houses on this side of 139th."

"I feel like I've heard that name, Stanford White."

"There was a movie made about his murder. White was a predator who liked teen girls. He even had a huge twirly villain's mustache. But he got shot in the head by the husband of one of his onetime victims. Guess he had it coming."

"I'll say."

She found herself enjoying showing off her knowledge to him, and that was…troubling. She cleared her throat. "This isn't the kind of detail I usually include when I talk about the history of the house to potential buyers."

He laughed, but his eyes were sincere. "I feel very special."

"At the time, the developer built up these blocks to sell to upper middle-class white citizens. It was planned so that white folks would settle up here. But that didn't happen, and they refused to sell to Black families, either, for years and years until about 1920. The houses ended up being bought by upwardly mobile and prosperous Black families—like my Uncle Byron's great-grandparents. That's how these houses got their name, Strivers' Row."

"Guess those developers had it coming."

His face shone with mischief. She had to admit grudgingly to herself that she liked that, too. "Thank you. I like to talk about that part."

"But now you're selling it. Don't you wish you could keep it in the family?"

"It's not my house, not my own background. My uncle Byron isn't related by blood. He was married to my late aunt. My family's Afro-Latina, not African American. But I am aware of how important this history is and how complicated it is, and I want to be mindful. It means something that my uncle trusted me to do this."

And despite how difficult Byron was, it really did matter to her. Who cared if everyone thought she was being set up for failure? She could do this. She wanted to do it right.

He nodded, and in the seriousness of his eyes, she knew there was respect. "I'm sorry. I didn't mean to pry."

"It's fine."

It *would* be fine. Eventually.

Another glance, and then he finally took a careful step over the threshold. "Then I apologize if I'm acting like such a gawker, but I've never been in one of these grand Harlem houses before. You must be used to it if your aunt lived here."

"It was divided into two apartments, with Uncle Byron's parents upstairs for a long time, so I didn't get a sense of how big it was. Plus I was a kid. When his parents retired and moved to Miami, and my uncle took over the whole house, my aunt became ill and it seemed like she got to enjoy it for a really short time."

"I'm so sorry."

"It was a long time ago."

She paused. "I was a teenager then and I have to admit I didn't quite understand what was happening. Maybe because my mom kept it from me, but also maybe because I didn't want to know."

"It's a shitty thing for a teenager to have to deal with."

"Terrible for the whole family. But I remember my

aunt couldn't take the stairs after a while, and they moved her into this front room. My uncle had it completely gutted after she was gone."

He'd redone it a few times. And then he'd moved down to Florida, too, keeping the house until maybe he'd taken stock and decided he couldn't ever change it enough.

She and Ty had moved into the kitchen now and she had to shake her head, reminding herself that she wasn't supposed to be giving him a tour of the place or of her family business. He was the enemy—sort of—she reminded herself. So instead of taking him upstairs to the bedrooms—*hush!* she told herself fiercely—she asked him to sit down and poured him a cup of coffee.

He also seemed to be trying to remind himself to stay on business as he perched on one of the kitchen stools. "I guess I should ask my questions. I'm not usually so easily sidetracked. I wanted to know if there was any chance that some of us from the garden could contact the owner to talk? We couldn't find much aside from a name. At this point, we're not even sure the owner knows that we've got a community garden established and that there are people who might be interested in maybe negotiating something with them."

Magda heaved a sigh. She had asked Keith some of these questions over the course of the week, but Keith had told her it wasn't her job. And since he was the one who'd given her work when she needed it, she couldn't quite question him closely. "You can send offers to me. But I'm not the person who's in contact with the seller. I'm mostly here to field inquiries to show buyers around. My boss is the one who's in charge of that side of things."

"You're not? It's just surprising to me that you don't have that responsibility. I mean, you're selling this place."

"It's more that my uncle is doing me a favor by giving me the listing."

"It's not really a favor if you're working for the money. It's early on a Saturday morning. It seems like you're earning it," Tyson said mildly.

"What do you do?"

"I'm a CPA, an accountant."

"My boss likes to remind me that someone as new to the business as me would never ordinarily land a place like this. I've only had my license for a few months."

"But someone more senior, how do they 'land' places? A lot of it is through who you know, your network of contacts, isn't it. And your uncle is in your network. That's what people are always saying, right? *Use your contacts.* And so you are."

"So I am."

He'd wandered away with his coffee cup to peek inside a closet. She could have told him she'd hidden a couple of industrial fans and the builder's shop vac in there, but instead, she was thinking about what he'd said.

She hadn't considered it that way before. Maybe she'd been so worried over the past few months that she'd concentrated mostly on the fact that everyone told her the listing was a lost cause. Sometimes it crossed her mind that maybe she hadn't gotten much at all, that nothing was what she deserved at this point. And yet, did Keith *deserve* his commissions? She was the one scouring the real estate database for his clients, and she was probably going to do the actual work at the lot, and deal with the people who were already there.

She shook her head. None of this helped her. "Listen, I sympathize, I really do. But I think you believe I have more power than I do here. I just started all this—" She didn't want to say she was in over her head, but she felt it. "I just started. I'm learning the ropes and I can try to talk to my boss, but I—"

Tyson Yang's face had gone flat. "So you won't help us."

"I said—"

He stood up. "No, it's fine. You're right. You're wasting your time with me. You obviously have a lot to do in this enormous expensive house that's owned by a member of your family—"

"Hey, I just finished telling you that it's not really my family's," she said, the frustration showing in her voice.

He took his cup and rinsed it in the sink. "Thank you for the coffee."

Without looking at her again, he walked out of the kitchen. In a minute, she heard the door close gently. The alarm system didn't even give a single peep.

Mrs. Espinosa marched up to where Ty was turning over compost, and pulled an iPad out of her bag.

"I asked a friend of mine who works for the city. She said we could talk to the Parks Department's Green Thumb program and the Trust for Public Land."

Usually, people did not disturb Ty when he was in the compost corner. But shoveling shit was the only thing that was helping him work off his stress. Although he'd been at it all morning if he counted how much crap Magda Ferrer had already given him in less than an hour.

He'd stopped to wipe his forehead and realized he was still in the good clothes that he'd worn in order to show up at her pricey house sale. He should send her the cleaning bill.

He was being unfair.

He didn't know her. No matter how much she seemed like a rich girl in a suit, she'd told the story about the house, about her aunt, as if it mattered. Maybe it did.

Anyway, what exactly had he expected her to be able to do? Call up her client, and with a twinkle and a laugh convince them to give the garden up to the community? He'd gone in thinking magically, just as he'd started helping the garden without being practical and considering the implications. It was unlike him to have ignored the fact that had been staring him in the face: none of the people here knew who owned the lot, and they'd never bothered to try to secure it. It was never theirs. It was always going to go away, like everything in his life that he cared about. He should have known better than to get involved.

He turned to Mrs. E and noted that a few others had assembled. Some of them had travel coffee mugs and were obviously getting ready to get in a couple of hours of digging under the sun.

From the back, someone called, "Are these Green Thumb Parks whatever really going to give us money?"

"I heard this place is worth a million dollars at least," someone else called.

"City's so slow about everything."

Mrs. E said, "We've got to get going, that's the important thing. We need to make a presentation at the community board—"

Someone in the back yelled, "Ty can do that! He cleans up nice."

Mrs. E ignored her. "We'll get a bunch of people. We want the community board to see all the different ages and colors and groups we represent here. We'll have to talk about the way the garden is good for the neighborhood. Maybe if anyone has any pictures—we need some before and after. Especially the before."

"I got a picture of a huge rat from that time. One of my favorites I ever took."

"Well, uh, good. If you can find more of those maybe we can use them. We should talk to our city councilor again, any community leaders. Your priest, your pastor, if you or anyone you know owns a business in the area. Famous people—"

Mrs. Freeman sang out, "My aunt's hairdresser knows someone whose cousin is Lin Manuel Miranda!"

"We know! You won't stop talking about it."

Mrs. E said, "I started a list of people we could talk to and we can expand it. Any of you who knows anyone, talk to them, bring them by to talk to me."

Ty looked around at everyone. "This is a great action list, Mrs. E."

Mrs. E raised her iPad and said clearly to everyone, "It's work, that's what this is. But we're gardeners. We're not afraid of work and we're used to being patient while things grow."

"But do we have time?"

"We're also not afraid of getting a little dirty."

The crowd laughed. There were a few cheers, and then, as if by agreement, everyone began to disperse.

Mrs. E stayed with Ty.

She seemed to be waiting for him to say something.

"That really was wonderful, Mrs. E. You know exactly what to do and tell people. It sounds like you know how we have to organize this."

"This ain't my first rodeo, sweetheart. It's not exactly like I've spent my whole life growing flowers in Harlem. I worked at City Hall for years. It can take a while and the system is frustrating, but stuff gets done, and I've still got a lot of friends there."

"We're going to need them."

"What we're going to need is your help, Ty."

"Well. I can try."

Dammit. It was hard to say no when she cornered him like this.

"I talked to the broker, Magda Ferrer, this morning," he said.

He scraped the ground with his shovel. For some reason, he couldn't look at Mrs. E, so he stared at his dirty oxfords.

He wasn't sure quite what to tell her about it. "I wanted to help at least get some contact information."

It was the least he could do. Then he would've been able to retire from the fray with a clear conscience. "It didn't go quite how I hoped."

"She didn't switch sides when you batted your eyelashes at her?"

Ty blushed. He wished it had worked. "We started off on the wrong foot and ended on another wrong foot."

"But in the middle, did you dance?"

"Mrs. E."

"Hey, old habits die hard. We'll keep working."

"I don't think I can do much more. This was a one-time thing."

"Let's make it a two-or three-time thing."

"Mrs. E, I don't know how else I can help. My job is really busy and it's not like I'm really affiliated with the garden—"

"You've been here since the beginning. I'm going to lean on you, especially because you know money and we're going to need some of that expertise. We can talk all we want with the city, but that's what it's going to come down to. So you're with me, right?"

"Right."

She started to walk away. "Love your enthusiasm, Ty."

"I only agreed because you're kind of terrifying, Mrs. E," he called after her.

She said over her shoulder, "Not scary enough if you almost said no to me."

Chapter Four

Early July

A few people came out to watch the city inspector do her business. Tyson Yang did not show up. It was a Wednesday afternoon. He was probably at work doing whatever CPAs did: making spreadsheets, reading up on taxes, calculating the student debt of people like her. Magda allowed herself one minute in which to picture him in a suit, but she couldn't manage it. The dirt-stained T-shirt and cargo shorts were too much a part of him. What was she doing mooning over him, anyway? She didn't even like him, despite how often he appeared in her thoughts.

A couple of gardeners doggedly continued their work, refusing to acknowledge that anything out of the ordinary was taking place. Some of the teens were curious, though, and went up to ask questions, and got to peer through the inspector's scope.

More gardeners, however, showed up for the early morning photo shoot. They also looked suspiciously well styled. In fact, Mr. Serra and Mrs. Freeman appeared to have had their hair done. A few people sported brand-new straw hats. Magda hadn't been planning to include any of them in the pictures. In fact, she'd tried to get Lou, her usual photographer, to take pictures from the emptiest angle possible. But Lou was charmed. It *was* charming, this crew of well-dressed elderly people and teens in a garden bursting with blooms and vegetables and butterflies. So even though Magda tried to downplay the fact that the lot was occupied—she instructed Lou to take the most forlorn pictures she could—Lou took it upon herself to get the gardeners back in and stood around long after her appointed time to point and click at people holding tomatoes and sniffing flowers. She heard Lou chatting with Mrs. E about the project to save the garden.

Magda gritted her teeth and reminded herself she needed to sell the lot. That she *wanted* to sell it. She wasn't out to make enemies with the gardeners. Who knows? Maybe they would raise the money. And she would be here to help with paperwork. Keith liked to remind her of it. Yelling into his phone from a cafe, he reminded her, "Property's bought and sold all the time all over the place. Neighborhoods change—you know that. You won't live long in this city if you don't get in on it."

"Well, that's the thing, lots of people *have* lived long in the city, in this neighborhood, and they're getting along in their lives."

"They're taking something that isn't theirs. Don't go all soft, Magda, especially for these people. You don't survive long in this business if you keep that up. Besides, it can be good for them, too. Think of the jobs it'll create, building this place."

"I know all that, Keith. But I was thinking we could explore options for the garden—"

"It's not a garden. It's *a lot*."

You could say that again.

Keith wasn't the one coming up to the neighborhood all the time; he wasn't the one who had to face all these sun-weathered faces. If anything, now that she'd been charged with showing the lot, he'd made himself scarce. She was the one who walked past people on the street and immediately knew they recognized her because she was selling their beloved community garden.

It wasn't that people were unpleasant. But she could feel them watching her as she bought cleaning supplies at the supermarket, or when she ordered coffee.

A few days after the garden had been photographed someone set the alarm off at the townhouse.

It was late on a Thursday night. Magda was in Crown Heights in Brooklyn showing a one-bedroom rental. She'd taken in ten applications. It had been a long work-day, but she needed the money. At least the apartment she was renting out was close to her place. But when she got the call from the security company she had to drag her tired self back into Manhattan and up to the townhouse to inspect it and make sure that nothing was wrong.

The security company had called the police who were waiting outside for her. It was a warm night but Magda shivered. She didn't feel comfortable taking the two bored male cops through the house so late, but she didn't have much choice.

It was pretty clear that the people who'd set off the alarm hadn't gotten the door open, but there were a few gouges visible enough that Byron would probably scold her for not wrapping the whole house in plastic each night before she left. She quashed her fear and tried

to seem pleasant and professional but it was past midnight by the time she'd given the cops coffee and answered questions. All because someone had scratched
up a couple of locks.

"Probably some homeless guy knows this house is
empty," the younger officer informed her. "Your uncle
should really do something about that. It's not safe having the place abandoned for this many years."

It wasn't abandoned, Magda wanted to point out.
She was here all the time. There were ladders and drop
cloths and all indications of construction being done,
even if it was quiet right now. And it was the freaking middle of the night. "Working on it," Magda said
through gritted teeth.

"How much does a place like this go for, anyway?"
the cop asked.

She wasn't feeling conversational. She wanted to be
rid of them, even though they'd turned out harmless
enough. She wanted to be home, in her bed.

"A few mil," she said through gritted teeth.

"Yo, that's ridiculous," the younger man said, although without any surprise.

He was clearly one of those people who wanted to
ask Magda the price in order to tell her it was too much.

The older officer finally finished his coffee. "Real
estate in New York," he said.

It was the most he'd talked all night. He got up and
put his cup in the sink and the younger one followed
suit.

They left Magda alone in the house shortly after. She
debated if she should bother to trek back home if she
was going to have to come back up here again in the
morning. But there was nowhere to sleep. There was

only one bed, and it was made up with an elaborate arrangement of pillows and cushions and blindingly white sheets that she'd never be able to smooth and refold to their current crispness. She'd have to *iron*. The thought made her shudder. Uncle Byron had reluctantly paid to have the bedroom staged as well as the dining room and he wasn't likely to spring for a touch-up. Still, she could have found somewhere to nap, but her hair was a mess and she didn't have her lucky suit with her, and that was what decided her in the end.

She locked up as best she could.

Magda felt better once she got outside. The streets weren't exactly empty at this time of night. People coming home from late shifts plodded down the sidewalks. Sirens wailed. Every now and then, a booming car cruised slowly down the block. Her sensible mid-height heels hurt, though. She'd made it halfway to the 135th Street stop when she noticed the jogger coming toward her. She braced herself. No one else was around, and she wasn't planning on becoming the first victim of someone who was clearly bananas if he was exercising at this time of night.

She shrank to the side as he appeared under the streetlight, still several feet away. His black hair was wet and his face was set in beautiful, serious lines, although she'd never seen them so grim.

But she didn't have time to wonder about his expression because in that swift flash under the lights, she'd also noticed a couple of other pertinent facts: the runner wasn't wearing a shirt. The runner was Ty.

The woman stepped out into the light just as Ty was approaching the spot under the street lamps. He'd angled himself off the sidewalk and onto the street and put on a burst of speed to get past her—slowing down would scare her into thinking he was a creep, especially at this time of night. But he'd already sprinted past her when he registered who it was—and that she had already seen him.

Magda Ferrer.

What the hell was she doing out here in the middle of the night, half limping? Was she hurt?

He turned quickly and almost ran smack into her as she came back toward him.

"Are you okay? Are you safe? Talk to me."

His eyes scanned her as best they could under the street lamp. He was aware that he wanted to run his hands over her, to check for himself to see if she was whole and healthy. But he didn't want to scare her more. She seemed unharmed. A little dazed. She was staring at his chest, which he realized belatedly was bare and sweaty, but it was dark out and he hadn't planned on running into anyone he knew. Self-consciously he shook out the T-shirt he was clutching in his hand and pulled it over his head. He noticed she followed the motions of his hand as he smoothed the fabric over his torso.

At least her eye movement was okay. She hadn't hit her head.

"I'm fine," she said after a long moment. "You're... you're out running at midnight?"

He blinked. "Well, yes. And you're out selling real estate?"

She paused again and he was starting to worry when she finally hung her head and laughed softly. She shook her head, then closed her eyes.

"You *aren't* okay," he said, looking around, wishing he could take her arm, wishing there was a bench nearby, a couch, a hospital cot, and an emergency physician.

He stepped closer to her, not caring if he was sweaty.

"No, no, I'm fine. Thank you." When she opened her eyes, Ty noticed she'd also leaned in and that her face was very close to his.

She must have realized it, too. She glanced away. "Someone set off the alarm at the townhouse."

"What? Were you inside? Did they get in?"

"They didn't. It's fine. It only set off the alarm. I wasn't here."

"Then why on earth are you here? Especially at this time of night."

"I'm responsible for the place. The alarm company called me because I'm the closest. Anyway, I talked to the police. A few scratches and dents on the door, that's all. I just want to get to the subway and go home."

Her voice, usually so calm, throbbed with fatigue. She'd had a terrible day from the looks of it.

"Let me get you a Lyft or something," he said. He reached for his phone.

She looked away. "No, thanks."

"But—"

"I live all the way in Brooklyn."

She let that sit. A trip downtown and across the bridge would be expensive. Had she gotten out of her bed to take care of this?

"I can put it on my account," he said steadily.

But she'd gathered herself and she was already starting to pull away from him and toward the subway.

"No. I can't owe you."

That stopped him. He wasn't sure how he felt about

it. He reminded himself he shouldn't feel anything. Much. "At least let me walk you to the train. It's late out."

"*You* are out running."

"I needed it. Bad day."

"So you decided to make it worse by exercising at midnight?"

At least if she was able to laugh at him, she was doing all right.

They walked slowly. Her shoes were hurting her, but it wasn't as if she could go barefoot on the sidewalk.

"It's cooler right now," he said, "and I couldn't sleep. I had a lot on my mind, a lot of excess energy. I wanted to clear my head."

His mind felt fuzzier than before, though. He had to stop noticing her curls, the way the dim light made her skin seem to glow like the softest velvet. He had thought of her on and off for weeks with a kind of irritation and restlessness that made him snappish. He tried to distract himself with the garden, sending out letters, fundraising. He exercised hard in the heat. But all of that, even the running, he thought grimly, seemed to circle back to Magda.

So here he was.

"I'll bet no one breaks into the garden," she was muttering.

Without thinking, he replied, "We get people cavorting there at night."

"Cavorting?"

Damn. He couldn't see her face clearly in the half-light of the city streets, but he could hear the laughter in her voice. And that made things better.

"They leave things. Like shoes. Erm, underwear. Condoms."

It was only a list. A list of personal items. Not sexy. *Do not think of sex.*

"Right. *Cavort* is a good word for that."

He was *really* not going to think of cavorting in the garden with Miss Business.

"Anyway, we want to have an open door—open doorway—policy. And that's what that means, sometimes. People are going to go in. Maybe they'll smash a few zucchinis in the process. Dammit. I didn't mean it that way."

But she had stopped walking and was laughing at him again; the sight of his face seemed to make her almost double over so that she had to hold on to the iron gate of a nearby brownstone.

He couldn't help it. It wasn't the greatest night of his life, and he was sweaty and smelly, and he was walking in the humid night air with the woman he'd slotted in his mind as his nemesis, and yet she was wonderful and her laughter was infectious, and he wanted to laugh, too.

"It's too much," she gasped. "Please tell me that they've left the eggplants and peaches alone at least."

"We can't grow peaches. Oh, you mean—"

Another burst of silent giggles from her. "I'm sorry. I'm sorry. It's been a really long night and I'm so tired, and the thought of Mrs. E having to break up a plant orgy is just too much for me right now."

It was almost too much for him, torn between laughter and the talk of sex and all of his warring feelings.

He took a deep breath and tried to get his head on straight. "It used to be worse, when it was vacant, of course."

"I'll bet," she said, wiping her eyes in that careful way of women who didn't want to smudge their mascara.

"It really was a dangerous place."

She gulped down a breath. "Tyson," she said.

It was maybe the first time she'd said his name. "Ty," she said, more softly. "You don't have to convince me that the garden is a good thing for the neighborhood. Even if it were just something beautiful, even if it were only a clean, quiet spot on the block it would be enough. I know it does a lot more."

"Well, if you do, how can you do what you do?"

"Because the seller owns it. Because we need more housing stock in this neighborhood—"

"Please, do you really think that anyone's going to be able to afford whatever fancy-schmancy glass-and-steel and Miele-appliance-filled apartments they put up?"

She turned on him, eyes blazing.

"Are you telling me you're not one of those people? That you're not someone who arrived here and drove up the prices so that these glass-and-steel buildings fill this neighborhood? Oh, look at how nice you are, helping out old ladies and trying to keep your pretty garden and participating in the community. You're even getting muddy with them to show your commitment. And then you wash the mud off and go to your corporate job and buy the very fancy appliances for your place. Now that you're here, you want to keep things the way they are, all that delightful *character*. But you didn't think of what you were doing before moving into the neighborhood, did you? What if I told you that there are a lot of developers interested in mixed-income and affordable housing in this area? What if some of them were interested? Would you step aside for the good of the neighborhood, for the good of your neighbors, your friends, who want to be able to stay here?"

"You aren't going to sell to those developers, though. You're going to sell to whoever makes you the most money." He added uncertainly, "Aren't you?"

"So what if I am? Listen, you can talk a good game about caring about the community, but people like you moving in was what caused an affordable housing shortage to begin with—not people like me, trying to make a living, trying to sell one empty lot."

They started walking again.

She was right, though, about people like him. He'd bought his apartment from a woman who'd lived in the neighborhood for nearly fifty years. He'd put in new floors, had the walls skim-coated, bought shiny appliances. He wasn't the only person in his building who'd done this. And when some of the people who, like him, had moved out after doing their own renovations, he had been pleased to see that the prices had gone up in a short time—that all his effort and patience had jacked up his property values. He'd been happy to make the money—theoretical though it was. When he moved in, he'd seen it as an investment. He'd never expected to make it his home.

He was attached to it. It was everything he'd told himself he'd never do again.

She was still talking. "Everything is so easy for you. You have no idea. You run around this neighborhood at night like you own it. But if you own it, you can sell it, too. You probably will."

They'd reached the subway station by then. Magda was

striding toward it. Anger made her taller, straighter—more right, or at least, less wrong.

He couldn't afford to think that way.

She was wrong. Nothing about this was easy. But he kept walking with her until they reached the stairs. She thanked him woodenly for escorting her, and they shared one last glance, too short, too loaded with hurt. Then she descended into the station and he stood waiting, listening to the click-click of her heels until he couldn't hear them anymore.

Chapter Five

"We're not like those other developers," the young white woman said, only half-jokingly. "We're *cool* developers."

Cool was maybe pushing it.

"I'm glad to hear it," Magda said, afraid to let that statement hang there for too long. "Anyway, let me tell you a little bit more about the property before we go see it."

Summer was always a slow season for home buying, lot buying, any kind of buying in New York City. Magda had spent the weeks sweating and worrying. The townhouse had gotten one half-hearted offer, quickly rejected, and even the rental market seemed to be stalled. Magda should have counted herself lucky to get this meeting with the rep of a potential buyer for the 136th Street lot.

She didn't feel so lucky.

It was a hot and bright Friday afternoon. She'd decided to ask Amanda Nott, from Eliot and Chase, to meet at the townhouse. Her uncle had, this very morning, called her and told her he was having the small patch of backyard re-landscaped. He wanted new trees, so new trees he was getting. Along with an entire island's worth of soil, which was currently sitting in the front vestibule because the driver claimed that the back lane was blocked.

Magda and Cool Amanda sat at the townhouse's kitchen counter going through the details on zoning for the land, the dimensions. Occasionally, workers trooped through the back doors.

"We understand there's an existing community garden there," Amanda said. "And that they're a pretty well-liked and vocal bunch. Like I said, we're also in the business of building neighborhoods and not disturbing the balance too much. So we do have some concerns."

"That's perfectly understandable," Magda said.

Understandable, but frustrating. Wouldn't it be nice to find someone without *concerns* and with lots of cash who'd come in with bulldozers and level the garden the way she'd be able to level her debt?

No, that wasn't true.

More than a week had passed since her argument with Ty at the subway station. She'd seen him from afar when she stopped by the garden, but she had not stayed to talk—or, more likely, argue. Judging by the way he seemed to prefer the compost pile to her company, he wasn't eager to see her either.

Besides, she didn't need to talk to him for his words to keep stinging. He thought she didn't care for anything except profit. Well, she did need money. She'd barely made her rent last month. She wasn't living so much hand-to-mouth as she was hand-to-gaping maw of debt, a life Magda was sure that Mr. CPA had never experienced. He might dress in dirt-smeared shorts, but she doubted he relied on the community garden for the servings of organic vegetables that kept his body lean and fit.

She had to stop yelling at him in her head. But although he might not believe it, she did like the garden. And she did want to find a buyer who would be good for the community. She'd sell her heart out to make it work.

Maybe Cool Amanda would save them all.

Magda glanced over to the young woman, who was scrolling through Twitter, and sighed.

On the walk over to the garden, Amanda talked about how they worked with planners to assess the viability of a development and if it fit the needs of a neighborhood. "Of course, we've done Harlem before. But every micro-neighborhood is a little different."

As they neared the garden, however, Amanda stopped talking.

Magda tried not to be hit with how, well, how pretty it was.

It was charming and not the least bit subtle about it, not this summer. That was the problem. It was in full bloom and the thick, wet scent of flowers and plants grew stronger with every step closer they took. All the various smells of New York—the garbage, cat pee, fried food, and asphalt—dissipated against the tang of fresh garden and green.

Straw hats bobbed up from between flower beds as Magda and Amanda approached. "Ah, Magda. Who have you brought for us today?" Mrs. Espinosa sang.

She looked at both of them like they were tasty sacrifices. Magda was starting to dread these meetings.

"Amanda Nott. I'm from Eliot and Chase," Cool Amanda said, sticking out her hand.

"Eliot and Chase. Of course. You did that project on 152nd and Amsterdam," Mrs. E said.

Mrs. E had been doing her homework in the last couple of months.

"Yes, we did. The Marisol. Mixed income housing."

"But how many people from the neighborhood ended up living in this housing compared to how many were driven out?"

"It's hard to keep statistics on that."

Mrs. E raised one eyebrow.

Amanda started, "The city's Housing and Development department sets income limits—"

Magda intervened. "I'm sorry to interrupt, Mrs. E. But we have to walk around a bit more before Ms. Nott leaves. She has another appointment."

Magda tugged on Amanda's arm. The woman wanted to argue and Mrs. E seemed pleased either way.

"It's mixed income," Amanda insisted on telling Magda as they moved away.

"I'm sure it is."

"We worked with HPD and consulted a lot with the community."

"I'm sure you did."

They stopped in front of the shed.

"We came up with a great solution. We can come up with one here."

A voice came from inside the shed. "I wasn't aware there was a problem."

Of course. Of all the Friday afternoons and of all the sheds in all the community gardens in the world, it had to be Ty.

He pulled open the door and Magda blinked at his

familiar, lean form. He was carrying a shovel. If she was lucky, he'd bury her and go away.

It was hard to make a dignified exit from a toolshed, particularly when he'd been caught eavesdropping. But Ty was too angry to care what he looked like in front of Magda Ferrer.

Still, he couldn't help drinking up the sight of her, the way her skin glistened lightly in the summer heat. She was in a fussy suit again, the one she usually wore when she came to the garden. It was funny how she never seemed to give up on that formality. He hadn't had the chance to gaze at her up close in a while and maybe it had been for the best. They made each other tense, even when they had good intentions.

Right now was no exception.

Magda gave him a tight smile. "Ty, this is Amanda Nott from Eliot and Chase."

Her expression said, *Don't fucking mess this up for me*. He had never been a messer-upper. Maybe at some time in the past, her silent warning would have been enough to make Ty subside. But he was thirty-two years old and he was sick and tired of the news, of the terrible anxiety of the last months, the last five years of his life, really, of watching his mother die slowly, of watching his father move away because he was unable to cope, of watching his world fold up in small important ways. He'd lost too much over the last few years. He'd only begun to rebuild himself again, and Magda and this person had come into his garden and were walking around like they already planned to slam five stories of concrete over the heirloom tomatoes that Mrs. Freeman had coaxed and cajoled into existence, and he wasn't about to let those hard-earned fruits go down without a fight.

He gave Magda a hard stare before turning his attention to the other woman. "Well, Amanda Nott from Eliot and Chase, I'm sure you already know that the lot was a problem before and the community came up with a good solution."

"It *is* really charming."

"It's more than charming."

Magda wedged herself right in front of him, her head right in the way of his line of sight. Unfortunately, she was also so close that her cloud of hair brushed his face, right across his cheek, like a whisper, and it was so unexpected and soft that it was more effective in shutting him up than the intrusion of her sharp shoulder.

He drew in a breath and stepped back.

"Amanda," Magda was saying, "I think we've seen most of what we need to see here. Maybe we could go to the townhouse and talk details."

"I'd like to say something to Mr. Ty," Amanda said.

"Just Ty—"

"You don't have to say anything to him. You don't have to justify what you do. And you—" Magda said, whirling around, "you've spoken your piece. You're getting plenty of opportunities to talk about it everywhere. Don't think I don't know about the presentations at the community board meetings, and the letter you guys have sent to the city councilors."

"What did you suppose would happen? How do you think people are going to react when you want to sell a neighborhood treasure out from under us?"

"I expected us to talk."

They were standing very close. Ty could feel every

angry puff of Magda's breath on his skin, he could see her eyelashes, the droplet of sweat curving its way slowly down her graceful neck. "We talked. And as I recall, you accused me of waltzing in here on a cloud of money and presuming everything in the neighborhood would fall according to my plans."

"I did not say that—"

"Listen, I've thought about this a lot over the past couple of weeks. I've replayed this conversation. Every time I open my stainless steel fridge or stare up at the ugly track lights that I thought were a good idea, I think about all the things I've done wrong."

Her face softened.

Too bad for her. "But it's not all about me. This garden isn't all about me. But it's about people and the ways we connect over it. You claim you want to talk. We've talked. But you're on your side and we're on ours. And at a certain point, there is nothing more to say."

He had a much better speech prepared in his head. But when he was faced with her big brown eyes, it came out disjointed.

"You two seem to have a history."

Amanda, Ty finally noticed, was looking back and forth between the two of them, lips quirked in a smile.

They both took a step back. This seemed to amuse Amanda even more.

"Definitely not," Magda said.

She didn't have to be so dismissive about it. Then again, it was true. "The first time I met her was when she came to announce the garden was up for sale," Ty said. "Not exactly a solid basis for a wonderful future together when she starts it out trying to sell the ground from under you."

"You say it like you thought of that future, though," Amanda chirped.

Even if his words were relatively innocuous, the blush that burned his ears and cheeks would be easy enough to read. And both women seemed to know it. "Maybe for a hot second," he said, then cringed when that came out meaner than he'd meant it.

But Magda was pulling at Amanda's arm. She wasn't looking at him. Well, maybe he didn't deserve looking at.

"We are not talking about this," she said.

But except for one swift, searing glance at him she avoided his eyes. It took him a second to realize maybe she had thought about the two of them, too. Maybe she had considered him, in those off moments, when they were not arguing.

But she was walking away—without her client, without looking back. It was probably for the best.

Chapter Six

"Men, amirite?" Amanda said, catching up to Magda. She put her hand up.

"Ms. Nott, forgive me. That was not something that should have come up, and I'm not—no, I'm not high-fiving you!"

"Why not?"

"First of all, nothing happened with Mr. Yang. And you're my client." *Not my BFF sorority sister whose bachelorette party I'm attending.*

Magda put on her suit jacket despite the sweltering heat and tried her best to seem *armored*. "I'm sorry that this whole visit was—well, as I noted, there is resistance to this project. I guess I'm going to have to get used to having them go that way."

"It was actually pretty entertaining."

Magda stopped in the middle of the sidewalk. She slanted Amanda a look.

Amanda twiddled her glossy hair between her fingertips. She'd probably paid more than Magda's rent to achieve those perfect, straight strands. "I'm going to be frank with you. I'm not going to be able to recommend that we take on this project. My boss isn't going to feel like doing anything too controversial right now, not after the 152nd Street thing, which *for the record*, I think we did a beautiful job. The building is gorgeous and it rented quickly, and we really helped some people get low-cost units, but there was a *leetle* bad PR—"

Magda waited.

"My point is, it's always going to be a little tricky up here." Amanda said hurriedly, "I'm actually pretty sure you'll attract a lot of interest, community buy-in or not. The location is getting really hot and the garden looks great. Well, it will until someone razes it. But we're not the people for you."

"Pardon, did you say it was a little tricky *up here*?"

"Well, you know."

Magda really didn't want to know, because if she listened too hard and thought too much about it, she was going yell at that skinny white girl, and then Magda would really get in trouble at the brokerage. Worse, knowing how the Amandas of the world usually fared, Magda could not afford to burn any bridges. At the same time, she wouldn't let it go completely.

"There are good reasons for people here to be wary," Magda said, trying to strike a balance. "No matter how helpful or *cool* you or your firm want to be, some of the changes in this neighborhood aren't fair and are really upsetting to longtime residents."

"I didn't mean anything by it. You know, the usual frustrations. You have to develop a thick skin in this business," Amanda was saying.

Magda wondered how tough Amanda's skin was and if she'd feel it if Magda thumped her on the head. Then again, in Amanda's case, it was probably thickest around her skull.

"Of course," Magda said through gritted teeth.

Well, it wasn't Cool Amanda's fault that the visit had gone like this, either. Surveying the land and getting photos had been one thing; Magda showing it to buyers, that was shit getting real.

She was going to have to start walking people around at midnight to avoid gardeners.

Then again, maybe she and her prospective buyers would come across people "cavorting," as Ty had put it and flinging those condoms and shoes and undergarments throughout the garden. Or they'd meet Ty running through the streets of Hamilton Heights. He'd probably deliver a stinging lecture about greed and development, all while standing there shirtless as Magda tried not to yell at him—or be distracted.

That left maybe safe one hour between 3:00 and 4:00 a.m. for showings?

She made a note to herself to get one of those powerful *X-Files*-style flashlights.

Magda quickly got a cab for Amanda, made her goodbyes, and went back to the townhouse.

She was going to have to tell Keith how it had gone. He'd been excited about Eliot and Chase.

The tree guys had left the townhouse and although the bags of dirt were gone, there were still traces of mud on the floor. There were contractors upstairs working on one of the upstairs bathrooms and she could hear them hammering and drilling. She put in her earbuds and started sweeping the floor. She really needed to talk to someone; her sister wasn't the best person to unload her feelings to, but Magda decided to call Flora.

Flora's kids were apparently loving their STEM summer camp. Her husband's recent spate of business trips had slowed down, thank goodness. Flora had started planning her organization's fall gala and she promised Magda a pair of tickets. "I'll only need one," Magda said, sitting heavily at the staged dining room table of her uncle's house. "I can afford to pay for myself."

At least, she hoped she could swing it. The tickets were usually at least a hundred dollars a pop, and she'd have to buy a new dress for this year's event.

"No, no. And if you can't find someone to come with you, I'll think of someone nice. You're still getting your real estate career off the ground. Mamí says you haven't sold Uncle Byron's place yet."

"I'm working on it. And really, I can pay. I only need one ticket."

Liar.

"But Magda, it's more fun with a date. And maybe afterward, who knows? Didn't you dance last year with that nice doctor Mamí found for you at the hospital?"

"I think he liked Mamí more than he liked me."

Who could blame the guy? Watching the poor man hang on to her oblivious mother's every word had been funny, although a little humiliating when he commented, "From what your mom said, I expected you to be really young. Not that that's what I wanted. I thought I was doing Lina a favor for her kid. I definitely like mature women." And his puppyish gaze had swung right around to Lina Ferrer.

Yeah, that had been a little awkward.

Magda rested her forehead on the dining table for another moment.

"Or maybe you could bring someone you know from work," Flora suggested brightly. "Your co-broker from the deal you're trying to do."

"Keith. No. Plus, it's not really going so well today. The gardeners scared off a potential buyer."

"It's not your fault."

"I *know*."

She hadn't even been assigning blame. But when Flora and Alma automatically said that, somehow they made it feel like a little kid pointing at a deflated balloon and bursting into tears. She wanted to tell her sister something serious. Maybe because Magda was so much younger, it was like growing up with three mothers. She didn't want to be pacified. She wanted to talk.

Ty, who didn't even like her, had at least listened. He'd recognized her work. *It seems like you're earning it*, he'd said. He hadn't made her worries seem small.

She should not be thinking of him.

Magda tried another tack. "I know it's not my fault that the buyer wasn't interested. But aren't you—aren't you wondering a little bit why I would be trying to sell this community garden out from under the people who made it?"

"Oh, Magda." And it was like Flora had reached out over the phone lines to pat her little sister on the head.

Magda couldn't complain about it, because it felt good. But at the same time, it seemed sometimes like her family didn't expect much of her at all.

"I was talking with the gardeners," Magda continued. "They do such good work. They really have transformed the whole feeling of the block. The space was full of garbage. People wouldn't let their kids play in it. Now it's beautiful and safe. *I* want to sit there and hang out sometimes."

"You don't have to try to sell it, Magda."

"So you think I should quit, try another career?"

"No. Yes. I think you should do what you want to do."

Maybe it didn't matter to her sisters what she did. "Why do you think I should do whatever I want to do, Flora? Why?"

A pause.

"I don't understand what's going on, Magda. I'm simply trying to listen to you. Clearly, you're in some kind of a mood—"

"Having a temper tantrum, like a toddler?"

"No, mija, all that all of us want is for you to be happy, to find someone—"

Magda let out a breath.

"Because I can't do anything on my own?"

"Of course not. But you're still so young."

"I'm twenty-nine, Flora! It's not old, but I'm trying to take responsibility for my life and that means I need you—all of you—to take me seriously, and listen to me. Sometimes I even need you to not let me off the hook every time I screw up. It just feels like sometimes you and Mamí and Alma try to soothe me."

"Oh baby, that's not true."

"I'm trying to tell you something important. I don't want to be a bad person here, Flora. I think I need to sell this lot to prove I can do this. But I'm wondering if it's the right thing to do. What if I'm on the wrong side? I know I have to figure out what's best for me— God knows, I need to finish something. For once in my life. And of course, I expected the gardeners to fight. But it feels so personal."

"You could never be a bad person, Magda."

Was Flora listening? Did anyone ever listen? Magda thunked her head on the dining table again. She was going to have a dent in her skull if she kept talking to her sister. And the next time she saw Flora, Flora would probably say a dent in the head did not make her a terrible girl and that she'd known many people with dents in their head who grew up to do great things.

Then again, it was Magda's own fault for calling and trying to change the entire history of their relationship during the workday, for not doing this face-to-face, for not talking to her sisters seriously about this years ago. There was nothing to do but thank Flora for taking time out of her day.

So Magda did, even though she was more frustrated now than when she'd begun.

"I know jobs can be hard, Magda," Flora said by way of goodbye. Her voice was already distant as if she'd moved on to other, more important problems. "Don't worry too much and call us whenever you need help. It's always good to talk things out."

"It's not really—"

But her sister had already hung up.

Sunday

"Remember Jojo's mom, Mrs. Shi? All the grown-ups used to say she made the best sticky rice but when we were kids, we thought it tasted like shit, but it turned out it was because her sticky rice was just sweet rice cooked in vodka? Like, straight up vodka. No water, no broth, not even a pinch of salt or sugar to let you know how you should feel, aside from numb in the mouth. Yeah, I could go for some of that right now."

Ty looked up blankly from the sink. He'd been washing the dishes. Jenny was drying—rather she was putting dishes into the dishwasher which Ty used as a storage rack because that's what Ma had done. Jenny still teased him about it, but she did it his way anyway.

"Ty, are you even listening to me?"

Her voice had taken on a familiar younger sibling whine, which was at least comforting in its ability to annoy him.

"I'm sorry. I'm preoccupied tonight. Did you say something about Jojo Shi's mom and vodka?"

"To make sticky rice. That's why the grown-ups loved it. I'd love to figure out how much alcohol cooked off and how much got absorbed."

"I do not remember one single thing about this. Is this a dish you're thinking of serving at Golden Egg?"

Jen didn't answer for a minute. In fact, she was avoiding his eyes.

He blinked. He'd been so preoccupied lately that he hadn't noticed his sister was jumpy. Jen had cooked a comforting egg and tomato stir-fry, for one thing, even though it was her night off.

"Jen, is everything okay with your job?"

Jen closed the dishwasher. "I'm thinking of taking a job in Portland. My friend, Amina, is opening a place there and she wants me to be her chef de cuisine. It's an amazing opportunity, and I'd have a chance to expand my skills. Plus, Portland has all those great farmer's markets."

"But that's—that's thousands of miles away. It's on the other coast."

"I'm glad your notion of geography hasn't abandoned you."

"Jenny."

She ducked her head.

"I've been thinking about a change for a while. And

watching you, how you've reacted to a lot of stuff that went on after mom died, that's made me think I needed to do something drastic."

"What's that supposed to mean? You think I'm stuck?"

"No. I think *I'm* still stuck. There's nothing holding me here, Ty. My job is okay—fine. But I'm not going to get promoted in that kitchen. Mom is gone. Dad moved. I'm twenty-seven and I have roommates I hate. My last two relationships didn't work out the way I thought they would. I'm tired. I don't want my job to be everything, but it's so competitive here. My old friends, the people we grew up with, they have regular 9-5 hours. No matter how hard we all try, it's hard to stay connected. A babysitter cancels, and I don't see some of them for another year. At least in Portland, I'd know Amina and a couple of other friends from culinary school."

"But I'm here."

Ty understood what his sister was saying. He sympathized. It wasn't easy making new friends at their age. But he was stuck on the distance, maybe because contemplating everything else was too much.

"Yes, you're here. And that's huge. But you've got a whole life here now. You live in an apartment you own, in a community you connect with. You're planning block party fundraisers and texting your friends all the time. Like during dinner I counted at least thirty pings, and for each one, your face changed, like you wanted to answer, but you were stuck with me."

"Jenny, I love having you around. You're my sister. You're important in my life. I'm stressed out, that's all. And the gardeners aren't my friends, really."

"What would you call them?"

He opened his mouth and shut it again. That was a good question. It's not like they went to each other's houses and hung out and played video games. He knew Mrs. E had kids—three, he thought—but no grandchildren yet. That she had nieces and nephews—at least one who worked at Dance Theater of Harlem and had gotten some ballerinas to agree to perform, and another whose choir had been volunteered. He knew Mr. Serra had been sick with cancer—he didn't talk about it and that was fine with Ty—that Mrs. Freeman had owned a shoe repair shop in East Harlem and had been married and divorced four times. That the teens who'd made their solar panel had hopes of entering the citywide science fair with an even bigger project which they talked about in hushed tones. But he didn't even know most people's first names.

Or maybe he had told himself not to learn them.

At some point, even before the idea for a block party started, he'd been invited to meet all the brothers and sisters and spouses and aunts and uncles. Maybe he'd even been introduced to one or two. But he had been polite. He kept his head down.

He didn't get involved.

"There are a lot of different ways of being friends with people," Jen added when he didn't answer. "It's not just if you've been to their house for Thanksgiving, or if you've known them since kindergarten. Sometimes, it's about what you've done. Have you been a good friend to them? Have you listened sympathetically? Have you walked them home late at night?"

If that were true, he was probably technically friends with Magda Ferrer.

As if reading his thoughts, Jenny smirked. "I mean, that's not all there is to it—"

"Thank goodness for that," he murmured.

"But I'm saying maybe the gardeners are your friends. You care about them a lot and they certainly adore you. They could be like family if you let them."

"Weren't you making fun of me the other day for hanging out with old ladies—not that there's anything wrong with that and a lot of them aren't old?"

"I was. And then I went back home and I thought about it and I decided I was an asshole. Like I said before, I'm jealous. You've found what I want. You've found a place where you fit in—"

"I wouldn't go so far."

"I would."

He wanted to protest. He didn't even plant stuff. He wouldn't know how. He didn't have a plot. What was holding him here? The answer was a dozen more texts, people to write, a fundraiser to help plan. Obligations held him there. A stinking compost pile. All things of which he'd been wary.

Fuu-huck.

This was the last thing he'd wanted. He liked his life just fine the way it was—pain-free. He'd watched his mom die for years and every one of those years had been a slow pull of nails on his flesh. He'd watched his father run away afterward, unable to deal with the funeral, the paperwork, barely able to look at his children.

Ty didn't want to lose anything or anyone ever again.

And here he was on the hopeless side of a fight, allied with people who wanted more from him.

He shook his head, trying to clear it. *It wasn't the same thing. The loss wouldn't be the same.* "You could be part of the garden," he tried, not managing to convince himself. "Think of the great herbs you'd be able to plant."

Jenny laughed. "I'll miss you, too."

"So that's it. The decision is made? You won't join them?"

"No, Ty. It's something you carved out for yourself. It's yours. I can see why you want to hang on to it."

But after Jenny left, after he turned off his phone, and turned off the lights, he wondered if he really did.

Chapter Seven

A Wednesday in Early August

"All of these open houses, and staging bills, floor plans, and photographs, and all you've gotten me is another lowball offer."

It hadn't seemed low to Magda. It wasn't full price, but it had been enough to get Magda's hopes up for the amount of time it took to check and double-check and, with shaky hands, fill out the offer sheet and email it to her uncle.

Byron had killed that with a message *Sent from his Android phone* in less than a minute. He'd rejected her work on the go.

Then, less than two days later, Uncle Byron showed up unexpectedly from Florida. He'd arrived in the middle of a tour she'd been giving to a record exec and her partner. And while Magda couldn't gauge whether they'd been interested, her uncle's heavy-browed presence made her stumble over her words. She'd shortened her usual talk. She'd been about to launch into the history of the house, but with one living component of that history casting a critical eye (and maybe ear) over her she couldn't dig into it with the same gusto. At least

Byron hadn't followed them from room to room, nagging her.

Like he was doing now.

"Don't see why we had to have new photos and floorplans made when we had perfectly good ones from before," Byron grumbled.

Magda kept her voice level. "You've made quite a few changes to the house since the last time those *other brokers at other firms* took their pictures and had plans drawn up."

"And this staging business," he continued as if she hadn't been talking. "I don't understand how people can charge to make up a bed and set a table."

"All the rooms are bare, Byron. It's a little easier to sell if people know what they're for."

"So get a label maker."

Usually, she tried to talk to Byron as little as possible. Other brokers must have gone over this ground with him in the past, although the last two hadn't bothered with staging at all. And of course, the last two hadn't sold the place. "It helps tell the story," Magda said. "People want to be able to picture themselves using the rooms, throwing a dinner party, reading on the couch, baking cookies, playing with their dogs in the backyard. We're selling a house, sure, but we need to help people picture their life in that home. The more real it becomes the more they want it. It's like…it's like we want buyers to think they'll have good memories even before they've lived here."

Something passed over Byron's face before he turned away.

In a moment, he said, "Is that hooey what they're teaching you?"

"Yeah, that's what they're teaching us."

"No one's table looks like that," Byron said, gesturing toward the gleaming glassware of the dining room table.

"It's an idealized version of the future."

"You don't need that many plates. There are plates here that are just for holding other plates—you don't even eat off of them."

"They're called chargers."

"They sure are charging me for them. Same with all those throw pillows upstairs in the bedroom. More like throw-money-away pillows."

"Well, like I said before if you're feeling squeezed, you could always stop renovating. While I've been here, you've already freshened up the foyer and the kitchen, the backyard and the master bath, and the security system. You got new trees. Not to mention all the other things you've done over the last few years. We're in good shape for September, when the market starts picking up more."

She tried not to shout that her uncle was willing to spend money renovating rooms that were perfectly fine—and that any new owners would likely redo anyway—but that he was grumbling to her about a few plates and pillows. It was like he wanted the whole house to be completely transformed into something unrecognizable. He didn't seem to care about the cost of constant renovation, and anytime she brought it up, he ignored her. And it was work—for her. She had to keep it all clean, ready to show at any minute. And the workmen would inevitably track in dirt, or the rumble of their machinery made dust drop from the ceilings. She couldn't be annoyed with the contractors and plumbers and landscapers. They were doing their jobs, and for the most part, they tried to clean up after themselves. But the place needed dusting. Plates, and glasses, and silverware, and tables needed polishing. She was cleaning his damn house, and supervising his workers, and mopping up after them because mess was inevitable and he took for granted that because she was here, she'd do it.

Byron was quiet.

This wasn't her real uncle. He wasn't related by blood. He certainly hadn't been around for the last ten years. He was a client. She couldn't take it personally. She could *not* quit. She put on her most professional voice. "We listed in summer. We've had two offers"— at least one of those was perfectly reasonable—"and I'm confident that we'll have more in fall. These things take time, I'm sure you know."

"I gave it to you even though you're young and you don't know anything because you're family and I thought—I thought I was doing one last good thing for Ariana. But you've come in and put in furniture, made it look like the place belongs to someone else."

Magda held her breath. She said as gently as she could, "That's sort of the idea."

"I know. I understand that's what we're trying to do. My great-grandfather bought this house. I grew up in it. I played with my brother in the backyard. We had dinners all crowded together in this room and spilling into the next, all the aunts, and uncles, and cousins and my parents. But over the years, we all dispersed. My brother got killed in Vietnam. I lived here with Ariana until she got sick. My wife died in this house. People want to make memories? They want to picture a life here? I got memories. I had a life."

"I'm sorry, uncle."

She didn't know what to say. She hardly knew him. Most of her recollections of him were of his worry and his anger when Ariana was dying for such a long time. The grief that cloaked the family during those long years had made it difficult for her, still a teen at that point, to see him.

She knew sellers often had a hard time letting go. Keith would roll his eyes and tell stories about people haunting their open houses, and reacting angrily whenever buyers brought their architects or held up swatches. But what could she say to her uncle? To a man who she'd hardly known a long time ago, who wanted to be rid of his home, but who couldn't let go?

She hadn't expected the pain.

Byron said into her silence, "Your sorry doesn't get me anything. You need to get rid of this place. I can't stand to look at it anymore. You want buyers to think they're going to be able to sit on couches and watch Oprah and do macramé and drink their fancy coffee while they feel good about their lives, or whatever you people do with your time, fine. But this house doesn't need any more memories. You need to get in a good offer by the end of September or else I'll take it to someone else."

He sat down heavily in one of the dining room chairs. Magda wanted to do the same.

Instead, she went to the kitchen and brought him back a glass of water. She watched him drink it.

It wasn't the time to argue with him, no matter how frustrated and sad and scared she was.

"Uncle Byron, can I get anything else for you?"

"I want to go back to my hotel. It's in Midtown."

"I'll call you a cab."

"No, I'll take the subway," he said sharply.

"Are you sure? I can—"

"I've been riding the subway longer than you've had all that hair on your head, girl."

"Let me walk you to the station."

"I know where it is."

"I know you know! I know you lived here most of your life. That you know this house, this neighborhood. But it's hot out and I want to make sure that you're okay. All right? Let me do this."

Byron huffed out a breath and said something about interfering women. But he rose to his feet heavily and waited while Magda fetched another bottle of water. He grumbled under his breath while Magda punched the code to lock the house. (A system he'd insisted on installing, Magda thought, although she said nothing.) They walked out into the hot, August air, slowly. Byron led the way, and, of course, inevitably, he chose the route that went past the garden.

Magda felt sweaty and self-conscious. Her hair was probably frizzing. She hadn't stopped by too often since the debacle with Cool Amanda, the developer.

She should have pushed Byron past quickly; she didn't need the two main disasters of her life to collide. They'd probably cause a third, even bigger catastrophe, and she didn't want to be responsible for a giant hole in the space-time continuum in the middle of Harlem. Think of what it would do to the property prices. But Byron couldn't be steered and, of course, like a bee to a flower—lots of flowers, actually—Byron was drawn.

There were signs up.

Byron knew how to strike at the heart of her, especially when he wasn't trying. *"SAVE THE GARDEN BLOCK PARTY,"* he read out loud. "136th STREET GARDEN NEEDS YOU."

He turned to Magda.

"There's a link for a GoFundMe. Any idea what this is? Where did this garden come from? Why does it need saving? Looks fine to me."

She was tempted to say she had no idea what it was. But no, she had to be honest.

She stood up straight. "They're saving it from me."

Byron looked at her for a moment.

He snorted. "Don't be dramatic. You're grown up and you wear a suit. Doesn't mean you're Godzilla."

"She's the one selling it," Tyson Yang piped up, coming up the garden path.

Magda snapped, "It's the middle of the afternoon. Don't you have work to do? Or does CPA stand for *chartered professional asshole*?"

"Magda Ferrer, you watch your language."

"It's okay," Ty said. "It really should be *certified public asshole*. Besides, she's called me worse."

She hadn't. But if they argued she might come up with something.

Byron wasn't paying attention to either of them anymore. He walked forward, into the garden, as if hypnotized. "There used to be a house here. Red brick. I know this place. Why is this familiar?"

Magda did not want to follow. "You don't live that far away—or you didn't used to."

Tyson glanced at her sharply, then at her uncle.

His mouth formed an O. Then his face softened. He moved closer to her. "Your uncle who owns the house."

Ty remembered.

"Yeah."

"Is he okay? Are you all right? You both look tired."

She wanted to laugh. "It's been a hard day for him."

"The house must hold a lot of memories."

"This whole neighborhood, it seems."

Byron was making his way slowly into the garden. She and Ty watched him for a minute in silence.

"I'm frustrated with him. But he's so lost without my aunt. Even after all these years."

Another pause. Then Ty said, "Same thing happening with my dad. After my mom died, he became angry and aimless. It was like he forgot how to connect to people. Not even his children could anchor him."

"I'm sorry."

"Let's be thankful he's not living here. My sister says he moved back to Taiwan so he could be an asshole to everyone in a language he's comfortable in."

Magda couldn't help laughing. "My mother and sisters definitely say all the good stuff in Spanish."

"You don't?"

"I speak, but not as fluently. I'm younger than my sisters. I went to different schools from them. My mom and sisters correct me a lot, or don't wait for me to finish sentences, which makes it harder to talk to them. I love my family and the language and I'm proud to be Boricua. I wish I spoke Spanish better, but I realize they'd treat me that way no matter what language I used."

"I get it. If you can't express yourself with the range and fluency, then it can feel like you don't have any power. I speak a little more Mandarin and Taiwanese than my sister, but the subjects I'm most comfortable with are food, and old people's health, or at least agree-

ing everything is bad. It's not like I could have a discussion about I don't know—"

"Gardening and being an accountant?"

"My only personality traits."

"I've gotten to know you well."

He slanted a glance at her and she shivered.

She was the first to look away.

With impeccable timing Uncle Byron came back and
interrupted the moment.

"Why didn't anyone try to save the house that used
to be here?" he asked, hands on hips.

"Did you know the previous residents, uncle?"

"I don't remember. You'd think I'd be able to recall
an entire solid brick building on a block I walked down
my whole life."

"It was an empty lot for a pretty long time," Tyson
said. "At least ten years. Long before my time."

Byron rolled his eyes. "The young sure do like to
remind old people they're old."

"I'm not that young, and you don't seem past your
prime, yet."

"Didn't Magda tell you? Talking pretty to me doesn't
work. Besides, what I want to know is what used to be
here and what happened to the building."

"I could ask Mrs. Espinosa. She's lived on the block
for at least thirty years. But this garden has been thriving here for three, thanks to the hard work of people in
the neighborhood. We really made something beautiful
here, which is why we want to save it."

"You shouldn't try to give me the hard sell on your
causes, young man. Especially when what you're ped-
dling seems to be a bunch of socialist vegetables."

"All that hippie-dippy shared work makes the crops sweeter, sir."

Byron raised an eyebrow and turned to Magda. "Your young man has a mouth on him."

"Your young man has a mouth on him."

Ty was beginning to like being this dirtbag who'd tendered his resignation without the prospect of another job in sight.

He'd quit his job! Well, effective two months from now.

And he'd taken a day off in the middle of the week because he felt like it and because he had to use his accumulated time off. He'd turned into a person who had so many texts that he had to block off times during the day when he could answer them, like when Mrs. Espinosa was all-caps excited because she'd learned a lot from her three-day grant-writing workshop and when Mr. S had waylaid their city council member into talking to the Parks Department.

Ty had turned into someone devil-may-care, someone who had a cause and allies, and a nemesis—a pretty one, no less.

Of course, if Magda were truly his nemesis, he probably wouldn't be thrilled that she hadn't bothered to correct her uncle when he'd called Ty her young man.

And if they were mortal enemies, he probably wouldn't be considering getting a T-shirt—two, one for him, one for her—that read, *Certified Public Asshole*. He'd also spent time getting Save 136th Garden gear made lately. Maybe she'd want some of that, too. He could make up a whole gift package.

Clearly, he had to work on this nemesis thing a little

more if he was contemplating sending his enemy free stuff. Jenny would probably laugh at him for being pathetic. *Trust Ty to try to give a present to the person he's supposed to hate.*

Then again, Jenny said she envied him, and he was enough of the stodgy older brother that he was thrilled his cooler, badass sibling admired him. But he was also torn up about it. He had known she'd been dissatisfied with her job, with her relationships, with everything. It was how he'd felt, too. The restlessness, the grief, had been part of both their lives for so long since his mother had died. He hadn't seen it for what it was. A certain numbness had become normal for him, and for his sister. And while he was sad he hadn't perceived it in himself, he felt worse that he hadn't detected it in her. It wasn't that he could really protect her from hurt, but he'd loved her, ever since she'd been a red-faced bundle brought home from the hospital, ever since he'd had to learn exactly how tightly and carefully to hold her, and later he'd learned how to let go when she didn't want to be carried.

Jenny was right. It was time for a change. For both of them. He would stick around to make sure the gardeners raised more money, of course. But there was nothing else really keeping him here. He was to find a job elsewhere, get rid of his apartment, start a new, uncomplicated life.

He watched Magda and Byron picking their way through the garden and a sharp pang went through him.

Okay. Yes. While he didn't consider the gardeners his best friends, he would miss everyone. He would even miss battling with Magda, hoping, waiting to see her every time he put down his tools. He would miss that cocktail of expectation and anxiety that stirred up in him every time he saw her walking toward him.

Magda and Byron left the garden shortly afterward, and Ty repaired the wire fences that kept the rats and squirrels, and possibly raccoons—there'd been a Tweet from the city sanitation department about them—out of the gardeners' precious tomatoes. He thought he'd heard the last of Magda's uncle. But later that night, someone named Byron Jackson left a hefty donation to the garden's GoFundMe. It could have been a coincidence. People from all over were contributing. But Ty's suspicions seemed to be confirmed by the message the donor left: *This better have gone through because I'm not entering all my numbers into these boxes again.*

The next week, Magda brought another potential buyer into the garden.

It was a stiflingly hot day—at least a hundred degrees Fahrenheit, and Ty didn't even want to think about the heat index. He'd tried to send most of the seniors home, promising he'd come back later in the evening to water their plots. But Mrs. Freeman had left a cooler full of drinks in the shaded corner near the shed. A group of kids was working in the back area, supervised by elderly Ms. Mosley, who at least had agreed to sit on a lawn chair, a hat protecting her finely wrinkled brown face. But the teens seemed subdued, poking sullenly at their panel. It was hard even for 136th Street to be magical. There were no breezes to make the leaves ripple invitingly. The brightness of the flowers seemed dimmed by the sun's relentless light. Worse, their combined forces couldn't combat the *smell* of New York City at the height of summer.

Into that walked Magda, tense and upright, a wavy dark line in the heat, along with her latest client. She was in the suit again. He was surprised she kept wearing the outfit because despite the short sleeves of the jacket it looked far too hot for a day like today. Maybe it held her up, held her in. It steeled her to whatever it was they would find here.

The woman beside her fanned herself.

No one went up to say hello.

Maybe it was the weather, or maybe it was Magda and the buyer, but the atmosphere seemed too stifling. Ty dropped back and watched them. This buyer seemed serious. She took a lot of pictures, including photos of the signs they'd put up, and thumbed notes on her iPhone. When she had a question for Magda, she asked in whispers.

Somehow, that seemed a lot more ominous.

It was eighty-year-old Ms. Mosley who started the heckling. "We don't want a building here!"

"No building!" shouted a couple of the teens.

"No building! No war! We don't want it anymore!"

Ty wasn't sure what current battle they referred to, but he couldn't really argue with any of those sentiments.

Magda was approaching, saying calmly, "If the gardeners come to me with an offer, then I will present it to the seller."

"How can we trust you to do that?"

"No building, no war!"

"I'm required to present all reasonable, good-faith offers to the seller by law. But also, I want to. If you can come up with the money, then I will help you."

Ms. Mosley waved her away.

The buyer said quietly, "We should go."

"No building!"

They were walking away. Everything was fine. It had only been a couple of minutes.

Then Ty saw Mrs. M get up. She shook aside the wire Ty had put up, stood, and pulled her arm back. She had something in her hand.

Rather than thinking, Ty reacted.

He dove in the missile's path, felt the shocking wet splat of it against his shoulder, the yielding of Magda's stiff suit as he brushed past her and fell to the ground.

"Ty, are you all right?"

He breathed.

He sat up and grimaced.

"I'm fine. It's just messy."

It was a tomato.

And judging by how juicy the damn thing was— it was seeping through his shirt, and parts of it were tricking down his collar—it had been a *good* tomato. Probably heirloom.

God, he'd learned enough about gardening to know this.

Magda had dropped to her knees. She was hovering right over him. He looked up into her eyes as she stared down at him and for a moment they breathed together.

He'd saved her from a tomato thrown by an elderly woman—one with a good arm.

He was *not* going to laugh. And judging by the tremble of her mouth, she was struggling not to either.

Why, of all people, did he have to share all this sense of humor, all of this understanding, all of these moments, with *her*?

He saw as she took another deep, calming breath—

smoothing the humor out of her face—and surreptitiously checked her suit. It struck him suddenly that maybe she didn't have another. But that was ridiculous, wasn't it? Surely she could afford more than one or two suits? He shouldn't make himself out to be more of a hero than he was.

The buyer was watching them, still curiously detached from the scene.

Tyson scrambled up.

"I'm so sorry," Magda began. She turned from him to her client and back again as if she didn't know where to start.

"It's fine," he and the woman said at the same time.

He let it go—let her go—and watched as they left the garden, much more quickly this time. He kept watching as they moved out of sight.

Mrs. Mosley was sitting again. She seemed quite proud of herself. The kids clustered around her and Ty made his way cautiously up to them.

"Mr. Yang! You're bleeding."

Ty picked some tomato pulp off of his shoulder and said, "First blood in the garden battle belongs to you, Ms. Mosley."

It wouldn't set a great example for the kids if he burst into laughter, he reminded himself. But also, he should probably say something about choosing how to protest? It wasn't like he knew any better himself.

Luckily, one of the teens, David, was already considering the numerous consequences of Ms. Mosley's move. He inspected the mess on Ty's shoulder, saying, "Da-ang, Ms. Freeman's going to kill you, Ms. M. You grabbed one of her tomatoes."

"I think it was an heirloom," Hector added.

"Okay," Ty said, trying to get people back on track, "while protesting is genuinely great as long as you do it safely and talk to your folks, I guess"—he was floundering—"maybe throwing tomatoes at a person who can also help us isn't the best idea? Also, if you're going to start throwing things at people and risk being charged with assault"—he made sure all the kids heard that part—"then, maybe instead of grabbing the precious tomatoes, you should consider throwing a zucchini. Because we've got way more of those."

No one was listening to him. Ms. Mosley's eyes gleamed. "Still got it," she said, shaking her arm.

"Living your best life, Ms. M!"

Ty sighed. Maybe they were right. It was hard to tell. It was not supposed to be his problem. He should walk away.

Chapter Eight

Later That Day

Magda was in the townhouse when she heard the buzzer. It was Ty, holding his palms up to the camera in the *I come in peace* stance.

Magda hadn't been expecting him—especially because of what had happened earlier, but she was perversely glad to see him. He'd *saved* her—or at least, her potential buyer, or the buyer's suit. Magda had taken off her own short-sleeved jacket and was considering putting on the workout clothing she'd toted from Brooklyn. She didn't have any more appointments today, but she needed to clean plaster dust off the floors because of the repairs to the second-floor bathroom and polish the dining room table before she could make her way to the subway. Even then, it would be a long time before she'd make it back home to her apartment, judging by how slowly the trains were running in this hot weather.

She jiggled with the door, which didn't want to open. The alarm beeped a warning, even though she'd disarmed it. On the fourth try, she finally succeeded in getting it to work. "Sorry. I'm having trouble with the system. I think too many people coming in and out is stressing it out."

"I get it. It wants to make sure I'm not armed."

She relaxed for the first time all day. If he were angry at her—and who wasn't?—a few words with him would probably be the best thing that happened to her all week. She couldn't help smiling. "No tomatoes?"

"Not one."

He smiled back.

The alarm beeped again for no apparent reason.

"This security smart-lock combo is going to kill me. Please come in so that the house doesn't freak out because I've left the door open for too long."

"Wow, it's cold in here," he said, stepping across the threshold.

"Central air. It's probably costing Byron a fortune. I do feel sorry for him, but he's also been a jerk, I figure I can't feel too guilty about it."

They stood awkwardly for a moment. Then Ty said, "I wanted to apologize," right as Magda blurted, "I wanted to thank you."

Magda recovered first. "You have nothing to say sorry for. In fact, you saved me."

"From a fruit."

"You dove in front of me so fast. And you saved the suit."

She waved at herself. Well, she was still wearing the skirt, which was wrinkled, but had taken off the short-sleeved jacket. Another housekeeping task she'd have to take care of. He had changed, of course. No more stains on him. His T-shirt stretched nicely over the chest she'd only briefly admired once long ago, and he was wearing a pair of crisp Bermuda shorts.

While she only had on a camisole, she realized.

And, of course, when she'd gestured at herself, he'd shot her a swift, encompassing glance that she'd felt all through her body; she'd invited him to gaze upon all this glory, after all.

Another slightly awkward silence.

"Well, I'm still sorry," he said. "I know we're on opposite sides, but I don't want people to throw things at you."

"It was startling."

"I, uh, also brought a peace offering."

He opened the canvas bag slung at his shoulder and pulled out a stack of neat boxes. "It's the deluxe dumpling assortment. My sister cooks at Golden Egg. It's my favorite thing on the menu."

Magda blinked. He'd brought her food. When she found her voice again, she said, "I love dumplings. And I'm starving. I haven't eaten anything since breakfast."

"In this heat, you should really make sure you feed yourself. I saw a woman pass out on the subway platform this morning. Luckily there were paramedics already there."

"It's terrible." She hesitated. "You'll join me, of course? In the air conditioning?"

"I was hoping you'd ask."

He grinned wide and she found herself staring helplessly at him.

With another start, she ushered him toward the kitchen. For half a minute, she considered bringing him upstairs to the dining room table. It was, after all, set with gleaming silverware and plates, and, as Byron said, plates to hold plates. But she'd have to clean up and reset everything and it wouldn't be the same. The place settings told a story, she'd told Byron, but that story was fiction—a romance.

That couldn't happen.

The smell of ginger and sesame oil wafted up toward her. Magda sighed and opened up a drawer, and pulled out some plastic utensils and a stack of napkins while Ty unpacked the dumplings.

They were beautiful, plump, and shiny, deftly pinched and plaited. Magda felt like she hadn't eaten in a long time; she hadn't cooked anything in even longer. It seemed strange that a plate of dumplings made by someone else could remind her so strongly of the things she loved and missed.

Ty said, "You also mentioned something about taking any offers. I wondered…so we might be ready to make a bid in a few weeks. We've been promised funding from the borough president's office and a couple of corporate donors. I wanted to see if we had a chance. If you've had any other people interested."

Magda carefully set some plastic forks and knives and chopsticks, a plate for him, a plate for her, aligning them precisely opposite each other. She wanted to be careful not to betray her disappointment. Of course, he was here to talk about the garden. He wanted to make sure the tomato hurler hadn't spoiled their chances of securing the garden.

It wasn't like her relationship with Ty had been warm before now.

"I'm not really at liberty to tell you much about other bids." Partly because there weren't any. "Like I said, I'll pass on any serious offers. Thanks so much for bringing all this food."

"Well, I wanted a chance to have the dumpling sampler before Jenny changes direction. She's moving to Portland and I—well, you're helping me out."

She looked up. "You said she's a cook?"

"She's taking on a position as executive chef. She trained at the American Culinary School."

"Oh, the ACS. I went there. For a while at least."

"Really? When?"

"I dropped out this past winter. I was there for a couple of years."

"After Jenny's time, then. Well, I can't blame you for quitting. Everything I've heard from my sister about restaurant work sounds rough. The hours are long. You get burned and nicked with knives. Pay's not great."

She nodded, not really wanting to talk too much about it. Instead, she picked up a solid, slightly translucent dumpling, and admired the chives glowing under its thin skin. It burst gently in her mouth, and then the juices hit her tongue. It tasted green, and brothy, and salty, and warm, and soothing. She didn't even want to chew. She just wanted that flood of comfort again and again.

They were both quiet.

"This is really good," she said.

She was not going to cry over a dumpling. She was not going to shed tears over one bad day in a string of bad days. She hadn't fallen apart because of her failure at school, and she certainly wouldn't now because she was faced with the knowledge she'd never make something like this one perfect dumpling, let alone three perfect boxes of them. She was not going to feel bad because Ty was here because of the garden. She wasn't even supposed to like him. Except she did. She liked his goofy, pleased grin, his floppy hair. She liked his hands, his wrists, the fact that they were engaged in subtly pushing the dumpling boxes toward her, even though she'd tried to place the food so carefully in the middle.

But this maneuvering was for the garden, and not for her. And she was going to take what time she could get with him anyway. She wasn't going to send him away any more than she was going to stop eating these dumplings.

"Try this one with the mushrooms," Ty said. "The textures are amazing and it's so rich, with a crunchiness, and softness, and that whole umami thing going on."

"Your sister taught you well."

"She has important things to say, so I try to listen."

She envied his sister—no, that wasn't what she was feeling. She didn't feel sisterly at all.

He stared at his plate, drawing little lines in the puddle of soy sauce with his chopsticks. "The funny thing is, what really made her want to move was this whole mess with the garden. She says seeing me get involved made her wish she had something similar in her life—some cause, some community."

"You sound like you don't believe it. But you've got a place there. You're loved. People respect and listen to you."

"And they don't you? Don't you have family here?"

"They love me a lot. And I have a place. Too much of one. My dad died before I knew him but I've never felt unparented, even now. My sisters have kids, and I'm still their baby. But the worst thing is, I feel like I haven't earned my way to becoming anything else for them."

"Why would you say that? Like, you wear a suit

all the time. You're…you're *polished*. Babies are many
good things but they aren't polished."

She laughed. "I don't feel that way. Especially on a
day like today, when it's hot and I'm walking around
with that suit sticking to me. A suit which I wear all too
often because I'm supposed to look *p*—"

"Say it."

"Professional. I'm supposed to look *professional* if
I ever hope to sell anything. At least that's the idea.
But it's been months and I haven't moved this house
or the lot—"

"The garden."

"Yeah. I get that it's a slow season for this kind of
real estate. But it's New York and I'm not getting bites
and I'm starting to wonder if it's me. If I'm not right
for this. If I should quit the way I've quit everything
else. At this rate, I don't think you have to worry about
whether you'll have the opportunity to make an offer.
Yours might be the only offer."

"Listen, I'd be really happy and relieved if that proves
true. But our money is money and people seem to like
it. I find it hard to believe your family could be disappointed in you if you're bringing it in."

"That's the worst thing. They love me a lot. They accept my many failures because they expect it. I'm not
disappointing. I'm confirmation."

"Hey."

"It's fine. They never expected much from me to
begin with. As far as they're concerned, I'm a kid they'll
have to look after for the rest of their lives. So when I
drop out of my graduate program, when I quit cooking school, when I fail to sell this house, they'll say to

me, *Oh, it's good that you tried.* And they'll pat me on the head and tell me to do something less challenging."

"I think my point is that you've set up challenges for yourself."

"Well, I wish someone aside from me would believe I'm up to taking them."

"If it makes you feel any better, you and your polished, professional suit strike terror into me every time you walk into the garden. So clearly *I* believe that you're up to doing your job."

"Terror? Really?"

She almost laughed.

"Fear, abject and complete. That's what you inspire in me. Well, other stuff, too. But I wouldn't be this scared, we wouldn't be working this hard on saving the garden if we didn't believe that you were able to sell it."

Magda sat back. She'd never thought of it that way. "That is the nicest thing anyone has ever said about me—and my suit. Which you saved, today."

He smiled at his plate, then looked up into her eyes. "Yeah, well, I can't regret it. I...as much as I don't want the garden sold, I was also scared when I thought someone might hurt you."

She stared back at him. "What was the other stuff that I inspired?" she whispered.

"I'm sorry, I don't follow."

"You said I inspired fear and abject terror in you whenever I showed up at the garden. But I also inspired other stuff. What was it?"

"Oh."

He glanced down again. He put down his chopsticks and very carefully wiped his lips with his napkin. He leaned over the counter, close to her, so close she could feel his gentle breath across her face.

She didn't pull away.

"I think about what it would be like if I"—he was speaking low, so low that only she would ever hear this—"if I kissed you."

She was dizzy, probably from holding her breath. And she felt herself nodding, as if he'd asked a question, as if the answer were yes. Because it would be. It was. "That's what I inspire?"

"Yes."

"Then kiss me."

Until now, he had hardly touched her.

Her eyes were cast down, her lips parted. He shouldn't—he definitely shouldn't—but then she glanced up again, right into his eyes, and he closed the small space left between them and pressed his lips to hers.

His hand came up to touch her cheek, to trace softly the voluptuous skin of her earlobe, down to the stubborn jut where her jaw began. He felt her breathe again under him, a sigh, and her mouth opened slightly so that the warmth of her curled around him, and they breathed into each other for a moment, until her tongue glided across his lips.

He couldn't hold himself back. His hand tightened, pulling her toward him. He banged his elbow on the hard, granite counter as she grabbed his shirt and pulled him closer. She slapped her other hand down on the counter and the crack of her palm on the surface nearly scared them apart—nearly. A quick breath and they were at it again: soft, hard, warm, wet. As if by agreement, they began to maneuver themselves to the end of the table, their teeth clashing, their movements labored as they slid awkwardly past their plates and chopsticks, bumped into a chair on his side, and—for one precarious moment—a box of dumplings on hers. They reached the end, and finally, their bodies closed the gaps between them, her arms around his neck, his hands sliding down the silky, thin material on her back. And always, their lips and tongues moved together.

And just when Ty was starting to press her into the counter, trying to get closer, to feel as much as he could of her, just as he was starting to move, his body was starting to scream it wanted more, the lights went out.

No, not only the lights, the stove and microwave clock went black. The sound of the air conditioning clicked off abruptly. The alarm system shrieked once, then fell silent.

Ty let go of Magda. Or she let go of him, and they both stood, holding the counter, breathing heavily. "What did we do?" Magda asked a little shakily.

"Our kissing shorted out the power?"

They both laughed uncomfortably. But it did feel like they'd caused some sort of electrical surge, although it felt too new and raw to mention it. Ty was still tingling. But ever rational, he volunteered to go down and check the fusebox. Whatever that meant.

"Let's go together," Magda said.

To the light of their phones, they picked their way carefully down the stairs. Ty stared at the box. He switched everything off, and then on again. Nothing.

"In my extremely un-expert opinion, I think we might need to call an electrician."

Magda was scrolling through her phone. "I'm on Twitter. Looks like there may have been a power outage."

"On one of the hottest days this year when everyone has their air conditioner on full. I guess that makes sense. I wonder how long it'll take them to fix it."

It had already started to get warm in the house. Not that Ty really noticed, because he was still hot from the kiss.

"Let's go upstairs and peek at the streetlights to make sure," he suggested.

They went back up again and opened the door. The security system—and the locks—gave another ominous screech.

Outside, the whole block was dark. But the sound of people shouting and horns beeping, the wail of ambulances down the block could be heard.

"I guess that answers that. Are those fancy locks on a backup system?"

"I—I don't know. My idea of a backup system is an actual physical key which I left at the office. I can deadbolt it from the inside, though."

"From the inside? You aren't staying. You don't live here, do you?"

"No, I have my own apartment. But I'm in Brooklyn, and I can't see going back tonight. Besides, I don't feel good about going all the way back in this mess, or about leaving the house alone with this one lock, not after someone already tried to break in."

"But—"

"Or what if the power comes back on in the middle of the night and the security system freaks out? It's on me to keep everything here together."

She was starting to look small, and alone. Ty didn't want her to look so forlorn.

"If the blackout goes on for a while, do you at least have somewhere to sleep in this house?"

She bit her lip. The same lips he'd been licking and sucking minutes ago.

Not the time and place.

"There is one bed. It's…the show bed."

"One bed," he repeated stupidly, his brain spiraling out in inappropriate ways. "A show bed. What does that mean?"

"It's staged to make the room look like a real bedroom so people can picture themselves there. Gives them some ideas."

He hadn't seen it, but it was definitely giving him ideas.

Magda continued, "The sheets have been ironed and the pillows are all arranged. I guess I could sort of take the pillows down and lie on the mattress. Carefully. Or maybe I could make a bed out of the pillows and plump them up again. I really don't want to have to iron the sheets, though."

She'd set her shoulders. She'd clearly already decided to suck it up and stay here. It was an empty house. It wasn't like an entire edifice could be stolen in the night. Still, he could sort of understand the urge to protect it. He wondered why she thought she was a quitter when it was clear she was willing to endure indignities and discomfort when she thought it was what was required of her. *He* wasn't sure she needed to do it. The house would be safe for one night. And even if it wasn't, what would she be able to do alone?

"You could spend the night at my place," he said.

"That's not a come-on, by the way. But my bed—for you—couch for me, is much more comfortable to sleep on than a bunch of throw pillows of different sizes and shapes that will scatter across the floor as soon as you try to lie down on them. Or move on them."

Another image in his head of her falling down into a pile of pillows in a soft, well-lit room.

Well, he thought, looking around in the dark night, that was definitely a fantasy.

Besides, she was shaking her head. "Thank you. That means a lot to me. But I can't leave. I don't feel right about it."

He thought for another minute. "Tell you what," he said. "I'm going to go back to my apartment. I'll get a sleeping bag for you. It's not cold out, but at least it's some padding if you sleep on the floor. What else would you like? A toothbrush and toothpaste? Something more comfortable than the suit? I have a T-shirt you could use."

"You don't have to—"

"Hey, it'll be fine. Kind of an adventure through an abandoned city."

"If you're sure. A sleeping bag and a toothbrush and toothpaste would be great. I have some workout clothing I can change into."

"Nothing else you want? Korean face mask? Seltzer? Extra flashlight?"

"How do you know about Korean face masks?" He heard the laughter in her voice. *Good.*

"I like to keep up with what the kids are into. Plus, I figure you must get your glow somehow."

"I think the glow is from making out."

Oh. Ty took in a deep breath. Yes, the air was very hot.

Magda said low, "No face mask required. But maybe a flashlight if you have one. My phone battery is low and obviously, I won't be able to recharge it. Thank you, Ty."

"It's no problem. Okay, I'm going to take off. You shut the door and I'll be back in"—the elevator in his building was probably out of commission. It would be a sweaty hike up to his apartment, and he'd be looking in the dark for gear he hadn't used in a long time—"half an hour, maybe? I'll text when I start back. I have your number from your card. Will you be all right?"

"I'll be all right."

They smiled at each other. It was going to be their first goodbye after their first kiss. Ty wondered if his life was always going to be divided this way: the life he'd led before he kissed Magda, the life after.

"Okay," he said again.

And then she leaned forward, he leaned down and their lips touched again, and they breathed together, they pulled closer, and then apart.

"I'll be back," he said.

"I'll be waiting."

Chapter Nine

After Ty left, Magda went inside and shut the door. She threw the deadbolt as a precaution. Then she took a deep breath to get her bearings.

The darkness made the house seem unfamiliar. It was so strange to be feeling her way around, trying to be careful of the buckets and building supplies left by workmen. More than once, she caught herself reaching for the light switch or flipping one to no avail.

She made her way back to the kitchen and snatched a now-cold dumpling—still delicious—and carefully boxed up the rest. No use putting them in the fridge. She checked Twitter one more time before tucking her phone away to save the battery. The blackout seemed to be concentrated above 125th Street. It could take hours before Con Ed fixed it.

A combination of excitement and nervousness still bubbled through her veins, heightened by the strangeness of the last hour. She was alone in a now-unfamiliar house. But she'd kissed Tyson Yang. At this counter. *Over* this counter. Her lips still felt sensitive; her whole body was still thrumming in expectation. Her palms tingled, her legs, her thighs, the juncture between them, felt heavy, thick with need. Because she'd promised— the kiss had promised—so much more.

But he wasn't there right now. And she had to be practical. After stumbling and stubbing her toe, she managed to find her bag and her workout clothing. She stepped out of her shoes, unzipped her skirt, and laid it neatly on a kitchen stool. She took off her camisole.

She was in her underwear in the kitchen of a large house, and a man who she'd kissed and kissed was returning to her very soon.

Her breathing heightened, she pulled out her T-shirt and the yoga pants and held them for a moment.

The fabric touched her bare thighs briefly, like a provocation. The night and the heat seemed to envelop her completely. It was almost frightening. It was exciting.

She was not going to do anything rash.

Her phone pinged. She reached for it, her heart pounding, and blinked for a minute at its too-bright face. "I'm coming," the message read.

She let out another shaky laugh.

It occurred to her that maybe she could take a cold shower, a rinse. Step in, step out in time for Ty to return. She rummaged for a towel and picked her way carefully to the small half bathroom off the kitchen.

Right. Be brisk.

She took off the rest of her clothing, turned on the water to cold and let it run. Her small shriek startled even her but the water did its business and she emerged tingling and far too awake. But at least the nerves in her body were confused enough that she wouldn't jump on Ty and ravage him when he returned.

The doorbell chimed as she was pulling on her yoga pants.

Make good decisions, she reminded herself.

But as the T-shirt slithered over her body, she was pretty sure that she was already ignoring her own advice.

Ty stood in the doorway, a bulky backpack distorting his shape.

By mutual agreement, it seemed, they decided not to touch each other. Slippery slope and all that, Magda thought giddily.

Ty handed Magda a light pack. "There's a sleeping bag, a toothbrush and toothpaste, and a crank flashlight. I guess I made an emergency kit at some point in the last two years. Go me."

"Thank you. For everything."

She should not invite him back in. She should shut the door and let him go home, let him sleep, or shower, or run outside shirtless in the enveloping darkness. It was already late and she should also definitely try to lie down and toss and turn and think about him all night long.

"I also brought the ice cream that was melting in my freezer," Ty said.

He pulled out two dented cartons.

"You'd be doing me a favor," he said. "They'll go to waste."

She never could resist ice cream.

They avoided the chairs they'd taken the last time

they were in the kitchen. They leaned against the cabinets. For a few moments, all they did was spoon rapidly melting ice cream into their mouths. She'd chosen the mint chocolate chip, leaving him the banana fudge.

There was something about darkness and ice cream that made her want to confess things. She felt like she had to tell him something about herself.

"I need the money," she said. "I have a lot of student debt. I still owe a lot to the culinary school. You asked jokingly earlier if I was…occupying the townhouse. I'm not. But I'm tempted. Every time the end of the month rolls around and I'm sweating and wondering if this is the month my rent check will bounce, I think about moving in here, just into a closet, not even the bedroom, so I can stash my blankets and pillows away. Clearly, I've thought about it. It sounds appealing, not only because I'd be squatting here rent-free, but because I'd be hiding. From everything that's gone bad, from all of my missteps. I know it doesn't make sense, because even if I stay here, eventually I'd have to face the consequences. Byron would find out, he'd be mad. I'd be out of a job."

"But you'll sell the place."

"I wonder."

"Everyone our age has debt. It's not easy to save these days."

"Even you?"

"Even me. I have some student loans, and a mortgage is debt. Believe me, it's not you, it's the economy."

She thought about that. She nodded. "What does it say about me that every day I pretend the house is mine. I stare at this oven and wish I could start baking, cooking, everything. I make up ingredient lists for pernil, for cookies, for a seven-course dinner that I could serve to my friends and family. I go into the bathroom to clean and think about leaving a toothbrush. I know exactly which table would go at the entrance, where I'd leave my mail."

"Do you really think you'd do it?"

"I don't know. Sometimes I feel like I could. I spend a lot of time talking to the people who come see it, telling a story about how they'd be in this house, the barbecues they'd have, the soups they'd cook on this stove in wintertime. In the middle of it, I manage to convince myself that the story is for me."

"It must be hard to be around it sometimes. Sometimes I feel that way about managing other people's money. But that's abstract. To hear people talk about how they'd arrange their furniture, or who could have which room. I think it would make me want a piece of it."

"Yeah. So if I gave in to the temptation of making myself at home here, I think… I think it would really hurt if I sold it, or worse if I didn't sell it and had nothing to show for the work I've put into it."

"And now you're going to stay the night."

"Now I'm going to stay the night. For the first time, I'm going to try to sleep here."

"Have you decided where you're going to sleep? Because I don't think a closet is a good idea. Too stuffy in this weather."

A pause.

She stared down at the soupy mess in her ice cream carton. Her mouth felt sticky and sweet.

"I was thinking of the roof."

She felt rather than saw his frown.

He put down his pint of ice cream. "Is it safe there?"

"Reasonably. My uncle started to build a deck there, but the neighbors objected because all the roofs are connected."

"He started, as in it needs some furniture, or started as in it has only part of a railing and you'll roll off in the middle of the night?"

"Give me some credit."

"I'm sorry. It's that the idea of you sleeping alone and outside on a roof makes me nervous. It's not about your competence, it's about my fears."

Magda confessed grudgingly, "It still needs proper decking if that's what you're asking. It's secure and I won't come crashing down, but it isn't polished wood up there. I love it anyway."

She took the remains of his ice cream and hers. Their fingers touched briefly. Then Magda turned and threw everything in the trash. When she spun around again, he was standing close.

"Take me to this roof of yours."

They went up and up the stairs, past the second parlor and dining level, Magda called it, up past the hallway where they peeked briefly at the room with the *one* bed. It did look inviting, and soft, and layered, even in the brief illumination of the flashlight. But it was much too hot for beds. At least that's what Ty told himself. They went up into a room piled high with boxes and then they emerged finally out into the night sky.

It hadn't cooled down very much in the night. Cars

drove by occasionally, booming with bass, their head-lights cutting through the thorough darkness of the blackout. Choruses of horns trumpeted in the distance, their brassy complaints coming from the larger ave-nues where traffic was no doubt a mess. Somewhere not that far off, someone had decided it was a good night to play music, and snatches of plaintive singing burnished the night.

Magda was staring up. "People say you can't see the stars in New York City. Too much light pollution. But on clear nights, I've always been able to make them out."

"Maybe those aren't stars, maybe they're planets."

"Even better," Magda said. "You can't live on a star. But you can always hope for a planet."

Oh.

He really, really liked her, especially now that he could see her soft silhouette out here on this rooftop under a clear sky. He wanted to hug her to him, to feel the length of her body pressed against his, to run his fingers through her curls. But aside from some acciden-tal brushes, they hadn't touched each other, not since he'd set out to bring her the sleeping bag.

And he shouldn't. She shouldn't. She should stay away from him, refuse to talk to him, refuse to kiss him. Because if she did, she might be disappointed in herself.

He didn't want to be her weakness. He wanted to be a part of her strength.

So, he kept his mouth shut. He helped her carefully spread out the sleeping bag across the rough surface of the roof. And he sat down beside her, and stared up at the planets, his bent knees beside hers, close enough that he could almost feel the warmth coming off of her, far enough that it wasn't enough.

"I can see why you love this neighborhood," Magda said.

"It grew on me. I moved here not long after my mom died. I wanted a fresh start and my apartment, the place I live in now, was somewhere that could happen. I remade it and it felt new. There was plastic on the appliances. There were even those foam spacers still gripping the fridge drawers, and tape to keep them from rattling. I remember at my old place, coming home late from the hospital, every night I'd sit down on my couch and drink a beer and stare out the window trying to shake off all the—all the anger and sadness. When I moved, I got rid of the couch. I can't stand the taste of beer anymore. I didn't even know why I did these things until recently. The couch was fine. Beer is probably fine. Same with the apartment. I tried to justify moving with saying my home was an investment. I was being sensible and planning for my future. But now I think I was so relieved to come to a place with no personal history for me. Although I guess I've managed to screw that up completely for myself by getting involved with the garden."

He lay back on the sleeping bag.

"My dad also moved not six months after she died. Just packed up, said a short goodbye, and he was gone. Left the house in Jersey for me and my sister to deal with. It seemed like he couldn't get away fast enough. But now, I think maybe I should have more sympathy for my dad. It's what I ended up doing after all. What I would have done if I could."

"There's no shame in wanting a fresh start after a long, tough time. Although I wonder if there is such a thing."

"Why not?"

"Well, there are memories, of course. I see it with Uncle Byron trying to rebuild this entire house, renovating it and renovating it until it seems completely different. But there's other stuff that we can't get rid of as easily. Like, I can start a new career, but it's not like I can magically erase the debt that came before."

"How did you end up with it, if you don't mind my asking?"

"School. All of the different kinds and varieties, all the kinds of education that I grew up believing was an investment in the future. I told my mom at the beginning of college that I didn't want her financial help. The more she pressed it on me, the deeper in I dug. I was in pre-med. I planned on following in my mother's footsteps. It would have been the best way to prove myself to my family. But I didn't like it. By the time I was done with undergrad, I'd decided to study psych instead. Then, I was in graduate school and it was all wrong for me, so I quit. I did a bunch of in-between jobs. I tutored kids for their SATs. I hostessed at a restaurant. And all that time, it seemed okay that I was trying out new things. That's what your twenties are for, right? Then, after working in restaurants I decided it was best for me to go to culinary school, which I loved. But that's when it really began crashing around me. I was denied financial aid and my loans couldn't be deferred any more. I tell people I couldn't hack it because, maybe because I'm ashamed."

"You shouldn't be."

"I should have paid more attention. I shouldn't have gotten myself in the hole. But I was so eager to prove all this experimentation was worth it."

"To who?"

"To—to my mom, or my sisters, I guess. But instead, I didn't. I don't want my family to know the real reason that I stopped was that I couldn't afford it anymore. The most responsible thing was to stop going to school and to work. By that time, I found a job at a real estate firm. I was good at some things. But also, I got paid regularly when I managed the office. I got more challenging work, and I'd get more money. Keith was fair that way, at least. That was more important than anything else."

"So you did the responsible thing."

"Well—"

"You said it. You can't take it back."

She sighed, but Ty was glad to hear there was a laugh in the sound. "No one told me being responsible would make me seem like a disappointment. That sounds so naive. But I have to get it together. I'm almost thirty years old."

"I'm thirty-two." A pause. "My mom died two days before my twenty-ninth birthday."

He paused. "If you want to talk about immaturity, in a way, I—I almost resented that. I wasn't ever going to forget about my mom. But now it's like that grief is cemented in the way I think about every passing year. But that's terrible and selfish and unreasonable, I realize it." He sighed. Why was it always easier to confess in the dark. "Birthdays are for kids."

"No."

Her voice was quiet and emphatic. "That isn't selfish or unreasonable. It's complicated. Like grief. Like the thing that drives Byron to want to sell this house as much as he loves it and can't let go."

"And now if—when—you sell it for him, you have a chance to take away a big chunk of your debt. For—well, for that fresh start for him and for you."

"Yeah."

"I guess I can't blame you for that either, for wanting a break, the thing I was able to give myself after my mom."

"Even though there's no such thing as a fresh start."

He hummed. "Well, it's like gardening—"

"Oh, no."

"Every seed or cutting must come from somewhere. You need soil and water to grow a new life."

Her voice was faint and sleepy. "And a big pile of manure."

"Or compost. Some sort of fertilizer."

She laughed softly. At some point, she had stretched out to lie down beside him. Now, he could feel her turn her head, the way her breath whispered across his ear. "You've got that covered."

It was stupid how much he was enjoying this. "What are you saying about my wise words about the glorious future that's within your reach? I think you need to spell it out."

She poked him. It hardly should have felt like an affectionate touch, but that's what it was, affection, pain, humor, understanding, a jab in his arm that warmed him all over.

He turned to his side to face her, to at least see the faint outlines of her face, the wet gleam of her eye. But her breathing had become slow and deep.

She was asleep.

He didn't want to leave her outside alone.

He didn't want to leave her.

So he settled back and stared up at the stars—no, the planets, the planets full of possibilities.

Chapter Ten

Later That Night

Magda awoke with a small start. It was so dark and so warm—warm because she was curled up against a body.

She was next to Ty. On the roof.

He'd stayed with her. He didn't need to, but he'd done it.

The power must still be out. She didn't remember falling asleep, but she recalled talking and talking with him. He'd given her a small bubble of happiness; she was still in it. That was what it was like to wake up next to him.

She couldn't think that way.

She felt for her phone to find out what time it was. Maybe if she shielded the light with her body. But of course, before she could close her hands around it, he woke up, and of course, he reached for her. Because he'd formed this bubble with her, because he wanted to stay in it as much as she did.

"Are you all right?" he whispered.

"Of course, yes. I'm sorry I woke you."

"It's okay. I didn't mean to fall asleep."

They both paused to take a breath.

"I know I told you a lot of things—"

"We probably shouldn't do this. It would mix things up. A lot."

Another pause. "Yeah."

But they were still lying facing each other, holding each other, though it was still too hot out for all this closeness. Every place he touched her—his arm on her, her knee to his—every place she touched him was damp with sweat. Was it hers, was it his? Who could tell? They'd already muddled everything.

"What time is it?" he asked.

"I don't know."

"Time has stopped. Light has stopped. Everything."

"We could be trapped like this forever."

"I wouldn't mind."

He rested his forehead on hers and stroked his hand down her arm, slowly but surely, lingering only at the damp curve inside her elbow, before smoothing down to her wrist. She breathed deep. Her body was tingling and restless. She shifted her legs, her ankle connecting with his calf. And suddenly it seemed like a good idea to smooth her foot along his, to relieve the pressure along the inside of her legs by pulling his hips in close, until she felt it, his cock, right at her groin.

"Magda," he said, "I would like…"

He exhaled sharply. Not, *I want. I would like.* A desire in his words that left room for her, room for everything she wanted, too. "I would also like this," she whispered. "I want this moment with you. Please, just once."

He pulled her closer—or did she pull him?—and now their bodies were aligned, stomachs, chests, his free hand tracing the neckline of her shirt, around to the back, then down her spine, each millimeter he traveled, tugging her closer to him.

"Yes, yes, yes, please," she said as he finally reached the bottom hem of her shirt.

With each yes, each breath, their mouths touched lightly. The *please* ended with a tease of her tongue, a breath before he rolled her on top of him.

They were kissing lushly now, in the dark, where no one could see them, where they could hardly see themselves, only feel the hurried breathing, her hands in his hair, on his face, the click and suck of his mouth as she leaned more hungrily forward. His hands, now both free, moved under her shirt, under the waistband of her pants, her underwear, squeezing, pulling the clothing more tightly around her until she wanted to writhe and scream from the teasing pressure around her thighs.

Her whole body was wet. Sweat and desire mingled together so completely, every part of her hot and wanting.

She reared up and his hands moved around under her shirt to cup her breasts. "Can I take this off?" he asked hoarsely.

"Yes, yes," she muttered, even as she ground herself against his erection.

He groaned "Fuck," and pulled her shirt off, pulled her down again so that one breast was in his mouth.

She grabbed his head and held it there until it was her turn to roll him on top of her, to grab at his tee and tug at it until they both managed to stop for a minute so that he could take it off. They paused for a minute, one minute. She could make out the outline of him over her, the gleam of his eyes and lips, the solid shape of his shoulders, down, down to where his legs straddled her. The tip of one breast shone wetly where his mouth had been.

She touched herself there and he groaned again and bent, his mouth taking in her fingers, her nipples, moving down, dipping to her belly button until he was pulling down the rest of her clothing and she was naked on the roof, her one leg over his shoulder, the other stretched almost too wide, held down by his hand, his breath cooling the wet between her legs.

But it was dark. Everything was all right in the dark. She could have this one small thing, this small moment to do something that she wanted—God, she *wanted*—instead of always thinking ahead to the task that she needed to complete.

Another glimmer from his eyes, a pause as his clothing rustled, a grunt as she imagined his hand moving over his cock before his nose and mouth nuzzled into her. She felt the slight rasp of his stubble, the gentler kiss of his lips, and he settled over her and he began to lick in wide strokes.

She felt the squeeze of one hand, the fingers holding her down, digging deep and filthy into her flesh. She whimpered and moved her hips again. "Ty."

He paused at her words. "Do you like this?" he whispered.

"Fuck, yes. Please don't stop."

She lifted her hips as much as she could, even as his grip tightened around her thigh. And then he let go and trailed one digit toward her clit, down the crease, and with a soft kiss from his lowered head, she felt him slide it into her and she let go of a breath she didn't know she'd been holding, and his lips and tongue found her again.

She was close. She was so close. She had to be quiet,

but her body was pulling her up and up in a long, deep pulse. She flung out her arm, scraping it against the hard roof where the sleeping bag ended.

Another suck, a firm push from fingers thick inside her, and she sobbed finally, long and loud.

She was never going to recover.

Ty kissed the inside of her thigh and cupped her briefly as she pulsed under him as if to capture something precious, to let her feel it a little longer. The gesture was so gentle so…so affectionate. And that softness was almost too much for her. She swallowed a sigh as he sat up, smoothing his hand along her. And then he was very quiet.

She said, "Is that all right with you? If I touch you? I want to."

Another pause. "Yes. I want to feel you everywhere."

His voice was everywhere, the heat was everywhere. He rasped quietly, "I also have condoms in my emergency kit. They were there so I…left them in. No pressure. No assumptions."

The last part of his sentence sounded strangled. But she could picture the expression on his face: determined, strong, yearning.

It wasn't pressure. It was freedom. To choose, to not have her life circumscribed by all the limits and responsibilities she'd felt for so long while she worked her way through the long days. Physical consequences could be swallowed up by the protection, any emotional ones by night. Her hand slid down to where he'd already partially undone his shorts, under the waistband of his boxers. She shifted herself down again. Her breasts still felt sensitive as they grazed along his chest and her thighs were sticky from exertion, from sex. His cock was so hard, for her. From her. Oh, she wanted this again. She wanted to feel reckless and powerful—both things she hadn't allowed herself to be or feel, in such a long time.

She smoothed her hand up and down the length of him, once, twice.

"Find that condom," she said.

He scrabbled away, cursing at the dark as he felt for the kit. "I don't know what I'd do if we kicked it off the roof," he muttered.

She smothered a laugh. But a minute later she let it out when she saw his cock, and almost nothing else, outlined faintly and palely by the condom. "You packed a glow-in-the-dark in your emergency kit?"

His laugh was still strained. "No, it's your standard latex. But it seems extra visible under these circumstances."

He moved toward her, taking her waist again. "But I can hide it," he murmured slyly. "If it makes you feel better."

"That's terrible."

But she smiled as she kissed him, and reveled in the feeling. Then he moved between her legs once again, kissing her breasts, nipping the undersides, then licking a path between them to her neck, and she felt him tense, and she moved her hand to guide him inside her.

She was already full and thick and sensitive from her orgasm and she grunted as he filled her heavily. A choked sound came from his throat, and excitement rose in her again. She dug her foot into his ass, commanding him to move. He began slowly, measured, despite the strain she felt in the taut muscles of his thighs, in the tremble of his arms locked around her, then he bent to kiss her again, and he gasped as they surged toward each other.

Maybe at some point, she'd thought they should be quiet, but maybe it was the pounding of her heart, his and her harsh breathing, the sound of their bodies pulling at each other, the wet smack of lips and skin, but everything felt loud and bright. He'd put his hand down between them as they moved, searching for her clit, touching her, but she wanted to do it herself. She moved his fingers away, and they rolled again to the side where he pulled her leg up and fucked her open like that. Then another rotation and she was on top of him, one palm on the slippery sleeping bag, another on the rough surface of the roof. There might have been a tearing sound underneath them as the material shifted, but she was past caring.

Leaning over him, she let him bounce her up and down, as she moved her hand between her legs to touch herself. He was close. She could feel it in his desperation, in his struggle with and against her body, his harsh breath and the moans he tried to swallow in his throat. She was close again herself, her body wanting to turn inside out with tension and heat.

As her body arched, she reached her hand down to his neck and felt the cords of his muscles stretch and reach until they seemed about to snap even as she suppressed the scream in her own throat. Then she felt him, the quick jab of his hips going upward, the wild jostle against her hand. And she was with him falling on him, her mouth open as she yelled silently into him.

She closed her eyes to the blackness of the night. Her body pulsed and opened and expanded and contracted the whole universe in a second. They both came down on a series of quiet sobs and quakes, gently, gently, until she could feel the sleeping bag under her numb knees, the hard roof, his body solidly under her, still in her, surrounding her. And when she finally opened her eyes again to look down in his face, she stared fascinated at the gleam of the stars—no, the planets, reflected in his eyes.

She was gazing at him, still gazing at him, when the power came back on.

Somewhere downstairs the alarm was beeping insistently. Lights had probably snapped on, like the ones in opposite houses, in apartments nearby.

And he was still inside Magda, she was still on top of him, raising her slumped form, her hair making a soft yet resiliently springy trail across his torso. In the dimness, he could finally, finally catch a glimpse of her breasts, her dark nipples, the curve of her waist, But despite the fact some of the lights were back on, it was too dark to see the spot where they were still joined. It was as if that part, at least, would remain concealed.

She pulled herself off of him carefully, the final slide making him grit his teeth. He paused for a breath then said, "I should go downstairs and get rid of this condom."

"And I should go to the bathroom, and, and—"

"We can take care of the alarm and the lights. And the melted ice cream and whatever else we accidentally knocked over."

They gathered their clothing and dressed, their bodies so much stiffer than when they'd flung everything aside.

Better not to think too hard about it. Better not to *feel* too hard about it.

Magda picked up the sleeping bag. "The underside is pretty shredded."

"Worth it," he couldn't help saying.

He was pleased to see the relief in her eyes.

She hurried downstairs to take care of her business, and he remained up on the roof a moment longer, stuffing things back into his kit. He let himself back down and found a bathroom. There was a hole in the ceiling and buckets of plaster on the floor, but it was useable. He took care of the condom, cleaned himself as best he could, and went to the kitchen. Magda had shut off the beeping alarm and was moving around somewhere else in the house. He rinsed out the recyclables and tossed the rest into a garbage bag he'd found under the sink. The house was getting colder again. The air conditioner had kicked on. By the time Magda appeared, he'd poured a glass of water for her, another for him, and he was drinking slowly at the counter.

The lights were on, and everything had changed again.

She stopped, and maybe he imagined it, maybe her eyes softened. She touched her wild hair a little self-consciously. But she didn't come much closer. "I, uh, I wanted to thank you."

He gave a small twisted smile into his glass of water. "It's fine. I know."

"If I had the time and energy to devote to a relationship, if things were different."

"But they aren't, are they?"

She shook her head.

"I see how you sacrifice your personal comfort, wearing your professional clothing in the heat of summer, spending the night here, probably not eating enough. And I know that I'm, if not on the opposite side, then on a different side of this garden issue. Tonight was good." He faltered. "It was more than good. But if I stayed, if we tried to have more, it would cause you stress."

He felt hollow, as if his own words had pulled everything out of him. *Bereft.* Could that be true if they'd been together for a handful of hours? He took his glass to the sink and after a minute, decided to wash and dry it. She said nothing.

He put it back in the cupboard where he'd found it and turned back. Magda was twisting her hands. She looked young and sad. But she didn't deny what he'd said.

"I like you." He almost laughed. "Still, I don't want to burden you with this, with my feelings. I won't start demanding we walk around holding hands or ride around on a bicycle built for two. So let me just say it. *I like you.* I know you have your work and you feel you need to be single-minded about it, and you can't get entangled in something with me. Anyway, I won't be in New York much longer."

An intake of breath from her that he felt. He felt it all over.

She said, "What do you mean?"

"I'm moving to Portland. To be nearer to my sister when she goes. I'm still making arrangements. Helping to find and train my replacement at work—"

"What about the garden?"

She'd put her hand on her stomach for a moment. But as he was about to ask her if she was all right, she turned and opened a kitchen cabinet.

"I'm going to be here to help, of course, with fundraising and figuring out some financial things. But I never was really a member."

"That's bullshit." She slammed the cabinet door and finally looked at him. "You're there. You help people. They like you. They depend on you, whether you like it or not. You're running away from them."

He recoiled. "So what if I am? Should I stay and watch a developer dismantle all these people's hard work? Tough out all the consequences for commitments I made to them when I was still trying to figure things out, like you are? How's that working for you?"

"That's a shitty thing to say."

"I'm saying you're brave and I'm not. It's a shitty situation for you. Are you saying you don't wish it away?"

"I want my debt to go away. But it's money. To like and to be liked is not always a *burden*."

"My liking you seems to be one."

She stiffened, and immediately he regretted saying it. It sounded too much like bitterness, although the tang of it was still on his lips.

He licked them and continued, "We want the same things. I want the people I like and love to live forever. I want them to be healthy and thriving for as long as possible, and I know that isn't realistic. Magda, this was one of the best nights of my life, all right? It was perfect because I got to be with you. And you are better and more warm and hopeful and beautiful than anyone I've ever met. But we can't. The lights are back on. The spell is over. You're still wonderful, but you told me going in that you have too much to deal with, and in my own way, so do I. I'm telling you I'm moving because I'm giving you an out. I'm giving myself one so that both of us can be okay again after this is over."

He would be fine after it was over—well, it was over now mostly, and it was not fine. But he'd live.

Her face had closed and although it hurt to see it shut to him, it's what they both wanted. She said, "You don't have to tell me you're giving me a gift. It's not some favor. You're right, okay? I can't do anything about any feelings I may have for you or for anyone. But relieved isn't how I feel."

"Me neither," he said.

He stepped closer to her, close so that he could take one last look, touch her hair one last time. She looked up and he kissed her cheek quickly. Then he slung his backpack over his shoulder and took the garbage bag— the rest of the evidence he'd been there—and he left, into the night, into the near darkness, and he went back to his empty apartment.

Chapter Eleven

Labor Day Monday

It was a perfect day for a block party. The sun shone, but a blast of rainy weather over Saturday had eased the rest of the weekend into cooler but still sunny and bright days. White tents lined the block. A bouncy castle stood at one end, ready for an influx of kids eager to get in some screaming and jumping before school started later in the week. On the other side, a small stage had been erected for the speeches and performances scheduled. Only the space in front of the garden was kept open so that people could wander in and admire it.

Early September had favored the gardens with a burst of stunningly vivid dahlias. A few students were stationed at the plots to show people the crops growing but Mrs. Freeman chose to guard her own tomatoes.

Mrs. Espinosa had an iPad and a lanyard. She strode through the street, Ty hurrying beside her.

"Did you check on the licenses? Are the vendors ready? Has the photographer shown up for the photo booth? Can we ask the sound man to turn down the bass? I always feel like I'm going to have a heart attack when the bass is too loud."

To every question, Ty answered an affirmative. They'd been through everything at least three times, but Mrs. E was nervous. And so was Ty. It wasn't as if he'd ever helped plan an event before. He didn't have parties.

He could probably throw one now, a really great one, considering how much he now knew about the ins and outs of renting bouncy castles.

At least when the fundraiser opened he would be too busy to think much about Magda. That was the theory.

"If I didn't know better, I'd say you were pining," Jenny said, during a slower moment at the Dumplings of the World booth.

"Pining is for trees."

Jenny wrapped a samosa in a paper napkin and handed it to a waiting kid. "What you are doing," his sister said, "is the very definition. Sometimes you're alert, you're looking around. Then suddenly you see something—*someone*—and you get this dreamy far-off look that I remember from high school, and then your eyes get sad and hungry, and I get an overwhelming urge to feed you another pastelillo. You've had five already this morning."

"I'll stuff more money in the till."

"I'm paying, and you're changing the subject. This whole time have you been doing this whole garden thing *because of a girl*? To think I'm modeling my life on you, looking out for my own purpose, and it turns out this whole time you've thrown yourself into this because you're mooning."

"I'm not mooning. I'm not pining. It's pretty much the opposite from what you think. I'm definitely not pleasing a certain woman because of my involvement.

But even if I were doing this because I was enthralled, what would be wrong with that?"

"It would be wrong if she didn't support your excellent work and was being a jerk about you spending time on it. Too bad I hate her, because one of us Yangs needs some action."

"Don't hate her."

"Too late," Jenny sang, handing three pastelillos to a harried-looking man. "Can you message Mr. S and tell him we're running out of the beef?"

Ty pulled out his phone and tapped out a text. Without looking at his sister, he said, "It's complicated and I'd try to explain, but this isn't the time and place."

"The time and place was a couple of weeks ago when you had a scrape on your leg and scratches on your arms, and a huge hickey on your neck."

"Oh, my God."

"But I didn't ask about them because *gross* and also"—she did a gruff imitation of a dad-voice, even though it sounded nothing like their own dad—"I was really hoping you'd tell me on your own."

It was at this very moment Magda walked up to the booth.

God, she looked beautiful.

He should treat her politely, but coolly. This was awkward. It should be awkward. But he was so glad, so overwhelmingly happy to see her, to look at her. Of course, he'd spied her in the garden and had called her once or twice to ask technical questions about real estate, questions he probably could have Googled.

He *was* pining.

They'd kept the conversations short. They talked in

daylight hours. Because a longer talk at night would mean silence and breathing and memories.

But as they stared soft-eyed at each other, his sister sprang out from behind the booth, wiping her hands on her apron, and said, "Hi, I'm Tyson's sister, Jenny. And judging by the way Ty is gazing at you, I'd say you were the person we were just talking about. Maybe you can give me some of the lowdown on what's happening here."

Jenny smiled wide, showing all her bright, white teeth, and Tyson had a sudden recollection that his baby sister was very good with knives.

She shouldn't have come.

A couple of gardeners nodded at her as she made her way down the block in sunglasses and a hat. A set of speakers blasted reggaeton while a band seemed to be setting up to play. Some of the local businesses and familiar street vendors had put up tents: a few people had taken out folding chairs and sat fanning themselves and chatting, others sold earrings and used books and records, clothing and bags pulled out of the backs of closets. And there was the food from all over: tostones, Jamaican meat patties, grilled corn smeared with cotija cheese and cayenne, coco helado.

But Ty was here, and despite the fact she told herself to chill, she was happy to see him, to be near him; she couldn't stop her legs from carrying her right to him. Instead of looking hurt, or awkward, or confused, that damn man beamed at her, his whole face glowed for her, or maybe she glowed for him. She couldn't stop the warmth, the longing, the happiness. No matter how much she reminded herself that he was not for her, that he was moving thousands of miles away, that she had not one single justification for spending her time with him, she *wanted*.

So much for playing it cool.

Then Ty's sister, the chef, had stepped out front, despite the line of curious, hungry onlookers.

Ty moved between them swiftly. He was always moving between her and danger. "Magda," he murmured, before turning to his sister. "Jenny, I'd like you to meet Magda Ferrer. She's a real estate broker in the neighborhood."

She felt a surge of affection at Ty's tone. *Play nice*, was the stern warning behind Ty's words to his sister. Magda and Ty had parted awkwardly, yet he still wanted to protect her. But as a sometimes bratty younger sister herself, Magda knew that wouldn't be effective at all, and for some reason, the fact that he wouldn't win this small sibling skirmish made her like him more.

She was really far gone.

Ty was standing so close to her, closer than he'd been in a long while. He smelled good, like fried foods, and his lips looked soft with the sheen of oil.

Do not take a bite out of Ty in front of everyone, especially his sister.

Magda summoned up all of her willpower and said to Jenny, "I've heard so much about you, but I shouldn't keep you because I think you're starting to get backed up."

Jenny opened her mouth to say something sassy no doubt, but Magda's words registered a beat later, and Jenny scrambled quickly back to the other side of the table.

Ty gave a brief laugh at Jenny's quick retreat. "You

are a talented woman to know exactly what to say to my sister to get her to back off."

She was blushing all over, even her heels tingled, not just at his words, but at his breath as he leaned down to speak quietly in her ear.

"It's only temporary," she said. "She's a pro. She'll have it back under control in a minute. Then she'll be back to question me."

"She's too smart," he said with some pride. "But I didn't say anything about you—I know you don't want…"

Well, she did want. Despite all they'd said, she still wanted. And he'd been standing too close, talking with her too intimately for too long already.

He's leaving.

She stepped away. "I'm going to go help her."

"Is that a good idea? It might get messy and you're wearing a sundress."

"At least I'm not wearing *the suit*."

His eyes were warm as his gaze took her in, lingering over the shadows and curves of her.

"I like the dress," he said.

She couldn't imagine why he did, because to her it felt overly constricting at this moment. She closed her eyes briefly and took a deep breath. When she opened them again, Ty was still staring at her, and behind him, Jenny glared.

Magda sighed. "Go help Mrs. Espinosa. I think she's arguing with the band. I'm going in."

"I'm not going to leave you to deal with my sister alone."

"At least she doesn't have any tomatoes."

Ty laughed softly. "Fine. Whistle if you need backup."

She watched him walk away. She liked his walk, the way he aimed his head right at a problem and the rest of him followed. But she shouldn't be his worry right now. She squared her shoulders, wishing she had the suit right at this moment—it would have been some armor, some authority—and strode toward Jenny's booth.

"You can't be here."

"I'll take the cash, you heat and serve. It's easier with two people."

"Should I trust you around money?"

"Probably not."

At Jenny's expression, Magda decided she probably shouldn't make too many cracks, not when the woman didn't want to joke with her. Magda cleared her throat and started handing people their change. "I'm not conning your brother into looking the other way while I steal the garden's fundraising money. Give Ty some credit. He's too—too good to want that or trust that."

"He *is*. At one point I might've even said he was a pure, straight arrow, but lately, he's been showing me that good can have a lot of shadings and dimensions."

Magda continued to work with her for a while, greeting customers and handing out change.

"So what is your story? What is my brother not telling me?"

Magda cleared her throat. No point in hiding the truth. "I'm the broker who's trying to sell the lot."

"The lot. What lot? Oh, the garden. That's you. You're the one showing it to developers."

"Yeah, it's me."

"But Ty likes you anyway."

"Yeah. And I like him."

Jenny shoved a selection of dumplings into a wax

bag for a waiting woman. When she turned again, some curiosity had diluted Jenny's fierce expression. "But he's leaving, and you aren't about to give up trying to sell the garden."

"If I don't sell it, my boss will. At least maybe I can help field the gardeners' offer. I can make sure they get a chance."

"But you can't do anything else? Plead their case?"

"You know, it isn't really their land. People seem to keep forgetting that part. I have to represent the actual owner. I have to do what's in their best interests."

"And what's in their best interests is making as much money as possible off the sale."

The line was getting longer and Jenny's movements were getting quicker and, if possible, defter. Magda could imagine what Ty's sister would be like in a professional kitchen. For a while, they were busy enough that they only exchanged terse sentences. It wasn't exactly the kind of situation in which she could endear herself to her—what? Boyfriend's sister? Not exactly. Her nemesis's sibling? That wasn't right either.

It was clear Jenny had been considering it the whole time, too. Because when the line cleared, she turned to Magda and said, "I don't want you to hurt him."

"I don't want to either."

"Then why are you here? Doing this? Guilt?"

She gestured around her at the booth.

Yes? No? Maybe? It was the chance to see Ty again.

That and her appointments had all canceled on her. No one really wanted to see an apartment on Labor Day and she didn't want to show one. She could have spent her time combing through the database or editing her listings.

But the truth was she wanted a couple of hours to herself. She wanted to wear a pretty summer dress she'd bought a lifetime ago. She wanted Ty to see her in it.

"I don't care about your guilt—"

"It's not—"

"But I do care about my brother. I'm sure the bouncy castle's doing big business, but you and I both know that our It's a Small World dumpling stall here isn't going to sell near enough. Ty knows it, too. Of course, he does. I'm sure he's already run the numbers and understands within a dollar how much we're going to make here. It's going to take something more to keep this garden. And the more is usually more money."

"They could raise enough."

"You're only going to hurt him. You're going to sell to some richy-rich person or company because that's who has the cash, that's who always wins, and when it happens, the garden is gone. You can have the best intentions to keep up with these people you care about on this project, but they won't keep it up. He's going to lose the friends he's made here, this entire community of people who like him and enjoy him, and get to see an entire other huge part of him that I—I didn't know existed. My brother who I've known all my life.

"He's leaving, you know. Because I don't think he wants to watch something he loves be destroyed again. Slowly. It's on his street. He won't be able to avoid walking past it. And you'll have helped it."

Magda found she'd been holding her breath. It wasn't as if she hadn't thought that way before. But Jenny saying it out loud scraped her wide open.

Ty's sister had already turned to straighten up her work area. She looked cool and composed because this was what she did daily: cut right through the meat and tendon, right to the bone in the most efficient ways possible.

Magda thought of abandoning the stall. It was easier than letting Jenny see her cry, letting Jenny see that she'd put into words everything that Magda had been afraid of—not that the other woman seemed to be paying attention after she'd delivered her opinion.

The fair was getting louder. A youth choir had gone onstage and they were singing to an enthusiastic, clapping crowd. In the distance, children screeched in the bouncy castle, and the roar of generators and the crackle of grills filled the air. But in the five square feet of tent occupied by Magda and Jenny, the silence stayed thick.

She straightened. She was going to tell Jenny that the reason his sister had never known Ty was so good was because she'd taken all of Ty's truth and kindness and generosity for granted. Magda was going to argue that Ty wouldn't lose his friends or his community— that what was making Ty lose it was the fact that he was leaving.

But that wasn't really what she wanted to say either. Before Magda could sort out the arguments in her head, a familiar voice piped up. "*Magda*, what are you doing in this booth?"

Magda turned slowly. This day was only getting worse.

It was her sister.

Ty had come very close to having to put out a literal fire. One of the men handling the grills had opened the hatch to a wall of flame. And Mrs. E, being Mrs. E, had rushed forward waving her iPad, and only Ty's hand on her arm prevented her from slamming the tablet down on the barbecue.

Apart from that near-disaster, the rest of the fund-raiser seemed to be going well. The food and craft vendors were doing brisk business, the youth choir trilled lovingly in the distance, the Museum of Harlem History and Heritage was handing out vouchers for free visits, and had set up a small exhibit of photographs, one in particular of which Ty planned to show Magda. He got to the garden's own booth, where some of the high schoolers were handing out free vegetables—mostly zucchini. The gardeners were willing to part with time and money to support the garden—but not their precious tomatoes.

Feeling relieved that things were running more or less smoothly and that they'd managed to avoid one conflagration, Ty moved back toward the dumpling tent only to encounter another potential disaster.

A woman was leaning over the table to hiss at Jenny. As he hurried up, the woman shout-whispered, "Why are you upsetting my sister?"

"What's going on here?" he asked.

But Magda was talking in low tones to the woman—a woman who looked a lot like her.

He slipped inside the tent. "I told you not to give Magda a hard time," he said to Jenny.

"She's a big girl, she can take what I dish out—and what I dish out is a hard serving of truth."

"Great. Put it on the menu in Portland, then. I'm sure some people will be interested in your version. But right now, you're operating a dumpling booth for charity."

"Are you saying you're eager for me to move?"

"No. I'm saying I want you to stop being an asshole right here."

A dangerous light appeared in Jenny's eye, one that he recognized from when they were children, but before Jenny could open her mouth, Magda's sister had come behind the table to buttonhole him. "Are you the volunteer coordinator? I found this woman"—she gestured at Jenny— "bullying my little sister. She's not a suitable representative for your fair."

Jenny started to turn her hand up slowly—her preferred way of giving the finger—but Ty shot her a warning glance. "I'm so sorry to hear it," he began.

"You—you don't apologize," Magda whispered fiercely at him, joining the fray. "You have nothing to apologize for."

"But he—"

Magda sent her sister a look. "No one asked you to interfere. I can take care of myself."

"Clearly you can't."

What the hell?

"What the hell?" Magda said at normal volume.

"Language, Magda," her sister hissed.

Wow, Magda's sister seemed to say the exact wrong things. Ty couldn't help shaking his head in warning. But the women weren't looking at him. They were too focused on each other.

"Flora," Magda murmured with admirable evenness. "What *the hell* are you even doing here, anyway?"

"You mentioned something about it yesterday. You never tell us about fun things you're doing usually."

"So you came to check up on me."

"I thought it sounded like a good place to bring the

kids. They're over there in the line for the bouncy castle with James."

"I'm surprised you didn't check to find *me* at the bouncy castle."

"What's that supposed to mean?"

"It means that this is none of your business. It means that even though I don't have kids and a husband and a career that I'm great at, I am an adult who is trying to get her shit together and you have no faith in me to take rejection, to work, to clean up after myself, to fight my own fights, to be an adult."

"I—I what?"

"You have no faith in me."

"What do you mean we have no faith in you? We've stood behind every shitty choice you've made, haven't we?"

Magda froze.

In the background, the youth choir's song about peace and belonging swelled to a crescendo.

The sisters continued their whispered fight. "So, that's what you really think, don't you?"

"No, that's not—you're doing great. I worded that poorly."

"Doing great. Yeah, I'm doing great, Flora. So you don't have to check up on me and intrude on my one moment of fun. You don't have to jump in to defend me. Because as you say, I'm doing great."

Magda pulled off her apron and stalked off.

Poor Mr. S, who had come up to the booth with an aluminum pan, watched her stride past. His gaze swung over to Ty, Flora, and Jenny. Jenny shrugged. Mr. S hunched over his famous pastelillos and crooned at them as if to protect them from the tension emanating from the group.

"Everything okay?" he asked, seeming reluctant to give up his food to people who wouldn't treat it right.

Ty took a deep breath. He wanted to go after Magda but he wasn't sure if that would be welcome. And even then, what could he say? What right did he have to say anything to her?

Judging by the confusion on Flora's face, she still didn't quite get it.

"What just happened here?" Flora asked.

She turned and pointed at Jenny. "*You.* You're the one who riled her up. She never talks like that to me."

At least they'd stopped whispering. They'd moved on to full-throated arguing now.

"But you're the one who made her stalk off. Think about that one."

Ty said as quietly as he could manage, "Jenny, I suggest that you help Mr. S. with his tray and maybe start selling some dumplings again. And you"—he motioned to Flora—"you aren't supposed to be back here."

"I'm tired of all of this lack of respect."

Ty said, "From the sounds of it, I'm sure Magda is, too."

He turned to Jenny, who was smirking. "Do you need any help?"

"I could use some as long as you don't give me any sass."

"I promise I won't. You're the professional here."

Chapter Twelve

Checking to see if you're okay, Ty had texted.

Mr. Serra just wants all of his dumplings to get along.

He sent Magda an image of Mr. S gazing at his paste-lillos, as well as a few other golden fried dough friends. Then Ty sent another attachment—a photo of a picture he'd taken at the Harlem museum booth that made her stop on the sidewalk.

A scooter zoomed around her as she stared. It wasn't the best quality—a photo of a photo—but it made her forget her anger for a moment.

More messages pinged. She grimaced. Flora, Alma, and her mother were confused—and not pleased with her.

Maybe she'd overreacted. Maybe she'd proven further that she was a spoiled child who needed careful handling, who they expected to have to rescue day after day. But there was so much in their past, in the way they treated her, that she was trying to navigate. It was as enormous as her debt and as difficult to handle.

By the time she arrived back at the townhouse, she'd received another couple of messages. One of them was from an unfamiliar number. She sat down at the counter to drink some water and checked her voicemail.

"Ms. Ferrer, this is Karima Carter. My partner and I viewed the townhouse on Strivers' Row last month. I'm sorry to call you on a holiday, but I wanted to let you know we want to make an offer."

Magda sat down. She remembered Ms. Carter and her partner. They'd come twice, once with a bored-looking broker, once by themselves, and seemed genuinely interested in the place—but they had also questioned her about how firm Byron was on his asking price. Then she'd heard nothing.

She couldn't allow herself to get her hopes up too much. After all, even if they did meet Byron's price, he still might reject it out of hand.

Unless she tried to do something about it.

She probably wouldn't be able to manage her sisters and mother—not when they could overwhelm her, not when she felt such an uncomfortable knot of love for them—but maybe she could figure out how to deal with her uncle.

Byron was not happy she'd asked him to fly in, although she knew he did so at least once a month. She arranged for a car to pick him up at the airport. She booked him his usual hotel—though he usually made his travel arrangements himself. In short, she did everything to make it as easy as possible for him to come up.

He still grumbled.

Worse, he really dug in his heels when she asked him to tour the house with her. "I don't need to walk this place from top to bottom. I know this house like the back of my hand."

"You've made a ton of changes to it over the years,

but I don't think I've seen you go up one floor beyond the kitchen."

"I'm old and my knees can't take the stairs," Byron snapped.

"You're fine. We're going to be examining everything you've done on each floor, so you'll have plenty of time to recover."

Byron opened his mouth again and snapped it shut. No doubt he was warring between wanting to prove he was hale and hearty enough to run up the stairs like a gazelle, and the desire not to contradict himself even further.

They started in the backyard and moved their way up. In minute detail, she showed him every repainted closet, every newly installed light fixture, every pipe and panel he'd ordered in the time she'd undertaken the sale.

Byron scoffed at the staged dining room and said something about how the bed had too many pillows for a body to get a proper sleep. But he grew quieter as they got higher up in the house and Magda felt a pang of worry that maybe she had overexerted him.

They got up to the level below the roof. Byron looked around. "What, you didn't fix up a garret so that buyers could pretend they're starving artists?" he asked.

"You only wanted two rooms staged, so that's what I did," Magda said. "Besides, this floor has some things on it."

Byron stilled. Then he said, "Well unless you find a buyer for this place, I don't see the point of renting out a storage space for a few boxes."

"I did find a buyer, uncle."

Magda pulled the offer papers out of her bag.

Byron looked furious. "What are you trying to pull here? I assumed you were trying to butter me up to ask me to extend my deadline. Or tell me about some repair you wanted me to make, or that you wanted the rest of the house filled with throw pillows or something."

"These people are interested in taking the house as is. They don't want any more renovations. A broker who they consulted with earlier in the summer discouraged them from offering, but they kept thinking about it. Karima Carter, she grew up in this neighborhood, and she knows the history. They took time to get their ducks in order so you'd take their offer seriously. They've really tried, Uncle, and maybe what's important here, they really seem to love the house. They came by to see it again last night and remembered everything about it."

Byron still clutched the papers in his hand.

"It's a good offer, Uncle."

"Get me a better one."

"You haven't even looked at it. They wrote you a letter. They're starting a family. They'd be really happy in it. I have to ask you, with all these compelling reasons, are you sure you want to sell it?"

"Of course I'm sure. You know how much it's costing me in taxes?"

"So why won't you sell it, then? Why won't you consider any of the offers? Why do you keep sending workmen? Why have you gotten rid of every stick of furniture but you still have these old boxes hanging around?"

"I don't have to answer any of your questions," Byron said furiously. "You're my broker."

"I'm also your niece," Magda added gently. "Please, take a look. Read the letter. Think about it. You can call your lawyer, and we could be all done in six weeks, as long as their financing checks out."

Byron was still looking a little lost.

She added, "I'll help you sort through the boxes, Byron, if that's what you want. Or I can ask Mamí to go through them with you"—if Mamí was still speaking to her—"or I can help you get rid of them."

"No!"

He stood straight, his eyes blazing. "No one is putting those memories in the trash."

"I didn't say we had to—"

"I am not looking at this offer. I am not calling any lawyers—"

"Byron, calm down."

"I will not calm down. You can't tell me what to do."

He sat down heavily on a trunk.

She assessed him warily. He was red-faced from yelling at her, but he wasn't panting or sweating. He looked tired but...

She shouldn't have pushed him so hard.

She took a deep breath. "Let me go downstairs to get you some water."

"I don't need any damn water."

"I won't be a minute."

She wanted to push. She wanted him to look at the damn papers that Karima Carter and her partner Sara had worked so hard to put together. Maybe he wouldn't care about the letter, but he should at least think about the offer. It might seem like nothing—a dollar amount scribbled on a piece of paper, some signatures, but it was important. It was a guarantee that they were going to have their financial lives scrutinized by their bank, by Byron's lawyer, by her. It wasn't quite like going up before a co-op board; they wouldn't need to produce reference letters from their friends and past landlords and managers. But it was still bad enough.

She was angry that Byron seemed like he was going to dismiss it like he'd dismissed all the other offers over the years.

When she came back upstairs, Byron had stood up. He was looking out the small window, a little too casually, as if she'd almost caught him at something.

She handed him the bottle and he drank it thirstily. "I wanted to show you something," she said.

She pulled up the picture Ty had snapped at the fair. He squinted at it. "I can't see anything on this tiny screen."

She enlarged a section and then moved the picture around so that he could read the caption Ty had included. "That's you, isn't it?" she said. "Outside this house."

Byron finished the bottle and set it down beside him. He didn't reply. He picked up the offer papers and started to make his way downstairs.

"Uncle," she started to say.

"I'm not going to talk to you right now, Magda. I walked all through this place, and let you talk all you wanted. I'm about due for a good dose of quiet now. Goodbye."

With that, he yanked open the door, to the beep of the alarm system, and started down the street.

Magda sighed. At least he'd left with the papers instead of crumpling them in a ball and throwing them in her face.

Thursday After Labor Day

"My Uncle Byron is missing."

Ty had gotten back from a meeting at Mrs. Espinosa's apartment when Magda called.

He'd been, well, happy. God, why was he excited to see her name light up when he should have felt all sorts of other things: sadness it wouldn't work out between them, resentful she'd chosen her path, and that it wasn't his? But no, his stupid pulse pounded and a smile leaked into his voice with his hello.

But then she sounded worried and his heart had dropped.

"He checked out of his hotel," she was saying. "Hasn't gone back to Miami either, according to his housekeeper. He won't return my calls, but he did text me saying he was all right after I checked in. His house-keeper must've alerted him I was looking for him. I know it's stupid. I know it's been a little over twenty-four hours and he says he's fine, but we said some things to each other yesterday—and now this."

"Does your family know?"

"Yes, I told my mom when I started worrying, and I called her after I heard from him. I didn't tell her everything. Then I needed to talk to you because—because I knew you'd understand."

They both breathed for a minute.

"I received an offer for the townhouse. I pushed him to take it and I showed him the picture you sent. I wanted—well, you know what I wanted. I got my hopes up and went at him too hard."

"Magda."

"It's okay. I don't want to talk about this. How are you?"

He gave a short laugh. "I'm okay." He gave her a minute to interrupt, but she seemed to want the distraction. "I just came back from a meeting. And now I'm going to make something to eat."

"What are you making?"

"BLT. Mrs. Freeman gave me one of her tomatoes."

"She must love you."

"I was never quite sure of her feelings until the moment she handed one over."

"Was there a ceremony?"

"Aside from the part where I knelt and she touched my shoulder with it?"

She laughed, and it was good to hear it.

She sobered quickly. "I shouldn't talk about this with you. I shouldn't enjoy this so much—calling you. But for some reason, you've become the person who doesn't make it worse when I say things out loud to you. It becomes almost okay."

"I feel the same."

He could hear her moving around.

"That picture you sent me, the one in front of the house with Byron's brother, the one from the museum, I thought—I don't know why I thought it would be good to show him his memories were there no matter who owned the house, that they'd been preserved. But it was clearly a shock for him. It was clumsy of me. I should have prepared him more."

"It's like you said, though. It's always going to be tough letting go of a home, especially when in Byron's case, it's been in his family for so long."

"I left him alone for a few minutes to get him some water. And then after he was gone, I went upstairs again to straighten out and I noticed one of the boxes was ajar."

"He was looking inside."

"Yeah. So I peeked, too."

She paused.

"No bodies, right?" he asked gently.

"No. More like…ghosts. Photographs. Hundreds of them from over the years. So many of my aunt—of Ariana—when they were young and newly married. Street scenes and pictures of relatives and friends. Some of them had been developed at the drugstore, you know the way they used to do that. And some of them, I think Byron did himself. Now I remember it used to be his hobby. He had a little darkroom in his parents' basement. It smelled bad so my sisters dared each other to go in. It had one of those eerie red lights and I remember trying to be like my sisters and hiding in there one day and I guess I flicked the switch and I was convinced I saw the Devil's eye. I started screaming. And of course we weren't allowed in anymore, and I forgot about it until a couple of days ago when I saw the pictures. All of these beautiful photos."

"That sounds amazing. What an incredible record of his family, and of life in this neighborhood."

"It is. It was. Ty, I don't know. Maybe it's wrong to try to make Byron sell this house when so much of him is clearly still there."

"That's for Byron to decide, isn't it?"

He'd been with her until that moment, but he didn't know what to say. Or rather, he felt frustrated—almost as frustrated as she clearly was—but for different reasons.

She couldn't give up now—now that she was close.

What difference did it make to him—to them? If she made the sale on the townhouse, she was still selling the garden—or someone else would take it up if not her.

He would still be leaving.

He shouldn't fool himself into thinking it would

make a difference to their situation—but it would help her, and he wanted her to be happier.

He closed his eyes. With her voice in his ears, it was almost, almost like being in the dark with her again, on the rooftop, under the night sky. "What are you doing right now?"

"I'm in Brooklyn. I'm making food, too."

So far away, yet so close. Well, that was their relationship—if you could call it that—wasn't it? Even her voice was a little muffled.

He asked, "What are you making?"

Her voice came more clearly over the line. "Pastelillos. After I tried the ones Mr. S made I wanted to give them a shot."

"Those sound better than a BLT."

"Even one made with prized tomatoes?"

"I'm a little afraid that the rest of the sandwich won't live up to this one ingredient."

It was her turn to laugh. He listened to the subtle clanging and scraping sounds. He closed his eyes for a minute and pretended his bacon frying was a part of it. He didn't even mind the little sparks of pain as hot oil spit and sizzled and hit his forearms.

"Okay," she said, "I'm getting ready to fold them."

Another couple of shuffles and noises and then she gave a small sigh that almost quivered in his ear.

He was burning his bacon. He quickly pulled the strips out with a fork—a fork he shouldn't be using in a nonstick pan, and dropped them onto a plate. Then he remembered he needed to toast some bread.

"How's your folding going?" he asked, switching the phone to speaker.

"Oh, they're beautiful."

"I'll bet they're perfect and uniform, and all of them have exactly the right ratio of filling to dough."

"Now, that is something I can take real pride in. I do make very good ones. Even when I was a kid, it was one thing I could do as well, or even better than my mom or sisters. I could sit in the same kitchen as them and we'd all fold them, and they'd talk, and I'd concentrate on making mine beautiful."

A pause as he finally got ready to cut into the tomato Mrs. F had given him. He looked around, but all he had was a steak knife. This was like a tomato steak, wasn't it?

He sliced into his tomato and the juicy flesh fell right onto the plate. There were seeds on his fingers and he couldn't help licking them.

There was a silence on her end. "Did you just—"

"I'm sorry. I'm being gross. I shouldn't eat on the phone. I'll—"

"No, no. It's—" He heard her swallow. "I guess I'm hungry. Or something."

The way she said *or something* was what did it for him.

He put down his knife and washed his hands.

"Magda?"

"Yeah?"

"Do you think about that night?"

"All the time."

There was a little catch in her voice, a longing, the click of her tongue against her palate. She sounded so close, but they were farther away today than they had been that night.

"I think about you," he said.

He cleared his throat. He'd never done this before. It was incredibly awkward, but he was also excited.

"I think a lot about the sounds you made."

He could hear maybe a swallow or a quick lick at her lips. She said, a little breathlessly, "I covered everything. I washed my hands. I'm… Are we going to do this?"

"I want to—if you do."

Another pause.

He had no impulse control when it came to her, he thought dizzily.

"I want to."

So softly. Almost whispering.

He turned off his kitchen lights and leaned back against the counter. If he worked hard enough, he could pretend the granite digging into his ass was her hands, gripping him. No, she had propelled him into the counter, she was pressing against him.

"I want to kiss you," he said. "I want to feel your hair getting in the way, the impatience in your whole body when you push it out of your face, the way you get a firmer hold on me when you really feel something. Like you're righting me, telling me to stay this course."

"I loved kissing you that night. In the hot kitchen, with the lights all off. I loved feeling your body on mine."

He put his hand on the front of his boxers and tried to imagine the weight of her whole figure moving into him.

"Hang on," she said. "I want to take off my shirt."

What could he say to that?

He heard some shuffling noises. He imagined her pulling up her camisole, the fabric as it traveled over the column of her waist, over her ribs. He put his hand into his shorts now and thought about her breasts, how his mouth had felt on them.

"On the roof, I felt so free," she said, rejoining him a little breathlessly. "We were outside and I was on top of you and I could throw my arms wide open when I—when I moved over you. This is difficult. I try to concentrate on your voice, on that feeling and I feel like I have to hunch over, to squeeze everything down to this point inside me."

He grunted and stroked himself.

"Are you all right?" she asked.

"I'm in my kitchen and I'm pressing against the counter. That's so awkward sounding. I'm sorry."

"Don't apologize."

He smoothed his hand over his cock again and gripped it. "Imagine me touching you," he said. "Down there. Imagine I'm licking my way down to your"—he squeezed his eyes shut again—"your *pussy.*"

He was glad the lights were out and she wasn't here, because he was sure his entire face had flamed red—red on top of the strain of trying not to come. His hips pumped, his ass banging painfully into the cool counter. He was in his kitchen with his shorts down and jerking off—and somehow this was supposed to impress a girl. "Is it possible to die of arousal and embarrassment at the same time?"

"I guess we're going to find out?"

He gave a choked laugh. "I remember how good you feel. How good you smell. How the insides of your thighs felt. I wanted to press my cheeks against them and rub all your wetness over me, over my face."

"Oh, God. Ty."

It was almost painful, how much he was panting, how loud his heartbeat seemed in his own ears. His head banged against the cabinet. "I can't—" he said at the same time she cried, "I'm coming."

He scrambled for a paper towel. The roll fell and unspooled across the kitchen floor. He was barely aware of a series of choked gasps over the phone.

He slid all the way down and put his forehead on his knees.

"I wish you were here," he said.

He liked her a lot. Maybe he was even beginning to think he loved her. Everything was a mess. "This half-together moving apart thing we're doing is really difficult."

He was rambling. He probably wasn't making any sense.

"You're leaving, though."

"And you've decided you can't anyway."

She didn't have to say anything.

"I wish things could be different," Magda said quietly.

Another pause. "Well. I should go. Thank you for—"

"No problem." He winced. "I mean, I like talking to you. I like you. But yeah, I need to"—he grimaced—"get myself together."

After he pressed the end button he sat for a while longer in the wreckage of his kitchen. He had no one to blame for this mess but himself.

Chapter Thirteen

Monday

"It's not enough," Keith said, dismissing the papers Magda laid out for him.

Magda muttered, "Why do people keep saying that? I am sick of hearing this."

Two reasonable offers from two great groups of people on two expensive properties, both of which had been difficult to move, both bids coming in within the space of a week. And it wasn't enough.

She took a steadying sip of coffee—the drink Keith had loudly announced he'd buy for her as soon as they entered this Harlem cafe. "The 136th Garden Association is making a sincere offer. They've lined up financing and grants from corporate donors and local government. Mrs. Espinosa, who I met with last night, has been amazing—" as had Ty, whose eagle eyes had probably been all over the offer. Of course, Ty hadn't mentioned that the group was ready to offer; yet another example of the distance between them, she reminded herself firmly.

She continued, "They've got a great profile in the community, and lots of people involved. It would be wonderful for the firm to broker this deal and I am sure that it would lead to a lot of other opportunities for us."

"Most of these garden people are probably *renters*."

Magda blinked. At some point, maybe even a couple of months ago, she might have not have noticed that remark. But now, she couldn't let it pass. "Wait a minute, first of all, that's a huge assumption based on what? And second, what is wrong with renters? Renters are my bread and butter right now. Yours, too. Remember, I'm the one who manages your database."

"But wouldn't you rather have brioche and jam? Caviar and crackers? We want to move this firm into doing more of these deals. You can't do big business without thinking big business."

She pointed at the papers. "*This* is what we could be. A great, motivated group of buyers who have deep roots in their community, who know all sorts of people from all walks of life. This pool, right here, is how you build a base. You told me yourself, this is a business of referrals. You could have bread and butter and fries and rice and pigeon peas and quinoa and everything in between by treating people with some respect and taking a look at their offer."

"Magda, who have you been talking to? Who's been filling your head with these ideas? Maybe you've been spending too much time up here, getting too close to the situation. You need an objective eye. That's why we're partners on this."

She snorted. "If we were partners, you'd at least take my recommendation to look at this bid carefully and give the owner a clear picture of it. If you dismiss it, the owner is likely to reject it out of hand."

If they were partners, she'd be getting as much say

as he was, and she'd make as much money from any eventual sale.

She tamped the thought down. "You keep on telling me you're giving me a chance. Well, this is a chance we're giving each other. I've been skeptical, too, Keith. Remember, one of the gardeners threw a tomato at me, so it's not like I've always been on great terms with this group of potential buyers—"

Body-to-body, mouth-to-mouth with one gardener, but he wouldn't even be here in a few months. It hardly mattered.

She cleared her throat and crossed and uncrossed her legs. "But in the end, they deserve a fair shake. And I like what they do."

Keith picked up on her wording right away. "Real estate is an investment—people think it's emotional and that's where they go wrong. It's business and you should remember that, especially because it is your livelihood."

But it wasn't simply business.

It was personal for the people making the offers. All this land meant something to the mysterious owner of the garden; someone had left that lot alone for so many years, someone had held on to it. Keith wanted people to make logical businesslike decisions in their own interest, but not everyone did that. Her uncle certainly wasn't, considering how he kept sabotaging any efforts to sell his grand old empty house. When it came down to it, business was personal for her, no matter what Keith wanted her to do.

But Keith was still talking. "Hey, you're a smart girl—woman, *sorry!* So I'm going to remind you, you never take the first offer that comes along. Don't sell yourself short that way. You shouldn't make me regret giving you a chance."

Funny how he managed to sandwich the aphorisms with threats and insults. She gritted her teeth and tried to inject some humble into her tone. She was a baby broker after all. "We're not taking the first. We're presenting it to the owner."

"But clearly you've got some *emotional* investment in it. But you have to wait, you have to learn to be patient in this game."

That was when she snapped.

"I do actually know a little something about waiting for the right thing to come along and about deferring what I want, Keith."

She didn't love this job, especially right at this moment. But she could be good at it given the chance. As Ty had pointed out, she was working. She was being responsible and thinking through the consequences. If only more people could see it.

But Keith was still spilling the pearls of wisdom, and she was starting to feel like the swine. "I like a pretty garden, too. I'm always telling clients to get a couple of plants—nothing too unruly."

"Oh my God, Keith. It's not about some greenery." She took three deep breaths. "We're still obligated to show it to the seller, no matter how you *feel* about the offer."

"Well, I'm saying we don't have to push it too hard. Just…leave it in her hands. Don't try to make it look sweet."

"You're going to have me send it?"

"Yeah. If it comes from me she'll think I'm pushing

for the deal. If I delegate it to an assistant, it's not important. I'll send you her email address."

"Can I at least get a phone number to follow up?"

"I don't want you harassing our client. She's an older lady."

"I won't pester her. I want to talk her through it."

"No. Email. That's it. And you cc me. Is that clear?"

"Crystal."

Keith nodded and left, saying, "This is for your own good."

Friday

Ty was coming out of the subway when he saw the missing Byron, looking hale, if sweaty, as he ate a rainbow coco helado.

Ty stood there a minute, blinking as people pushed past him on the stairs. But it wasn't the ghost of Magda's escaped uncle. The man was leaning casually against a wall, enjoying an icy treat, and acting as if he hadn't worried Magda by disappearing or crushed her dreams of selling the townhouse and getting out of some of her debt.

The fucker.

"Sir," Ty said, because he couldn't very well call the man Uncle Byron. "Mr. Jackson. I'm Tyson Yang. I'm—" *your niece's not-so-young man?* Except he wasn't, was he? "We met at the 136th Street Garden last month. You gave us a generous donation."

Byron looked Ty up and down. He noted the neat work trousers, the briefcase, the rolled-up sleeves. "Well, you better not be asking me for more because you seem to already be doing better for yourself, young man."

Right. Byron was clearly *fine*. He wasn't confused. He hadn't been mugged or hit on the head. He wasn't being held hostage by a group of mutant, pizza-eating turtles who lived in the subways.

Ty was determined to let Magda know her uncle was enjoying a nice break in the neighborhood. But he should probably get Byron to contact her first. He took in a deep breath. "Mr. Jackson, your niece has been looking for you. She's very worried about you."

"Worried about me running off without getting her money, you mean."

"No, she's anxious about you. She blamed herself for pushing you too hard."

Byron blinked at that. "It's not that easy to push me where I don't want to go."

"I'll say," Ty said.

"What was that?"

It had been a long day. His boss had asked Ty to consider commuting remotely when he moved to Portland, and while sensible Ty might once have jumped at the chance at steady, familiar work, this new Ty tried to imagine what it would be like to move to a strange place and work from home, not having friends to goof off with in the break room, or to haul dirt for, or help with the squash vines.

Wow. His friends were really all old garden ladies.

Plus, the last thing Ty wanted to do was talk about moving. He'd been avoiding the topic with—well, almost everyone, especially with Jenny. To be fair, right now he also didn't want to talk about work, or the garden, or any reality past a shower and a cold drink. He was sweaty and he'd planned to change out of his work clothing and go and avoid his email. The collective still hadn't heard back on the offer. He hadn't talked to Magda, but he felt like he couldn't contact her—he shouldn't really. She was mixed up in this garden sale; even now she could be recommending that they work up a counter bid to ask for more money—money that the gardeners didn't have. And if that wasn't enough pressure, in front of him was this man who'd gone missing when someone offered him a pile of money for a house he didn't live in anymore.

So while Ty hadn't called her after their last—erm—warm exchange, he couldn't stop thinking about her, worrying about her. Hoping for her sake that she was getting what she wanted.

Although if Byron was here on the street instead of in some lawyer's office signing some papers then clearly that wasn't happening.

"This is none of my business," Ty said curtly. "But if you won't contact your niece, I will. I want her to know that you're doing great. Or at least, you seem to be the same as ever."

Byron crumpled up the tiny cup that held his coco helado. He threw it in the garbage. "You clearly have something to say to me."

Ty stared at Byron for a few seconds more.

Then he sighed. "It's been a long day for me and I'd like a cool drink. Why don't we go somewhere there's air conditioning and sit down?"

"Are you buying?"

Ty rolled his eyes. "Yes."

They found a cafe on Frederick Douglass. Ty ordered sparkling water and some fries. He texted Magda to let her know he was with Byron and gave her the address. Byron got a beer. They sat in silence for a while.

"What I don't get," Ty said, "is why you dragged Magda into this in the first place if you never planned to sell."

"I'm going to sell. I don't want to keep paying the taxes on an empty house. A man can't help it if he keeps getting these subpar offers."

"What's wrong with this latest one? Are they meeting the asking price?"

Byron avoided Ty's eyes. "Maybe."

Jesus fucking Christ. Byron was getting his asking price, and he still didn't want to take it. What chance did the garden collective have if everything was left to the whims of people who couldn't make up their minds about what they needed to hang on to?

"Do you know how much work your niece has been putting into this?"

"I've been putting in the work."

"No, you've been in Florida dreaming up delays and construction. She's been here cleaning up after the workmen, supervising every new light fixture change, every alteration to the security system, updating the listings, showing it to people who keep opening drawers and tracking mud and ripping down shower curtains. She's keeping it all up under the threat you'll yank it away from her, because she's responsible and because she cares. Did you know that on the night of the blackout, she even spent the night in that place because she wanted to make sure it was okay? She's doing this all while trying to rent out other places and sell that garden so she can pay off her student loans. Then she brings in an offer before your deadline, and you disappear on her.

"I'm not going to argue with you, but I hate what this is doing to her. If you don't want to sell the townhouse, that's your damn business, but why keep dragging other people into it? You jerked her hopes up by giving her the listing, and then down again by telling her she needed to get an offer. And then when she did, you didn't even consider it."

"I've been thinking about it. I've been thinking about it for days. Do you believe any of this is easy for me? My wife's been gone for ten years now. The rest of my family, even longer. I've moved on with my life, except for this one piece of it. Every time I'm about to sell it feels like losing the people I love all over again."

"Some of us don't have those choices, Byron. I would have loved to be able to grieve after my mom died, to not have to take care of things. For my dad to have stayed awhile after she passed. But also I know that my choices now—to do things or not do them—affect the people around me. And you're holding back the family you have now."

"They aren't really my family. They're my wife's."

"They visited you when they were kids. They remember the darkroom you used to have. You kept up with them enough that you knew Magda was working in real estate—"

"That was her mother's doing. She's always calling to check in on me."

"They worried when you went missing. They could be your family if you'd let them. I'd love to go away and leave all this pain behind. My dad tried to do that. It's only made him worse. But I'm always going to feel those losses. When you care about something, anyone, anything, a person, a pet, a garden, a home, you feel it."

God, he already cared, didn't he?

Jenny had told him, but he hadn't listened. Maybe she'd been teasing him about his gardening friends. Maybe she'd been jealous. But it came down to the same thing. He didn't have to chase down his sister. His sister would always be his sister, his family, his mother, and father, no matter where they were, would always be loved by him. But the friends he'd made at the garden—they wanted him around, too. They welcomed him, even in the face of his reluctance.

And there was Magda, who'd told him the same, who was trying to do the right things for herself and for everything else even if it wasn't always the pleasant or easy thing.

Could he build something with her? The answer had always been yes, but maybe he'd faltered because he'd been too afraid to turn that question on himself, to find himself unworthy.

But before he had a chance think more, Magda stormed in. "Uncle Byron!" she said, her face a mixture of the fury and helplessness that he often recognized on his own when he dealt with family. "Where have you been?"

Chapter Fourteen

All she felt was relief. Deep, deep relief that Byron was all right—made even sweeter by the fact that Ty was with him. For some reason his presence made her know it was real—it comforted her.

She hugged her uncle and ended up with a fry squashed into her shoulder. She didn't care. She turned to Ty and she almost wanted to cry with how grateful she was, how glad she was to see her uncle, even though he thought he had never been lost.

There were probably some other feelings in there, too, but now was not the time to analyze them.

Uncle Byron was still looking a little startled by her enthusiastic greeting. "I checked in with you. I told my housekeeper I'd be staying on. I don't see what the fuss is."

The heartfelt part of the reunion was over, apparently. "You left the townhouse in a frail emotional state. You checked out of your hotel."

"I'm not frail. I don't have emotional states. I get mad when people feed me nonsense, and I certainly didn't think anyone was keeping tabs on me."

But Byron did at least look a little ashamed.

Ty intervened. "Why don't we find somewhere quieter to talk about this? We could go to my apartment."

Byron said, "We could go to the townhouse."

To the waiter, he added, "Can we get these fries wrapped up?"

On the way there, Magda texted her mother to let her know Byron had been found and where they'd be going. She received a reply in thirty seconds flat. *On my way.*

She stared at the phone. She knew her mother wasn't pleased with her right now, with the way she'd behaved with Flora at the fair. But sometimes that instant show of support *was* comforting and sincere.

She hurried to catch up with the men, who'd already reached the door. Uncle Byron was having trouble with the lock. "Don't know why this system has to be so elaborate," Byron muttered.

Magda refrained from telling him why and took over.

They emerged into the house. It was hot and stuffy. She'd turned the air conditioning off as she hadn't shown the place for a couple of days.

Byron blinked, looking around. Then he said, "You kids have strong backs. Why don't you help me move some of those boxes from the top floor downstairs."

They were already sorting through Byron's photographs by the time Magda's mother and sisters and their families arrived with food from Mamí's favorite restaurant: a big aluminum pan of arroz con gandules, chicharrónes de pollo still warm and crisp, and pastelón with dark cheesy bits at the edges that Magda couldn't help picking off and popping into her mouth as she cut squares to serve everyone. There were tostones, and surullitos, and fresh green salads, and there was even a little mac and cheese for Magda's nephew Sebastian, who had recently declared that was the only thing he'd eat. Although Seb did also happily consume a handful of the fries that Byron contributed to the table. It was good Mamí had brought food and the children were there; otherwise it could have been awkward, considering Flora was still angry with Magda over her remarks at the block party, and how Ty and Flora remembered each other from that same event, and how Alma had taken Flora's side, and how Byron had scared everyone by going missing.

Yet, with the kids racing around, enjoying the novelty of spacious empty rooms and stairs and with everyone walking back and forth and getting in everyone's way in the kitchen, the atmosphere relaxed to a degree. They'd pulled the chairs from the dining room. For a moment they'd debated whether to use the plates and fancy napkins and glasses, too. "It seems a waste that we have these place settings and we can't use them," Mamí lamented.

But it was better this way, to be able to move around and get up and sit down and talk. Magda couldn't help noticing that despite the tension between Ty and Flora, Mamí liked the way Ty made sure that she and Byron filled their plates. Ty answered her mother's questions with good humor and convinced Seb to eat a surullito.

Mamí gave her youngest a look of genuine approval; she had made a good choice for a change. But Magda was slightly deflated by the fact that she and Ty weren't really together. Ty wasn't staying.

"He's nice," Mamí said. She nudged Magda's sisters to say something as she went over to talk to Uncle Byron.

"He's great," Flora said without inflection, watching their mother depart.

Magda snorted. "Somehow I doubt that's what you think."

"You wouldn't be able to take my honesty."

Magda took a deep breath. "Maybe that there is the whole problem. You don't respect me. You don't think I can handle things and so you try to take the hurt away."

"We love you," Alma said.

"That isn't the same thing."

From the way they both stared blankly at her, she knew she wasn't explaining clearly.

"I need you to start treating me more like an equal. I understand it's not easy for you. I'm younger. I haven't always made great decisions in the past. I got in debt—"

"How much?"

"It's not your business. It's all mine. I am taking responsibility for it. It's why I quit culinary school and why I've been trying to sell this house and the lot. It's why I can't go to your benefit, Flora—"

"I can pay."

"I don't want you to rescue me. I'm not saying all of this because I want or need help. I'm telling you because I finally feel—I finally feel like I *can* say it to you—that I need to clear this up."

Judging by the way they were staring at her, they were concentrating on what they thought of as her failures again. But she owned all of it; they didn't. And that was something.

Flora was muttering under her breath, "This is what happened because Mamí spoiled her."

"Flora," Alma said, a warning in her voice.

But Magda said clearly, "I'm almost thirty years old.

You don't have to blame anyone else about how I was raised and how I turned out. You can talk to me about what you think. Why didn't you ever say anything to me if you were worried?"

"Would you have listened?"

"I wasn't really given a chance, was I? I mean, I don't like being criticized more than the next person, but I do like being talked to like I'm an adult, and that I can handle myself. I'd appreciate being included. I know it's a lot to demand respect right now after admitting I've screwed up. But I deserve to be treated like your sister, not your child. It's what I always deserved."

Flora rolled her eyes. Alma shrugged.

But although it stung a little bit, at least she'd laid out her thoughts to them. Was it better that they addressed her as an imperfect adult rather than a kid who needed placating? She laughed to herself. *Not much.* But it made a difference in her mind. Plus, there was something Magda enjoyed about Flora and Alma's awkwardness around her right now. They swerved away from her like a fish in an aquarium for the rest of the evening, but in that avoidance maybe they were really thinking about how to treat her. She and her sisters weren't finished with this argument. But family was never quite finished, was it? The tension wasn't comfortable, but something had shifted in Magda's heart, at least—something might really change if she stuck firm.

"I still say your debt's not about you. It's the economy," Ty murmured.

"How much of that did you hear?"

"A little. Are you sure you want all this honesty with your sisters?" he asked. "Because I have that with mine, and it's a pain in the ass."

"And yet, you're leaving because otherwise, you'd miss her," Magda said lightly. "Which is too bad, because I ought to hire you as my financial adviser."

His look was inscrutable. "That reminds me I should hire you as my broker because I'll really need to sell my apartment."

She opened her mouth and closed it again.

This was a very bad time to realize she didn't want him to leave. No, more than that; she was halfway in love with him.

In her silence, he'd gotten up to get himself some water and it seemed like he was now going to avoid her, too.

She sighed.

Across the room, Mamí and Byron were sifting through more boxes of photographs.

"I remember you used to love to take pictures," said Mamí, wiping her hands on a paper napkin. She reached for a portrait of Ariana in what Magda recognized as one of the house's window seats.

Magda leafed through more. Ariana in the backyard with sunglasses. Ariana in the kitchen—a greatly changed kitchen from this one, waving a spoon menacingly at the photographer.

Magda hadn't known Ariana very well. She'd been a child, then a self-involved teenager when her aunt died. But she could see that each picture carried with it so much love.

She closed her eyes. Too much. It was all too much. She could feel the love, the love in the picture, the love in her heart, searing her from the inside. She had to tell Ty before he left. She had to tell him she loved his voice, the gentle murmur of it in her ear, strong and tender, she loved the way he listened to her, the way his hair flopped when it was hot out and he'd been in the sun, she loved how he fed her and how he watched her to make sure she was enjoying herself. She couldn't leave these things unsaid, trapped in time and distance.

She had debt hanging over her, but she didn't want to also live with regrets that could fill an entire house. When they were alone, they were going to talk.

"Byron," Ty was saying to her uncle. "Have you ever thought about taking these pictures to the Museum of Harlem History and Heritage, maybe to donate or lend them? I'm not an expert, but this seems like something they'd like. You have an amazing trove here."

"Your boy here is always hitting me up for donations," Byron grumbled. But he looked pleased. "My pictures in a museum. It would be a nice way to be remembered."

"Like we could ever forget you, Byron," Mamí said, swatting him on the shoulder. "You or Ariana."

"I don't stay in touch."

"You called me when you wanted to sell the house," Magda reminded him.

Mamí added, "You could take us up on our invitations."

Byron hummed noncommittally and pulled out a picture, which he gave to Ty. "There. That's your garden. That's the Joneses' old place."

Ty took the photo. A huge smile came over his face. And because it seemed he couldn't help it, he looked up for Magda because that's how he was—he always shared with her.

They bent over the picture together. A long sweep of solid stone steps, flanked by elaborate ironwork on the railings leading up to a narrow three-story townhouse.

In front of the steps, a woman in what looked like late-sixties garb posed with a young boy.

"Do you know who they are?"

"I didn't take this. I think my brother must have done. But that's the mother of my old classmate, Katherine, and maybe the younger brother. We were in first through sixth grade together. She had to sit next to me quite frequently—Jackson, Jones. You know how it is. It was a big family. Always a lot of mischief going on at the Joneses'."

Byron's face glowed as he talked about the photo.

Ty was asking about a couple of the other houses on the block. Magda pulled out her phone and looked at the reply she'd gotten from Katherine Jenkins-Jones, the owner of the lot. It was only a couple of lines, thanking her for the offer papers, and saying that she'd take a couple of days to consider it.

Byron's old classmate Katherine.

"It's still in the family," Magda said slowly.

She thought for another moment. "Are you still in touch with Katherine?"

"Everybody likes to remind me I'm bad at keeping in touch," Byron grumbled. "Of course I'm not. It's been years."

Magda pulled out her phone.

"Would it be okay if I gave her your contact information?"

Byron seemed intrigued, although he tried to play it cool. "Why not?"

He watched closely as she started tapping in Katherine Jenkins-Jones's email address. Keith had told her that he didn't want her pestering his client. But surely it wasn't a bother if she simply passed on some information. And a picture or two.

Magda snapped a photo of Byron's photograph of the house. She attached it along with a picture of the garden in full bloom. *Tell a story*, Keith had said. Of course, he'd probably never expected her to weave one for their own client.

Chapter Fifteen

Saturday

Ty hadn't planned on going to the garden the next morning, but his phone started pinging while he was trying to dutifully down his Greek yogurt and granola. Jenny's hoarse morning voice drifted from somewhere near where the couch should be. "These messages! How many gardens are you planning on buying?"

Jenny had given up her apartment and was staying with him for the next few days before she packed up her U-haul and drove across country, and her boxes had somehow managed to take over the whole living space.

Ty tried very hard to ignore his sister as he scrolled through his messages. There was such a thing as too much closeness, and he was experiencing it right now.

He stopped at a text from Magda and stood up abruptly. "I gotta go."

He started looking around for an unobstructed path back to his bedroom. What a time for him to die Collyer brothers–style, crushed by the weight of his sister's belongings.

Jenny appeared in front of him, hair sticking straight up.

"In a couple of months, this will be you," Jenny reminded him.

"Right," Ty said. He was starting to dislike being reminded of his impending move.

"What's the rush?"

He tried to sidestep his sister, but there was no room for the maneuver. "Something's happening at the garden and I need to get there."

"What, are they paving it over?"

He pushed past her. Jenny called after him, "Hey, I guess we don't need a bulldozer if we've got Ty Yang here to mow everyone down."

He gave her the finger.

In less than five minutes, hastily dressed and hardly washed, Ty was pounding down the sidewalk toward the garden. He met Mrs. Espinosa near the front. "The owner is here."

Mrs. E looked nervous. She never looked nervous. She patted her hair. "It's only that over the years I've had thoughts about what I'd say to her. Sometimes I thought I'd yell at her for letting the lot get so bad. Sometimes I wanted to thank her for turning a blind eye and letting us set up here. Sometimes I wanted to shake her. But now she's here and she's tiny and I just want to give her a couple of tomatoes."

"Let's not get carried away," Ty said.

Katherine Jenkins-Jones was indeed a scrap of a woman, and Byron was leaning over protectively and seemed to be pointing out various features of the garden—maybe all the cucumbers and string beans she now owned. Ty looked around to find a knot of his friends were gathered around them, muttering uncomfortably as they watched Magda and these strangers stroll down the well-tended paths. It was as if he and his fellow gardeners were locked out of their paradise as Ms. Katherine Jenkins-Jones, Uncle Byron and Magda decided their fate.

But he stood, surrounded by his friends—yes, friends—in their floppy hats, and he gazed out at the mass of morning glories tangled around the border, and past at the rows and rows of vines and curling leaves, the stout low trellises holding hidden fruit—all of this he'd helped nurture, all of this he'd brought to life, all of this potential. Who would ever give this up without a fight, without staying to see what could happen?

His gaze went to Magda again and he found her gazing right back at him.

He was planning on abandoning this. But he'd never really leave, would he? The grief would still follow him, as he'd told Byron, and the happiness he'd felt here, he'd leave behind.

But before he could really let that thought settle in, the trio came out and halted.

There was a moment of silence.

Magda broke it by saying, "Ms. Jenkins-Jones, I want to introduce you to the 136th Street Garden Collective. Mrs. Espinosa here has been the driving force behind rehabilitating the lot. She headed up the fundraising campaign that brought their offer to the table."

Mrs. Freeman nudged Mrs. E forward.

Two tiny women faced each other, Katherine Jenkins-Jones, compact but commanding, with her silver hair pulled back in a bun, and glasses behind which glinted a pair of sharp eyes, and Mrs. Espinosa, diminutive herself, dark skin gleaming with vigor from many hours spent outside.

Mrs. E barked a sudden laugh. "Can I try to sweeten the deal with some homegrown vegetables?"

Another pause. Then Ms. Jenkins-Jones put her hands on her hips. "Are you trying to pay me with crops grown on my land?"

Everyone sucked in a breath and the woman turned her gaze on all of them. Her voice softened. "I looked at your offer. It has been—it has been difficult to come back to that burned down, empty lot where my family's home once was."

Byron reached out and held Ms. Jenkins-Jones's shoulder.

After a minute, the woman continued. "I wanted to forget it for a long time. And I did that. I buried it. I think this year was the year I was finally ready to face it again. But when I did, I found I couldn't hang on to the land anymore. It didn't make any sense."

Around her, it was quiet. Even traffic seemed to have stopped for one moment as they all waited for Ms. Jenkins-Jones to continue. The only noise was the steady hum of the bees and insects hovering over flowers and leaves, disregarding all the tension of human activity.

Ms. Jenkins-Jones said, "Imagine my surprise to find something really different here, something beautiful and something that honors this neighborhood. It's as if all the things buried here rose up again, thrived. They always wanted to live and they created a new life for themselves. What I'm trying to say is, I love this. My mother would have loved this. And I am happy to accept this 136th Street Garden's offer. I think we have a deal."

There was another silence, then a roar came up from the crowd. Mrs. E was hugging Ms. Jenkins-Jones and sobbing. Ty had his arms around Mrs. Freeman and they were both crying. But Ty looked up and his gaze locked with Magda's. "You did it," she mouthed.

"You did it," he mouthed back.

Then there was another wave of hugs and tears. It seemed like another party was about to start up when a white man in a suit came barreling up to Magda and Ms. Jenkins-Jones.

Keith did not look happy.

For once, Magda was glad her boss lost his ability to navigate when he crossed 125th Street, because if he'd been a few minutes earlier, he might have utterly ruined the moment instead of merely causing it to lose some of its shine. He paused only to glare at Magda before greeting Katherine Jenkins-Jones with a panicked heartiness. "Katherine, what are you even doing here?"

"I was visiting my daughter in New Jersey when I got the email from your associate Magda here, and my old friend Byron Jackson. So I called them up early this morning and said I'd come down. And then I accepted the offer for the garden from the 136th Street Collective," Katherine said calmly.

"You can't do that," Keith said.

Katherine Jenkins-Jones raised one perfect eyebrow. "Oh. Can't I?"

Keith seemed to remember himself. For a minute. "Listen, I want you to think about this. You haven't signed anything"—he gave a sharp look to Magda—"have you?"

"I *have* thought about this, Kent—"

"Keith."

"Keith. I've given a lot of thought to this over the

years, as a matter of fact, and this is better than anything I could've come up with by myself."

"But this land is so beautiful. It's on an up and coming street. It could go for a lot more!"

Katherine seemed amused. "It's gorgeous because these gardeners made it so. No matter if it could go for a lot more, it's still a lot of money. I'm not some poor gullible widow who can be easily bilked."

Keith threw up his hands. "This is only the first offer! This is not how we make sound decisions."

"It seems a sound decision, me having enough while also ensuring future generations have something to grow."

With that, Katherine dismissed Keith and waded into the exuberant crowd.

Keith stood for a moment. Then he turned to Magda and hissed, "We need to have a chat."

Ty had already stepped up to Magda's side at that point. So had Byron.

"Well now," Byron said, "Magda here has gone above and beyond to sell my townhouse. In fact, I'm so pleased with this latest offer she fielded that I've accepted it. I interrupted my lawyer at dinner last night—she was pretty surprised to hear from me—and told her we're starting the process of getting the place sold. I hope," Byron said, fixing Keith's face with a stare, "that there won't be any hitches. You might want to know, Kent—"

"Keith."

"Keith, I specifically wanted Magda to broker this sale because she was instrumental in convincing me it was finally time. And now that I know it's time, I want to get it done."

Magda stared at Byron. She hadn't known this was

coming. Not last night, not through all of this morning when he'd called her early to meet him and Katherine at Penn Station. But from the way his eyes gleamed, she knew he meant every word of it.

She wasn't going to pass out, but she needed to hold on to something and there was Ty. She turned to Ty, whose face had lit up. Wordlessly, she went into his outstretched arms and they held each other for a moment—not long enough. Reluctantly, she turned back to Byron and Keith.

Poor Keith. He had gone through a range of extreme emotions in the last five minutes. His face was almost like a study in ombré, with traces of his red-faced anger fading into glowing wonder at the knowledge Magda had sold the impossible Strivers' Row townhouse, and then paling at Byron's implied threat to take the triumph away if Keith did anything to her.

Thankfully, Keith also knew a done deal when he saw one. He took a deep breath and gave Magda a beaming, if insincere, grin. "I guess you sold it. I wasn't sure you had it in you, kid. But—but we sold both of these properties." He shook his head. "And in record time, too."

Magda thought of all the instances when Keith had told her she wasn't aggressive enough, that she was too naive, and she didn't have enough experience. And she reminded herself of how this business was built on relationships—clear-eyed relationships.

She smiled and inclined her head. "*I* did have it in me. And yes, I did it. I'll have the paperwork on your desk on Monday morning."

Keith shook his head. And because he wasn't a complete idiot, he'd taken out his business cards and started

introducing himself to the crowd of gardeners and onlookers who were laughing and chatting in the garden.

Magda turned to her uncle again. "Uncle Byron.
Thank you. I know this hasn't been easy—"

"I said yes, but we've still got at least a month or two
before closing, so you're going to be seeing a lot of me
and hearing a lot of my complaints."

"So I shouldn't thank you until the check's in my
hands?"

She stood on tiptoe and kissed him on the cheek and
laughed when he turned red.

"Ariana always told me you were the smart one in
that family." His eyes had softened. "But thank you,
Magda. Thank you for being patient with me."

Byron touched her gently on the shoulder, then went
up to talk to his old friend, Katherine Jenkins-Jones.

Ty nudged her. He eyed the two older people specu-
latively. "Think something's going to happen there?"

"Might be. At least on Byron's side. But right now,
I think we need to talk."

"You don't have to take care of business?" Ty asked,
quirking his eyebrows at Keith.

"I've been taking care of business for enough time.
I want this. I want you."

In a strangled voice, Ty said, "My apartment—Jenny's there right now—"

"The townhouse, then?"

He nodded. Then he turned to face her deliberately.
He put out his hand and she took it. For a moment, they
stood, palms together, eyes locked, in the middle of the
hubbub that had taken over the garden. She pulled him
toward her and kissed him.

It was brief, a touch of their lips, one shared, inhaled

breath. But it was intimate because it was so public.
"Let's get out of here," Ty whispered.

"In a minute."

They started to make their way out, reluctant to let
go of their hands, but by the time they were on the sidewalk, they were running, flying along 136th Street and
laughing like children.

They arrived at the steps of the townhouse disheveled and breathless and Ty kissed her sweaty face and
tangled his fingers through her hair. "It's been so long
since I've been able to do this," he said, before taking
her lips once more.

"Let me get the door. Let's go inside," she muttered
into his mouth.

They stumbled to unlock the door and tap in the
code and struggle and swear, and then they'd grabbed
each other again.

"You said"—Ty kissed her again—"we have to"—a
nibble on her lip— "talk. We're going to do that"—his
hand traced down her spine and up again, to a magical place between her shoulder blades and up her to
her neck, to her cheek, even as he kissed her greedily
again—"in a minute. Just another minute."

A couple of minutes passed, maybe hours, before
they pushed away from each other, panting.

Magda said, "We do have to talk. You're going away
and I need to say some things. I can't apologize for trying to do a job I needed to do. For trying to save myself. But I also couldn't live with myself knowing"—she
took a breath—"knowing you would have resented me
if things had turned out differently with the garden.
That you'd leave angry with me."

She tried to laugh as she backed herself against the

wall of the foyer, holding her hands out in front of her as if to push him away—or hold him. She didn't know.

She couldn't do this. Because despite how relieved she was, how happy she was she'd managed to get this work done, there was still the fact that Ty wasn't going to be there at the end of it all.

She closed her eyes. "There I am again, wanting it both ways—wanting...*feelings* from you, but also wanting them a certain way. Maybe I am spoiled. Maybe I'm never satisfied, demanding my sisters to speak to me with respect even though I don't know that I've earned it, wanting you to give me more, but only if it's given freely and without strings. Not that it matters. Never mind. I'm spoiling the moment."

Ty shook his head. He'd stepped back, too.

Magda curled her fingers. They had been so close—so close—and then she'd had to speak up again.

Ty said slowly, "What if I said I wanted more from you, but I'd been afraid to ask. Because of course, I have feelings for you. I could—I'm half in love with you. But I also want things my way and I'm afraid to ask for more from you because you've already said you can't give me much. You don't have time, and you shouldn't have to spend energy worrying about how I feel. I don't want to take more from you, but I've spent so much of my life giving my all to people I love—only for them to withdraw, or go away, and I can't do that again."

Magda's heart started beating faster. "That scares me, too. I keep thinking, what if I'd helped sell the garden to someone else? Because I know I could fall in love with you. But I can't do it knowing if I screwed something up, then it would change how you feel."

"The point is you didn't. You didn't want to. That's

why I admire you and respect you, and why I stop in the middle of the day when I should be absorbed in my work, and think of you with awe, and remember how serious you get when you're listening to someone, when you're trying to figure out a solution, the way you brush your hair out of your eyes like you're impatient with it for trying to distract you, the way you never look away until someone has stopped talking to you. That's beautiful to me. Even your suit is beautiful to me."

She blinked. Was he saying what she thought he was saying? Her hands needed something to do, someone to hold. She clasped them in front of her. "We can do long distance," Magda blurted. "I know it's across the country and it's expensive but—"

"I won't leave."

Magda stared at him.

"But—but you quit your job."

"I can get another. What happened to, *Stay and be my financial planner*?"

Seeing her stricken expression, he added quickly, "I'm kidding. My boss would probably be relieved if I begged for my job back. But this summer has taught me I'm looking for more, too. Which is why I thought I wanted to leave. But I've also learned I don't have to find everything in my job, or in my family. Maybe I'll put more of myself in the garden. We're going to have to form a board and write a charter, among other things. But also, I want to start something with you. We don't have to figure it out now, but I need to be here, by your side, not that you need me. But I *want* to be here. I want to see the garden into another summer, years and years of summers. I want to see things grow between us. So I'm staying, because it's right for me and it could be right for us. You might not always have time, but *I* have patience."

Magda wanted to laugh. And cry. *Again.* Then she had to sit down, but there was nowhere to sit in the empty foyer, so she slid to the floor and Ty did the same. Their feet met in the middle.

"Ty," she said, wiping her eyes. "Do you know what my plan was for today as I went to meet my uncle and Katherine? I was going to get fired. I was going to break my lease on my apartment. And I was going to see how you'd feel if I moved to the same place as you—how you'd feel if I started over, beside you, this broken, debt-ridden person that I am. That was my whole plan."

"But you were never broken. Not if you were willing to risk that much. And none of it happened that way."

"Yes, I am glad it didn't go according to my plan. It—it turned out better than I could have imagined. So, new plan. I'm still going to be debt-ridden. After Keith takes his chunk, I won't be in the clear. But it's a start."

"What happened to putting things off until you're in a better place?"

"That doesn't mean I have to sacrifice every part of my life. I want to choose at least one path that will make me happy right now. And that one leads to you if you'll let me follow it."

Ty kissed her again. Then he pulled her up to her feet and into his arms. "I absolutely want to choose the path that will make me happy right now. So let's go up to the bed."

She groaned. "The show bed."

"Not for show anymore," he said impressively, then added, "unless you mind."

"As long as you help me with the laundry and to make it up again."

"I will even iron the sheets."

They scrambled up the stairs, kissing on the landings. When they reached the bed, Ty made a show of sweeping the many cushions off with one arm and looked so pleased with himself that Magda ended up laughing so hard she doubled over.

He took the opportunity to tear the duvet off, too.

He set her on the bed, which was firmer and higher than she expected, but she was past caring. Slowly, he tugged off his T-shirt. She remembered his chest in the light under the streetlamps. But now she was allowed to look at the way his wrists corded as he undid his belt, the flop of his hair filtered in the sunlight. She caught the first real glimpse she had of his bare hips as he twisted to toe off his shoes and pull off the rest of his clothing.

She reached out to touch him, to feel his slightly damp skin, the ridge of rib and muscle under her thumb. She rose on her knees to walk her hands along the ladder of muscle, better to see the small mole under her pectorals, which moved up-down, up-down more quickly as she wisped her fingers over his nipples and pressed her palm along the collarbone, his neck, his jaw and then leaned forward to settle her body into his, to rub her face along his shoulders, to kiss his chin, the sharp line of his cheekbone, his lips again.

He sighed. She loved it. She loved seeing him, feeling him, breathing him in.

"I want you," she said. "Do you want me?"

"Right now. Always," he whispered.

His hands helped hers pull off her dress and underwear. They fell onto the bed and he rose up to look at her and she loved how his gaze took in all of her. She loved how the morning sunlight shone behind him, making it seemed like his skin glowed, how it picked up the glints of his dark hair and made every strand shine.

"Look at you," he said.

"Look at *you*."

He sat back, running his hand down her body, warm and quick, pausing at the juncture of her thighs to press down, and oh, it felt good, good enough to make her swing her legs wide open to let him look down deep into her, and as his hand played on the delicate skin inside her thigh, she moved herself restlessly up toward him.

He bent down and kissed her there, licked her in thick strokes. She pulled at the short hairs at the back of his neck and he raised his head again. His lips were wet, wet with *her*. He said thickly, "I have to be inside you."

They were both scrambling to grab his pants and the condom in them. She made him stop for a brief moment so she could look down at his cock, so she could remember. In a long, aching moment, his hand sloppy and shaking, he covered himself and then she pulled him with her arms and legs and all the muscles she had inside her, she pulled him deep into her.

They kept their eyes open as they kissed now, as if they were both eager to see everything. If she'd closed them, she would have missed the small drop of sweat traveling down the side of his nose, jarring down with each thrust into her, each cry she made. She wouldn't have glimpsed the flare of his nostrils as she pulled him tighter into her, as he answered her with a hard pump.

It felt so good, so good to be alive, to be inside, around each other, to be hot and to feel their muscles working and to hear every stuttered breath, every lush smack of her thighs against his. It felt strange and good and new, and in a moment, just as she felt the smile spread over her face, over her whole body, she felt herself lift up as if to the sky, to the sun, and she threw her arms wide open, even as his body moved in her, as he worked and worked through his own gasping pleasure.

And then with a sigh, they both came down, back to the townhouse, to the high, hard bed in that sunlit room, back to each other.

In a moment, their phones would probably start ringing. People would ask where they were. They'd have work to finish.

"But we can have this," Ty said, in response to her unspoken thought.

"Not *all* this," she said, gesturing at the townhouse.

"Some of it. The important parts. Each other. A start."

* * * * *

Acknowledgments

Huge thanks to my editor, Alissa Davis, for her keen and compassionate eye, and to everyone at Carina Press, who have been a pleasure to work with.

Much gratitude for my agent, Tara Gelsomino, who continues to be my biggest booster.

A hearty thank-you to Ana Canino-Fluit, whose patience and recommendations were invaluable. It is a gift to be able to show one's work to such a careful and empathetic reader.

Thank you to Amber Belldene, whose insights into my very rough manuscript were so important.

I wrote most of *Open House* at my branch library and it's safe to say that I am thankful for librarians every single day. I'm also most grateful to the members of our local urban garden for their cheerful work, bright flowers, and for the community.

Special thanks to my husband, who keeps it together even when times are stressful.

Finally, during the writing of this book, I had the pleasure of hearing Ysaÿe M. Barnwell's "Wanting Memories," performed by a local choral group. Dr. Barnwell, a member of the seminal, all-female African American vocal ensemble, Sweet Honey in the Rock, grew up in New York City. In the composer's notes for this song, she writes, "When my father died and then my mother, and I prepared to sell the house I grew up in, I found bags of photos, letters and other memorabilia—the kind of things especially an only child hopes for…"

Many of these photos and letters (and a recording of "Wanting Memories") can be found at http://www.barnwellarchives.com/. Thank you, Dr. Barnwell, for your words, and your music.

Author's Note

"House Rules" deals with topics some readers may find difficult, including discussion of endometriosis and infertility.

HOUSE RULES

To those of us who never get it right the first time.

Chapter One

The last person Simon Mizrahi expected to see when he arrived at the uptown apartment he was looking into renting was his ex-wife, Lana Kuo.

He'd caught only the quickest glimpse of her profile, the back of her dark head, her decisive shoulders as she disappeared into another empty room. It was nothing but an impression, a ghost crackling with Lana's energy, before the real estate broker asked him to sign in.

It couldn't be her. Could it?

He was still distracted when the broker, who introduced herself as Magda Ferrer, began telling him about the building, and extracting information from him.

"I'm a music educator," he answered, trying to peer into the next room. Maybe there was no one there, but no—he heard a creak, a door opening and closing.

He fumbled through his email address and telephone number on the tablet, dimly aware he'd probably be getting a flood of emails from this broker because he'd given out too much information. But instead of protesting and stalling, he wanted to get this over quickly. To get into the other room. To make sure it wasn't *her*.

He hadn't seen her in years.

Magda Ferrer was looking blankly at him, so he

added, "I teach, and I work with the Manhattanville Youth Chorus."

"Oh, I think I've heard them. They sang at a street festival I was at this summer."

She tugged a little self-consciously at her suit jacket. She seemed quite young.

Brokers always seemed so polished, so unlike his rumpled self. Part of the job, he supposed. He'd been hunting for apartments for a few months now, ever since the noisy renovations had begun on his neighbor's place, disrupting his concentration when he tried to work from home, knocking bits of plaster from the ceilings and onto his books, his piano. His tiny one-bedroom felt dustier and smaller, more oppressive than ever.

But try as he might, he was never going to find a deal like the one he had on the rent-stabilized unit he'd lived in for the last twenty years, the place that he'd shared, for a brief time, with Lana.

He plugged a few more answers into the broker's form before heading toward the open door of the bedroom to see if he could find the ghost. He was half afraid the broker would follow him and talk. Half afraid of what he'd say to Lana when he saw her.

She wasn't there.

He stood for a minute in the empty room. There wasn't another door, and it wasn't as if there was furniture anyone could hide behind.

Maybe he was dreaming. That would make more sense. Lana lived somewhere across the country, maybe the world. He didn't keep track of her. She wasn't on Facebook—and yes, he'd gone looking for her a couple of times. Once or twice he found mention of her in online newspapers. But she hadn't kept up with the rest of their friends, hadn't kept up with him, so that excused his occasional curiosity. They'd shared a life. And now, well, he didn't think of her obsessively every day. It was a long time ago.

In dreams he still saw her, though. On familiar and unfamiliar streets, in empty rooms like this one, in his bed—or rather, not in his small depressing bedroom, but a different bed, a better one that still somehow belonged to him.

He walked to the window, unbuttoning his heavy pea coat as he looked outside. It was snowing in great, thick tufts. There'd been no hint of this weather as he'd walked out of the subway to get here.

He'd been given a respite, and he was going to enjoy this, the quiet, warm empty room, so unlike his own apartment, the light from the snow outside reflecting on the walls. He was not going to rent this place, he already knew it, because he wasn't going to change. He needed to get out of his cramped space—should have gotten out years ago—but the thought of moving all of the stuff he'd accumulated over the years, the thought of paying double the rent every month even though he could afford it, the thought of changing everything he was used to, everything that annoyed him, every one of his small daily joys, with no dramatic compelling reason, it made him tired.

He frowned even more at the unexpected sky.

Definitely a dream.

He pinched himself, knowing that didn't work, and even if it did, he wasn't likely to be more pleased on waking. But a startled sound behind him made him swing around.

There, in the doorway, was his wife. Her eyes were

round with disbelief, and she was clutching her puffy coat in one hand as if she was going to fling it at him.

But she dropped it. And it hit the floor with an unexpectedly heavy thunk.

She was probably real.

So was the coat.

They both looked down at it, and then back up.

"Simon," she whispered.

He took a deep breath. "Lana."

There was a moment when they stood, not sure what to do next. Then Lana's face softened into a bittersweet smile. One palm opened, beckoned for him.

He was going to have to touch her. He was going to get to touch her.

And he stepped up for a hug.

Lana Kuo had not expected to end up with her arms around her ex-husband that day as she set out to view potential apartments before she went to work.

But here she was gathered into him, her forehead against his shoulder, her nose pressed into the lapel of his slightly scratchy wool coat, her arms tightening of their own accord around his lean familiar yet unfamiliar body.

She pulled away to look at him and he stared right back at her with his bright blue eyes. He didn't bother with the polite cheek kiss she knew he might have given an acquaintance, and somehow that made her more and less comfortable.

They dropped their arms. They both took a single step back and began talking at once.

"Have you moved back to the city—"

"You're looking well—"

"Here for a job—"

"You haven't changed."

They stopped. Luckily they both laughed. If it was a bit forced, Lana didn't care.

She hadn't seen Simon for years, and he was as handsome as ever, the asshole. Same soft, floppy dark hair, now touched with gray at the temples, same sad eyes. He had a few more lines around them now, but they only made him more elegant, less stern than he'd been when he was younger; they crinkled as he smiled at her. She resisted the urge to touch her hair, to remember with dismay about how she must look several years later, to think of how she had changed.

Because despite his words, of course she had.

She wasn't in her twenties anymore. Her skin was no longer smooth, and while her hair was still dark and her body relatively strong, she felt so much more utilitarian. Youth had been so effortless; she knew this now because back then she hadn't thought about her health much at all except when she enjoyed it. She'd enjoyed it a lot when she'd been with Simon. Now, more of her efforts were geared to making her parts function correctly.

Most days, they did.

The broker luckily chose that moment to pop her head in. "How are we doing here? Have any questions for me?"

Judging by the speculative glint in the young woman's eye as she measured the small distance between the two people looking at the apartment and took in Lana's coat still on the floor, it seemed Magda Ferrer had more questions than Lana and Simon did.

Simon recovered and took another step back. "It's

such a coincidence. We've known each other a long time," he said.

Which was true, if he didn't count the last absent seventeen years.

She didn't. She knew nothing about him now. Why was he thinking of moving? She never imagined he'd leave the rent-stabilized apartment he'd "inherited" from his father. Was he with someone? Not that she cared too much about that, of course, but after all, she was curious.

"We knew each other," she corrected, more for her own sake than for anyone else's.

She grabbed her coat and smoothed it down, trying not to blush. The broker glanced between the two of them again. "What are the odds?" she said, giving them a brief smile before withdrawing again.

A small silence.

"Why are you here?" Simon must have realized how abrupt that sounded, because he added quickly, "How long have you been in New York? Are you moving back? Planning to stay this time?"

She wanted to laugh again because she remembered him enough, still understood him enough to sense he was trying to hold back, but he had too many questions. *She* had them, too. It was like carrying a brimming cup of hot coffee that was threatening to spill even as she tried to take sips that inevitably burned her tongue.

"I arrived a few weeks ago. Crashing on my cousin's couch. I'm taking a temporary job at Lore in Chelsea, one that might become more permanent, depending."

"Depending?"

"On whether they like me, or whether I like them, I guess."

He thought about that for a moment. "Do you have time right now to catch up?"

She'd planned to view a couple of other apartments, and she had to be downtown at her new job before three o'clock.

She was not going to be finding a place to live today, and she didn't care.

Ten minutes and one slippery walk later they were perched side by side in a cafe, looking outside as the snow continued to fall.

"You used to be a coffee hound," he said, inclining his head at her green tea.

She pulled the lid off and sniffed it. "Can't drink it anymore. It makes my heart race. But I guess you're the same if you're drinking a cup in the middle of the afternoon."

"It's a new habit. I need the kick if I want to stay up past eight nowadays. Not that there's much call for it."

Even as she knew she shouldn't take the bait, she did. "Not out tripping the light fantastic?"

"Not so much. I mean, I've dated since. You must have, too."

"Sure."

There was another short pause as they digested the implication that they were both currently unattached.

He gave her a sidelong glance. "This is weird, isn't it?"

"It is. I want to ask you all these questions, but I don't know if I can or if I should. But at the same time—"

"At the same time?"

"I want to sit and look at you for a little bit."

"Same."

They hadn't screamed at each other over the divorce,

but they'd both been angry and hurt and…shaken. She hadn't exactly asked him to vow to always be her friend, either. Because it was no use. She'd loved him, she'd tried to stay with him in the graduate music education program. But she'd been barely hanging on and he'd been a rising star. She'd needed a change and he kept believing until the very last day that if she just kept at it she'd be all right. But she wasn't all right, and she knew—she *knew*—he still considered it a failure, a failure of his love and belief. While she thought of it as her own personal failure, one that had almost nothing to do with him. She'd known she couldn't stay in New York anymore, not if she wanted to ever find a path that made her happy with the course of her life. But he couldn't see it that way.

They couldn't be friends. Even after more than fifteen years of silence and distance, the prospect seemed doubtful.

There were a lot of reasons why she wanted to stare at him without talking.

So she didn't tell him she'd missed him. She didn't tell him about the immediate years after she'd left. No use dwelling on the mess she'd been because she'd chosen to leave school, New York, and him. She gave him the abbreviated version she gave everyone else. "I ended up apprenticing with a master noodle maker. I learned to shape a long log of dough into hundreds of thin strands, all by swinging and pulling the dough through the air." She mimed the gesture with two hands and he laughed, not really understanding. It did sound like a circus trick. "I moved to Taiwan for a bit, then Singapore, then to Seattle, cooking and learning the whole time."

"So now you're a master noodle maker."

"Not quite. Plus that makes it sound dirty."

His eyes lit briefly, and then he cast them down again. He sipped his coffee.

Lana realized she'd been holding her breath.

"Well, my life hasn't been quite as exciting," he said a moment later. "I'm sure you could've predicted the whole thing. Finished school, taught for a few years and started a chorus for teens."

"I heard it won a few awards."

He raised an eyebrow, which she saw although he wasn't quite facing her. "You kept up with me?"

She looked into the reflection of his eyes in the window. "I checked in every now and then. Of course I did."

He shook his head. "I thought… Well, I thought when you left, that you really left everything behind."

This was not the time and place to get into this. The time and place had been seventeen years ago, when neither of them had had a clue how to talk.

So she picked up all those old feelings that had been unravelling around her and gathered them into a tight ball and shoved them deep, deep down where they usually lived. "And you've been teaching the teachers now, right? That's your new gig?"

"It's been over ten years, so I wouldn't call it new. No, now I'm also trying to write a book about choral programs across America. Still living in the same apartment."

"The one we—the one your dad lived in?"

"Same one."

"Wow, you've been there a long time now."

"Yeah."

"And now you want to move?"

"I've wanted to leave for years. I feel like it's holding me back. I'm in a rut, but my rut is so reasonably priced and centrally located. Besides, not moving feels easier than moving, you know? Maybe you don't. After all, it seems like you don't like to stay in one place for very long."

That was a kind way of putting it. "Maybe it's not so much that I don't like to stay in one place as much as the place doesn't necessarily want me to stay."

It was her turn not to be able to look at Simon.

She glanced at her phone.

"Shit. I have to go to work."

She stood up and pulled her jacket on. Simon got up, too.

He said, "Well, if you're in town, we should meet up again. You know, for old time's sake."

"Of course, yes."

She gave him her number and when he called to give her his, she saw how familiar it was. "Your old landline."

"Yeah. I got it transferred to this hand computer."

He held up the device.

"Kicking and screaming into the 21st century. Does it mean I get to text you, like the kids do?"

"I'm not great at that. But yes, everything else is the same. You could have dialed up anytime, you know."

"I could have. It's not like I don't have that number memorized."

It was supposed to be a joke, but it didn't come out as one. Simon sent her another swift, searching glance, and she knew he'd seen the truth of it.

He probably also sensed that she had almost called him many times. She *really* had to leave now before she said too much.

This time, when she went to say goodbye, she kissed him on the cheek, the way an acquaintance would. "You take care of yourself," she said, before giving him one quick last squeeze.

She dashed out before he could answer, and once she was seated on the train, she closed her eyes.

Well, against all odds, she'd run into her ex in her first month in town. It likely wouldn't happen again.

Not unless she wished for it.

Chapter Two

"Does she look the same?" Maxine asked.

Simon was on the phone with his sister, who lived in Toronto. He was supposed to be finding out what gifts her kids wanted for the holidays. Maxine had four children all under the age of fifteen who she shuttled to school and tae kwon do and piano and skating lessons, but she had only one ex-sister-in-law who she never got to gossip about, so of course she wanted to hear everything about Simon's accidental encounter with Lana.

Simon was not quite as eager to recap events, although he couldn't quite say why. "Yes. I mean, no. Of course, she's going to seem a little different."

She wore her hair in a braid now instead of loose, but the tip curled up defiantly. She was thinner. Her skin probably wasn't as firm as it once was. Around those golden-brown eyes he'd loved, he noticed little wrinkles, but those made her look softer, where before sometimes her face seemed stretched tight with worry. He liked how she appeared now, more still, more serene, even as he'd glimpsed her reflection in the cafe window, he'd felt slightly startled by her appearance—no, by her presence.

There you are, finally.

He hadn't wanted to look away, dammit.

Maxine was saying, "Men never notice anything. I want details."

"There wasn't much to it. We updated each other about our lives, and she had to go to work. I got her number. In a city of nine million people, we're probably not going to run into each other again, especially now that she's doing something so different."

"So you're not going to talk to her after this?"

Max sounded disappointed.

"You didn't even like her."

"I liked her fine. I didn't like that she left and cut off all contact in order to *find herself* like some *Eat, Pray, Love* cliché, and that you clearly never got over it."

"I'm—it's been years. Of course I'm over it. I've dated. I've had long-term relationships—"

"Two."

"I've got a very full life. It's just strange encountering someone, *anyone*, after so many years. You'd be confused, too."

"I had dinner with my ex-boyfriend when he was in town and I didn't feel flustered at any point."

"Were Allen and the kids there?"

"Of course they were there."

She said it as if she'd proved a point.

Simon shook his head. Maxine dragged them everywhere. They were a complete set. Simon's once-foulmouthed, glamorous, rocker of an older sister was now a person whose life was tethered completely to her kids and husband.

People changed over the years. Simon didn't understand it.

"Well, I'm at least glad to hear you're moving," Maxine said.

"Who said I'm moving?"

"You were looking at apartments. And your place is crumbling, and tiny. You could afford more."

"I'd think you'd want me to hang on to the lease to pass the old family homestead to Noah."

Noah was Maxine's oldest.

Maxine snorted. "What gave you that idea? I tell you how crappy your apartment is all the time!"

"But it's rent-controlled, and it's in a great location."

"At the rate things are going I doubt Noah's going to want to move from Canada to the United States even if it is New York City. Get rid of the place, Simon. The windows are drafty. There aren't any closets. Who knows what color the tile used to be or the bathtub—"

"Hey, I clean."

"There's so little light that I'm surprised your eyes haven't migrated to the top of your head like those fish who live at the bottom of the ocean. It's you against the years, Simon. You can scrub and declutter and patch up every damn day, but let's face it, grime is the only thing holding those old walls up. I know you hate change, but sometimes I can't understand how you're still there. Part of me can't believe that you and Lana used to both live in that tiny, cramped space together. With a piano. Sometimes, I don't blame her for leaving."

Oh, that hurt. He didn't know what to say.

"What?" she said into his silence. "I thought you said you were over it."

He breathed in and out. "New York is expensive. The place I saw with Lana yesterday was almost triple the rent of this one without much more space. And it wasn't that near the subway."

"You can afford it. You need a change."

"It's an adjustment that I don't know I want to make right now. Plus it's almost winter. A terrible time to move."

As if on cue, his neighbor's workers started drilling again.

Maxine was saying something else, but he couldn't hear. Unwilling to let her know what was happening, he covered his head and fled to his bathroom, shut the door, and folded himself down so that he could sit on the lip of his bathtub.

The construction noise continued, and Maxine was saying something about the kids that didn't require his full attention. He bent down and scratched at the tile with his fingernail. His sister was right. No matter how hard he scrubbed the tiles (and truth was, he didn't scrub them that hard anymore) they were discolored and needed replacing. He was forty-four years old. He'd lived in this five hundred square foot apartment for more years than he cared to think. He'd kept the same job, more or less, lived in the same neighborhood. Sure, he'd traveled and had relationships and to most eyes probably had a fine life. But he also never invited friends over anymore. The old wooden floors sometimes gave him splinters, and he couldn't open his kitchen window unless he tapped the frame with a mallet. Management dragged its feet because the rest of the building had gone co-op years ago, and they wanted him out so that they could finally sell the last of these rent-stabilized apartments to someone like his renovating neighbor.

It made sense to move. It was why he'd been looking at new places to live. But, of course, scoping out rentals also became incorporated into his routine, until looking for apartments and *not* moving was part of what he did and how he was.

"So you'll remember all that and think about what I said?" Maxine asked as the drilling stopped, and a steady thumping began.

"Sure."

Maxine sighed and said goodbye. She could always tell when he wasn't listening.

"A bunch of us are going to O'Dells. Wanna come?"

Almost all of Lana's coworkers were in their twenties, cynical, beautiful, with bulging biceps and intricate tattoos. Much smarter and surer of themselves than she'd been at their age, that was for sure. They could probably drink her under the table, not that she planned on testing the theory.

Lana was slowly cleaning up her station at Lore, the Pan-Asian restaurant in Chelsea where she cooked. She'd been on her feet for hours. Her legs were sore. Her arms were tired. She didn't want to socialize, or end up much later in someone's apartment smoking weed, as these nights generally went. She wanted to go home—not that she had one right now—and put on her wrist braces and sleep forever. She would settle for her cousin Julia's couch and six hours of tossing and turning.

Talia came up beside Lana and eyed her slow progress, but said nothing.

"I'm probably going to take too long," Lana muttered. "Have fun without me."

"Not trying to push you, but it would be better if you

came. All that bonding shit so that we can pretend like we don't want to go at each other's throats with knives half the time. You know how it is. You have to be seen talking and drinking with everyone."

Lana sighed. "I've been seen all night."

Like many of the large, showy restaurants in this far western section of Manhattan, a good portion of the kitchen was on display. Patrons could watch her toil. Of course, the customers were probably more focused on the flashy sushi chefs at the front counter, but her work making hand-pulled noodles was showier than most. Flinging and twirling dough in the air, stretching, and doubling, and pulling at it until it became 2, 4, 16, 32—sometimes hundreds of distinct filaments.

She liked the shaping and making the dough itself. She liked how different it was every day, testing the flour with her fingers, measuring it against the humidity in the air, against the strength she brought to it. She was always learning, though, and it made her self-conscious sometimes. The title "noodle master" felt like a bit of a misnomer. She'd started later in life and was probably still technically an apprentice, or whatever Western equivalent people used. There were many other true masters in the city, but at this circus of a restaurant it probably didn't matter. The patrons got their show and their hand-pulled noodles, cooked fresh as they scrutinized her. The other staff were all right to her, probably because they didn't see her as competition, partly because she had weird specialized skills, and partly because she seemed willing to teach them when she had time. Talia, especially, seemed interested in learning.

"I can't compete in drinking games. I'm old and

tired. My arms would fall off if I lifted a glass," Lana tried joking. Except it was true.

Talia shrugged and moved off. Lana had probably offended her by not taking the young woman up on her offer—again. It was hard to know the right way of taking care of herself: should she get the sleep she needed, or should she do the work of making nice with her colleagues?

It was tiring. And when she was tired, she started to see flaws in everything. Especially herself.

As Lana finally headed for the subway, she wondered once again if it had been a mistake to return to New York. But the job seemed suited to her, and working for a well-known Manhattan restaurant would certainly burnish her resume. Plus, it offered health insurance, which was rare enough that even if the pay weren't that great, she would have jumped at it.

On the other hand, there was Simon.

Cousin Julia's place was a walk-up in Hell's Kitchen. After a longer-than-planned rest on the couch, Lana downed the sludgy smoothie she'd left in the fridge and began her nightly routine. It was funny. When they were younger, Simon had been the one dedicated to schedules, and at first she'd tried to shake him up. Maybe she'd even been a little angry about it. She stopped practicing, and her playing became sloppy. She didn't exercise. When it was time for him to work or study or practice, she'd sometimes distracted him with sex. It was hard to think about him, to see him, without a bloom of discomfort over what a mess she'd once been.

As she washed her face and rubbed in her skin serums and moisturizers, as she carefully put salve on the nicks in her hands, and smeared lotion over her skin, she thought about everything she'd done wrong, everything she'd seen on his face earlier today. Despite asking for her number, he wanted to keep her at a distance. She knew him too well for him to mask his unease at seeing her. And of course, he knew her too well, too, not to catch sight of the regret for hurting him that she'd felt.

It wasn't guilt exactly, but it was something like it. It had been the right thing for her to leave, but doing it left so much pain and confusion. She'd loved him better and more deeply than any other person in this world. Probably still loved him more than anyone, for all that she didn't really know him anymore.

She fell asleep, as she had too often over the years, thinking about him. At 6:30 in the morning, her cousin Julia woke her up, sounding bubblier than anyone had a right to be at that ungodly hour. "I found you an apartment!" her much younger relative squealed.

Lana rubbed her eyes.

"A friend is moving to New Zealand. Isn't it amazing? And he wants a long-term subletter for his two-bedroom in Harlem. It's near the 2-3 and the C. You could just zip down to work and zip up again. It's perfect."

It was taking Lana a long time to process what her cousin was saying.

"Plus, he hasn't put it on the market yet, so you'd save on the renter's fee to a broker," Julia babbled.

She swung her shiny hair and started to make coffee.

Lana sat up and tried to get her brain to function. "A two-bedroom. It's probably more than I can afford."

Not that Lana could remember her budget numbers right now. Or what a number was.

"You could get a roommate," Julia said.

"I'm forty-two years old. I don't want a roommate."

"You're forty-two years old, and you're crashing on my IKEA KIVIK couch."

Tou-fucking-*ché*.

"I'm going to tell your mom you were mean to me while I stayed with you," Lana muttered.

"At least wait until you've seen the apartment," Julia said. "It may turn out I've been nicer to you than I've been to anyone in my entire life."

Chapter Three

"Simon, it's Lana."

He knew it was Lana. Of course it was Lana. He'd saved her name to his phone even though he had been pretty sure he wouldn't hear from her for another seventeen years. Usually he let calls go to message, but he answered this one. He'd been in his apartment trying to work on his book and idly considering going online to find a date to distract him from thinking about the very person who was now speaking to him and whose call he'd scrambled to answer with such alacrity that he'd sent three pens skittering across his desk in his haste to pick up the phone.

"I know this is going to sound kind of weird," Lana was saying, "but I'm looking at an apartment in Central Harlem right now. It's sort of a railroad-style with the living room and kitchen in the middle and two bedrooms on opposite ends of the house. And I was wondering if you'd like to come see it."

Simon blinked. He hadn't been sure why she'd begun telling him any of this, and how her last sentence would conclude, but he never could have predicted that particular ending. And now she was waiting for him to answer.

"I don't quite understand. Are you asking me to see it because you think I should move into it?"

Simon pressed the phone more firmly into his ear as he waited for her to answer. There was something about the way she was hesitating. "Yes. I mean me, too. It's really nice."

He heard other voices in the background, and then she must have moved away.

"It's a two-bedroom," she said again. "And it's split so we could have privacy."

"Wait, who is this *we*? Lana, are you sure you're okay? Did you call the right number?"

A huff. "Yes. And I'm talking about me and you. You're not going to make this easy are you?"

"Maybe I'd like to, maybe I wouldn't. But I don't understand what you're saying."

"Simon Mizrahi, I'm asking if you'd consider being my roommate."

Maybe he was the one who wasn't feeling all right.

"It's really, really nice, Simon. It's on the top floor of a brownstone, and it's bright even on this cold November day. It has a beautiful kitchen with a big stove, and exposed brick in the hallway, and crown molding. We wouldn't have to pay a broker's fee because the owner is my cousin's friend, and he hasn't even put it on the market yet. And the rent is really reasonable. He wants someone trustworthy, that's all."

"If it's so reasonable, why don't you take it on yourself?"

"I know you're looking to move, and it's a little bigger than I need, and more than I was hoping to have to pay. I could probably swing it, but I wouldn't have money for anything else."

"So you can't really afford it."

"Whatever, Simon. It's too good to pass up. You could have the larger room facing the front, if you want, and it would be almost the size of your entire apartment right now. And… I thought we could make a go of it because I know you. That's the main thing. I'm sure you'd take care of it and be considerate. You're exactly the kind of person this guy is looking for."

But was Lana the kind this landlord would like? No, that was uncharitable. She hadn't been irresponsible in the last year they'd been together so much as she'd been trying desperately not to have those particular responsibilities anymore. One of those responsibilities being, presumably, him.

Why was he even a little tempted to say yes to her?

He closed his eyes. "You know why this is a bad idea—no, it's not just one bad idea. It's several bad ideas rolled into one large column of highly suspect ideas supporting a sign that reads, BAD IDEA."

"I've talked to other people already, Simon. If I had better choices I wouldn't have asked. But still, what is so awful about this? What could be worse than what you've got now, Simon?"

"Well, first of all, how do you know that we'd get along after all these years? How do you know I haven't turned into some psychopath who stores people in my freezer?"

"Please. If it's the freezer I remember, it barely has room to keep a pint of ice cream."

He glanced at the ancient appliance then looked away. "I'm old and set in my ways."

"We'd have different hours. You could do all those things you used to love in the mornings. Go running.

Eat toast at your desk, and get crumbs stuck to your arm. Sit at the piano for a couple of hours arranging parts. Heat and reheat that one huge cup of coffee—"

Oh God, he really hadn't changed.

She was still talking. "I'd come in late at night, but I know how to be quiet. I don't want to have parties, and besides I don't have that many friends left here. We'd hardly have to see each other at all. I know I can trust you and, well, you know me."

She didn't, he noticed, say he could trust her.

"For all my faults, you know I'm mostly not so difficult for you to live with."

That was true, too. She'd barely taken any room in the tiny space they'd shared. When she left, he'd noticed she didn't have many belongings. In fact, if anything, in those last months, she seemed to shrink into herself, sleeping more and more.

He frowned at the memory.

But she'd taken up space in his brain, that much was true. She still occupied it. "Then there's the fact I used to be in love with you," Simon finally said.

He heard her breath catch.

When she answered again, he was glad—oh, it was terrible of him—he *was* glad her voice sounded strained. "Well, you're past it now, aren't you?"

"That's not the point. We shouldn't. That's all. There's too much in the past. It'll confuse things. No good could possibly come of it now. I'm surprised you even thought it was a good idea to ask."

A pause.

Then Lana said, "I told myself after—after we separated I would always ask for what I needed, no matter how hard it was, no matter how long it took to work up to it, no matter how afraid I was of the answer. I'm still trying to do that."

She said goodbye quickly and hung up.

Simon put down his phone.

It was unsettling. How could she ask him after all they'd been through? But at the same time, he couldn't help the pure shaft of joy at the knowledge she'd thought of him first, couldn't stop thinking about him.

Living together was a bad idea, though. A terrible one. But the worst thing? He could picture it. A clean, white-walled apartment. The sunlight streaming in through the wide windows making the strands in Lana's black hair glow with red and brown as she opened her sleepy eyes and—

Stop.

He did need to move. He knew it. Everyone else did, too.

But to live with Lana again, to know she was in the same apartment as him, it would be too difficult. It wasn't simply about the fact he might still yearn for her physically, because, yes, if he were honest, he still did. He didn't want to mistake his memories for feelings.

But Lana was right about a few things. His present setup wasn't working for him.

The neighbor's contractor thumped in agreement.

He went into his office early.

It was hard to work there, too. Too many people who wanted to gossip about who was going to be the new department head, or complain about the upcoming renovations to the offices. Too many people asking about the non-progress of his book. At least later he got to oversee practice. The chorus had holiday events to gear up for: they were leading carols at Marcus Garvey Park, singing the national anthem at a hockey game, and they had a lighting ceremony for the trees on the West Side.

He liked to run the kids through their warm-ups himself. The chorus was open for anyone ages ten to eighteen without audition. He'd never excluded people who really wanted to sing, and the really dedicated ones tended to stay in once they got to high school. Once warm-ups were done, he let his interns take over the practice, while he played accompaniment, supervised, and occasionally helped lead smaller groups.

The hour always seemed too short, though, and they'd be starting their performance season in two weeks. When the last kid was out the door, he turned to his staff. "We're going to need to give extra attention to rehearsing 'Gaudete' next time."

Abena agreed, "The harmonies aren't really meshing."

"They need to learn the parts better and maybe sectionals will help. They sound tentative and the song really needs to ring out. The soloists need some support."

Abena and Dion had this well in hand. He half listened as they hashed out a plan for the chorus's practice pages and next week's rehearsal.

It was so much quieter here in the practice room, even with the two of them talking. He shook his head.

"You okay, Simon?" asked Abena.

"The noise in my apartment is really getting to me. Who knew I prized silence so much?"

He tried to laugh it off and started straightening the stands and picking up stray pieces of sheet music, but his interns were exchanging amused but concerned glances.

Dion laughed. "We all compromise living in such an expensive town."

"I feel like I do that enough already. This new noise is rattling my old bones. Maybe I should take up the offer someone made me to live in their apartment."

"A sublet?" Abena asked.

"More like a roommate. Can you imagine?"

Both of the interns shrugged, and he winced. The chorus's grant paid them for their internship, but it still wasn't as much as he would've liked considering how much work they took on. They were in graduate school, young. They both had roommates.

"Especially at my age," he said, trying to take away the sting. "And the person offering would be my ex-wife."

Now they were interested. He didn't usually talk about his personal life, not that there was much to say.

"Your ex?" Abena said. "Do tell."

Dion pulled up a chair and theatrically put their chin in hand.

"I was married a long time ago. We're fine with each other now." Because they hadn't lived in the same city for years.

Abena was shaking her head. "Living with a former partner is bad news. What if you want to, you know, have someone over? Can you imagine explaining it to your date? Think of the introductions."

This was why Simon had never brought up his personal life at work before.

Dion was saying, "My brother lived with his ex for three months. It was awkward. But real estate in this city..."

"Yeah, you do end up putting up with some wild stuff to hang on to reasonable rent."

Well, that was what Simon was doing now.

Abena asked, "You're okay with your apartment, aren't you?"

Simon started to tell her yes, but he couldn't really.

"Aside from the endless drilling," Dion said as they finished their last sweep of the room.

"And hammering. The demolition was the worst part, but I think that's mostly over now."

Abena shuddered. "I hate that kind of noise more than anything. The sounds of the city—fine. A garbage truck or some sirens don't bother me. But construction? I'd have to wear earplugs and a set of noise-canceling headphones."

"And wrap those in a scarf," Dion said.

"More like a blanket," Abena countered, shrugging herself into her heavy coat.

Simon looked back and forth between them. "Noise-canceling headphones?"

He wasn't the most technologically advanced person, but by the end of the night, he'd purchased a handsome, heavy set from a store Dion recommended. He pulled them on when he sat down to work the next morning and listened expectantly.

The neighbor's contractors started their thumping and drilling again. And Simon, in his headphones, could barely hear them.

It wasn't perfect. He didn't love how ponderously they rested on his head. And he could swear he felt vibrations. But he could live with that.

Maybe he'd been going about this all wrong, trying to find drastic solutions for small problems. He could ask around for help about what to do with windows, and his tub and tile. He might spring for some renovations himself. Better yet, he could watch YouTube, learn how to regrout…whatever it was people regrouted. He could put in new cabinets, maybe build some bookshelves. Why move into a beautiful, sunny apartment with his ex-wife when he could make what he already had acceptable?

What a funny story he could tell if he ever had a party again: Real estate in Manhattan so bananas that exes considered living together.

The high whine of the drill was barely audible.

But just as Simon leaned back in his desk chair to look fondly around his old apartment, he saw a thin crack splinter his wall, starting right above his most prized possession, his Steinway upright.

More fissures spider-webbed out.

Simon jumped up, and his new expensive headphones clattered to the floor. A shard of plaster fell onto the piano's top board. Simon watched the drill head spin through his wall and then disappear back.

Silence.

Simon cautiously approached the hole. He put his eye close to it to find another eye gazing right back at him.

The eye winked.

Or blinked.

It was probably not the time to try to figure it out.

He backed away, still staring at this new, messy complication, and fumbled for the phone to call his ex-wife.

Chapter Four

Simon didn't want to like the apartment. But he was afraid he might love it.

It was on the top floor of a handsome brownstone on a quiet street off Malcolm X Boulevard. Bricks and trees and a fine stone stoop weren't going to impress him. The owner, a gregarious Black man, met him downstairs in the worn foyer and told Adam a little about the neighborhood as he led him up the gloomy stairs. "You're a musician, your roommate told me," Raoul said.

Potential roommate, Simon thought grimly. *Not-really roommate. Bad idea roommate.* "I teach music."

"Cool. Cool. Lot of great places to hear stuff around here. You like a jazz brunch?"

"Two of my favorite things."

Raoul laughed. "My kind of man."

He opened the door. "Well, here it is."

And Simon stepped in and turned to his left and he immediately was drawn toward the light.

"Excuse the mess. Who knew it would be hard to pack up your life and move halfway around the world?"

Simon hardly noticed the boxes and Bubble Wrap and packing tape. He'd started walking forward.

"I put French doors between the front room and the living room to let in some sun," Raoul said. "I think Lana said you might like that one for yourself. She said she could picture you there."

He could imagine himself here easily, waking up in the mornings, fixing coffee at the counter, running down to Central Park.

But no, that must be another person, another life.

He could be that other person.

He stepped into the bedroom, then left it again. He closed his eyes, but the brightness still filtered through his eyelids.

"There's also a washer-dryer in the bathroom," Raoul called from the kitchen.

Simon let out a muffled moan.

Raoul came back and handed Simon a bottle of water. "Feel free to explore more. Open the closets, you know. I already took all the important stuff out of the medicine cabinet."

Simon accepted the water and squared his shoulders. He was not going to weaken. This was a bad idea. He was here because he had to be a responsible piano owner and at least contemplate a safe place for his beloved Steinway...which would look perfect right in the corner of Raoul's living room beside the white painted fireplace.

He took a deep breath, marched himself down the hall, and opened the next door.

He turned on the light.

Never in his life had he known he cared so much about bathrooms.

It was so clean. The deep lapis tile had to be new. The whole space *sparkled*.

Simon wanted to weep. And if he did, he could always splash his face with cold water from the gleaming pedestal sink.

From the other room, he heard the door buzzer. Maybe it was a sign, a warning.

In a moment, Raoul was greeting someone. Simon supposed he should probably leave the bathroom but he didn't want to move. He sat on the edge of the polished white tub and let his fingers caress the smooth surface.

His own was pockmarked and peeling.

Raoul was laughing at something the other person said, and as the voices came nearer, he realized it was Lana.

Damn. Damn. Damn.

If he came out of the bathroom looking like he wanted to live here, she'd see it. She knew him too well. She could use it.

At the same time…

Well, he did want to live here. It was like Abena said, people put up with a lot for reasonable rent. And this was more than reasonable rent; this was beautiful, sunlit, and clean, and in a gorgeous old neighborhood.

After a long-short time, someone knocked on the bathroom door, which Simon had left slightly ajar.

He said, "Come in," which he knew was a weird response when one was sitting on the lip of a tub in a stranger's bathroom. But weird was how his life seemed right now.

Lana poked her head in, and when she spotted him, half-hidden by the shower curtain, her face seemed to soften.

He didn't know how that made him feel.

"Hey," she said, cautiously. "You've been in here a while. Are you okay?"

He nodded.

She glanced out the door and back in at him. "Raoul's on a phone call. Would it be all right if I sat there?"

She indicated the spot beside him.

"Pull up a tub," he said.

They sat side by side, both still in their winter coats, hands in their pockets, staring at the pattern of blue on white in front of them. Raoul hadn't packed up his towels yet. They matched the tile. Dammit, even his towels were perfect.

"I realize maybe I put you in a tight spot and it was unfair to ask you to do this."

"This apartment isn't fair," he said, perhaps a bit petulantly. He took a breath and tried to sound like a grown-up. "And as for asking me, it's not a question of fair or unfair. You're right. You should ask for what you need. And… I can understand why you did. In a lot of ways, this is a really logical solution to both our problems. We're both mature adults now, and surely we can figure it out, you'd think. But it's not the logical part of me that's worried."

"Yeah. I totally understand."

"Do you? Do you really? Because I don't know how to feel myself. Because for the last seventeen years, it hasn't been perfect, but my existence was mostly fine. I have work that fulfills me, and I have a place to sleep, and I got over you. I—I had a life. A routine. And then you come along again—and you show me this thing, this other possibility that seems brighter and sunnier, but you have to be in it. I know it probably hurts you for me to say I don't want you in my life again, even in a different, limited way. This hurts me, too."

For a while, there was silence.

"You know what, I'm not sorry, Simon. I'm not going to apologize about your hurt feelings. You're a success. Congratulations! You're solvent. Your apartment was crap and is crap, but you can afford to fix this part of your life. You don't need me. You don't need this place. *I* do. I want to live here so much, and after seeing it, I bet you understand why. If you don't want this, you don't have to take it. And you certainly don't have to try to make me feel guilty again."

"I'm not."

"Aren't you?"

She crossed her arms and pulled back to look at him.

He cleared his throat. "Maybe a little."

She stood up. She went to the sink, ran the water, and washed her hands.

"Is this really so easy for you, Lana?" he asked.

She seemed to study herself in the mirror. "No, of course it's not. But I have limited choices, and I have to pick the things I think will work out best for me in the long run."

"And you think this—us—is a good idea?"

"No, I don't."

He flinched slightly. But at the same time, he felt a little surprised. Lana of seventeen years ago had not been so blunt.

"But I don't have many friends left in the city, and the ones that I do are past the roommate stage of life and don't know anyone to recommend to me. Before and after we talked last time, I tried putting up an ad online, and both times all the people who answered either tried to pick me up or, when they heard how reasonable the rent was, attempted to poach the lease. And this was before they'd even seen the place or me. I have limited options. Believe it or not, you were the best I could come up with. If you have a better idea, you should go for it."

"How do you know *I* won't try to steal this place from under you?"

"You wouldn't do that to me. Because you're honest, even kind of noble in your own way, Simon. I trust you. And that's why I ended up thinking of you. Not that you weren't in my mind before. But that's why I supposed I could share a space with you."

They stared at each other. Simon couldn't help it. He drank her up, and she seemed to do the same with him.

It was strange, and maybe too intimate being in a bathroom with her. He stood up. They both walked out.

Raoul grinned at them. Lana had probably told him their history.

"I... Do you mind if I go make a call?" Simon asked.

He needed a moment. He couldn't quite deal with it, deal with himself.

He went to the front room, the beautiful room with all the light, while Lana and Raoul talked quietly at the other end of the apartment. When Simon finally finished arguing with himself, Lana was gone.

Raoul slid a contract over the counter. "She signed the lease and left with a set of keys. There's a space for you here on the agreement, but she said you still weren't sure."

Simon glanced at the pen. He took the keys. "I'm not sure," he said. "But I guess I can't let it stop me."

Moving took place over Thanksgiving weekend. Luckily, Lana didn't have much stuff. She bought a new bed, which Julia helped her set up. Her cousin even stuck around to put fresh sheets on it. Lana suspected her baby cousin was hanging out in hopes she might run into Simon, who Julia had never met but who she'd probably heard much about through the extended family's grapevine.

But Simon wasn't set to get his boxes and furniture in for a few more days. He had a lot more to wrangle than she did. She wasn't going to enquire more closely, or volunteer to help. *Hands off* was her policy about everything Simon. She was tempted to have it cross-stitched and hung on her wall.

While Julia lounged in the bedroom, no doubt sending pictures of Lana's sparse belongings to all the aunts and great aunts, and adding that the infamous ex-husband still hadn't yet shown up, Lana wiped the cabinets clean, and poked around the boxes holding her kitchen equipment. Over the counter, she could see the one big piece that had already arrived: the piano.

Simon hadn't been around for that, either. He'd called her earlier today sounding harried, asking if she could supervise as the instrument was delivered. She was already here, so she agreed to watch as the Steinway was trundled up the three flights by one burly Russian guy with a special moving belt. A skinnier older man whose main job seemed to be to tell Lana and Julia stories about which houses in the neighborhood had which kinds of staircases was there to warn the younger man about the angles to take when maneuvering the instrument through the brownstone's landings. The move hadn't taken more than an hour, but for Lana, it felt like forever. She hadn't realized how stressful it would be to wait for the piano to arrive, to hear the shouts and orders as it came up the stairs, to see the instrument in person once again.

She did not touch it.

"I wish you'd play for me," Julia said, coming into the kitchen.

If only Lana had a fainting couch on which she could fling herself dramatically before she answered. "I don't play anymore."

But there was no furniture other than what she'd put in her own room. She hadn't talked with Simon, but she'd expected him to provide most of it. She wondered if he still had the tweed foldout that sagged in the middle.

She could definitely spring for a couch.

They'd seemingly spelled out everything else, though. They agreed to a trial period of four months. If it didn't work out, Simon would be given time to find another place to live, and she'd be allowed to show potential new roommates around. In the meantime, quiet hours were between 8:00 pm and 10:00 am. They split utilities and internet and shelves in the bathroom. They both agreed to try to keep clutter to a minimum and have honest conversations about housekeeping. Top shelf of the fridge was for shared food. Middle was for her and bottom for him. They each had one crisper. No dinner parties or large gatherings unless one cleared it with the other.

And if they had, uh, more intimate guests over, those people could not stay more than twenty-four hours.

Lana hoped there would be no such visitors. Not because she was jealous. It was just awkward.

Simon was right, as usual. The whole thing was a terrible idea.

She stared harder at the damn piano.

She hadn't been as sure of herself as she sounded when she'd sat in the bathroom arguing with him. But she had to let him know he wasn't dealing with the person she used to be; she needed to remind herself often of the same fact. She'd learned over the years to keep her knives sharp, to show no fear, whether she was trying to keep her place in a restaurant kitchen or find her way out of a strange and confusing airport. Sometimes that meant sounding steelier than she felt.

Julia sat down at the piano bench and lifted the keyboard cover. "Your dad says you were really talented."

Lana shrugged. "He's biased."

"He's a music professor and former concert pianist. That's an informed bias."

"Despite his opinion, a lot of people play the piano and talent only gets you so far. You can practice and practice and be the best you can be and better than anyone else in your circle, and still only be the 2000th best pianist on this earth."

"What about your dad?"

"In his prime, probably top 1000."

Her dad lived in Ohio. He'd always loved Simon and was delighted Lana was moving in with him again.

Her father had been disappointed when she went into music education instead of trying to have a career as a performer. But by the time Lana had grown up, the industry changed. Dad might have been able to work and thrive teaching and holding recitals. But Lana didn't have his drive, probably because she didn't feel a spark for performance. She'd studied what she had in order to please him, and that had been a mistake because her heart wasn't in it. And now here she was raising his hopes in a different way, by seemingly reconciling with Simon even though she'd been very clear that was not what was happening.

She reminded herself she wasn't responsible for her father's ambitions. She could only be in charge of herself, and judging by how tediously slow unpacking was going, she wasn't sure she even wanted to be responsible for that.

Julia opened the lid of the piano and began to play "Chopsticks." "Aren't you at least going to do the bass part with me?"

"Tempting."

Julia stuck out her tongue, and Lana gave her the finger back. It was on this warm scene that Simon arrived, slightly out of breath, hair flopping in his face, coat unbuttoned.

Eyes sparkling.

This was definitely going to be a problem.

Lana hadn't seen Simon in person for a while. They'd conducted their business in the intervening weeks through phone calls and texts, which Simon was slow to respond to, but at least they effectively avoided having to see each other. He'd viewed the apartment one more time with their landlord to take measurements, and conferred with her on the phone. She may have eluded the invitation (though she probably should have taken her own measurements) because she hadn't wanted to see him. Ridiculous considering they'd soon be living with each other again.

And now, here they were.

Julia was delighted. Lana's cousin, her baby cousin, leaned against the piano and extended her hand, palm down, like a society dame. Simon crinkled his eyes charmingly, flashing Lana an amused look before turning his attention back to the woman draped across his instrument.

Ugh.

Lana barely managed to suppress the exasperation in her voice. "Simon, this is Julia, another one of my cousins. She's the daughter of my dad's youngest brother. She went to NYU Law, and she's with a firm downtown."

"Your dad's the ornithologist, right?"

"No," Julia said. "Uncle Yi-shang is the ornithologist. My dad's the ophthalmologist."

She sent another wide smile Simon's way, and when he turned to Lana for help, Julia mimed clutching her heart and pretending to swoon.

Why couldn't one of her other eleventy-million cousins have moved to the city and offered her their spare couch?

Simon was asking Julia about her work and about all of the various aunts and uncles. He remembered more than Lana expected. His eyes coasted around the rest of the apartment once or twice. Maybe he was looking for an escape hatch, or maybe he was trying to imagine how little he could move in before he moved out again.

Lana stayed in the kitchen behind the counter, her fort, and kept her head ducked. She pulled spices out of her boxes and put them back in.

"I'll leave you two alone," Julia eventually trilled.

With a sweep of her scarf, she left the apartment. Lana and Simon listened to her clatter down the stairs.

Lana realized she couldn't also make a grand exit. This was her home now. This was where she was spending the night.

She glanced up to find Simon's eyes on her.

He put his hands in his coat pockets. "So, settling in okay?"

"Yes."

"And I see the piano's all right."

"As long as Julia didn't sully it by playing 'Chopsticks.'"

"At least it wasn't 'Heart and Soul.'"

"You take that back. You know I love me some 'Heart and Soul.'"

"I remember."

He laughed and looked down.

She'd told herself she should stick to the present when she had to speak with him, but it was harder than she'd thought. One day they'd get over this awkwardness. They had to. She wanted to tell him it wouldn't be so bad. It was just a trial period. It didn't have to be forever.

Simon cleared his throat. "The movers will be here tomorrow morning, we're thinking around noon, and depending on parking. All my things I've accumulated over the years, turns out it's not as bad as I anticipated."

"Famous last words."

He laughed again.

"Did your landlord give you a hard time about breaking your lease?"

"No. They've wanted me out for about the last ten years. Now they can finally renovate and sell the place for half a million or so."

"No. That's ridiculous. It's tiny."

"Manhattan real estate. Maybe my dad should have bought it when he had the chance. But now, the last Mizrahi is leaving apartment 204 after fifty years."

"Wow. How do you feel?"

"It hasn't hit me yet."

Another pause. "I'll manage, though." He began pacing the room. "This place makes up for it. It's almost too bad we're going to cover up these dark wood floors with rugs. I love the way the sunlight looks on them."

"I can contribute furniture if you'd like."

"Do you want to? This place should be furnished in your taste, too."

"I don't have a strong opinion—"

"I don't either."

"I don't want to step on any toes—"

They talked over each other and stopped.

Simon seemed to take a deep breath. He was avoiding her eyes. "I wanted to apologize for the other day. In the bathroom."

"It was fine. I was pushy, too. It's going to take some time for us to adjust."

He didn't answer.

She laughed a little awkwardly, and put down the spice bottle she'd been fiddling with. "Still time to back out."

Please don't back out.

Simon shook his head, then gave her a brief, piercing glance. Her stomach seemed to drop as he said, "I'm not going to change my mind at this hour. I'm living here for four months. I'll try my best, and so will you."

She bristled, not so much because of what he'd said but that he felt he had to say it. Still, it was true. They'd set out their guidelines for how to live together. They'd follow them.

But later as she grimly cleaned out an already clean cabinet, she decided she wasn't going to have trouble sticking with her own, private number one rule that she wouldn't fall in love with him again.

New number one rule: She was not going to let him boss her around.

Chapter Five

It was surprisingly easy for Simon to abide by his privately formed dictum not to get involved in Lana's life. Her hours were so different from his that he rarely saw her. She slept late and left sometime in the afternoon, not returning until way after he'd gone to bed.

Some nights, he wondered if she'd come back at all. Not that he was keeping tabs on her. He had unpacking to do, a grant report to write for the worryingly opaque foundation that funded the chorus, a book to avoid working on, and a handful of seasonal concerts the kids would perform at, along with the end-of-semester grading.

But he saw evidence she'd been there in the damp towels spread out to dry on the rack near the bathroom radiator, the green vegetables she left in the fridge and the disassembled blender parts drying in the dishrack in the evenings. Their living quarters were indeed split, so thoroughly that when he was in the living room he could barely see down the brick-lined hallway to her door, which was always closed. He hadn't caught one glimpse of her room since he'd moved in. Not that it was his business. He'd taken the large front bedroom with its tall windows and its ghostly painted-over crown molding. At first he'd worried about noise coming in from the street, but it wasn't as if his former apartment had been perfectly quiet. At least no one would be drilling through these walls. The branches of a tall tree cast friendly shadows in the room, and in summertime the leaves would shield him from some of the sounds of cars and passing people.

Not that he was sure he would stick around long enough to find out. Although it was surprising how quickly he'd managed to adapt. The quiet helped. The light did, too. And seeing the red brick of the townhouse as he rounded the corner was an unexpected— what could he call it?—it was a *pleasure*. Never in his life had he thought he would become so attached to a building. A few weeks into December, he still paused, no matter how cold it was, to enjoy the black, wrought-iron gate, its solid bars ending in fleur-de-lis, lumpy and thickened with layers of paint. He smiled at the steps, slightly higher on the right side to make up for the sloping of the street, and he enjoyed the solid *thunk* of his key entering the old lock.

It was after such an evening, after a concert in which the kids had performed exceptionally well, he came galumphing up the stairs, a little drunk with pride and on the single glass of prosecco he'd downed at the post-recital reception, that he came up the stairs to find Lana in the kitchen.

God help him, he was happy to see her. He was so warm and full of fellow feeling, so grateful she'd suggested this whole arrangement. And she looked soft and pretty with her hair in two braids, her slim figure clad in navy blue pajamas piped in contrasting white, her bare feet peeping out from under the rolled hems. His eyes went down, then up briefly to the shallow notched vee above her throat, to her delicate skin. He moved toward her in three full steps ready to give her a hug.

And stopped short. Before he had a chance to say a word—before she did—he raised his index finger. "Hi. Let me go to the bathroom."

He swiveled unsteadily and fumbled for the door. Shut it. And looked at himself in the bathroom mirror.

He'd almost hugged his ex-wife. He'd raised his finger when she was about to speak to him. He'd lurched for the bathroom.

He was still in his coat.

Suave.

Not that he wanted or needed to look any particular way to her. She'd seen far worse from him. But this old, *ex*-er version of her hadn't.

He took off his coat, and cleaned himself up so he didn't look quite so *jovial* and tried to pump some sense into his veins. His chorus had done so well, these kids, their faces glowing, their voices strong. The audience had been on their feet.

"Good performance?" Lana asked as he came into the kitchen again.

She handed him a plate with some cheese and crackers, and an orange sliced up in fat segments, the peel still on.

She still cut up her oranges that way.

"How did you know?" he asked, sitting on one of the new stools at the end of the kitchen counter.

She smiled and looked down. "It's in your face. It glows."

He cleared his throat, embarrassed to hear his

thoughts echoed. "Probably from the sparkling wine. I didn't have anything to eat."

"You never could before a performance."

"I wasn't even the one who was up there singing or conducting. One of my interns, Abena, she was in charge of selecting the music and teaching the kids these parts. They really responded to her. She has a great future. I'm so proud."

He pulled the peel from the orange and put the entire segment in his mouth, sucking the juices dry. It seemed to taste better than anything he'd ever eaten before.

Lana was still standing there watching him, amused.

Amused was good. It was better than slightly alarmed, which was the expression that had flashed over her face when it seemed like he was going in for a hug.

The cheese and crackers were also the best he'd ever eaten. Hands down.

"You are a wonderful chef," he said, his mouth full.

"It's Breton biscuits and store brand cheddar," she laughed. "You're still like this. You just love everyone and everything when people make music."

He grinned through a mouthful of crackers. "It's a beautiful experience."

"Yes. Yes, it is."

She looked down again. And suddenly he felt a little bad. Maybe she missed music.

If she did, it might explain the way she veered away from the piano the few times he'd seen her in the living room.

He was about to pose some indiscreet questions. Maybe find out things he didn't want to know the answers to, when she asked him, "Would you mind if I adopted a cat?"

He blinked, completely thrown.

Her face had pinkened as she said hurriedly, "I wasn't trying to take advantage of your mood. I didn't know you'd be—it's my night off from work and I was up so I wanted to ask…"

"You want a cat?"

"Yes."

He thought about it for a moment more.

"Why? You never wanted one before."

"I never asked for one before."

She turned on the sink and started to wash the knife.

There was something in here that he should probably try to think through. But although he wasn't really drunk, he seemed to be having trouble understanding her request.

She dried her hands. "I'd try to keep it mostly in my room. We could store the litterbox in the bathroom. Cats are nocturnal anyway so you wouldn't really have to do anything unless I went somewhere for a trip. But that isn't likely to happen."

She added, "I'd like the company."

It wasn't a judgment precisely. It was better for both of them to keep out of each other's way, to attempt to lead separate lives. But a part of him, rather childishly, wondered why she didn't take his companionship. Not that he was offering.

"I guess it's okay with me. I never thought of—I suppose pets weren't allowed in my old place, and it would've been too cramped. I put it out of my mind."

"So you'd be fine with it."

"I think so."

"Thank you. Maybe I'll try to find a cat who's older,

more settled. One who won't want to go running all over the apartment at all hours."

"Right."

He picked up an orange peel.

If she wanted a cat, maybe she was feeling more settled than he was. Maybe this meant she was going to stay.

He should not feel a burst of joy from thinking of it. But he wasn't supposed to like seeing Lana in her pajamas in the kitchen in bare feet, to be aware of the subtle curl of her toes, to wonder how they'd feel brushing up his leg.

Of course she was going to settle here. That was part of the agreement. He was the one who had to move out after four months if he didn't like it. This apartment was supposed to be the next step in a new him, one who didn't get stuck, one who tried new things.

But as he dropped the peels in the freezer compost and tried to calm his unruly body, he couldn't help thinking that if he had to stay here with her, he wouldn't mind. He wouldn't mind at all.

Christmas Eve

"I wasn't planning on asking if I could adopt until after the holidays. But he came into the apartment looking like I remembered, just while I was thinking of all the ways I'd changed. So I blurted it out. So much for never apologize, never explain."

Julia snorted. "Who said that?"

"Some rich white person, no doubt."

Julia had called Lana up to ask her to help with her baking. Lana reminded her cousin she wasn't a baker and didn't make pastry, but Julia sounded desperate and Lana did owe her for all the weeks on the couch, so she'd pulled herself out of her bed on her day off and slumped down to Hell's Kitchen, her tired body cursing her all the way as she thought of the shift she'd agreed to pick up tomorrow.

But so far this was all right. Julia's apartment was warm, probably too warm for pastry making, and Lana had installed herself on the couch and was looking through a pet adoption site while "coaching" Julia through the dough.

Julia raised a flour-and-butter-covered hand and rubbed her forehead with her wrist. "Is Simon coming to the shelter with you to pick out the cat?"

"No. It's not like we're a couple or something."

Julia pursed her lips in disappointment. Or maybe she was concentrating on the butter and flour.

"That might be easier with the food processor."

"I hate cleaning that thing. Plus doesn't making it in the food processor make it tough?"

The glutens were probably already overworked, but Lana didn't say anything. Instead she told Julia to add more ice water.

Fear of a tough crust wasn't going to divert her cousin from her favorite subject, though. "What's Simon doing for Christmas? Does he celebrate?"

"He doesn't, but he's planning to go to Westchester to see his aunt Rose. He's got a lot of cousins. They usually go see a movie and order takeout."

"So you two won't be trapped together in the apartment with a big snowstorm blowing outside."

"It's supposed to be 45 tomorrow. Practically balmy."

"The fire roaring. A blackout threatening…"

"The fireplace doesn't function."

"He slowly takes off his button-down shirt and puts it on you to keep you warm."

Lana snorted.

Julia inspected her work, her face a mask of innocence. "It's just the unresolved sexual tension coming off of you two."

"What are you talking about? We were married. There's nothing unresolved about it."

"Ah, so you admit there is sexual tension."

"Are you sure you don't want to be a criminal defense lawyer, Perry Mason?"

"Who's that?"

"I think my hip just broke from the old."

"Anyway," Julia was saying, "it's clear when you're in a room together. That's all. He's very aware of you."

Well, Lana was certainly alert to him, too. They'd stopped avoiding each other since that last encounter, and it was much better this way. The most awkward part of living together seemed to be over. But still there was tension, as Julia called it, a not-unpleasant pull that she felt for him. When they were both in the apartment's shared spaces, she involuntarily tracked what he was doing. She watched him hum quietly to himself when he was going over a score, thinking about how the slight buzz of his breath might feel against her skin. Her eyes would flick to his hands, his elegant fingers, swiping over a tablet. It was usually a short distraction. Then she would get back to doing whatever it was she was doing: making her to-do list, checking her messages, getting her jacket on before she ran off to work. Her small fascinations weren't something she wanted to admit out loud, but there they were. It was only natural wasn't it? His face was still beautiful and elegant, if a little careworn, and it had been some time since she'd left. The reasons why they'd gotten divorced were long over, and memory had dulled her guilt. Plus, they had more breathing space, both in the apartment and because they didn't work in the same field. Of course she was going to have a tiny crush. Except could she call it a crush when it was her ex-husband?

Admitting she still had those kinds of physical reactions didn't prevent her from knowing they'd separated for good reasons.

She cleared her throat and tried to change the subject. "How about this tuxedo cat?" she asked holding up the screen. "His name is James Bond, but we wouldn't have to keep it."

"It's just everyone wants to know why it happened," Julia burst out.

"Everyone?"

"Everyone in the family. You know how they are."

She did. But it didn't stop her from narrowing her eyes. "Don't put this on all the relatives."

"What do you mean?"

"They aren't here. You haven't texted at all this afternoon. This is you. You are really pushing some sort of reconciliation hard. I want to know why."

Julia appeared as though she were about to argue. It came naturally to her. But then her head dropped. "I don't even really know. Because all of this happened to you and Simon when I was a kid, and I feel left out of the discussion like I don't know something important. Because he's cute and you're cute, and you're both single. That's what we're supposed to do, isn't it? I know I sound like all of the aunties and uncles when I push you together. They all have this black and white idea of what it's like, not marriage itself but staying. But I also know it's more complicated than that—you keep saying. Maybe I want to know why love doesn't work out, or that it does. Maybe I want that story."

Lana put down her phone. She sat at the table and started helping Julia peel fruit. She had to stop thinking about Julia as her baby cousin.

"Are you interested in someone?" Lana asked carefully.

"I had a thing with a classmate in law school," Julia said. "We even lived together for a while. I didn't tell Dad. He wouldn't have approved. You know how they are."

Lana thought of her churchy older relatives and nodded.

"We ended it because school is hard, and we didn't know where we'd end up going. But I think I told myself we'd get together again after we had our careers a little more mapped out. I dated and all. I got over it, except maybe I didn't because now he's engaged, and all I have is this hard pastry disc and a pile of unpeeled pears I'm supposed to make into a pie."

"Oh, honey."

"I'm fine. At least I'm not over thirty and alone."

Lana very carefully put the knife she'd been using down so that she didn't accidentally commit the terrible crime of infanticide.

Julia, blissfully unaware of her tactlessness, added, "It's so hard to meet people when all I do is work. Which is why I'm making this pie. To take to church on a Christmas Eve."

"For all the hot religious singles?"

"Something like that. It's not that I'm competing with the ex. I want to feel like I have something of my own going on."

Lana nodded.

She picked up the knife again. "I was floundering back then when I was your age. Simon knew exactly what he wanted to do, and I wasn't quite as sure. Not only that, everyone else was there for him. There aren't as many men studying to be music teachers, or there weren't when I was in school. They tended to stand out."

"Oh wait, are you saying all these people fawned over him?"

"Some people did. People tended to smooth the path for him."

"Did you catch his attention by being the person who didn't giggle and swoon? Was that why he noticed you?"

"No. I was wild about Simon from the first. But even the people who were cooler toward him, they listened to him. The department administrators laughed at all of his jokes no matter how corny, and people tended to be quiet when he spoke up. He wasn't a jerk about it. He didn't talk over people. But it was easier for him to be heard. That's a measure of his personality, too. He's single-minded when he wants something. But also I think the two go together. It's easier for people to pay attention to him, and it makes it easier for him to talk to them. I mean, I worked hard but even my own supervisors seemed to praise Simon to me when it came time to evaluate *my* work. It made me feel…"

"Invisible."

"Yeah. It's funny, because now it's pretty clear that being a music educator wasn't what I wanted to do with my life. But Simon was convinced I was good. The more he tried to put me forward and encourage me, the more painful the whole program became. I don't know how to explain without sounding like I'm jealous, even though it wasn't what I wanted to do, even though it wasn't for me. Maybe I was, a little. Or maybe a lot. It's sort of like you said, it wasn't that I was competing with him. It was a tough position for both of us. This is so much easier to understand now. At the time, the only thing I felt was like I had to get out of that tiny apartment, out of that life, because I was all wrong. I couldn't figure out how to right myself while I was there."

"Please, I get it. It's starting to sound like law school. Or, like, real life."

"Well, yeah. It's not like professional kitchens are less sexist. But I'm not married to another chef, so my life is slightly less complicated in that way at least."

They were quiet for a couple of minutes, both probably remembering their own stories.

She *had* been jealous. She could admit it to herself now. She'd envied her own husband, his skill, but even more, his assurance. He knew what he wanted. He didn't have doubts. She'd held that helpless lump of fury about him even as she'd been proud of him. Now it was easier to articulate those feelings, now that she wasn't married to him or in that apartment sleeping next to him. She didn't have to convince herself to rise from a bed she shared with him anymore, and go out and face another day with increasing dread. But it felt different saying it to another person. Maybe she'd have cared less if she'd been happier with her own work at the time. But because their lives had been mixed in that particular way, there was almost no path to untangle herself from the accumulated hurts and insecurity without letting go of him.

"Sounds like you made the right decision for you at the time."

"I think so." Lana was surprised by Julia's support. She blinked away the sudden and completely unnecessary tears. "No one has ever told me that."

"Did you ever explain it to anyone else?"

"A couple of years ago, I talked a little to my dad after he'd brought what up Simon was up to for the umpteenth time."

"You picked the worst person to try to tell."

"Well, I chose better this time."

Julia smiled briefly. Then she looked at the mess of fruit in the bowl in front of her. "Ugh. I'm not going to get to the church dinner in time," she said.

"I'll finish and bake it off while you get ready."

"Thank you, thank you! I knew I could count on you!"

Lana sighed and preheated the oven. She made the streusel topping and piled it onto the pears and cranberries. Julia was singing "Silent Night" loudly and making herself beautiful. Lana had no doubt her cousin would bounce back from her sadness; in a way, it seemed she already had.

As for Lana, she'd get over her temporary crush on her ex. After all, she'd done it before. She could do it again.

Chapter Six

January

The cat had arrived three days ago. But, like all of Simon's roommates, it seemed she was too skittish to come out of hiding. The cat was a little messier than Lana. The tabby left trails of grit from the litterbox in the bathroom, and slopped water on the kitchen floor. Simon didn't mind, though. In truth, he was more curious about the cat than the cat seemed about him.

"At least she's eating," he observed.

"She seemed so friendly and outgoing at the shelter," Lana said, bending to wipe up bits of cat food with a paper towel.

"Give it time."

Simon watched her from his side of the counter. She seemed tired and anxious. He felt slightly and irrationally annoyed with the cat for worrying Lana, but telling Lana wouldn't exactly help, so he tried to inject some joviality into his voice. "Maybe she's still getting used to these grand surroundings."

Lana washed her hands. She did that a lot these days. She kept a basil-scented lotion beside the bathroom and kitchen sinks, and he had to admit he loved the scent of it.

Oh God, he was not going to start perving on his ex-wife briskly rubbing lotion into her hands.

"I think she's interested in the piano. Or the sound. A couple of times, I've been working and she'd sneak out to listen."

Lana didn't even look at the Steinway or at him. "Maybe a really smelly treat. One of those fishy tube things. I could pick one up at the pet store."

He thought about this for a moment. If she could ignore his words, he could ignore hers. He went over to the piano and opened the lid. He realized he hadn't played in front of Lana in years. For some reason, he avoided music when she was around, and clearly so did she.

He pressed a couple of chords, soft and easy, the piano's tone shimmering tautly in the air. Then he dipped his fingers into one of the songs the chorus would be singing in their next concert, a melody that was probably unfamiliar to Lana, something new. And as he played, he could feel it working. He could feel her creeping closer, the warmth of her presence moving toward him like the sun in the morning. Except it was never the sun that moved, was it? He sounded the deep resonant notes of the bridge, pulling her closer, but the tune was almost done, the final chorus already rolling through under his fingers. Then it was over as quietly as it began.

He stayed very still.

A scrabble of claws told him the cat had come out, if only for a moment. And when Lana spoke, her voice was quiet and low. Nearby. "Well, I guess your music worked."

"I'll try and play more to lure her out from wherever she is."

More distantly, "You don't have to do that."

He looked up again, but she had moved to the hallway and was smoothing her hair back. He loved watching her run through her set of checks and measures before she left for work, the way she pulled back her hair into its shiny, black braid, the way she stared intently and dispassionately at her face before she checked her bag. Keys, wallet, phone, water. He could almost hear her going through her list. Next came the first scarf, a wisp of a thing that she wound around her neck. He always wanted to reach out and help her with that one, to touch it, to feel it grow warm under his fingers. Next came her boots, and he admired each leg as she turned them and zipped them matter-of-factly, then the soft marshmallow of a jacket, the slouchy hat, the second woollier scarf, which, depending on the weather, she knotted or tied around her nose. Finally, a pair of soft leather gloves that he had handed her once or twice.

Then came the slightly awkward part. Because he was so often near the door when she was leaving, because he frequently made up an excuse to linger near the hallway, there was the goodbye. If she was in a hurry, she called out a soft farewell, and scampered out the door and down the stairs. If she seemed to be feeling shy, she quirked up her lips and waved, and it was both the most adorable and least satisfying of the iterations. If he managed to look a little busy at her departure, she'd touch his arm, his bare wrist. Sometimes he held the door open for her, as a courtesy, of course. Sometimes he watched her walk away, her head and shoulders disappearing as she went down each step. The downstairs neighbor had caught him staring after Lana once, and now Mrs. Pierre's eyes twinkled at Simon whenever they ran into each other.

More embarrassing things had happened to him in his life. Probably.

But today he stayed at the piano bench. He watched Lana go down, heard the heavy door slam. He wondered briefly what the hell he was doing, playing for her, trying to seduce her like a goddamn siren.

He got up and opened and shut the door more firmly, locked it. Right. Time to get down to business. If he worked, he wouldn't think about Lana. This was the perfect time to make progress on his damn book. He'd already told himself he wasn't going to go out today. He wasn't allowed to read, or listen to any music, or clean the cabinets until he'd organized his notes, and finished writing the chapter he'd been working on for the last week.

Simon settled himself at the small table near the kitchen, his laptop in order, his coffee in front of him in his favorite mug, his noise-canceling headphones at the ready, not that he needed them in this apartment. He'd even opened his document.

He took a congratulatory swallow of caffeine.

His phone trilled at him, and he leapt for it. It was his sister. He couldn't exactly ignore his sister. She never called during the day.

But it wasn't Maxine's face who appeared on his screen. It was his youngest niece, Ronnie.

"We're on winter break until tomorrow. Mum says

I should talk to you because she needs just one single minute to herself," she said by way of greeting.

Ronnie was a solemn-looking child with glasses, whose placid facade hid a swirling mass of pure, anarchic energy. Currently, this energy seemed to be concentrated on adjusting and readjusting the position of the phone.

"Are you having a good vacation?" Simon asked the blur.

He propped his own device against a stack of books, grabbed his coffee, and leaned back, settling in for a long chat.

"It's okay. I read thirty-three books so far, and we went sledding and skating."

"Thirty-three. That's a lot."

"It is."

"Are you a good skater?"

"I'm very good. I'm better than Mum. She likes to sit on the bench and watch me."

"I'll bet."

Ronnie launched into a story about a raccoon that had gotten into their garbage bins, and was telling Simon about how she was going to have baby raccoons as pets when she stopped and yelped, "It's a kitty! You have a kitty."

Simon turned very slowly. The cat was crouched behind him. When she saw his face, though, she streaked under the couch.

He turned back to his niece. "She's very shy. Maybe if you sing her a song, she'll come out."

Ronnie wasn't about to be fooled into a performance. "What's her name?"

"I don't think Lana has given her a name yet."

"Lana. That's my aunt, isn't it?"

Simon didn't know. Had she ceased to be their aunt when she and Simon divorced? Ronnie hadn't even been born yet when they split. It seemed oddly heartless to tell this to his niece. At the same time, it probably wasn't healthy for Lana to keep the aunt title.

Was it any healthier to hang around the door in hopes his ex might pay attention to him as she got ready for work?

While Simon puzzled this over, Ronnie had moved on. "The kitty's name is Muffin," Ronnie said confidently.

"I don't know—"

"She looks like a Muffin."

"You only saw her streak by. You didn't get a good look."

"She's brown like a muffin. When she curls up she's going to look like one."

"She might be what they call a tabby cat. So, she's actually—"

Ronnie stared at him.

He was mansplaining to a seven-year-old, and she'd called him on it.

"I'll see what Lana thinks of the name," he sighed.

Chapter Seven

It started out as an ordinary day. By the time Lana had risen, Simon was already out and the cat had been fed. Muffin, which was what Simon had reluctantly told her his niece had suggested calling the tabby, had gotten bolder as the week wore on. Bold enough that when Lana came home last night, she found the arm of the new couch scratched up and streaks of claw marks down the curtains of her bedroom. The cat had gotten into her closet and torn up one of Lana's old sneakers. And she'd knocked several books down from the chair Lana kept beside the bed.

Lana picked up the novels, threw out the shoes, covered the couch arm with a blanket, and hoped fervently that Muffin hadn't gotten into Simon's room.

Now, the cat was still in hiding. Lana made and drank her chard and mango smoothie. It was a cardio day, so she went for a run down Malcolm X Boulevard and along the top edge of Central Park. On the cold, half empty playground, she went through a series of stretches and resistance exercises that helped her arms and wrists and core for the night ahead. Years ago, she'd consulted a physiotherapist to help her deal with the strains and possible repetitive injuries that came from tossing and twisting pounds and pounds of dough around every night; she'd been careful about going through her routine ever since. Her roommates at the time had called her dedication to it her Olympic training.

If only they could see her now, she thought, giving herself a good stretch on the dome-shaped climber. She grimaced slightly, feeling a twang—several twangs, a banjo chorus, really—somewhere near her midsection.

The exercises were supposed to make her feel better for her work. But more and more lately, even the warmups themselves were exhausting her to the point where the idea of going in to work all night made her tired.

She thunked her head against the cold bar of the playground climber and breathed in deeply. She had been officially working at Lore for three months. A month left before she was assured of a more permanent position, a month left before she could sign up for insurance and maybe go see a PT again.

She jogged slowly back up the wide, spare expanse of Malcolm X, turning onto the tree-lined street. By the time she'd made it up the stairs, she was holding her side, and she probably looked like a swaybacked farm animal.

She stood a moment in the hallway trying to catch her breath.

"You never used to exercise."

Lana jumped. Or she would have if that hadn't required using her limbs. She hadn't seen Simon coming up behind her.

Half of her braid was probably sticking right up from the wind. The smaller tendrils were plastered to her head with sweat, the heat of the apartment mingling with the lingering cold of the outdoors to create streams of moisture running down her red cheeks.

"We could go running together," Simon added before she could say anything.

The cat peered from behind Simon's ankles. Muffin seemed to prefer him. Catching a glimpse of herself in the hallway mirror confirming her suspicions about her hair and face, Lana could understand why.

She shook her head, partly to dismiss those thoughts—why did she care what Simon thought of her looks?—and partly to put him off the idea of them being running buddies. "I don't know about the exercising together. I wouldn't want to disrupt your routine."

He'd been a runner since high school and in his forties he was still built like a fucking gazelle. There was no way she'd be able to keep up with his pace. She'd barely made it home.

Of course, some days were better than others. Today was…not a better day.

She bent down slowly to pet the cat, who sniffed at her curiously, accepted a couple of scritches before hissing, and darting away.

"Of course," Simon said, stepping back, his face in shadow again.

Leaving, like the cat.

Maybe she'd hurt his feelings, putting him off. But he liked running alone, he'd told her long ago. He liked the opportunity to get his thoughts in order, to have the wind rushing past his ears. Simon had made running sound exhilarating. Just like he'd made school sound fascinating, and the kids and other people seem endlessly good.

But these things came easy to him. Maybe that's why her experience of it never matched his.

She could call him back to explain, but she wasn't here to get close to him again. She went and took a hot shower, letting the water revive her somewhat. When she was dressed and neat again, she came out to check Muffin's food bowls and put on her jacket.

Simon really had disappeared.

She sighed. She'd gotten used to him seeing her off. It was probably the wrong thing for her to enjoy. But it seemed like such a tiny, harmless pleasure to have him hand her scarves, hats, to have him hold open the door. In those moments, it was as if she knew she could—she would—come back to someone who cared about her.

She trudged down the stairs, back out into the cold, and to the subway station, not paying attention to the audiobook she'd downloaded for her commute. Once at work, she greeted her coworkers, and got herself ready for the long evening ahead.

She felt off.

Who knew what it was. Maybe it was the fact that Simon hadn't said goodbye. Her mouth twisted ruefully as she thought about how she'd been irritated by his routines when they were married, and how she now had her own.

Talia came by her station. "We're down a few prep cooks and we're already behind. Can you pitch in?"

Lana nodded. In a few minutes, she was coring, quartering, and chiffonading napa cabbage.

The atmosphere was tense. At least four people were out with what was probably the flu, although no one liked to speak out loud about illness in the kitchen. The front of the house was set to open in two hours. Out back amongst the prep cooks, it wasn't exactly quiet; the ventilation fans roared and pots clashed. Knives chopped frantically. But even the cursing was down to choked-off mutters.

Lana cleaned off her board and started on the next batch.

"Did you do any formal training, Lana?" Talia asked, sidling up.

"In Singapore for a little while. But most of my learning comes from working."

"I'd love to do that," Yara, one of the other cooks, said. "Travel and cook my way through places."

They were keeping their voices quiet. "It was good for me in a lot of ways, but it wasn't glamorous. And the credentials don't translate as well as you'd think, especially when you're a woman and not white."

All three of them grimaced.

Yara muttered almost to herself, "This is my first gig out of culinary school."

"And it's a big one," Lana reassured her.

"Yeah, I don't want to mess it up. But at the same time." Yara lowered her head so her nose was almost touching the counter. "It would be nice to be able to travel and learn more."

"You're better off staying here longer and getting job experience that looks good on paper," Talia murmured. "Having the health insurance you can't use because you can't ever take time off to go to doctor's appointments and then getting fired if you really do get sick."

"They aren't really going to fire those guys, are they?"

"Shhh." Talia looked around. She lowered her voice

more. "They might try, depending on how long they're out."

Lana kept chopping grimly.

"Well, I got my—" Yara glanced around "—my F-L-U shot, so I should be okay."

"I did, too," Lana whispered.

She'd paid fifty dollars out of pocket for one. No use taking chances.

They managed to get through 'til about 8:00 without too many disasters. Luckily it was a slow night. But by 10:15, as Lana was finishing up a last batch of noodles to be cooked, she started feeling a familiar cramping.

"Oh, no, no," she said through gritted teeth, as she did a quick mental calculation.

She should have started taking painkillers yesterday, just in case. But with the cat, and her new place, she'd been distracted.

She fanned the noodles with a grimace, and managed to cut them before bringing them over to Talia. "Can you take over? I need a minute."

Talia eyed her, but gave a terse nod.

A moment later, Lana hobbled to the employee bathroom. The nausea was getting worse. She dialed Julia, who didn't pick up. Then she called Simon. "Can you please come get me?" was the last thing she remembered saying before the pain rolled over her and she passed out.

Someone had wrapped her in her jacket and scarves and propped her in a metal folding chair before Simon arrived. "Just get her out of here," a bulldoggish white man in a chef's coat muttered.

Simon knelt to take her hand. He glared up at the man.

"It's not the flu," Lana breathed, her eyes closed.

She looked gray, in sharp contrast to earlier today when she'd come in flushed and breathless from her run.

"It's endometriosis," she said in a louder tone.

Chef Asshole reared his head back, but the tall Black woman, Talia she'd said her name was, snapped, "It's not catching. You don't have to worry that we've made customers sick."

"Is it some kind of cancer, then?"

Talia rolled her eyes. "No."

She strode out saying, "Do I look like Google?" as Chef Asshole followed, still asking questions.

"I'm so sorry," Lana whimpered as Simon helped her get up.

"It's all right. You'll be all right," Simon told her.

He didn't know that. He took one moment to put his face in her hair, and then went through the checklist of all her things he seemed to already know so well: the scarves tied the way she liked them, one on the inside, one on the outside, the jacket, the hat over her ears, the bag, the gloves. He peeked in her purse to make sure she had her keys, wallet, and phone. Then, half carrying her, he bundled her out to the waiting car.

"I'm sorry," she whispered again, and he wanted her to stop. The last time she'd apologized so much was when she'd told him she'd decided to leave New York. She'd told him she knew his life was here, but she couldn't stay. She asked him to come with her, but he'd been too angry and hurt that she hadn't wanted their life, that she could think he could give up everything he wanted for some whim of hers, that he wasn't enough to hold her there.

But he didn't know what was making her sick now, and he didn't want anything terrible to happen to her. He didn't want her to leave. So the whole ride back, he held her. He kept her in his arms as they climbed up the darkened West Side Highway, even as they slowed to a crawl on 110th Street and the driver murmured into his headset, and the cab grew too warm. Every time his body complained about how hot it was, Simon tightened his hold on her against the thought. When they finally turned onto their street, he reluctantly let go. He tipped the driver generously, checked again to make sure they had all of Lana's things, and the two of them slumped slowly up the familiar and welcome steps. Back home. Home where they belonged.

Lana got her things off and stumbled to the bathroom as soon as they came up the stairs, and she stayed in there for such a long time that Simon wondered if he should go in. He took off his shoes and coat. He was in the T-shirt and sweatpants which he'd donned hastily before running out the door. The cat rubbed herself against Simon's legs and then, in a perverse moment of camaraderie toward Lana, chose to wait by the door behind which her dear rescuer had hidden herself.

The cat mewed, a rusty, breathy croak that would have been amusing if Simon weren't so tense.

"I know how you feel," Simon muttered.

He took out his phone and tried to search the thing Lana said she had. But in truth, he couldn't remember the term. The only part he recalled was "not catching" and "not cancer."

That left a lot of other ailments.

He heard the door of the washer-dryer slam and Lana exited the bathroom a few minutes later, wrapped in a towel even though she hadn't taken a shower, and then padded to her room.

It had only been a glimpse. The white bath sheet, her hair loose, her bare shoulders, and Simon felt everything roil through him: relief she was all right, fear she wasn't really, lust, disgust with himself at his lust, and finally grief, overwhelming, almost incomprehensible. Why grief, of all things?

He stared at her door for a couple of minutes more, then took a deep breath. He walked the ten steps through the hall and knocked. She made a sound and that was enough for him. He opened the door and peered inside, almost afraid of what he'd find.

A nightlight glowed softly and Lana huddled in the bed, covers pulled around her ear as if she couldn't get warm enough. The towel lay neatly folded on the chair. "Lana," he whispered. It was still too loud. "Are you going to be all right?"

She nodded and seemed to shiver. How could she be cold in this warm room?

"Are you sure you don't have a fever?"

He came closer.

"It's endometriosis," she said. "Let's just say I recognize the symptoms—in me, at least. It's not always this bad."

Her voice was fading, and he didn't know what to do with the new fear sweeping him. He knelt down. The bed was a low platform. To be sure, he checked her face for assent and laid his hand on her forehead. Not feverish, not at all.

"You're cold."

"It's like this sometimes."

She reached her own hand to where his fingers rested

gently on the covers. For a few minutes, they were both still, both watching those places where her skin touched his. Then she drew his arm in underneath. She pulled him as she turned, until he was under the blankets with her, his chest against her pajama-clad back, his legs twined with hers.

He let out a long, shuddering breath and pulled her closer to him. It was never close enough. In a few minutes, her trembling stopped. Her breath deepened. She was asleep.

He told himself he was afraid of waking her in order to justify not slipping out of her bed. But that didn't explain why he smoothed her hair and pressed his lips to it before closing his own eyes.

Chapter Eight

Lana woke up early in the morning with an unexpected companion in her bed. Muffin, the cat, was sprawled in the center, taking up more room than a creature that size should be able to occupy. Lana had been pushed almost to the edge of the mattress, her fingers clutched around the duvet as if to save herself from falling onto the floor. She tried to ease her way back into her own bed, but the cat was immovable.

"Now is when you decide you like being around me?"

Like was perhaps too strong a word. The cat gave Lana an indifferent stare and stretched her limbs wider until Lana was almost over the edge.

"I thought pets could sense when their people were sick and try to comfort them instead of kicking them out of bed."

Muffin closed her eyes and Lana sighed. She wasn't about to get any consolation from that quarter. Worse, the events of yesterday had started coming back in sharp, humiliating flashes.

Lana sat up and rubbed her face. On the chair beside her bed sat a tray holding a glass of water, a plate of saltines, and a selection of Motrin, Pamprin, and

Midol. In the bed, beside the cat, was what looked like a brand-new hot-water bottle.

Fucking Simon, that fucker.

He must have risen from her bed, the one she'd dragged him into, and gone to an all-night pharmacy.

She was *not* going to cry.

A knock sounded, and Lana muttered an oath. It was loud enough for Simon to take it as agreement to come in. He came up to her and knelt beside her. "You're not okay. Go back to bed."

"I'm fine," she said, squeezing her eyes shut.

"You're crying."

"I'm not in pain. It's more…"

It was because of everything. Because she'd fainted at work, and because she might lose her job. Because she'd had to call her ex-husband after trying to establish distance, because she seemed to need him. Because he'd been kind to her.

The image of the array of medicines stayed in her mind no matter how tightly she kept her eyes closed.

"Are these like those cramps you used to get, you know, before?"

Before. When they were married.

"Yes. I got a diagnosis of endometriosis a couple of years ago when it started getting worse."

"When you started passing out."

Something about his flat tone made her eyes snap open. She felt oddly defensive.

"It doesn't happen every time. So much nausea and pain, I mean. They usually prescribe a hormonal IUD to keep it under control, but I didn't react well to that. So I take the pill, and I use an app to track my period to make sure I dose myself with painkillers before. But last month with the moving and the holidays I didn't keep up, and I've been so busy I probably forgot."

She stopped talking. She didn't want to tell him about the ways she couldn't seem to care for herself. It had taken her a long time to feel competent, equal to her job, to any job, really. And now, in front of so many people, she'd collapsed.

He stood up again and rubbed his face. For some reason, his small gesture of weariness made her feel a bit better. But when she started to get up, too, he held his hand out, almost as if to push her down, but not quite touching her shoulder.

"I'm sorry," he said, perhaps realizing he'd gone too far.

"I need to use the bathroom."

When she came back, she saw he'd sat on the floor next to the bed, his head on his knees. It was still early and he probably hadn't gotten much sleep last night. She sat down next to him.

"I'm doing this all wrong," he said without raising his face.

"No. It's not that. You're—" she gestured at the tray, at him, not that he could see it "—you're perfect. As usual. You didn't have to come for me last night."

He snorted. She winced over how dramatic the whole thing must have been. "Well, you didn't have to do the rest. You didn't have to get me this medicine or come in and check up on me or—or hold me."

She added, "I'm sorry about making you sleep here."

"I wish you wouldn't apologize. I…wanted to. I held you in the car, too."

The tiredness and worry, and yes, affection seeped

out of the edges of his voice, there to be heard by anyone who was listening for it.

She shouldn't have heard it.

She nudged him with her knee. It was supposed to be a friendly touch, casual, to tell him she was okay, that he should go easy on himself. But it was too affectionate, too intimate. Her pajama-clad leg sliding briefly against his reminded her of how familiar she'd been with his limbs long ago, how she'd sometimes started with his calf, twined her leg with his until the rest of her body followed. She'd done some of that last night.

Lana jerked back.

She had her period. She had dark circles under her eyes and while she didn't have the cramps anymore, her insides felt tender. She was in her uniform-like nightwear. There was nothing sexy about the situation.

As if to confirm her thoughts, Simon started to get up. "You're probably hungry. Let me bring you something."

"I can make my own breakfast."

"Please, just let me."

Lana took a deep breath. "Thank you. But can I at least come into the kitchen? I'd feel weird eating in here by myself."

He nodded and offered his hand to help her up.

She took it.

They had never really eaten together in their time as roommates, Simon realized.

But he was hungry, too. It had been a long night.

He got butter out of the fridge and cracked some eggs a little self-consciously. His ex-wife was a chef and could definitely make fancier things than he could.

But this wasn't the time to wish for a demonstration. He pulled out a few tomatoes and sliced them, put some bread in the toaster.

The cat came out from Lana's bedroom and weaved around his legs. "I already fed you. There's food in your bowl," he said, trying to get to the stove.

The cat yelled, first piteously, then angrily when she realized her demands were going to be ignored.

Lana laughed, and he couldn't help it. His heart leapt.

He'd always loved her laugh. Big, bigger than her, it started down low and opened into a wide sound. Sometimes, when he wanted his students to sing loud and happy, he tried to laugh like that for them.

Out of the corner of his eye, he watched Lana, who was leaning down to coax Muffin to come to her. Her hair was loose and messy, but he could see the clear line of her neck, her soft jaw, her ear.

He loved that ear.

His eyes jerked back to the stove. No ears. No jaws, no delicate skin, no collarbones just visible beyond the points of her neckline, no hips, or legs, or bare feet.

Eggs. Eyes on the eggs.

The pan was a mess of streaky curled layers. He scraped the bottom. "It's not the best. I always leave more egg in the pan than we get to eat," he said apologetically.

"Eggs and toast with butter are always the best."

She'd poured him a cup of coffee and added just the right amount of milk, and he didn't—he shouldn't—say, *You remembered*. But he was thinking it.

They ate their eggs and toast and slices of tomato side by side in silence. It wasn't exactly comfortable but he wasn't unhappy. She was recovering and he'd slept badly, although again, not unhappily, beside her.

This was the whole problem. It would have been easy to simply let himself go there. To tease her into smiling. To let his elbow touch hers when he picked up his mug. To forget all the painful things that were in the past and think only of the present. And it would be easier if he didn't know she was struggling against the same temptation.

That was the problem with knowing someone so well, even if it had been a long time ago, even if she had changed.

So now, he was aware that she was glancing at him from the corner of her eye. He was gloriously alive to every quiet swallow, every word she didn't say. They both got up to take each other's plates.

"I can do the dishes. You cooked."

"You're ill."

"I feel fine. It's just washing up."

They feinted left then right, both trying to be considerate, both trying to get to the sink, to not impose, to be good.

They stopped. Lana still hadn't looked up. "This is silly," she said. "We can both do them. You wash, I'll dry."

"Fine. Yes. Good."

They stood side by side as he conscientiously rinsed off the plates and silverware and soaped everything up. He didn't know why he was being so careful. He handed off dishes to her, she moved off to put everything away, taking, it seemed, equal care to make as little noise as she could. At one point, their wet fingers met, and she jumped back.

In a small corner of his mind, it pleased him that she was skittish, because it signaled that their contact meant something to her.

"The thing about endometriosis," she said, clearing her throat, "it means I probably couldn't have had kids very easily."

He picked up the pan he'd used to cook the eggs. It was a mess. He was completely unprepared for this.

He ran hot water over it and squeezed dish soap into it and looked at the bubbles rising.

When they were married, of course he'd wanted children. He was a teacher. He never questioned that he wouldn't have them. Except here he was, forty-four years old and he hadn't had kids and, although he hadn't really thought about it lately, being a parent didn't matter to him that much. The only person he ever considered being a parent with was beside him, but not with him. Right now the absence of Lana seemed more important than those hypothetical lives he'd assumed he would nurture long ago. "Why are you telling me this right now?"

"I need to remind myself why it would never have worked out."

"I don't need to have kids," he said, abruptly shutting off the water.

Let the pan soak.

She scoffed. "Really? You."

"I've taught a lot of people by now. I have nieces and nephews and they are…a lot."

"And this is enough for you? You're still plenty young enough to go out and father some children."

"As appealing as you make it sound, I think I'll stick with what I've got."

"You've changed," she said slowly.

"Of course, I've changed. You've changed. Why are you the only one who gets to do that?"

"Well, you didn't have to. You're still in the life you envisioned for yourself."

"I'm in the career. I fulfilled some of the ambitions—"

"Most of them."

"Some. I am doing those things, and sometimes I love it, and sometimes I go through the motions. But as for that whole life, well, you altered it. You, Lana."

"You mean I ruined that part of the plan by leaving."

"No. Yes. It's not that. I shouldn't have said it that way. It's more that at the end of it all, when it was really over—really over—like the anger and the hurt and the numbness, when it was more or less over, I was a different person. And it wasn't about categorically declaring things like, *I will never trust again.* Although I'm sure I did it. I became more cautious. About wanting things."

"Oh, Simon."

"Don't say it that way."

He stopped, then started again. "Maybe it was good for me. No, I know it was good for me to learn that I couldn't always get everything I wanted my way. It was good, but still painful."

Lana gave a short laugh. Her eyes came up briefly to meet his and his heart gave another painful thump. "You don't have to make a lesson out of everything."

He moved closer. His fingertips were inches from hers, resting lightly on the kitchen counter. "Sometimes I wake up and I can't believe you're here, in the same city, under the same roof, not a hundred feet away. You're not the way I remember in some ways, and the same in others. We're both in a different place. It's confusing. Because I still like you. I still want to be around you. It isn't at all what I thought it would be like to live with you again. I can't even say that it's worse or better than before, because what it's like now seems to swamp and erase all the memories of what it used to be. I'll recall specific incidents, but it's like watching two different people act out some words that I already know. So yeah, despite resisting it, I've changed. Are you so surprised?"

She raised her head finally and closed those remaining inches. "I like being surprised."

A moment. A flicker. The air seemed to grow heavier between them.

He slid his fingers carefully over hers as she rose on her tiptoes. There was a short, sweet breath of a pause between them, and his lips were on hers, her hand came up to rest lightly on his shoulder.

At first it was as if they were simply exploring being close again, feeling each other, the texture of skin and lips. It wasn't better or worse than he recalled; it was another thing entirely. His memory would never have supplied him with the glory of the sudden tightening of her fingers on his shoulders as she pulled him down closer. He'd never have remembered the slight breath she took as she swayed into him, her body tensed and stretched, overbalanced but not wanting to put her weight on him.

His other hand had traveled up the intriguing strength of her arm, mapping dips and cuts of muscle that spoke of years of discipline and dedication. He moved up and around, and his fingertips traced the architecture of her shoulder blade. When had she become all of this? His mind was still marveling over her even as his body kept him from thinking too clearly.

Then her mouth opened wider and she grunted, drawing a breath before returning to him with more intensity. At the feeling of her teeth grazing his bottom lip all he felt was want, helpless and overwhelming. He wanted to pull her closer to him, to let her fall into him, to feel her body against his. She licked him gently and the curl of her tongue made him never want to let go.

But though she gave her mouth to him, her cheek rubbing softly against his, she didn't pull him closer, and the thought of her restraint was enough to keep him to his own careful line. In another moment, she took one more breath, and he seized the opportunity to kiss his way up to the fine skin at her temple, to bury his nose in her hair. A sigh. A blink. He reluctantly stopped and pressed his forehead against hers.

She exhaled long and deep, from the very bottom of her, and he felt it vibrate through him. Her hands were still touching him, caressing him, not quite letting go. He could feel the desire in her, the need to be closer, the way she held back. He closed his eyes: her want was almost enough for him, almost enough to feed his greedy soul.

But not quite.

She was starting to disengage herself now. Her palms smoothing a path down his shoulders, pausing a moment to cup his biceps, her thumbs kneading his muscles in a way that made him want to seize her again. But she was stepping back, her hands moving down his arms.

And she was looking at the floor again, at their interlaced fingers.

"Are you all right?" she asked.

"That should be my question to you."

She winced a little, as if that were enough to remind

her she'd been in pain last night. He regretted his words. But he couldn't feel that way about anything else that had happened.

"I am…all right. I think this can be okay."

"Be still my beating heart."

It was supposed to be a joke, a bad one. She jerked his arm a little. "Hey. Hey. This is not easy for either of us. It is understandable if we're both feeling cautious. Even if our hormones are ready to do a lot more."

Yes. At her words, his body once again perked up even as his brain sounded a warning.

She was going to be sensible, despite her feelings. He had to be, too.

He let go of her hands, and they were facing each other. Not touching.

"We'll be talking about this," he said. "God knows, since we live together, we'll have plenty of time to talk. But for now, you've been feeling bad, and you should go lie down again."

And I am going to take a shower. A cold one.

Chapter Nine

She was forty-two years old, long divorced, and she was sitting on the floor of her bedroom listening to her ex-husband take a shower, and wondering if he was jerking off.

She squeezed her thighs together and concentrated on the ache of her cramps. She wasn't grateful for the now-dull pain. She would never go as far as that. But she needed space to think, and the gray edge of discomfort had been enough for her to want to preserve the border between her body and his. Another thing preventing her from sinking into him, another reminder of how hard she had to fight to keep herself intact, to keep herself in this place she'd worked too hard to get.

But she still wanted him. It was hard not to long for the comfort of him, of his arms around her, of the way he listened to her. She looked at the tray, still on her chair, at the medicine he'd gone out to find. She pulled the hot-water bottle out from under the duvet. It wasn't as warm or all-encompassing as him, but she clung to its rubbery form for a minute.

The shower shut off. It was easy enough to think of him, his forehead pressed against the shower tiles the same way he'd leaned on her. His hair would be dark and slick, his lashes thick with moisture, his eyes closed as he remembered, as he stroked himself, as he thought of her.

The cat bumped her knee, bringing Lana out of her reverie. The tabby probably sensed how unsettled everyone in the household was, and had finally decided it was all right to be affectionate and needy. But as Muffin settled down for pets and scritches, it seemed she was the only one getting any satisfaction.

Absently, Lana turned on her phone. She sent off a message to her boss and another to Talia telling them she'd be coming in tonight. If she still had a job.

Talia texted back saying they were shorthanded, and even though it probably spelled another tough night, Lana felt somewhat relieved. She swallowed a few pain pills, checked on her alarm, crawled back into bed, and fell asleep with the cat pressed against her side.

He was gone when she awoke at her usual workout time. She found a note saying he was at class, and he'd left her a turkey sandwich in the fridge. She found it wrapped in white deli paper, along with some fruit, several different kinds of yogurt, and various sports and vitamin drinks. She grabbed the sandwich and a banana. Why not? She'd slept without her arm braces and in the same bed with her ex-husband. She'd kissed him and kissed him. Why not go whole hog, skip the workout, eat the sandwich. It had slices of real turkey, with lettuce and tomato, mayonnaise and cheese, no mustard. The way she used to make them. He remembered.

Yes, he made it easy to slide.

At least that's what she told herself as she sat down with the sandwich.

She was still eating when the first text came from him.

"Should I pick anything up for dinner tonight?"

She considered it for a moment. Then typed back. "Going to be at work."

It didn't take long for him to call. He sounded like he was outside. "Are you sure you should be going back today?"

She breathed in deep through her nose. At least he wasn't here to see her expression. "I have to. I'm still in my trial period. I don't even know if I still have a job."

"It doesn't sound like a great one."

This wasn't the conversation she wanted to have with him. "It's a good stepping stone. And it's not like I have a lot of choices. I don't have my pick of work."

Not like he did.

Another whoosh of air and a faint crackle.

Maybe he sensed he was losing her, because he tried another tack. "I was hoping we could talk. Maybe pick up where we left off."

He'd lowered his voice. She could almost picture him, the collar of his dark, wool coat turned up, a private smile playing on his face, the intimacy of their conversation warming him against the cold wind. And this time she wished—oh, she wished—not that she was up to taking him up on everything he offered, but that he were here instead of out wherever he was, that his later was their now.

"You're trying to tempt me."

"I'm doing it because it hasn't worked."

"And it's not going to because I have to be a responsible adult."

"It's the worst."

"Sometimes it really is."

He hung up, but not before asking what time she thought she'd be home, and telling her to wear three scarves tonight, and to sit down if she needed to, and to call him if she had to leave early, and he could come pick her up and yell at her boss if she needed it.

She wished he could be there to yell. It was a tiring night, and Danny was terrible about yesterday's incident, but not *extremely* terrible because he didn't have time to really let out the full extent of his terrible, and he needed all the bodies he could get. At the end of the night, she stumbled onto the subway, sore and exhausted and almost missed her stop. The cold winds blew up the wide avenues of Malcolm X Boulevard. And when she finally got home—she thought of it as home, now—she was chilled and tired. She found Simon asleep on the couch with the lamp still on. He'd had a longer day than she had. After all, he'd brought her home last night, let her cling, gotten her medicine and the hot-water bottle, made her breakfast, and then taught his full day. She looked at him for a minute, at his long, dark lashes, his messy hair, his crumpled collar. Then she nudged him down into a more comfortable position, put a blanket over him, and turned out the light. He hardly stirred, never moving even after she'd brushed her teeth and gone through her nightly ritual with washes and serums and creams. She finally left again, reluctantly, as if hoping he'd wake up, and they could have their conversation. Or that he could at least hold her the way he had last night.

One night and she'd already gotten used to leaning on him again.

But she did have to be sensible, and she did have to

be an adult. So Lana put on her braces, got into her own bed, and she went to sleep.

Simon woke up in a terrible mood. He'd fallen asleep in his clothing and missed talking to Lana again. He'd been wanting to speak with her in person for nearly a week, but between his schedule and hers, they hadn't been able to find a moment when they were both present and conscious.

He couldn't even tell what time it was when he opened his eyes, because it was so dark in winter. He got up to go to the bathroom and on his way there, peered at the light on the microwave. Five forty-nine. Almost near his usual waking hour. Not enough time to crawl back into bed and take a decent nap. But early enough that he felt resentful at being up at all.

Lana's door was closed.

Well, what did he expect? If he was asleep on the couch when she returned, then she was too considerate to wake him, or kiss him or sit on his lap. She'd been in such pain only a few days ago, for God's sake. She needed her rest. She should never have gone back to work to begin with, and the fact that she had—the fact she'd dismissed his concern so breezily—needled him, even though he knew he was being immature.

Mouth full of toothpaste, he gazed into the mirror. He didn't usually worry too much about his looks, but he felt haggard. The highs and lows of the last week had been too much.

The rest of the day didn't go much better.

Abena pulled him aside at the end of practice and said, "What's going on with you? You've delivered your lecture about grit at least four times today."

"They need to hear it, don't they?"

"If they're listening to the same lecture from you over and over again then they're showing plenty of it."

"Concert's in less than two weeks and the second sopranos are still muddy in 'Wanting Memories.' Did anyone hear back from Monroe Webb about whether he's going to be there?"

"An extra practice was rescheduled for tomorrow. They'll work on it. And Mr. Webb is coming."

"Great. Fine. I forgot about the sectional."

"You seem more stressed than usual."

"Our grant's up for renewal. We're using a different venue for our concert. The kids need to be in top shape. We have to have our board members out in force. And I haven't been sleeping well because of Lana."

Abena raised a perfect, dark eyebrow.

"It's not the way it sounds. She was sick."

"God, I'm sorry."

Well, Lana hadn't been sick for the past few nights. Or maybe she had. He didn't know, did he? The thought that she'd been hurting and going to work all week made him angry. But he couldn't exactly tell that to his intern.

"She's fine. She always is. I'm just tired. Maybe I'll take off. You guys can handle cleanup?"

"Of course."

He started to walk home, cutting across 120th Street, down the slippery steps of Morningside Park and past the elementary school. It was still early, but the winter sun was already setting. A man pedaled past him, boom box playing Otis Redding, the singer's voice bright against the cold gloom. Simon tried to keep the sound in his head, to follow the thread of the melody home.

As he swung open the door, his neighbor was checking the mail.

"You kids, out 'til all hours."

It was six-thirty. "Hi, Mrs. Pierre."

"Where's your wife?"

"Still at work."

"Where's her job?"

"Downtown," Simon muttered vaguely.

"And she has to come back up in the cold and dark alone?"

Well, Simon had just returned in the cold and dark alone, but he saw Mrs. Pierre's point. "She's a grown woman. And she's stronger than she looks. She could probably braid my limbs like a challah."

Mrs. Pierre gave a crack of laughter. "You young people," she said as Simon started his slow climb toward his apartment.

But rather than collapse onto the couch by the time he got inside, he was jumpy. The warmth he'd craved was suddenly stifling. The cat was too wild to want to cuddle, running back and forth through the hallway for no reason Simon could understand. He watched for her progress—or lack thereof—for a while, drinking a glass of water.

He should go out.

And why not? He was still young, according to Mrs. Pierre. Single. Restless.

A man had to eat.

Before he knew it, he'd taken a shower, shaved, and changed into a clean shirt. He hopped onto the subway at 116th Street, and rode down to Chelsea.

As the hostess asked him if he had a reservation, he realized he hadn't thought this through. He wasn't down there to harass Lana. He didn't want to make her talk to him while she was working. But he was lonely for her, and he wasn't sure she felt the same way. Once, long ago, he'd been sure of her. Certain they were completely and utterly in love with each other and that they would be together forever.

That had turned out great.

"Well, since you're alone," the hostess said brightly, "we could squeeze you in at the counter."

She led him out into the loud, cavernous restaurant. Some sort of boy band K-pop was playing, while beautifully rumpled people talked loudly at each other. Servers dressed in black dodged nimbly from table to table, ferrying drinks and food. Billowing red ceiling draperies did little to reduce the noise, but at least it was all very dramatic. Simon paused for a moment to gape at the huge iron fountain in the middle of the floor and then trotted after the hostess once more.

He'd noticed none of this the last time he was here. He'd been too worried about Lana.

Simon quashed the memory. He got to the counter and slid cautiously onto one of the high-tech stools, doubtless made of some dense polymer that was also used on several space stations and was now being employed to hold his ass. The hostess handed him a black matte menu folder, which he promptly smudged with his greasy, plebeian fingers.

But his attention was diverted almost immediately by the view of the kitchens, by the sight of a station behind a line of sushi chefs, of Lana.

She was standing in her chef's whites, sleeves rolled up, arms dusted with flour. Her hair was pulled back neatly and covered by a dark kerchief, and she was holding a hank of dough, spinning and manipulating it like it was magic and elastic, not some ordinary mix of flour and water. At first, it seemed to be all one thick, smooth piece but after she doubled and stretched it several times, she paused a moment to sift it with her fingers, and it was revealed to be made up of smaller strands. She swung her dough, and lifted it to twist it together again. Another quick comb through the now even finer strands. She went through the process over and over. It was almost hypnotic. In another moment, she was handing the lengths to another white-jacketed chef to be cooked.

He started to understand where she'd gotten the muscles he'd felt when he held her the other morning when they'd kissed. His tiredness was gone. All that remained was awe. When had she learned to do *that*?

"Would you like a drink to start with, sir?" His server had been standing patiently while Simon stared.

"No, thanks," he said. "I'll just have the noodles."

Chapter Ten

Simon was waiting for her. But she didn't find out until she'd already cleaned up and was getting ready to leave.

"Is anything wrong?" she asked, hurrying to the front where the crew were vacuuming and stacking chairs.

He looked disheveled. Tired. She shook off the urge to reach up to him and touch his hair.

But as he shook his head, he took her hands and kissed them, and she knew Talia, who had followed, was probably raising one dark eyebrow at the sight.

Lana didn't care. "You should have told me you were coming. I'm all right, you know."

"No, it wasn't that. I know you can take care of yourself. It was—I wanted to see what you do."

"Oh."

She examined him more closely. At first, she'd assumed he was worried and exhausted, but a strange light was shining in his eyes when he gazed back at her.

"It was really good," he said. "I don't even know how to say it."

They stood in the way of the rest of the staff, so she pulled on her things. He helped her with the jacket and scarf, and they headed out into the crisp night. He held onto her hand as they walked to the subway and as the train squealed into the station. They stepped onto a nearly empty car.

He was still quiet, bright-eyed, watching her.

It wasn't until they reached 34th Street that she finally said, "So you ate at Lore."

"The fresh hand-pulled noodles."

The food she'd made.

She said slowly, "And you liked them."

"I loved them."

His voice was low and fervent, so intense that she could hear it even above the rumble of the subway.

She glanced down at her lap. She was still holding his hand.

"Noodles," she said. "It's such a silly sounding word. Just flour, water, salt."

"What you did with it wasn't simple. You must have spent years learning those skills. I can't even begin to understand, especially because it was you."

"What do you mean?"

"I've witnessed you do other spectacular things. I've seen you get a roomful of little kids to hush and really listen to music with you. I've watched you handle all of your rambunctious older relatives, how you switch so easily from English to Taiwanese to cajole them. I've heard you play. I remember the way you touched the keys when you performed *Gymnopédies*, the reverence with which you'd play old folk songs. I've seen you, well, when we were together in bed, I saw all of you."

His voice had dipped even lower and he had pulled her—or had she leaned?—so that his voice was close to her ear, stirring the escaped tendrils at her temple. She shifted in her seat.

"I always knew you were amazing," he continued softly. "I think young, arrogant me congratulated my-self a lot for seeing so much in you. But I feel foolish now, because I realize I didn't see half of it. I didn't see how much you work, how dedicated you can be. How, given half the chance, you can make something ordi-nary—flour, salt, water—make it move for you, trans-form it into something else entirely. I didn't see half of anything in you. It came out of left field. And I guess the thing I feel now is strange, because I feel like I don't know this whole part of you. I'm ashamed for how little I realized about you."

"Simon, this isn't—"

She was going to say that this wasn't something he could have known about her. She'd hardly known it her-self when she started out. It had taken years of appren-ticing, years of messes and lumpy, recalcitrant doughs that broke or stuck together. It had taken forearms that trembled from fatigue at night, stiff shoulders, strange but obvious dreams about being tangled in noodles and cooked in soups, to come up to this point to make it something she'd gotten used to, to make noodle-mak-ing part of her muscle memory.

She didn't feel like a different person, because she'd been there the whole way, but she *was* different now. And so few people who'd known her for a long time seemed to be able to understand it—to *see* it. And Simon, in a way the last person she'd ever expected to want or acknowledge that, could. He did.

He was amazed by her.

She felt amazing.

She turned her head toward him and kissed him.

She kissed him as they traveled uptown, under the

too-bright lights of the rattling, rumbling 2 train, her hands stealing up past the thick collar of this coat, to his warm neck, to his hair.

"We're disgracing ourselves," Simon murmured, even as he nipped her earlobe and his fingers found the zip of her jacket and pulled it down. "Making out on the train, like teenagers."

He watched the progress of the zipper avidly, as if it would reveal more than her scarf, her sweater, more layers and layers of clothing, as if he could see down to her skin. Then he tipped his tongue up to catch her again in a lush kiss.

She pushed her breast, or the area of her clothing that covered it, shamelessly into his hand, and he gave a muffled gasp that only made her wilder. The train seat felt too smooth and unsatisfying against her restless thighs.

Every stop on the walk home was marked by where they paused to kiss, where Simon pushed her up against a wall, and she ground her hips against his. A car slowed once and honked while they were pressed on the brick beside a beauty salon. Its headlights illuminated their desperate bodies, causing Lana to bury her head in the front of Simon's coat. Simon laughed softly, an edge of incredulity in the sound.

"We should get back."

"Yes."

They hurried now, swinging around the corner and down the block, through the gate and up, up the stairs, the thumping of their footsteps loud and urgent. Lana couldn't help blushing at how impatient their running sounded. She and Simon burst in the door and into their dark hallway. Before the door fully closed, they'd fallen on each other, tripping in their haste to kick off shoes and unzip and unbutton each other, to unwind. It was as if they expected someone would stop them, someone wise and mature who'd tell them to think this through. But of course, they were the adults here, they were the ones in charge.

The fact that this was a bad idea only made Lana want it more.

She groaned.

Simon stopped unwinding her scarf and dropped his hands, panting. "Are you okay? Are you feeling all right? I should have asked first. We should slow down, maybe talk."

Talk, now?

But he'd turned around and hung up her scarf. He was trying to get a grip on himself, and maybe that was what got to her again. Or maybe it was his erection, which when he faced her, pulled insistently against the line of his jeans under the thick fabric.

She wanted it.

Lana hooked her hand around his waistband and it was his turn to moan. He fought her with difficulty, the drag of her arm reeling him in until he was so close to her. She fumbled with his button, with the zipper. When she looked up again, he was watching her hand intently.

"I don't want to talk about anything except whose room we should go to."

"Mine," he choked. "I have a bigger bed."

She reached into his pants and squeezed him. They stumbled awkwardly toward the bedroom.

Simon's bed was occupied. The cat yowled as soon as they fell on top of it—and who could blame her?—but instead of giving them space, the tabby hissed and dug in. Lana scrambled off the mattress and fell on her ass beside the bed. She looked stunned and outraged and messy. She wasn't wearing a shirt, and the straps of her pink bra had fallen so that the cups were opening like the petals of an overbloomed flower. She was the most beautiful thing Simon had ever seen, and he dropped to his knees and pulled her down the rest of the way to the floor.

The cat was still complaining.

"Cock blocker," Lana muttered as she pulled Simon's shirt off and threw it onto the bed. "The cat, not you."

Simon laughed, part giddy, part relieved, that she seemed so determined, so eager despite the fact if they stopped to think about it, this was probably an extremely terrible idea.

The cat yelled again. Lana stood up. She'd shucked off her jeans. The bra was somewhere on the floor, her eyes were blazing. "We're going to my room," she announced.

He pulled the rest of his clothing off, then grabbed the box of condoms that he'd bought in a fit of optimism, and he followed her, his eyes taking in her messy hair, the strong curve of her shoulders, the intimate line of her spine. He reached toward her and ran his thumb along the valley of her back, and she stopped, trembling, her hands moving down her own sides, her ass curving up in invitation.

They were in the living room. They weren't going to make it to another bed.

He hooked his fingers into the seam of her underpants, gliding them along her soft, firm skin. She made a sound like a whimper and he stopped. He fell—that was the only way to describe it—he fell on his knees so he could lick her right there, bite gently on the plummy curve, kiss her in the places he remembered in dreams.

She buckled soon, too, and he caught her, his hands splayed over her smooth, soft stomach, lowering her down until she was kneeling on the rug and he was right behind her, his mouth at her shoulder. "Why don't you sit on the couch?" he managed to say, his breathing harsh.

For some reason, this was what made her stiffen. "You want to—you want to eat me out?"

"Why not?"

Did she not like it? Had she ever liked it? Did he not remember?

"It's been so long…since we did that," she said.

She turned around to look at him, her eyes wide. Then she buried her face in his shoulder. "I don't know why this feels so different. And new. I don't know why I'm—I'm shy?"

And why did this confession make him want her more?

He tried to calm his breathing, his body, his cock, so he could listen.

She said, "It's not that I don't want this. I do. I've hardly been able to think about anything else for days. Weeks, to tell you the truth. But memory is a different thing, and fantasy is different, too."

She lifted her head.

"Like for instance, I don't remember your shoulder being so sharp." She pressed the point where his arm met the socket and traced her hand down. "I don't remember the texture of the hair on your chest. I can tell myself how I thought it felt, but it seems different."

"Maybe it is different. My body has changed."

"So has mine."

With aching care, he skimmed his finger up her stomach between her breasts, then down again, down to the tuft of hair between her legs. He breathed in and out, then he cupped her, letting her get used to the warmth of his palm before he moved his hand down.

She was right. Somehow everything had changed. Maybe the blue of her veins stood out more in her strong arms, the soft skin on her neck was more yielding, more fragile. His own body had definitely changed, because this body had never felt hers in this way. *His* fingers were the ones that felt different as they moved down into her damp folds, his eyes were the ones that were opened to wonder, his tongue and lips felt new as he kissed her and kissed her.

He couldn't stop kissing her.

She murmured and moved herself onto the couch, opening her legs wider. "Okay, yes."

Her hands had moved up, flirting with the undersides of her breasts. She circled her fingers around her nipples, and Simon gulped in one breath and pulled her forward to place his head between her thighs, brushed his cheeks and chin against them, held her knees. Once upon a time he'd loved her knees, and as his hand closed around one, he remembered why. The idiosyncratic bumpiness of bone and cartilage, the way she managed, even through that one hardy joint, to be so much herself. He kissed both of her knees and went back slowly to begin to lick her clit, trying to remember what she had enjoyed, trying to put himself back in the skin of the person he'd been.

But it was difficult to concentrate on memory under

the exciting scent of her now. His recollections were overlaid with the reality of her dampness, her present softness. He had forgotten the way she moved when she enjoyed a nip, a touch at the spot she liked, the way she kept up a low hum, the feeling of her hand curved around his head, the restless pull of her fingers in his hair. He knew the eager jolt of her hips when his tongue hit a sensitive spot.

Her thighs tensed around him and she couldn't seem to hold still anymore. One upward movement caught him on the lip, the shock making him see sparks for a moment. But it was good. It was better this way, a reminder to keep a rein on his own arousal.

He couldn't help looking up at her head thrown against the back of the couch. Her cheeks were warm with pleasure, her lips and tongue moving, murmuring. At the last moment, she opened her eyes and looked down at him, and she watched him, she watched him taking her with his mouth and hands. She cried out, and her body shook.

He had been waiting for the memories to come back to him, but he'd been wrong. All he wanted was now.

Chapter Eleven

Lana should probably be worried. This was Simon. *Simon.* He was straightening up, his face intent on her. Desire stretched over his skin, pulling his eyes tautly to her. And although she felt lazy and liquid and warm, part of the warmth that bathed her was from a sense of her power.

She eased herself up on the couch, extending her arms, her legs, down to her toes, enjoying the way he followed every movement. Simon rose to his full height in a sudden surge, and she smiled to see the tic in his lean face that showed he was barely controlling himself. His body was strained everywhere, his toes almost digging into the floor. She admired him, her gaze going down the line of his chest, down the dark hair, to his cock, hard and thick. She tilted her head so that her eyes could trace lovingly the muscles of his ass, tensed, ready.

Lana reached out with her leg, touching him musingly, her toe trailing along his calf, and he let out a harsh breath, and dove to tear open the box of condoms, the strips of shiny plastic bursting out as he pulled it apart in his haste.

She laughed.

"I'm glad you're so pleased," he grumbled, smoothing the condom over himself. He kicked aside the unused strips and stood above her.

"I'm very satisfied with how things are going."

Despite the heaviness of her limbs, she did want to help him out. She reached up and grabbed his hand, yanking him to sit on the couch, arranging his limbs, sliding her hands over him. Then she crawled into his lap, straddled him, put his hands on her breasts. "Kiss me."

It was almost too much for Simon, she could tell.

She lifted her ass and closed her hands around his cock, then slid down around him in one full, satisfying movement. She could feel him, feel herself, expanding, her hips loosening. Even his hands, reaching down to grip her ass in a deep, deep hold, seemed to be pulling her outward and upward as he began to pump into her.

For a while there was no sound except for the creak and thump of the couch and the pant and wet slap and suck of their bodies. They both worked furiously. She brushed impatiently at the sweaty strands of her own hair, caught between their faces and lips and clashing teeth. A strangled gasp broke out from him, and the sound of it filled her up, making her wild and powerful. She opened her arms and threw her head back, pushing herself up and down on him until her thighs were trembling with the effort of her motion.

But he was turning them now, flipping her under him so that she lay on the couch, one leg over the back, the other over the side, while he braced his foot on the floor. He was holding himself over her, sliding her up the cushions until her back burned from rubbing herself against the material. She needed to hold something.

There was nothing anchoring her against his relentless movement. Another wave of pleasure crashed over her. She should let it carry her.

She arched, trying desperately to grab something, anything, but there was only Simon pulling her along. She could feel him—she could feel herself—losing control. She banged her head against the arm of the couch even as she felt herself coming, as she felt Simon's last powerful thrusts.

The tears were from pain and pleasure, and her first breath came out deep with the weight of Simon's body collapsed on top of hers. He raised himself after a moment, the last wet drag of his cock leaving her body making her gasp again.

"Are you all right?" he asked.

She sighed and rubbed the back of her head. "Yes."

He kissed her hair gently, her cheeks, and her lips. He pulled her up, so they were both sitting, and touched her gently as if to make sure the rest of her was all right. Then he walked her to the bathroom. When she came out again, he'd disposed of the condom, and cleaned up the mess they'd made of the living room. The tang of sex still lingered in the air, but she was too tired to care. He held open a blanket for her, which he used to bundle her to her bed, where they slept for the rest of the night.

"You're thinking too hard," Simon murmured.

Lana had been awake for a while. She needed to go to the bathroom. She felt grubby and uncomfortable, and she suspected there was a small bump on her head from last night's activities. But the bed was warm, and Simon was in it, his palm resting lightly on her belly, his even breath tickling her ear.

For a while, she let herself match her inhales and exhales to his. She almost, almost took his hand to feel the long fingers curled with hers once more. His hands had always been so expressive and active. When she and Simon were still married, they'd often sat doing their reading, hand in hand, the little jumps and squeezes and jostles telling her exactly what he thought of the material he was studying. But she didn't want to wake him now, no matter how much she wanted to hold him. So she held herself in bed with him but away from him. She stared at the ceiling, her eyes following the curves and dips of the crown molding, imagining faces in the shapes, wondering what they thought of her lying in bed with her ex-husband, the person she'd vowed to avoid.

"Don't think about it too much," came Simon's voice again, more clearly.

She rolled to her side, moving her belly away from his hot hand. He tried to keep her for a moment, then pulled his arms away when he noticed she'd stiffened. She found it difficult not to feel a small edge of resentment from his words—a tiny crack—but whether that was because she didn't want him telling her what to do, or because he knew her too well, she didn't know. And that was also irritating.

He must have understood, because after a moment, he said ruefully, "It's as much a warning for you as it is for me."

Oh. Of course, it was hard for him, too. She said, trying to gentle some of the panic in her voice, "I have to go to the bathroom. But I feel like the minute I leave the safety of the covers, reality is going to set in. I'm not ready for that, either. Also it's cold out there."

This time his arms came around her. And he pulled her close. "Real life is cold."

"Were we really stupid? Did we complicate things too much?"

He kissed her forehead. "Everything is complicated all the time."

Simon laughed at her dubious expression. "I'm serious. It's never just putting your shoes on and running. It's stretching, and not eating too much beforehand, and having a shower afterward, and having clean clothes and shoelaces, and worrying this whole thing is too hard on your knees. It's never just getting a bunch of bodies in a room to sing together. It's coordinating with venues and getting programs printed, and chasing down permissions slips, and making sure kids can come to extra rehearsals and fretting that your grantor is going to withdraw funding. It's never just a bowl of noodles. Life is constant complication on top of complication. So right now, I'm going to try not to worry that we've done something terrible when we're warm together under these covers, when you've energized me. Right now, I'm happier than anything."

He kissed her neck, her shoulder. His body was interested, and hers, too. But in the end, real life came to them. The cat slipped in the room and leaped onto the bed, or rather onto what felt like Lana's bladder, and yelled about her breakfast. And Lana really did have to go to the bathroom, not to mention she should brush her teeth.

So she kissed him, and he knew her well enough to understand she was going to get up. He said, "I'll feed this cat."

She went through her morning routine, feeling self-conscious and oddly tender, as if she'd shed her old skin for new growth last night. But there was nothing new that she could see in the bathroom mirror, except for her smile. At least she was dressed by the time she got into the kitchen.

"Of course I'm wary," she said by way of greeting. "Of course I'm going to think too much."

He handed her a mug of green tea. "We can try to be casual about it. Take it day by day."

She almost laughed. "I don't know if we can, judging by how intense it was last night. And by the fact that we have a past."

He moved closer, his hand went to his waist. "But you are new. You're different. You were always wonderful, but you've become an amazing manipulator of flour, apparently. But it's not only that, the way you talk—the way you talk to me—has changed. You're braver and more complicated. In a lot of ways. I'm the one who's stayed the same. Living in the same apartment. Going through the same routines. Teaching. Worrying about students and grants and department politics. Doing the exact things I said I'd do."

"Do you really think the grant isn't going to come through?"

"Yes? No? We have a solid board and good business management. But the best thing is this group of kids. And it isn't just their voices. It's how dedicated they are. How much they really seem to love singing and performing. They're so engaged. They volunteered to choreograph some songs we hadn't done movement with, and they came up with such great moves. I'm constantly impressed by them. But the grantors, they've been funding us for a few years now and they've been making noises about changing things. You know what that means."

"It could mean that you'll get more money. And I'd like to point out, you're not living in that apartment anymore. You're with me now."

"Yeah, I'm with you now."

He drew her closer, his hands smoothing up her waist, and she felt like a flower about to unfurl under the sun. There was a question in his eyes. She nodded as she stood on her tiptoes to meet his lips. It was so soft and searching. He snuck up on her until all she could feel was the pressure of his tongue on hers, his hands working up and down seeking the sensitive spot between her shoulder blades, or cupping her ass just right, always pulling and seducing her toward him until she was an open well of want.

When he pulled back and asked suddenly, "Will you come to the concert? It's the Monday after next. Your day off. No pressure, though. I don't know how much you like to attend these things anymore now that you're—I mean, you haven't gone near the piano... Anyway, I can get you a ticket, if you'd like."

She blinked, still dizzy with lust and with the change of subject. Or was it one? "Ye-es? Yes, sure. Can I bring Julia?"

His smile was a bright ray, and for a moment he looked just like he did when he was younger. She felt a stirring of unease. But he'd spun her around and out of the kitchen. "Yes! I'd love that. I appreciate it. I really do."

He started maneuvering her toward his room, his hands sliding under her shirt, hot and eager.

"I'd forgotten you get like this," she said.

He pulled his head up. Something flashed over his face. "Like what?"

"All the energy you have when a big performance is coming up. Remember that time you put together an impromptu benefit for the college? I think it was your first big production, your first time coordinating all that—"

"You did a lot. You helped."

"Sure. But you were running around frantic all the time, booking a venue, getting people to type up programs for you, and printing off the lot on the school's photocopier, convincing our friends to perform even if they had another gig that same evening."

"I could be a bit much."

"Yes, you could. But I remember at a certain point each day, you'd snap your phone shut. It was one of those little slider cell phones and it made a really final sound when you closed it. And then you'd apply that same frantic energy to me."

He blinked, hands still on her as if remembering this all for the first time.

"The concert was a huge success. I remember. All our classmates performed, solo and together, and it wasn't competitive. We were all so talented and young and hopeful. We had lots of wine, and we came home, back to your apartment. You were so relieved and happy. And you pulled me to the bedroom and took off all my clothing, slowly, like you had all the time in the world. And maybe you did. First you took down my hair and unzipped my dress, that long black concert dress."

"I remember it. The neckline came down in a low vee. I always wanted to rest my face right there."

"The dress was so stiff it would've supported you."

She moved her hand down his chest. He was breathing lightly and quickly, his eyes bright.

"It was like you built up all of this energy, all this feeling inside, and then after it was done, you felt like you were allowed to let go."

He swallowed. "I remember that. I remember all of it."

Without taking her eyes from his, she unbuttoned and then unzipped him, her hand slow and certain. He looked like he wasn't sure of what to do, which was unusual for him.

She liked that.

"Come on," she said softly.

He followed.

Chapter Twelve

"I can't believe you're with her again," Simon's sister said.

"I'm not with her with her. We're still figuring it out. Trying to take it slow."

It was well past noon on the Thursday before the performance, but entirely too early for this conversation.

Maxine had called because she was asking him, as she did every year around this time, to come visit for spring break. Usually he managed to avoid her. But this time, he'd been walking to his office, preoccupied, and answered without looking at his phone.

He was still not sure how Maxine had taken his usual "No, I really can't make it this year," To indicate he'd gotten back together with Lana, but she'd done it and he hadn't denied it, and now Maxine had to talk to him about it.

"Take it slow? You were *married* to her. If your relationship was a car, then when you got divorced you ripped out the brakes. And now you just got in and started driving again. You can drive it fast, you can drive it slow, but you can't stop unless you crash."

"Wait, why would anyone rip out the brakes of a car?"

"It's an analogy. It doesn't have to be perfect."

"Perfect? It doesn't even make sense. If anything it's more like we were on a long-distance journey, but Lana got out, and I don't know, hitchhiked or pedaled a bicycle or rode in an ox cart or something, while I kept going. And now she's back in, and we're on a country road driving responsibly and carefully while enjoying the scenery."

"Sometimes you can take an analogy too far."

"You started it. Listen, when I say we're taking it slow, I mean that's what we're doing."

Except he and Lana already lived together, and they were definitely sleeping together. Or not sleeping. Taking each other hungrily the minute one of them arrived home, with hardly enough time to remove all the complicated layers of winter. How many times had he looked up from his frenzy to realize they were having sex with most of their clothing still on: scarves and hats wet with sweat as they moved together. The only slow thing was that they weren't talking much about where this was going. Partly because so far they spent most of their time together in bed, and partly because he had a concert he was getting ready for, and she was working, and they had very different hours. And partly because maybe he didn't want to think about where this relationship vehicle would end up.

He tried to switch the subject over to the concert, but Maxine took the opportunity to ask if Lana would be attending, and, without him answering said, "Of course, she is. Of course, she is. Because that's how you get around performance time."

Did everyone assume he got horny when he had a show coming up? That was a humiliating thought.

Maybe he should change the subject again.

Maxine was not done. "I'd have thought you'd pick someone younger, at least. She must be more than forty now. What about children?"

"Maxine, you're out of line. And I don't have time to discuss this."

"I mean, I always assumed you'd have at least a couple by now. I kept some better hand-me-downs for you until a few of years ago. Not too many, because we didn't have that much left that was decent. After they've cycled through four kids, you know."

"I have to go."

"No you don't. You don't want to talk to me."

He thought for maybe half a second about protesting. But they'd never been polite to each other. Why start now? "You don't make it easy."

He added, perhaps rashly, "I don't really want children."

He heard a clatter from Maxine's end, as if she'd dropped something. "What do you mean you don't want children? You're a teacher."

"I work with teens, not little kids. Plus, nowadays I teach adults."

"But you're so good with your nieces and nephews."

Maxine sounded genuinely frustrated with him, as if he'd suddenly changed the terms of a deal they'd had, although what deal and when they'd made it, he couldn't say. He felt somewhat trapped, and because of that, a little guilty and a lot irritated. "I don't remember having this discussion with you or even having to clear this with you."

"I assumed—"

"You assumed wrong. And maybe I've changed.

Maybe I want the life that wasn't mapped out for me. I am allowed to want different things from what you want for yourself."

He was aware he sounded like a child. Which was all the more reason he shouldn't have one. Not that he was going to use that particular point in the argument.

He'd stopped near the top of Morningside Park. Through the bare branches, he could see down into Central Harlem. He spotted the crossing guards for the local school in their fluorescent vests waving at kids, cars moving carefully down the roads, friendly buildings with their bright bricks and windows. If he squinted, he could almost see his house, the apartment he shared with Lana, the place to which he'd almost refused to move. It wasn't quite what he'd envisioned for them all those years ago.

"Is Lana the one who made you think you didn't want kids?"

"This has nothing to do with her. I've been considering what I want and what makes me happy. I was stuck because I kept mistaking what people thought I should want for things I actually strove for. For the first time in a long time, I feel like I'm finally figuring myself out. And if it means my life doesn't turn out exactly like you planned it, then fine."

"What is that supposed to mean?"

"It means you tell me how to live all the time. *Move out! But don't live there! Or there! You need to date more! Why don't you get married? But don't get involved with Lana!* Less than two months ago you were telling me I was in a rut."

"You were. But this is not how I saw you breaking out of it."

"Maybe that's the problem. Maybe you've got this firm, completely full-color vision in your mind of how things ought to be."

Maxine started to laugh. "*You* are telling *me* about full-color visions? Mr. Artistic Director, Mr. What-I-Say-Goes-and-If-It-Doesn't-I'm-Going-to-be-Very-Disappointed-in-You? That's rich."

"Since when am I like that?"

"Since I got married? Since I had kids?"

"I'm not disappointed. It's just you're different from how you used to be. Which of course, you should be. But you're such a wife now."

"I'm married."

"You were also my badass older sister. You were in bands. You guys even played at The Knitting Factory. You traveled the world. Then one day you came back with a boyfriend, you got married and you moved away. And it was like you became more about your husband, about him and the kids."

"You think my life is narrow."

"No."

Maybe.

"Well first of all, have you ever considered that I have interests I don't talk about with you, because I don't think you'd care to hear about them? You think I don't notice when you scoff when I talk about learning tae kwon do?"

"Because it's always with the children."

"Just because I'm doing it with them doesn't mean I didn't want to do it for myself. Do you think I don't notice how you sneer when I talk about family activities."

"It's just weird for me, okay? To think of you being such a mom."

He knew he sounded selfish even as the words left his mouth. Of course she was a parent. She had been for more years than not. But she used to be other things, too.

"Well, my life didn't turn out exactly like yours. I chose not to pursue my music, but I didn't lose myself simply because my priorities changed. Do you want me to be my own person or do you want me to be a person you thought I was?"

"You were so talented."

"So what, Simon? So what? I'm happy. I chose this life. I like it. For someone who claims to not want kids, you sure have a lot of opinions about how I'm raising mine."

"It's not about my nieces and nephews. I love them."

"Right, it's about me, and the potential you think I've squandered. I wanted to show you at one point how happy it makes me. But you have this image of me from when I was your so-called cool sister, and you don't want to let that change—let *me* change. So now, I don't tell you things. I don't try to include you as much in my life because I'm tired of you thinking I'm not enough. I don't even expect respect at this point, just a little understanding."

"I respect you."

"You respect what I was. But that's how you are. You say you want everyone to do their best, but you only think one way is right, and you steamroller over every opinion to the contrary. You're the narrow one, Simon."

How had Maxine done this? They'd started out talking about how she was the one who bossed him around, and somehow he was the one who was judging her choices?

Of course, he did judge them a little.

It was cold out and he couldn't pace the park forever.

"Maxine, I have to go."

"Go, then. I'll be here, because I'm your family, and I'm what you've got left. Other people might not stick around."

With that, she clicked off, and Simon was left listening to nothing but birds and traffic.

Lana was nervous about the concert, which was ridiculous considering she wasn't the one performing. But apparently none of those old feelings ever died. When Lana's dad called as she was getting ready, she didn't have her usual coping mechanisms in place.

"Lana, your stepmother and I are thinking of coming to New York for a visit in the last week of April. Of course, we don't want to intrude on you and Simon," he said in his careful, formal tones.

"It's not intruding, Dad. We're not—it's not intruding."

"Nonetheless, we will stay at a hotel. If you could recommend something central, we would appreciate it very much. It's been a long time since I was last there. And of course, we'd like to see you, if Simon's schedule permits."

"I may be able to take a couple of days off. Also, I can get you a reservation at a few restaurants, and at mine if you'd like."

"That would be nice. Your stepmother and I do not eat red meat."

"I know, Dad. I'm sure we can figure that out."

"Thank you. I assume you're well. See what Simon's schedule is like. I'll follow up with email."

And that was it.

That was enough.

She was not going to think about it.

It wasn't exactly that she was estranged from her father; obviously they were still speaking. But somehow in the years between when her mother died and he remarried, he'd almost started acting as if she wasn't quite there. Simon existed; she did not.

At least Lana had her extended family, especially Great Aunt Setzu, who'd lived with them on and off during Lana's teenage years. Her father's sisters, brothers, aunts and uncles were a much warmer, more gregarious lot.

She took a deep breath and put on an aggressive stripe of red lipstick, stuck her tongue out at her reflection, then went to meet Julia.

The recital hall was warm, and between the crowd and their puffy winter jackets, it wasn't easy for Lana to find her cousin. But when Julia whispered, "So you're *together* together?" she wished they hadn't taken their seats so quickly.

"Just one together. A little together. Together-ish. We're still figuring it out."

While Julia smirked, Lana occupied herself by looking around at the crowd and tried not to think about how her arms tingled. She had been spending so much time with Simon that she often fell asleep without putting her wrist braces on at night. Because she didn't get as much sleep, she'd also been skipping or half-assing her workouts.

Her body felt fantastic, though, hopped up on sex endorphins and riddled with tender areas and bruises, small physical reminders of how she'd banged her forearm on the frame as he'd taken her over the side of the bed the other night, or the still reddish spot on her chest where his stubble scraped her over and over. Every time she shifted it seemed, she found one of those secret places, and every time she found a place, she crossed and uncrossed her legs. She was nervous about the concert, yes. Tired? Also yes. But the tiredness added something to her excitement.

This wasn't exactly information she could share with Julia, though, so she watched people struggle into their seats, the proud grandparents and wiggly siblings, people poring over programs, and pointing out names and song titles, singing snippets of melodies they'd probably heard rehearsed often in their homes. It felt like a real community. People knew each other. All these brown, golden, pale, dark, beautiful faces in the audience. She wasn't naive enough to think this gathering solved the world's problems, not in this fraught age. But she was optimistic enough to want it to mean something.

Julia was scanning the crowd, too. She said, "All ribbing aside, I am happy you're happy. Although, I thought a lot about what you said. About how you lost yourself when you were with him. But like you said, you have a completely different career now, right? You've changed your life, switched careers. You're almost a new person. So there's no danger of that anymore."

"Yeah, absolutely."

Julia looked at her narrowly.

"I'm trying to be careful, follow the rules I set out for myself, take it slow."

It didn't feel like they were taking things slow, because of the way her heart raced whenever she saw him. Lana was maybe more infatuated with him now than she had been in her twenties, which was why she really had to be careful. She'd found her voice later in life; sometimes she had to remind herself to use it.

The lights dimmed and the chorus members filed onstage. Simon came out last, and a warm rush of applause filled the hall.

Simon nodded easily at the audience and raised his hands.

The kids were so good. Lana sat forward as soon as she heard their first notes. They had a big, open, full sound that grew in enthusiasm as they moved through the song. They weren't absolutely perfect. Another musician would probably argue that they needed to blend their vowels more, to make their voices more uniform. But Simon had always wanted to include everyone who wanted to join. And these kids so clearly wanted to be there. A few of them began to sway, their heads moving back and forth in rhythm with the music as excitement hummed through the audience. Their smiles grew bigger. By the last note, the crowd, which was admittedly partial to begin with, was cheering wildly.

Lana clapped giddily, almost relieved, definitely moved, even though she'd had nothing to do with it. But Simon was giving a modest bow, gesturing at the choir and the pianist before leaving the stage. Next, a beautiful Black woman strode up and the kids rearranged themselves with some nervous giggles, and a guitar and drums struck up the opening chords.

Lana's program had fluttered to the floor but she didn't bother to retrieve it. A few of the songs were familiar, gospel tunes, a few classical and haunting modern pieces, a choral merengue arrangement that had the audience clapping along, and a soft almost doo-wop song. For some arrangements, kids came up to the mike and took solos that were by turns awkward and affecting. Despite the teenage gawkiness and drama and flash on display, their voices bloomed out with beauty, and every time they all retreated to sing together once more, Lana found tears aching in her eyes.

She'd been worried she'd be envious. A small corner of her mind had told her that she'd come to this concert and think of all the things she couldn't do. She worried she would compare her own meagre talents to Simon's. But the concert hadn't been about Simon. It hadn't been about one person's perfect playing, one perfect note. It was so much an effort of love from everyone involved, and she couldn't help it, she was proud, happy he'd invited her, that he'd brought this together, happy to be here for something so important. She'd forgotten what it was like to be surrounded by music, to have that sound come at her from all directions, harmonious and beautiful.

At the end of the program, Simon and the other conductors, Abena and Dion, were all out together on the stage, along with a few former chorus members.

"It's time for the last song. In what has become our tradition, we want you to sing along. This time we're going to try 'Shalom Chaverim.' It's a canon. The words are easy but we've got them up here."

Abena pointed to a rather small white board. But someone had printed the words out bold and tall, and Lana could make them out easily enough despite her middle-aged eyes.

"Let's all do this together once, then we'll divide you up." And she and Simon and Dion launched into the song with the kids giggling behind them.

"All right, are you ready? This third of the audience will start singing, and this third will follow with the same, and then this third will be last."

The piano played a vamp, and the audience started, quiet and tentative at first. At least the chorus knew what they were doing. People were looking around, stumbling over melodies, coming in at the wrong spot, but as they carried on, the song seemed to gather momentum. They sang over and over, in a mixture of Hebrew and English, the music chasing itself, the audience growing in confidence, in awe of the harmonies they could make, until they were all standing. *Till we meet again. Till we meet again. Shalom. Shalom.*

They held a reception in the small mezzanine area immediately after the concert. It was usually a good time to get all the board members together, lubricated with music and wine. But Simon found himself waiting anxiously to see if Lana would show up. And when she did, a little glassy-eyed and bewildered, his heart gave a twist.

He hugged Julia and thanked her when she told him how moved she'd been by the concert. When Lana turned to him, he couldn't help himself from bending and whispering, "There you are," and putting his palm on her back. "I'd love for you to meet some people."

He handed her and Julia glasses of wine, and made space for them in the throng of people. Soon, Julia was in a lively conversation with a local gallery owner and Lana had been introduced to some of his choristers and their families, and Simon was just watching her talk to them all, enjoying the way she seemed to fit in his present life.

It felt husbandly. Or rather, it seemed like he was in a dream where she had been his wife all along, there'd been no separation between them. He'd be lying if he didn't enjoy the fantasy, the warmth of her back, the shine in her face, not just for the performance, not just for the kids, but for him.

And she was proud of him. He could see it shining in her face when she turned to look at him, before she murmured that the concert had been wonderful, before she lifted his hand and brushed a kiss over it. That much hadn't changed. And the light touch of her lips, her eyes, her warmth, it kindled another fire in him.

He could not wait to get her out of here.

But one of his longtime board members was clearly lingering to get a word, and there were other donors and grantors he had to shake hands with, so he gritted his teeth and smiled. "Lana, this is Monroe Webb and his partner, Annie Wu. Monroe's the chair of our board of directors. He's been with us since his son Cal was a member of the chorus. Cal's a musician now, too, and a musicologist."

Monroe, nattily attired as always, gave them a friendly nod, but sprightly Annie, much less reserved, was studying Lana with open curiosity.

"An early success story," Lana said, smiling.

Simon replied, "I can't take credit. Cal was already incredibly skilled when he decided to join us. He was one of those kids who wanted to make music all the time. He's got so much curiosity. How is he doing, Monroe? I'd love to persuade him to perform with us again, or come down and talk to the members. They'd love him."

"I'm sure he'd enjoy that, too." Monroe turned to his

partner. "We'll have to get our heads together, see what his schedule is like."

Annie Wu grinned. "I'll bet we can lure him with the promise of adoring fans. But I have questions for Miss Lana here. How long have you known Simon? Are you a musician yourself?"

"A long time," Simon responded without thinking. "She's a pianist."

He felt her spine stiffen under his hand.

"I'm a chef."

The way she said it, the way she stepped slightly away from him, made him realize he'd made a mistake. And even as he felt sorry for answering for her, for having discounted all those years of her life, all the hard work that made her new and magnificent…it irritated him slightly because he'd been enjoying this dream and she'd reminded him it was one-sided and not true.

"Well, I can't sing a note," Annie Wu said cheerfully, ignoring Lana and Simon's sudden silence. "When I was a kid I had piano lessons, and I was terrible and everyone let me know as if I hadn't figured it out. The best thing about the lessons was my teacher had seven cats. Possibly more."

Monroe Webb looked at his partner, his expression horrified, and he brushed the sleeve of his dark bespoke suit as if he could feel feline hairs accumulating.

"Oh, please," Annie said. "Don't tell me when you were a kid you wouldn't have been delighted with the idea of having hundreds of cats."

"I would not," Monroe said.

But Annie's response seemed to relax him. "Another wonderful concert, Simon. The kids, especially that second-to-last song, 'Wanting Memories,' it was incredibly moving."

Simon found his voice. Good thing he'd been giving and rehearsing some version of this pitch for months. "All the credit goes to Abena. We're lucky to have her, and if we could bring her on as co-conductor and organize a larger stipend for her, who knows how much better the chorus could become."

"It's definitely something we should consider."

Monroe's smile flashed in his dark, handsome face. "You be careful with this one," he warned Lana. "He's seems gentle but he can roll right over you when he gets an idea in his head, and make you think it's what you wanted all along."

"Don't I know it," Lana said so softly that probably only Simon heard it.

Monroe and Annie were already waving to someone else they knew, leaving Simon and Lana alone in the crowd.

"I'm sorry. I got excited, and I didn't mean to discount your work."

But his apology seemed to be swallowed up as someone else approached wanting to talk to him about making a donation. She gave him a quick squeeze of her hand; it should have been reassuring, but like his apology it was rushed and not quite enough, and she slipped away.

The last he saw of her at the reception was when he spotted her talking to Julia. Then the crowds started to thin out, the last of the kids arguing with their parents that they should be able to stay up late even though it was a school night. And finally, he knew she was really gone.

Disappointment cracked across him, unexpected and heavy. Of course she shouldn't have stayed to the end. It wasn't her show. And if she'd asked him if she should wait, of course he would have urged her to go home, perhaps walked her out the door and handed her into a cab.

But she hadn't, and really, why should she?

The fact that he had no real right to his feelings was perhaps the softest, most killing blow of all.

But Lana was still asleep in his bed when he got home. He watched her for a minute, her face pale in the light from the window, her dark hair disappearing into the night. Although he was tempted to wake her up, he knew she hadn't been sleeping as much as she should have. She'd been drained by the end of the evening, and as much as he wanted to hold her and ask her for some sort of reassurance, he couldn't right now. He crept quietly around the room, thinking about how it was usually she who did this. She knew how to slip under the covers so gently she didn't even wake him.

He was struck by how generous it was—not in not waking him, although that was thoughtful—but in how she was there to share her mornings with him, her warmth, her body. So he tried to be generous, too, although she gave a start when he slid in and the cat sprang up, disgruntled. "Don't you have your own bed?" he whispered to the cat.

She did. She had Lana's old room all to herself. She'd peed on the bed to underscore her possession. But Muffin was an ambitious little taker, yowling noisily for food that she ignored when dished out, demanding scritches until she was ready for them to cease immediately, which she signaled by biting.

The cat stalked away now, giving Simon a baleful glance. He would probably pay for it later.

Lana hardly seemed to stir. She was probably exhausted. He knew he was tired, too, but his brain pinged with adrenaline, and it was a surprise when she pulled one of his hands to her belly and slid it right down into her underwear where she was already wet.

"Am I the one who gets revved up after performances, or are you?" he asked, his fingers already busy on her clit.

"Shut up and get under me," she said tenderly.

For some reason, her small irritability mixed with affection made him feel more reassured than anything else that had happened that night.

She rolled on top of him and pulled off her arm braces, the decisive crack of the Velcro surprisingly loud and erotic in the silent room. He'd already been ready, ready as soon as she'd grasped his hand in her strong fingers. But now as she raised her ass to take off what little clothing remained on her, he felt himself almost trembling. Part of him wanted to take over, to roll her under him, and to move himself on a short, straight line to completion. But another part of him knew it wouldn't be as good as if he let her surprise him. His jaw clenched with the effort to hold himself still, to let her do this in her own time. As she leaned over him to the nightstand, he took the opportunity to lick her nipple, to smooth his hands down her lithe waist, coiled and strong. He moved his hand around the front to her thighs and slicked his fingers down and into her pussy.

She ground against him for a moment, then sat down

hard on him with a gasp so that his hand was almost crushed against his stomach. But he worked, and she worked, and soon, she was sliding down him, leaving a trail of her arousal down to his cock. At least any effect she had on him, he also had on her. He had doubts, yes, but he didn't doubt she wanted him, and that knowledge was sometimes more than enough.

She rolled the condom on quickly—thank God for that—and when she took him inside he nearly choked with relief and pleasure. For a moment, he watched her moving on top of him, the jounce of her small breasts, the upward movement of her head and shoulders as she looked to the ceiling then down at him again. Then he pulled her toward him to kiss her, to feel her mouth, still fresh with toothpaste. Her tongue and lips slid against his, hot with the rhythm of their movements. He felt surrounded by her, by her skin and smoothness and the wet warm scent of sex and sweat, and he was lost.

She was murmuring against him, inhales and exhales, her teeth against his lips and chin and back up again. He grasped her hips to steady her and pumped up into her, breathing against the strain of trying to slow himself down, concentrating on her mouth, on the push of his tongue on hers.

Her hand tugged at his hair now. Through her fingers, he could feel her entire desperate body. She was so strong and he loved it.

Then like that, she'd pulled up, up and away from him, her breathing gone as her body bucked on him. He watched her with wide open eyes, following the outline of her in the dark. Everything about her moved upward then crashed down almost as if she were trying to take off, as if he were holding her here. He had to let go, he had to let her go. His hips and hands moved her higher and higher. Even as his own orgasm started to lash its way through him, he felt that effort of hers straining toward the sky.

In a moment, she took him with her, the pleasure tearing through him until he couldn't see, couldn't hear the sound that left his throat.

When he came back down she was a warm heap on top of him. He brushed her hair gently from her face, and out of his mouth, wanting to hold on just a few seconds more. But she rolled off him quickly, a little too quickly, and padded to the bathroom.

He couldn't move. Who would want to? But when she came back, he went and got rid of the condom and cleaned up, too, like a grown-up, and jumped back into bed like a kid and listened to her giggle.

"Go to sleep," he told her.

"I can't. I'm riled up." She yawned and stretched beside him. "I feel like I could spring up, play Scrabble or chess or something."

"Sing a song, play the piano." He was half asleep.

"Our neighbors would love that."

"Why don't you play anymore?"

A pause. "Because I don't have to."

"But you still love music. I could see it tonight. It moved you."

"Yes, it did. But maybe I loved it because I wasn't doing it."

She buried herself into his shoulder. "Where is your dad's old chess set, anyway?"

"In storage. With a lot of his old stuff and some of mine. I moved it there when I came here. You know, I wasn't sure it would take. Us living together, I mean."

Another silence. Maybe she was asleep. He was half asleep himself, hardly aware of what he was saying. "It's our trial period together, after all."

He couldn't fight it any longer, sleep was claiming him. Maybe he heard her whisper, "Right. Trial period. How could I forget?" Maybe he didn't hear it at all.

Chapter Thirteen

Lana hadn't expected to be offered a job when her old friend came into the city.

Hester was a couple of years younger than Lana. She'd grown up in Hong Kong, cooked in Vancouver, and now she lived on a farm a little upstate and ran a culinary school and restaurant with her partner. Lana had visited last fall before she'd started working at Lore. It felt like a lifetime ago.

"Our curriculum is expanding," Hester explained over late, late-night drinks. "I thought of you immediately."

Lana was tired. She'd been in Simon's bed when he came home after the concert. They'd never bothered with the pretense they'd sleep alone, and the cat had grudgingly taken Lana's smaller bed as her own. When she and Simon had sex last night, his eyes had stayed open and glittering, following her, seeing her as she smoothed the condom over his ready cock, taking in her every movement as if to make sure she wouldn't disappear. When he watched her like this, she didn't think she could.

But afterward, he'd reminded her they were still in a trial period, and even though she'd fallen asleep after talking about it, the phrase had struggled its way up through her memories, repeating itself throughout the day. What did Simon expect would happen? Maybe he was judging, and she was on trial.

Lana brought herself back to reality by taking a tiny sip of her drink. Some terrible '70s hard rock played over the speakers, and the table was scratched, but judging by the gloss on the crowd and the price of the drinks, this bar wasn't the dive it was hoping to be. She grimaced at the glass rather than meet Hester's eyes. "Me, teaching at a cooking school. I went to college to be a teacher, but I haven't dealt with students in years."

"Don't talk your way out of feeling qualified for a job that you're already being offered, Lana."

"I see where you're coming from, Hester. But chiding me when I'm cautious isn't helpful. Trying does actually cost something, no matter what they say. You and I have both been told about opportunities only to have them taken away, or to be told we don't have the right credentials when we do. It erodes your confidence even when you know you're right. So let me have a moment."

"Fine. But this is me, and this is a real offer. I ate at that place Lore tonight. You've gotten better and better. The other chefs there pay attention to you. They watch you because you have skills they want to learn. But that place is a pit that eats young people up even though they think it gilds their CVs. You probably don't want to stay there long-term. I can't see you planning on it."

"I'm not exactly known for my planning, Hester."

"Well, don't stay there forever. Put aside your fears, because that's fear talking you out of this. We have plenty of people who've gone to European schools and can teach pastry making to middle-aged weekenders.

But for our regular curriculum, we want a truly global school with people with diverse backgrounds who've learned their techniques in Singapore, or India, or Ethiopia, to teach our young chefs."

"You're really offering?"

"Yeah, I am. You have a unique skill set and experience. And as you mentioned, you do have teacher training, which is more than most of the other people we've hired. I want you to really think about this. The pay is not extremely high but we offer healthcare, dental, and regular hours. And you'd still be cooking."

It sounded too good to be true.

"How far is it again? Say, if I wanted to commute?"

"A couple hours. Longer in rush-hour traffic. You would probably want to move or rent somewhere for weekdays, but housing's a lot cheaper up there than in Manhattan."

Hester spoke with the assurance of someone who was independently wealthy, waving aside the cost of an extra living space with one careless hand. "Take a little time to think about it."

Oh, Lana planned on overthinking it, starting now.

But Hester was frowning at her drink. "I can't really do these late nights anymore. I don't miss it."

"Do you need a place to stay?"

"No worries. I booked a room. I have to see a couple more people tomorrow."

As Lana sat on the rattling, bright 2 train back home, she thought about picking up and moving again, this time to a small town. She remembered her fainting spell at work. Her period would be coming up again soon, and she hoped it would be gentler this time. She was otherwise healthy, but she was getting older. Not counting the endometriosis, how much longer could she keep this up? Especially when her wages as a cook weren't so great to begin with.

It was a good opportunity, and with Hester living in the same town, she already knew she wouldn't be friendless, nor would she be the only Asian woman for miles. It was the offer she'd been waiting for, even though she hadn't known it.

Of course, she loved the apartment and didn't want to think of leaving their tree-lined street, the warm brick walls, the sun-filled room at the front of the house, Simon's bedroom, Simon's bed.

She still cared about him. And she wanted to know where this would go. They'd only really been together again for a few weeks. *They were still on their trial period.* There was still time for him to change his mind about how he felt, if he was holding back, if he had never really moved in. After all, he kept his important mementos in storage as if half expecting to leave. He was apparently still weighing options.

She, on the other hand, was pretty sure she'd fallen for him again.

She could admit this to herself now. But to say the words to him—it seemed almost overwhelming, given the weight of everything they had been to each other. It seemed too soon to bring up separation or commitment, to articulate clearly what she wanted from him when she wasn't sure herself, to ask him what he wanted from her. No, that wasn't true. Then again, as everyone kept pointing out, what did *too soon* mean when they'd already been married and divorced?

They would have to talk. She would have to ask for what she wanted, because that's what she had promised herself she'd do from now on. But it was going to take time to work up to it. Probably because she was so afraid of the answer. And didn't being afraid mean she already cared too much?

The lights of the 2 train were harsh and although it was almost empty, it seemed narrow. She had a headache. Probably the two sips of alcohol she'd had. Definitely the alcohol, and not the worry that long ago Simon had refused to give up any of his dreams so she could pursue hers.

Early February

Lana had to work on the first day of the Lunar New Year, and although she hadn't made a big deal of celebrating when they were together, Simon decided to try to cook for her. She'd started her period again, and while it wasn't as bad as last time, she was clearly tired and uncomfortable. He wanted to do something for her.

But even as soon as he formed the plan he felt… somewhat daunted. She was a professional chef and she worked at a Pan-Asian restaurant; he wasn't going to attempt anything like that. But he could make some kind of dumpling. A ravioli? He fell down an internet hole of pasta shapes for an hour, leaving him unprepared for the class he was supposed to teach. He got through it by relying on muscle memory and letting the chattier students drone on for longer than usual. When class was over he promptly started looking at the internet again in his office.

But Abena and Dion knocked on his door and barreled in, as they usually did.

Abena stopped short. "Are you browsing recipes?"

Simon closed the lid of his laptop.

His interns glanced at each other and grinned.

"Was there something in particular we needed to discuss?"

"No, it's more that we've been getting emails about the kids not being able to access their practice pages," Dion said.

"Oh, shit."

They looked at each other again as Simon pulled up the website.

"You don't usually swear in front of us, Simon," Abena ventured.

"I'm a little on edge."

He'd absentmindedly left off the extension of the file he'd uploaded this morning. It wasn't the first time he'd done this, of course. Abena and Dion were constantly sending him texts he'd forget to read about some sort of broken link or other. He wasn't exactly the quickest at adapting to technology, so of course that had led to numerous little irritations but— "Why are you *both* here?"

"You haven't been checking your messages again, obviously, and we wanted to see how you were."

"You know we haven't talked much since the concert."

"To which you brought your ex-wife."

Simon fought the urge to fidget. After all, he had wanted to show her his work, and he wanted everyone to see her. But…he didn't want to answer questions about it. He opened the laptop again and let Abena take over. She said over her shoulder, "And now we find you planning some sort of Valentine's Day surprise."

"It's not for Valentine's Day."

They all watched the music file upload.

Dion said, "It's just you haven't seemed quite as present as you usually are and we were wondering if you could shed some light."

Classic Dion, trying to be tactful while extracting information. Even Abena was smirking at Dion's efforts.

"This isn't really appropriate." Simon sighed.

Abena leaned in. "Please. We're your interns and apparently we know nothing. The whole department is gossiping about you. Some of the old-timers remember your wife—"

Guess that made him an old-timer.

"And they have opinions. You have to give us something. Are you officially back together? Have you forgiven each other for the things that drove you apart to begin with?"

"One of the old admins, Ms. Frey, she said your ex was jealous of your success."

Simon snorted. "Jealous of what success? Lana was amazingly talented."

"No one remembers that part."

He paused. *He* remembered. He felt an irrational flare of resentment against Ms. Frey, who was the only one who could ever produce an extra ream of paper from the supply room, and who was a whiz at figuring out what was wrong with his iPad. No, it wasn't Ms. Frey's fault that she half-remembered something about some silly kids from long ago. People's personalities, their talents, their quirks and the things that made them who they were—they were flattened by memory. Even he had done the same thing in some ways with Lana. And he'd known her better than he'd known anyone.

Now she didn't play the piano at all anymore. She didn't consider herself a musician. She'd said it didn't make her happy. But he hadn't asked her why it made her unhappy. At the time he'd assumed it was a product of being around him. Maybe that hadn't been the problem at all.

He said aloud, "She was really talented. I spent a lot of time trying to get her to see how good she was."

Abena and Dion raised their eyebrows at each other.

"She's doing a different thing entirely and she loves it. She's very good."

Abena frowned. Dion smirked.

"I don't understand. Why are you both looking at me like that?"

"It's just that we've heard this before. You always say things like, *I want them to know how good they are.* You see the best in people, Simon. No, that's not the right way of putting it. You see how people can be their best. You see the potential. Of course, you're fine at critically evaluating people, but it also makes you push sometimes. You believe so fervently that it takes a big personality to push back."

All right, maybe that described him, but he often knew what was best. "Lana is very strong."

"Saying she can take it doesn't mean we ought to always force it."

This was getting far too personal when really his assessment of her talent shouldn't be. But he wasn't about to get into that with his interns.

He glared at them.

"Anyway, he's clearly trying to win her back," Dion said, turning to Abena.

Was he? He did want her, but that phrase held a lot of possible meanings.

"I approve of the way he's going about it, at least. Cooking is so nurturing."

Was he even here?

"It's better than yelling at her about her talent and potential."

"I didn't do that. I don't do that."

"No, it's like *The Parent Trap*."

"This is nothing like *The Parent Trap*. We're not parents. You two are not Hayley Mills."

"Who is Hayley Mills?"

"I think you mean Lindsay Lohan."

A pause. "Right. Of course."

"Although who knows if it was a good idea for those parents to get back together," Abena said.

"No, the bad idea was for each parent to take one twin and not tell the other. That's the real fucked-up thing about that movie."

"Good point, Dion. So can you really trust the judgment of people like that?"

Simon interrupted their delightful trip down pop culture memory lane. "But do you think that Lana and I should get back together?"

"Yes!" Dion said. "Finally, you're asking for our opinion. A thousand times, yes!"

Abena, however, blinked. "It's clearly what you want," she said cautiously. "So I support that."

"But?"

"But I don't have all the information."

"I don't know that I do, either."

"Well then, I think what you really have to do here is prove you can listen."

"I can listen. Of course I can listen. I'm a musician. *What is so funny?*"

Dion couldn't even answer, they were giggling so hard.

"It's just—it's—you're such a *conductor*," Abena finally said.

Like she wasn't one.

Dion shook their head and wiped their eyes. "Thanks for that laugh, Simon. Now open up that laptop. Let us help you woo her."

What was he was doing? He wanted to do something special for her. He needed to show her he appreciated her. How could he signal a new start? Was that why he was worried about messing up the symbolism of the meal?

And if he was wooing her, did that mean he was afraid he hadn't won her back? Would he always be afraid of that? "This is inappropriate. I am not taking advantage of you in this way."

"Think of it as us taking advantage of you."

"You'll be satisfying our nosiness and we'll be propelled to the top of the grad student gossip tree. Win-win for your interns who aren't paid enough."

Simon groaned. "I'm working on that. Believe me."

"We know."

"You are not helping 'woo her' as you put it. But if you could let me bounce some ideas off of you."

Dion clapped their hands and Abena beamed. "First thing you need is a haircut."

Chapter Fourteen

"I hope we're all ready for Asian Saint Patrick's Day."

Standing next to Lana, Talia muttered, "That doesn't even make sense."

The only thing Lana was ready to do was to roll her eyes at the fact her bosses had come up with another reason to get people trashed and spending money in February.

Apparently, they were debuting a new drink in honor of Lunar New Year, and they seemed gleeful about charging a lot for some cranberry juice, a splash of an alcohol they hadn't been able to move, and one of those little umbrellas. But at least someone sensible had convinced them no one wanted to drink a bright red beer. There was a special menu involving spicy fried chicken wings and soft-shell crab with a batter spun out to look like a dragon—to her it seemed more like a spider, but she wasn't about to say anything about that. She concentrated on her noodles—at least no one had suggested she dip them in gold or something—and tried to avoid thinking about how the smell of the deep fry was going to be really hard to get out of her hair.

But other than that, it was just another work day. Maybe she should be thankful to have a job at all.

Lana half expected Simon to appear at the restaurant tonight. He made it a habit now of showing up at least once a week, usually on a Wednesday. But raising her head and peering into the main room, she could see why he might have chosen to listen to her and skip tonight.

She was tempted to do the same. She kept rolling Hester's offer around in her mind, like a heavy, shining pinball. Maybe if she moved it around long enough, she wouldn't have to make a decision. Then again, she thought, wincing at the crashing sound coming from the front, she was pretty sure she didn't want to stick around Lore to suffer through an Asian Bastille Day.

She watched another elaborate deep fried creation being ferried out, then put her head down and tried to concentrate on her own work. Today people were supposed to eat Long Life noodles, drawing the strands up from a bowl with their chopsticks. The longer the noodle, the longer you lived.

Well, her noodles were a lot of things, but metaphors for life, they were not. Especially not her own existence, which was lumpy and many-stranded and which could definitely not be pulled up from a bowl in a single, smooth movement.

Maybe on her next day off she could make a celebration dinner for Simon. They'd skip the Long Life thing, but she would tell him about the job offer. He'd also clearly had something on his mind for the last few days: determinedly cleaning and trying to be unobtrusive about it, shutting the lid of his computer when she came in the room, or simply observing her.

It made her oddly happy he was keeping a secret from her—from her specifically, a secret that made him grin when she thought he wasn't looking, a secret that made him watch her carefully. He wanted to surprise her and he was terrible at it. Partly because his song choices always gave him away. The other day he'd been smiling to himself and singing "You Did It" from *My Fair Lady* under his breath. This morning while he was cooking eggs, he'd hummed, "Hey, Big Spender."

It was adorable, and later as she left work she couldn't help mentioning it to Julia, who'd called her to wish her a happy new year.

"He's going to propose again!" Julia immediately squealed.

"No."

Was he?

She paused at the entrance of the subway.

It didn't make any sense. After all, they were, as he'd put it so casually and sleepily, on a trial period. He hadn't moved all of his belongings into the apartment. And sure, she hadn't loved the reminder, although later on she'd appreciated it. Because she had to be realistic.

"After the concert he was introducing you to his colleagues. He had his hand on your back. He was looking at you adoringly. That's practically a public declaration."

"We haven't talked about marriage. It sounds romantic but we haven't thought it through. That was part of our problem last time. We ought to be sensible."

"Screw sensible!"

"Aren't you supposed to say something lawyerly like, *You of all people should go into this with your eyes open*, or *Get stuff in writing?*"

"Your eyes are open. Annoyingly so. And besides, your problem last time was that you were doing the same things, and okay, you needed to figure yourself

out. But you did it. And now you have a job and en-
viable muscle tone for a woman your age. Plus, being
sensible isn't passionate or interesting!"

"We're different people now, which is why we have
to talk about it. Plus, we don't have to worry about the
passionate part."

Or about being interesting, considering how curious
people seemed about the two of them.

"Do tell," Julia said. "You never give me any of the
sexy bits. And it sounds like there are plenty of those."

"I'm not saying anything. I refuse to corrupt your
innocent mind in the new year."

"You're making that rule up. There are a lot of rules
for this celebration, but that's not one of them."

"Go to bed, Julia. Happy new year."

"You're no fun. Happy new year."

On the subway ride home, Lana allowed herself the
brief fantasy of marrying him again. Not the ceremony.
They'd gone to City Hall the first time, and then shared
French fries in the park. Simon had to fend off an especially aggressive city squirrel that had developed a taste
for fast food. That had seemed quite romantic enough at
the time, and nothing could touch that memory.

But she could entertain the dream of *being* married
again, of being sure of him, of knowing no matter how
much furniture he had in storage, he wasn't about to
move out. Of someone who might care for her when
she got sick, of having his health insurance. Maybe if
they were together, she could quit Lore and stay in the
city. She wouldn't have to go upstate. She could start
up her own modest restaurant. Or a food truck. And
she could be with him at regular hours. They'd stay in
his bed and sleep-in once in a while. To be well-rested

and have sex? She could so easily slide into the role of faculty wife, attend his concerts. She'd have the right to feel proud of him.

The living room lamps were still on when she got home. When she'd taken off her boots and coat and scarves, she saw why. Simon was sprawled asleep on the couch, the cat tucked beside him. On the counter were covered dishes and two place settings, unlit candles, matches, a bottle of rosé swimming in a bucket of melted ice. She picked up the lids to see what was under them: a glistening filet of salmon with slivers of golden ginger, two small meatballs in a nest of red sauce and pasta, a simple salad.

It was a New Year's meal. This was her surprise. And he'd fallen asleep before he could deliver it.

She should probably put her coat on again and make a lot of noise to wake him and pretend to be astonished. But instead, she sat down gently on the sofa beside him and fitted herself under his arm. His hair was different. Shorter. He'd had it trimmed. She reached up to touch it, and despite the severity and newness of the cut it felt as soft as ever, He didn't wake up. Neither did the cat.

The things she'd dreamed about, the feeling of security—well, she'd been married to him and that hadn't prevented her from doubting herself and him. Now they were unmarried. Curled up underneath his arm, she was aware at that moment she felt more secure right here, right now than she ever had before. And with that realization, she knew she loved him. She didn't *still* love him. She simply loved him, and it was like a new wound on top of the old, a fresh surge of love where there'd been a scar.

All that feeling must have made her twitch. Or maybe

it was the breath that she was struggling to take with this wonderful, horrible realization. Because Simon woke briefly, his long lashes fluttering, special dinner clearly forgotten. He smiled at her as if she'd always been there and pulled them both down in that uncomfortable position on the couch to sleep again.

Simon knew he had a failing—several, actually. But the one most people seemed to focus on was not the fact that he was always the last to get his grades into the system, or that his shirts were perpetually wrinkled, or that he was maybe too hard on his sister.

No, the thing that people became irate about was the fact that he didn't check his messages often enough.

He had a flurry of texts from Maxine, as well as a message or two. Some of them were probably from Ronnie, who now asked constantly for pictures of Muffin. Simon didn't like texting, but he did know how to attach photos. He'd take a few when the cat was asleep, because otherwise she was a scratching, complaining whirlwind. He had a slew of voicemails from unknown numbers that were probably telemarketers. Lately a lot of his calls had been in Mandarin. He also had a couple from Lana.

But he was in a department meeting and couldn't really check the messages now. Of course, being bored by his colleagues' sniping was why he'd found himself glancing at them for the first time today.

He sighed. The New Year's dinner had not gone according to plan. Not only had he failed to stay up, he'd been so deep into sleep he didn't even remember Lana rousing him and leading him to bed, where she hadn't bothered taking off his clothing and had let him curl up into her with his shirt and khakis still on.

It was maybe a little dismaying to find out he didn't look noticeably more rumpled when he'd slept in his clothes. It was, however, very dismaying he and Lana had not managed to have their romantic dinner. They also hadn't managed to talk.

"Simon, do you have anything to add?" Nancy Charles-Dubois, the interim head of the department asked, interrupting his reverie.

Ugh. *Teachers.*

"Nothing at this time. Thanks."

He was full of thoughts, but none to do with the plan for their relocating offices while his floor was being renovated. Luckily, he didn't keep as much there as he did at home, otherwise yet another move in less than three months would have distressed him.

But his thoughts were preoccupied with Lana. When he'd asked her why she hadn't woken him, she'd told him she would've had to prop him up at the table, and he very clearly needed to sleep. And as he yawned his way through the rest of this meeting—his office neighbors were *not* happy with their temporary quarters—he realized Lana was right. He was still exhausted. He checked some of the messages on the way home, but it was windy, and everything sounded garbled, and he was already irritated by his long-winded colleagues, and the fact that Lana was probably already at work, which meant he'd hardly seen her this week, which meant he missed her and—well, that was something to think about later. He was faintly and irrationally annoyed, and tired, and angry with himself that not so long ago he'd have been able to concentrate on his work, make love to Lana, plan and eat late dinners, run, feel sure about his future, not miss his wife when he hadn't seen her for a few hours, and above all, not be tired from missing a couple of weeks of sleep.

He fell into bed almost as soon as he got home and woke up late at night, disoriented. Lana wasn't home yet.

He got the sudden urge for a strong cup of coffee. He could still drink at all hours, couldn't he? After this night, he felt like he had to prove it. But his frankly terrible single cup coffee maker wasn't what he wanted. He had the sudden longing for one of those thick Turkish coffees in a small cup. He hadn't had one for months, not since he'd moved, and he decided he'd make the coffee and stay up with Lana and make her something to eat if she needed something. They could talk and it would sort of make him feel better about how Lunar New Year had turned out.

The Turkish coffee maker was behind this teapot that had been a wedding gift. He was sure Lana and he never used it, but Lana recognized it the minute she'd opened the cabinet. He'd kept it all these years, and he wasn't sure why he had bothered unboxing it to bring to this new place. Optimism, he supposed. Maybe he'd imagined they could sip tea together because she was off coffee nowadays. Plus, tea seemed to imply the kind of hands off, formal relationship he'd envisioned with her. But of course, they never drank tea and they'd definitely not kept their hands to themselves, and what they shared most often was water from the same glass that he brought to her in bed after they'd been kissing and fucking and whispering to each other in the night.

They'd put the teapot on a high shelf. It would be safer there, he'd reasoned. Now it was in his way.

He reached up, just able to feel the cold handle of the coffee maker. If he could move the teapot's spout sideways he'd be able to—and with a crash the surprisingly heavy piece of crockery fell, bouncing off the edge of the cabinet where it still seemed miraculously whole, and then when he unthinkingly reached out to grab it with both his hands in a last-ditch attempt to save it, it fell apart under his palms, the body of it disintegrating as it shattered into the dish rack in a pile of shards.

He stood there a minute and let the adrenaline course through him before he unbent his fingers. At least he hadn't cut himself.

God, he was stupid. He could've hurt his hands trying to catch it. He might have brained himself trying to get it down in the first place. And now he was going to have to clean the dishes it had fallen into, the counter, and the floor.

He picked gingerly through the clean plates and cups to see if the teapot had broken any of the other glassware in the rack. Miraculously, it seemed it hadn't.

Fuck.

He took another minute to breathe.

When Lana returned home, he was still cleaning.

He heard her come through the door in a rush, straight to the kitchen where the light was on.

"Good, you're still up," she said coming straight into the kitchen.

She looked worried and tired. He noted that she'd come into the kitchen without taking off her jacket and scarves and bag. She'd kicked her boots off, though.

"I'm sorry," he said, holding up the two fragments he'd just found.

"No, I'm sorry," she said, pulling the hat off her head and shaking out her hair. "I feel like this is all my fault."

"How could it be? I'm the one who was careless."

She'd been preoccupied with putting down her bag and unwinding her outer scarf, and she frowned up at him.

"I shouldn't have unpacked it," he said. "I knew we wouldn't use it. But I'm sure I can replace it by tomorrow. We'd probably be able to find another on eBay."

She stared at him. "There's no point in replacing it, not right away."

"Well, it's not urgent but you loved it and—"

"Simon, haven't you gotten any of the messages?"

She was still in her jacket. He wanted to take it off her shoulders, but for some reason he felt like she wanted him to touch her. Instead, he looked down at the two shards in his hands. "What do you mean?"

She huffed out a breath. Was she irritated or was she sad? Either way, once again, he was having to catch up with her on bad news. "Our landlord. Raoul? The one in New Zealand? He says he's selling the apartment. We're being evicted."

He blinked. He understood all the words, but together they didn't make any sense. He stared at the pieces of crockery in his hands and for a moment thought about how they'd never fit together again. "But he said we'd have at least a year. He told us he'd be coming back. This was supposed to be a temporary job."

"He got an offer on the apartment he couldn't refuse. From the downstairs neighbor. She wants to restore the whole house to its original glory."

"What original glory? Is she going to rip out all the plumbing and heating and put in lead pipes? Move in a bunch of cats and trash?"

His voice had become too loud. He could tell from the way she narrowed her eyes and winced. But he was frustrated and tired and the only sleep he'd gotten lately had been at the expense of a dinner he'd planned with the help of two of his interns who weren't paid for that sort of thing, and that he'd cooked and let congeal while he snored on the couch. And all he wanted was to simply settle down in this apartment he loved with this woman he loved, and he couldn't even spend one god-damn minute of peace with her before he broke things and was kicked out.

"I've already moved once in the last few months. Isn't that enough for one decade? I hate change. I hate it."

Something like frustration flashed across her face, but her tone remained patient. "I know."

He was behaving badly, and he couldn't help but agree that Lana was right for getting annoyed with him.

"If you'd checked your messages—"

"You're blaming me?"

"No, of course not. But at least I wouldn't have to deal with you being this way after a long night if you did."

She turned away.

God dammit.

He watched her shoulders go up and down. She was tired, and she'd had to sit with this knowledge this whole time, and he hadn't made it any better for her. Instead, he'd yelled and it wasn't even her fault. He was an asshole.

An about-to-be-homeless asshole.

"I'm sorry," he said.

He finally put the fragments down and moved toward her. He pulled her to him and she came willingly into his arms. He kissed her forehead and her cheek, and her chin, and unzipped her jacket and unknotted the scarf around her neck.

"I'm sorry I wasn't better at checking my messages and that I got angry—"

"You're allowed to be annoyed. I was."

"But there's a place and time and you're already stressed enough."

He pulled the jacket off her arms and hastily put it on the counter behind him without turning around, then he ran his hands up and down her body as if to check for injuries, to make sure she was still here and intact and he hadn't done some other damage through his carelessness. The important thing was that she was still with him, after all.

This had been the best thing to come out of moving. They'd gotten together again because of this apartment—and that's why he loved it, and why he didn't want to leave it.

"Maybe we could buy it," he said aloud. "I wonder how much the downstairs neighbor paid for it. Maybe I could ask Raoul if he'd consider another offer. How far along is the sale? I mean, even if they're in contract—"

"We're not going to be able to buy it, Simon."

"I have savings, and I'm sure that you—"

"No. I don't have any money, really, Simon. Not that kind. I could never afford this neighborhood."

He pulled her in again, he sighed. "Who'd have thought all those years ago that Central Harlem would turn into a hot zone? I guess it was always beautiful, though." He smiled ruefully. "But now a bunch of gentrifying jerks like us figured it out."

"Like us," she agreed, her voice muffled.

He took a deep breath. Concentrate on Lana, on their new relationship. That was more than enough to give him strength.

At least he hadn't moved all of his stuff in. "How long do we have?"

"Around two months."

"So it's not that bad. We have some time to find another place, hopefully in this neighborhood."

Chapter Fifteen

This was the moment to tell Simon—no, talk to him about it.

It was the worst time.

"I don't know if I can stay here, in the city, I mean."

Lana pulled back to look at his face. He was confused, but that wasn't even the worst—they hadn't gotten to the hardest part yet.

"What do you mean? Oh, is it about not being able to afford rent? That doesn't matter to me. I can probably afford it. Or we could try another neighborhood. But we can—" He stopped for the first time to look at her. To really look at her. "*If* we're together…"

He held her gaze and said, "We are together, aren't we?"

"I want us to be."

He stepped back. His hands left her arms slowly, as if he were already letting go. "But?"

She tried to swallow the rising panic in her throat. She hadn't said anything and already she didn't like the way Simon was taking this. "But. I was offered a job, a little upstate, at a cooking school."

Her breath was too loud in the silent kitchen.

"You want to go back to teaching?"

"It's not quite that. I don't know how much longer I can keep up with the restaurant job. It's not because of the endometriosis. It hasn't stopped me before. I've worked through it. But I'm getting older and slower. And the kids who are doing this, they're so young. They can take the long hours, and they stay on their feet, and they can cope with…with the constant stress. This job, it has better benefits. It means regular hours. No more night work. And I can still practice my craft. I can still learn and teach and do what I want to do."

"You can teach. You want to go back to teaching. Well, you could've stayed in school if you wanted to do that? Why didn't you finish your degree? Why didn't you—"

Why didn't you stay with me?

"It's not the same, Simon."

He gave a short laugh. "It feels the same. No, it feels worse. Because I knew this would happen. Because Maxine warned me and I was stupid and I fell for it again. I fell for you. I love you, and you don't love me enough. Again."

She struggled to talk at a moment when she really needed him to understand. "Simon, I loved you then and I love you now, but we can do something different this time. I love what you've become, what you've done with your life and we can work with this. I wouldn't be so far from the city. Hester says on a good day, you can get into Manhattan in an hour and a half. I could get a car with the money I save on living here. We could have weekends. I'd actually have Saturdays and Sundays free sometimes! Or you could come with me."

His mouth pressed in a tight line. "I am not going

anywhere upstate. I'm not moving again. My entire life is here."

Her shoulders drooped. "I know. And you've worked hard for it."

"I have."

"But what about weekends? And now it's easier to stay in touch. We can Skype and my hours are going to be like yours."

He was shaking his head, not looking at her. "These things never work, Lana. I've seen this with my colleagues. They get married, and then they reside in different states—"

"It's the same state!"

"And after a couple of years, they get divorced. I guess I should thank you because at least you left before we could try out something that untenable. Saved me a lot of time."

"You're being unfair."

She couldn't help it. He'd retreated to the far end of the kitchen. He was gripping the edge of the counter. And she was still standing in the middle, under the light, barely able to keep her hands from reaching out to him.

"Am I being unfair?"

He wouldn't look at her.

"Back then, it wasn't about you at all, Simon. I asked you to leave with me. I had to find something else to do with my life. I was suffocating."

"You're saying *I* was suffocating you."

"You aren't listening, I was trying to be someone who I wasn't! I needed to find the thing I wanted to do, because being the person I thought everyone else wanted me to be was killing me."

"And it turns out that what everyone else wanted you to be was a teacher, which is what you want to do now."

"You keep making this the same thing when it's different. *I've* changed and you have, too, even if you think you're not. I thought you saw how much I'd grown, and were happy about it. You seemed excited I'd learned new skills, that I'd found a thing I was capable of doing better. But maybe I'm wrong."

She was furious at him, so angry and so mixed up in her ball of love and frustration and hurt. She'd handled this badly. Was there another way? It didn't matter. She had to focus. She didn't want to let him go, the fucker. She refused to let go without a real fight this time, because this time she was stronger. She didn't want him to be hurt, or worried, but goddamn him for being stubborn and hurt and worried. "Things do not have to end between us. I love you."

"Well, I love you more than I thought possible. I love you and can you blame me for not being happy at the idea of being separated from you, because now I know what it's like to have you back in my life?"

He turned around. He couldn't even face her. "I'm an idiot."

"No. Simon."

"How can I help loving you? But it doesn't do me much good, does it? You know, all those things you worry about, if you'd just asked me I could give them to you. I'm not rich or anything, but we could have health insurance. You wouldn't have to work. But you'd rather swing noodles around."

"My work is not swinging noodles around any more than yours is telling teens to sing pretty songs."

She tried to make herself sound softer. Calmer. But

the frustration cracked through each syllable. "I am asking you to try and work this through. I wanted you to do that back then, too. We have more now. Simon, we could make this work if you'd just try."

"No, you're asking me to change who I am."

"If that's true, then you're demanding the same of me."

She wanted to sink down onto the kitchen floor. Her legs were strong. She'd run miles and miles over the years. She was so much more than the last time she'd faced Simon down. Her back, her entire core, had been strengthened with constant work. Her arms were full of muscles she hadn't even known she possessed. She could make things. She'd fashioned her own life on her own terms. But right now, those legs and arms felt numb and weak. She knew they would haul her up again eventually. They didn't want to do it right now.

It would have been so easy to take him up on his offer, to have him carry her.

It was past midnight. She was tired and heartsick, and she could see from the bowed lines of his back that he felt the same. But his voice, when he spoke again, was unwavering. "You're right, Lana. It's not like last time. Now we're older. We're supposed to have learned our lessons. At least last time, I had a place to stay when you left me. At this point, you want to leave again, you want to live away from me, but I have to haul up my life and find somewhere to make my home, too. The only thing that's changed is this time you didn't make any promises."

For a moment, Simon thought he felt terrible because he'd woken and Lana's warm body wasn't nestled into his. The scent of her hair wasn't tickling his nose.

Then he remembered he was going to have to get used to it. Again.

He wasn't sure how long he'd slept. But it was Saturday. He didn't have any classes, so he hadn't set an alarm.

He heard a knock on his door. It was Lana, fully dressed. "I'm sorry. I'm sorry to bother you. I just—have you seen Muffin?"

Of all the things he expected her to ask, that wasn't one of them.

"I'm sorry I woke you. I didn't know you were still here until I saw your shoes. But I can't find her and I realized I haven't seen her since yesterday afternoon. Maybe even before then."

Lana was worried. His first instinct was to get up and pull her into his arms, but he held back, and it hurt like the pain he'd felt the time he'd broken his ribs and he'd tried to suppress a laugh or a sneeze. Except now when he breathed the desire out of him, even when he relaxed his arms, the band around his chest didn't let up.

So instead he tried to be logical. "I haven't seen her since…"

He couldn't remember.

"She hasn't eaten her food from yesterday. And I've looked everywhere. Even tried to move the fridge."

"I can check behind there for you."

"I'm bad at this. I'm a bad cat mom."

"That's not true. Cats are wily and they disappear sometimes. I'll search my room and a few other places. She can't have gone far."

He didn't know why he was offering to help. He had things to do. He probably had to pack up his office. And this apartment.

No, he knew why. It was because he was now worried about the cat, too. And because Lana was beating herself up. He'd never even known she wanted a pet before.

"You don't have to. It's my cat."

"Lana. Just go. You have to get to work about now. I'll search for her, and I'll text you when I find her. All right?"

"All right. I'm sorry."

"Stop apologizing, please."

She turned back. "Well, I am sorry, and I am going to say it. But I am not about to apologize for wanting to do my work and looking at taking care of my future. I told myself I would ask you to figure it out with me, even if it was hard, even if you were angry. I love you. And I am sorry you're hurting. I am sorry that you won't think about it. And I'm sorry you have to look for my jerky cute cat who I also love."

She was gripping the doorframe but whether it was to keep herself from coming in or going out he didn't know.

He had one single slicing moment of sympathy. This was painful for her, too. It had been difficult for her to knock on his door. It was an effort for her to ask for everything she'd ever asked of him.

And why was that?

Had he made it so hard?

But Lana turned, and in a minute he could almost hear the thumps and rustles of her routine: the scarves, the zip of her jacket. He could almost smell her shampoo as she turned around one last time and closed the door. He wasn't going to be able to have that small joy for much longer.

Had he ever really had it?

It was only then he got up, sweeping the room with his eyes for signs of the cat before going to brush his teeth.

Well, Muffin was his cat, too, in a way. He fed her, cleaned out her litter, and talked to her, and maybe spent a lot of time every day trying to interest her in a crinkle ball when he should have been doing other things. She curled into him when he read on the couch, and sat on the piano purring whenever he tried out a new arrangement, not minding all of his starting and stopping and swearing. He hadn't known how much he'd enjoy her company until Lana had adopted her.

How much was he missing by following his own long-established path?

No, people shouldn't think that way. Besides, Lana would probably take Muffin and Ronnie would be sad he wasn't sending pictures anymore. Or would his niece simply forget and skip off, not even momentarily puzzled when she learned she'd lost an aunt and an animal? Would it matter to her?

He ate a piece of toast standing up over the sink and looked over at the untouched cat food bowl. Dammit. Something really had happened to the cat. There was no way it was afternoon and there was this much food left. Lana was going to be devastated if he couldn't find her.

He dropped the rest of the toast in the garbage and checked under the sink to be sure. He looked behind the fridge, even though he was sure that Lana had already done that.

He eyed the unusable fireplace and stuck his head in it. It seemed safely sealed and painted. He looked in the bathroom, the duct behind the washer-dryer, or where he supposed a duct like that was likely to be because he'd heard of cats who got stuck trying to crawl into those kinds of things. The machine only had a water hose, and he doubted the cat had anything to do with that.

This was worrying.

Lana had had all morning to search and she hadn't turned up anything. She'd probably wanted to wake him to rifle through his room. And even though he tried to tell himself he had good reason, he was mad at himself for sleeping so long.

He checked his bedroom again, even poking the pillows he'd slept on, as if expecting the cat to pop out covered in stuffing with a malicious grin on her face. The jerk.

He peered in his small closet, poking amongst the shirts, always the same blue and white shirts. He stood on a chair to check the shelves.

Nothing.

Maybe they'd accidentally let the cat slip out the door when one of them had opened it. Muffin was uncurious, for a cat, but of course thinking that would have made him and Lana careless.

He got dressed, and headed out, first walking to the top of the stairs, inspecting every dark corner of the staircase for what? Pawprints? He was a city person. He knew which trees not to stand under so he wouldn't get pooped on by pigeons, not how to track wildlife. And Lana had actually offered to bring him upstate? She thought he'd be able to survive outside of New York. Although admittedly, an hour-and-a-half's drive didn't sound very far.

Maybe he should look for scratch marks, or holes where a small cat could slip in for a nap. Or if he was lucky, he'd find a large neon sign that said, MUFFIN WAS HERE with an arrow pointing down to Muffin neatly caught in a cat carrier.

That didn't happen.

He walked downstairs and knocked on the doors of his neighbors. But neither of them was home.

What now?

Time to check the rest of the neighborhood, then.

He was aware he probably had other things to do: marking, a couple of arrangements that he'd book-marked to check out for the choir, another grant update to write. He should probably follow up with the board to see if they'd had any word. Oh right, and there was the book he had been trying to write for a year now.

None of it was as important as this.

He went out the door and inspected the bushes. He walked around the garbage area and lifted up the cans as if expecting to find Muffin asleep inside with a fish skeleton in her mouth, like some sort of cartoon cat. Nothing.

"Muffin," he called half-heartedly, realizing that even if she heard it she was unlikely to respond to her name.

He widened his search, walking down the street, checking discreetly in bushes, and inside gates and bins.

The street was quiet. A few sparrows hopped along the sidewalks in search of crusts and crumbs. A couple of men chatting on the corner said hello. As he passed he asked them if they'd seen the cat. Their noses crin-kled sympathetically as they shook their heads.

He didn't want to leave this neighborhood. He was going to have to figure out how to stay here somehow.

Over there under the awning of the salon, he and

Lana had paused to kiss that night they got back together. At the opposite corner was a deli where they
played merengue, and when he'd mentioned something
about one of the songs the counter guy had given him
a CD he'd recorded himself.

He walked around the neighborhood as if he were on
a farewell tour of all the nooks and crannies, and then
he bought himself a cup of coffee and a sandwich, sat
down to eat it, and thought about how he'd sat in a cafe
looking out the window with Lana when he'd first en-
countered her again after so many years.

He'd been so sure he'd gotten over her then. Maybe
he had.

What was it to get over someone? If it meant he
stopped thinking about her every day, then he had. He'd
been able to remember her without pain for a long time.
He'd gotten to the point where he could recall happy
moments without bitterness, like the way she'd start
humming a tune while washing the dishes and he'd
harmonize until the dishes were forgotten and they'd
stand there with soapy hands singing to each other. If
he'd been able to think of her with fondness, that meant
he'd been over it. But last night had showed him that
wasn't true, hadn't it?

It was stupid to be angry over this.

He walked around aimlessly and without a plan, his
thoughts circling back to how Lana was going to be
hurt because he'd failed. Again.

His toes felt cold by the time he plodded back home.
For the first time, the iron railing, the stoop, and the
handsome, solid door failed to cheer him. He'd started
on the steps when Mrs. Pierre appeared.

There was Muffin, in his downstairs neighbor's arms, purring.

The little asshole—the cat, not the neighbor.

Relief swamped him. The only thing preventing him from snatching Muffin from Mrs. Pierre's arms was his desire to call Lana and shout out his relief and triumph. Not that she'd be able to pick up. Besides, he realized right then that he was going to have to be thankful for Mrs. Pierre, the person who'd bought their apartment from Raoul.

Her smooth, brown face was stretched in a welcoming smile. "Is this your cat? I found her out on my ledge early this morning, but she wouldn't come in. I had to lure her with some tuna, but even then she was pretty suspicious until after she'd eaten. What a good kitty she is."

Muffin gazed smugly at Simon through half-closed eyes.

"I can't thank you enough for finding her. My— Lana is going to be so relieved. We've had an eventful twenty-four hours."

Simon held out his arms, but Mrs. Pierre didn't seem quite ready to cede the cat. "I had a kitten like her a few years ago. Quite an escape artist, but she was such a purr-monster."

"Ah, we haven't experienced a lot of her cheer so far."

"She's got it in her. Haven't you?"

Mrs. Pierre still had a soft smile on her face. She wasn't thinking of it, of how she'd upended his life, a life he'd only had a chance to love for a brief time. Why did she even need the upstairs? She was a single, older woman, as far as he could tell. It wasn't as if she had a growing family.

"I heard from Raoul about the sale," he said a little abruptly.

"Oh, yes! I'm so happy."

There was not a cloud in her face. What did he expect from her? Guilt? Apologies? But she was scratching Muffin under the chin, and the cat was loving every minute of it. When Mrs. Pierre stopped for a second, Muffin thrust her tiny head under her hand again.

"It's my daughter and her kids. They're moving back to the city and they want to be close by. She looked around for a bit, but the market is hard, you know. Well, I told myself, what can be closer than upstairs? So I asked Raoul if he'd be willing to do this for me, to sell, not expecting him to say yes. And miracle of miracles, he agreed."

Mrs. Pierre laughed, and the sheer joy and relief in it made Simon realize he was being a self-involved asshole. Yes, he wasn't pleased to have to pack up his belongings again, but he'd done it a few months ago, and it had been the best thing that happened in a long time. He didn't want to make a habit of jumping from apartment to apartment, sure, but he'd clung to his old place, his old ways, his old life and thoughts for too long. And Lana had seen that.

He'd even *expected* to move again. After all, wasn't that what their agreement had been? Didn't he still have a chunk of his belongings in storage? If it hadn't worked out in four months, one of them would have had to go anyway.

But it had worked out.

"It's too bad you kids will have to find a new place, but it's harder to move an old body like mine. And I can't pass up the chance to be with my loved ones after so long."

Mrs. Pierre smiled so sweetly at him. She hadn't intended to upend his life. She'd found and fed Muffin, and Muffin was the only thing that could make Lana happy right now. Certainly not his selfish ass.

It was difficult and unreasonable to be mad at his neighbor, to be mad at Lana. All they'd done was ask for what they wanted.

Maybe it was time he sat down and asked himself what he really wanted, too.

Chapter Sixteen

When Lana got home that night, she was met with a familiar sight. The lights were on. There was a pot and two place settings on the counter. And Simon and the cat were sprawled on the couch. Asleep.

She wanted to curl up with both of them, to hold on to them. But she didn't have that right with Simon, and the cat would be grumpy. Simon had texted her after he'd found her. He'd taken her to the vet. She was no worse for her adventure, but Muffin was better off asleep with Simon.

All Lana had done was lose her. Lose them both. She felt sorry for herself, and she supposed she was allowed to wallow in five damn minutes of self-pity in her life. She was tempted to put her things away quietly and go back to her room and hide and sleep. It wouldn't have been out of character. She was irresponsible: inattentive of her pet, unmindful of her health, careless with Simon's feelings, with her own.

No, that's what years-ago Lana would have said about herself.

She took a deep breath.

The cat was fine. She'd even had an adventure. Simon would survive. After all, he'd gotten over her once and thrived. Demanding he come with her was asking him to change, and it wasn't her right. She should never have asked him to live with her, never have contacted him again. How could she have thought that a silly set of rules would protect them?

It was done, and she was still alive. She had made the right choices, and she had to honor the hard work she'd put into her career, her hands, her brain, her life. She'd hoped Simon would want that, because it was what she'd become. But it was not to be.

She stood up straight, not that anyone was awake to see her. And because she couldn't help herself, she lifted the lid of the pot. A squash soup—butternut or pumpkin—bright and warm, spiced with curry. The next little bowl held chopped cilantro. A small loaf of bread sat to the side.

"You should have woken me."

Simon was up and next to her, close but not touching. His short hair was rumpled and his shirt—well, it looked the same. He smelled faintly of the curry he'd been cooking.

She wanted to dip her head toward him and sniff him. No, she wanted to bury her face in his shoulder and never stop leaning on him. But she had to stand firm. It was what she'd chosen, and she'd go by that. Besides, he was holding himself stiffly. So she crossed her arms in front of her and straightened her spine.

"What's this about?" she asked, pointing her chin toward the food.

"I wanted to apologize."

He didn't look very apologetic. The words seemed to emerge unwillingly out of his tight jaw, and he looked anywhere but at her. She wanted to fling those reluctant words in his stupid, beautiful face.

Except. He was almost vibrating. She could see it in the tension in his hands, the slight tremble of his fingers as he brought them forward, then down.

Always follow a conductor's hands.

When she finally searched his face, it wasn't anger, it was…fear? Well, she understood that all too well.

"What's this about?" she repeated more softly.

He glanced over at the food. "Maybe we should sit."

They settled opposite each other at the counter. Muffin circled Lana's legs curiously, as if she hadn't scared the living daylights out of both of them.

He cleared his throat. "So I have this whole speech planned out. And this food. I'm sorry it isn't what you're used to, and you're probably tired after a long day."

"It's good, Simon. It smells delicious. Thank you. People hardly ever cook for me and you've done it twice, no, three times."

He ladled out the soup. "Well, the Lunar New Year dinner didn't exactly work out the way I envisioned it. I wanted to surprise you. I hoped to make you happy, to make you laugh. Instead I always seem to be asleep for the important parts. Or I haven't checked my messages, and I'm oblivious to the important things that happen to you, and to me. I don't want to miss everything that matters."

Lana was holding her breath, watching Simon's face—she didn't know how to describe it—was it falling? Maybe it was just loosening, as if all the tension and fight and fear started to unspool.

She gripped her spoon and tried to control her sudden rush of hope. Because even if Simon apologized,

if he still loved her, if he soothed her, it still wouldn't
necessarily be right for her, or for them.

She cleared her throat and poked at the swirls of
cream and squash in her soup. "Thank you for looking
for Muffin. For finding her."

"It wasn't me. It was our downstairs neighbor, Mrs.
Pierre. She's the one who's buying this apartment."

"Oh." She pursed her mouth. "I guess I'll have to
thank her, too."

Simon laughed, just a short bark that startled her
(and the cat) into realizing how quiet it had been. The
sound was so unexpected and welcome that she started,
to her horror, to cry.

Fuck. Fuck. Fuck.

She'd made it so far without shedding tears, and now
she was going to break down in front of this man.

She stumbled off the stool to flee the room, but
Simon caught her, he held her, and for one moment,
she allowed herself to lean into him, to sob on him,
even if it was about him, before pulling back.

Dammit, she couldn't stop crying. Her valve was
broken.

"Lana. Please. I'm sorry."

Simon's voice was frantic. Through her tears, she
could see the watery outlines of his arms reaching for
her—just short of her—but she'd pulled away, and he
was trying to respect that.

She felt his hands again briefly as he pressed a napkin into her hands. Cloth, she registered dimly—*fancy*,
the part of her that wasn't crying said—before she buried her face in it and wiped her eyes and nose, her
cheeks and even her chin. And she wondered if she was
going to have to wear the damn thing for the rest of her

life, because she couldn't face him after this. After all the shit they'd said to each other, all the things they'd done, she'd lost it because his laugh had startled her, and because she'd miss it.

"Lana," he said, softly, "are you going to look up again?"

"Probably not," she said. "I hope this napkin goes with my hair, because I'm not taking it off."

The line would have been funnier if her voice weren't broken and hoarse. Somehow, she sensed Simon's third meal for her was probably not going to work out exactly as he'd planned either. She gave another little sob-hiccup into the damp cloth.

"Lana, Lana, sweetheart. I love you."

"I know," she blubbered. "It makes you unhappy."

"No, it doesn't. I'm the idiot making me and you feel bad."

She lifted her eyes and saw his hands were hovering over her, never quite touching her, so close, but not quite there. It may have been her own blurry eyes, but he seemed to be teary, too.

She dropped the napkin and reached for him. He took her hands. Together they touched his wet cheeks. She felt his stubble, the small grooves of worry so close to the laugh lines.

"Lana, I want to do this. I want to move with you. If you want that."

"But your work. Your life. I don't understand."

Abruptly he let go. "I found some apps!" he said excitedly, showing her his phone.

It was not what she'd expected him to say.

"I saved all of these listings. Did you know we could buy an entire house with bedrooms, and an office for me, and a real dining room, and the mortgage would be less than rent? Like this place here? All these beautiful old floorboards and these huge windows. I can see the piano going in this room where I could work. And yeah, the kitchen needs updating, but that would be a fun project to try. Look, it's even got an herb garden out back. And a chicken coop. Although I don't know how Muffin would handle a bunch of hens."

She watched helplessly as he scrolled through photos and listings. Until he looked up again. He seemed to remember himself. "I do steamroll over people," he said, worriedly.

"Sometimes."

"But this is all up to you. We can figure out where we want to live and divide finances. Or maybe you don't want to live with me at all, which is up to you, of course. Or there's this place I found which has an upstairs apartment and a downstairs. Or—"

He stopped.

She said gently, "I want to live with you. And I love these houses and all the work you did. But what happened to your entire life being here?"

"It's not really true that all of it has to stay in New York. Not anymore."

"Are you sure? Because I'll worry about it if you give up too much of you for me. I love you and I want to be with you, but that's not an easy thing. I want to be an important part of your life, but I can't be your everything."

He was shaking his head and kissing her hands as she spoke. "It's because you're already an important part of my life, Lana. Being with you, seeing what you've done, has taught me that I can have more of everything. It doesn't have to be limited to what I have right now. You make me want to want more. You make me brave enough to ask for more, even if it means asking it of myself."

His words were slowly starting to penetrate. She felt herself vibrating. Was this what Simon was feeling? It must be, because her own heart was bursting with possibility.

He touched her hair now, gently, and it was a question. "You've changed a lot. Well, I've changed, too, only I didn't realize it. The list of things I aspired to when I was in my twenties doesn't have to be the same as what I look forward to now. In fact, it shouldn't be. I should have new goals, new ideas of where I want to go. I'm not going to lie, I'll have difficulty with adjusting to new things sometimes, but I need to try."

"But I still don't understand what you'll do with the chorus and your job and, well, everything?"

He laughed, and she felt it again, that ache, almost a loss, almost hope. She pressed her hand to her chest, and his fingers followed and closed around hers.

He stared at where their hands were joined. "I'm going to do the same things. I'll shift my teaching around so that I do it only two or three days of the week and fit rehearsals on those days, too. We got more money from the grantors, by the way—"

"Simon, that's wonderful."

"That means I can give Abena a bigger stipend to step up as the conductor of the chorus, with Dion as her assistant. I'll still be there to put my oar in, but I've been evolving into a different role for a while. It isn't perfect. I'm going to have a long commute, and sometimes I'll have to stay in the city overnight. On the other hand, all the train time means I can work, do my grading, and write this book I've been putting off."

She stood on tiptoe and kissed his chin, his lips. "Maybe you don't want to write this book."

"Could be. And perhaps this new town will give me some space to figure out if that's what I want to do."

He looked down at her, his eyes shining and eager. And while there was still so much of that energetic young man in him, the person he was now, the person he'd become, was the one she loved.

She knew what she wanted to do. She pulled him down, her fingers sliding through his short hair, down his neck, where she could still feel the pulse of tension, the uncertainty. This was new for him, new for both of them, but his eyes looking into hers were sure. He was ready, and that was all that mattered right now.

They kissed each other slowly, leisurely. Now they knew they wouldn't be apart, and she could savor the warmth of his palms on her elbows, gentle on the soft skin of her arms.

He groaned. "I love you. You know I love you, don't you?"

"And I love you."

She watched him move up slowly. She helped him take off her T-shirt and trace his hands along her rib cage, then under her breasts until he abruptly pulled the cups of her bra up and over her head.

He slid his hands down her jeans next, and she helped him by unzipping herself and stumbling out, laughing a little as she kicked them aside. Then she was bare to him and cold. "Take off your clothing," she breathed.

He tore his shirt off, getting briefly tangled in the buttons, and pulled off the rest in a few quick movements.

There they were, naked in front of each other, wanting each other after all these years.

She knelt down. "Lana," he groaned as her breasts slid down along his thighs. She adjusted her own knees on the hard kitchen floor and ran her palms up his legs, pressing herself to him. She liked feeling the wiry hair against her nipples, against her stomach. She drew her hand up along the tensed muscle, so hard now, waiting for her, and up to his cock. Carefully, carefully she slid her fingers over it, then breathed and licked him, smacked her lips, and filled her mouth with him.

He was moaning, holding her head, trying to gentle her, telling her to be patient, saying the same to himself. But she wanted the fullness of him, every overwhelming experience. She was hungry for him, and the ache between her own legs intensified enough that she tried to seek some sort of relief, pushing her body against his legs as she sucked, rubbing herself up and down.

It was too much for him. He peeled her off his body and cleared a spot for her on the counter where he set her down decisively. The stone felt hard and chilly, and she cringed from it even as she was stuck to it. But he'd put his forehead on hers and was breathing hard, trying to take a moment. They both needed it.

"I have to go get a condom," he said thickly.

"I think I'll be okay without one, if you are."

His nostrils flared, and he nodded. Then, as they both looked down, he put his hands under her to cradle her from the cold of the granite. It was only his palms, but it made all the difference. She felt supported.

She pulled him closer, as close as he could get, and they both watched as she took him in, letting them both adjust to this heat, this feeling. Her arms closed around his solid form. His lips met hers. And for a moment, they were still. They kissed, their heads dipping and bending until their bodies began to move, slowly, awkwardly, and she felt the pleasure making her body supple and warm and wet. She rocked into him, enjoying his harsh gasps, her palms moving restlessly up and down his back to urge on the flex and thrust of his muscles.

His own hands moved up until his fingers dug into her hips, his thumbs so deep in her flesh that she felt it almost on her bone. The press of him seemed so good and wild.

The insides of her thighs became slippery now, and she arched up grunting, past the point of caring, and then as the release started to throb out of her, he was coming inside her in a hot rush, and she was open wide, her heart and throat and legs and chest a pulse of bright red pleasure.

Then Simon was leaning on her. Or she was sagging against him. They held each other up, still panting, maybe laughing or crying with relief.

After a minute, he murmured into her hair. "I don't think I can move. Except I'm going to have to because my legs feel weak."

He pulled out from her, and helped her down from the counter. They held each other for a moment. Then she headed for the bathroom, and he turned to clean up and put on some clothes. Within half an hour, they were back in his bed—their bed—warm and sleepy. The rest of their plans could wait until morning.

Lana was about to drift off when a thought made her head pop up from the pillow. "Again, we didn't get to eat that beautiful dinner you made."

Simon laughed quietly and pulled her close. "It'll keep."

Epilogue

They held their housewarming on the Sunday of Labor Day weekend, in the big backyard of their new up-state home, under the shade of crabapple trees which had already begun to yield small, sour fruits that Lana and Hester were scheming to turn into wine when the time came.

They'd made a brisket outside in the barbecue, and everyone brought more and more food. By late afternoon, the buzz of chatter between Lana's and Simon's colleagues, Abena, Hester, Dion, Julia, Maxine, mingled with the perfume of smoke and flowers and herbs. Ronnie and a couple of kids darted around, chasing Hester's dog. Two picnic tables groaned with platters of fried dumplings, pungent mustard greens tossed with ginger and sesame oil, summer rolls with mint and cucumbers and slippery noodles and peppers, spicy chicken wings, macaroni and cheese, meatballs, sweet Taiwanese sausages, and beef hot dogs for the kids, yeasty rolls and breads, a salad redolent with summer herbs, and fresh corn from a local farm stand. And then there were the pies Julia had insisted on making early this morning, the piles of berries with a bowl of lemon crème fraîche that Simon would happily have spooned down his throat, and a big tres leches cake that people protested was too sweet and rich, even as they helped themselves to larger and larger wedges through the evening.

It was, Simon reflected as he stood on his back porch, surveying the crowd of friends new and old, pretty much a perfect day.

As if in response, Maxine sidled up, and slid her arm into his, imprisoning him in her loving grip. "Where's your wife?"

"Not my wife. Lana's inside mixing more sangria."

"You two should get married again."

Simon rolled his eyes. He'd been hearing clunky variations on this theme all weekend from her. At least she and Ronnie would be flying back tomorrow.

"If we decide to get married again, I'll let you know. But moving and owning a house together pretty officially says that we don't want to be apart again."

"But—"

He untangled himself from his sister, and shook his head. "For someone who was against us getting involved after all that time, you sure are pushing it."

"Because I know when I'm wrong, and I support you."

"Is bossing a way of expressing support?"

"In our family it is."

He had to laugh because it was true. "I think Dion brought a guitar. Go and sing with them."

Then he turned to go into the house to find Lana.

Lana and Julia had their backs to him, their dark heads bent over the kitchen island as they cut up fruit. He paused at the door to look at Lana, to look at his love.

Her hair was pulled into one of those intricate braids,

ending in a soft curl that he wanted to tease even as it
teased him. His gaze touched her shoulders, the round-
ness of the muscle which he knew would be smooth and
warm under his fingers. She was wearing a sundress
that flared at the hips, and if her cousin weren't there, he
would have come up behind her, and put one hand right
there, where the material puffed out, and bent to kiss
her neck, while with the other hand he'd have reached
under the skirt to caress her knee, her thigh.

Okay, this would be a perfect day if only his guests
would leave.

But Julia was saying laughingly, "I mean it! I feel
like I should move here with a handsome husband and
buy a deceptively gorgeous money pit of a house. We
could get into fights over paint color and the cost of
plumbing and yell at each other about why we're stuck
in the middle of nowhere. And then we could have
makeup sex in front of the non-functioning fireplace."

Without pausing in her chopping, Lana asked her
cousin, "You sure you want to stay a lawyer? Because
you've definitely got a couple of stories in you."

"Lawyer to novelist? Doesn't sound plausible. But
seriously, you seem to be doing great. And Simon is,
too. I'm really surprised he's adjusted so well."

He probably should have made a sound to let them
know he was there.

Lana didn't answer for a while, and just when he felt
himself getting anxious about what she would say, she
spoke again, her voice dreamy, "I don't know what it'll
be like when school really gets busy. But these couple
of months, even with the unpacking and getting lost
and me figuring out my new job and home ownership,
it's been wonderful. Perfect."

He breathed out, relieved to hear his own thoughts echoed.

Lana dropped more fruit in the pitcher. "There are little things. Like he's not the greatest driver, so I end up doing most of it."

He snorted. But it was true. He didn't feel comfortable behind the wheel yet.

"Maybe down the line when we've saved up money, he might get an apartment in Inwood. One of his friends lives in a beautiful old Art Deco building, and apparently there are always units for sale. That way we can stay in the city a couple of nights a week when Simon teaches, or has rehearsals or a concert."

"You'd come with him on those nights?"

"If I'm not very busy, yes. I love being with him. And I love the city. I'm sure I'll miss it."

"And me."

"Yes, I'll miss you, Julia. But you're going to have to leave for me to do that."

Julia turned around and spying him, smirked. "I know my cue."

She picked up the pitcher full of fruit and wine and stuck her tongue out at him as she passed.

Lana was leaning against the counter now. She looked flushed and warm in the worn old kitchen of their funny little house. Her feet were bare, and as he gazed at her, her toes curled. When he looked up, she seemed warily amused, and he knew they were both thinking it wouldn't do to start having sex in the kitchen when they had a yard full of company—much as they wanted to.

Simon stalked toward her nonetheless, not stopping until he was right over her, the hem of her dress billowing around him, her breath wisping down his open collar.

He stroked his hand along her back. "Do you know, I think we've broken a bunch of our house rules. We're having a party. We've got significant guests staying for a long stretch of time."

He put his arm around her and drew her into him.

"A couple of days is not a long stretch of time," she murmured into his neck.

"It is when it's an eight-year-old and my sister. And it must feel considerably longer in cat years."

Muffin, who was currently hiding from Ronnie in one of the upstairs closets, probably agreed.

He said, "It's a good party, but I can't wait for them all to go home and leave us to ours."

They stood that way for a long time, close, but not kissing, touching each other gently, glad to be in this proximity with each other. They would have continued this way, but the sound of a guitar drifted through a window. Then a voice started up with a folk tune he recognized as "I'll Never Find Another You."

"Is that Maxine?" Lana whispered.

"I think it is. I haven't heard her sing in a long time."

She kissed him and craned her neck toward the music. "Let's go out and join everyone."

He didn't want to, he didn't want to change a single thing about this moment. But even as he resisted, he knew he'd be happy out there, too, as long as she was with him.

"Lead the way," he said, letting go, but taking her hand. "I'll always follow."

* * * * *

Acknowledgments

Thanks and love to my editor, Alissa Davis, whose keen eye and enthusiasm have made this series a pleasure to work on. Much gratitude to Kerri Buckley, Stephanie Doig, and the wonderful editorial, marketing, publicity, and subrights teams at Carina. Special shout-out to Deborah Peterson at Dandelion Design and Krista Oliver of the Harlequin Art Department for the amazing covers for the Uptown books. I am also very grateful to Angela James for agreeing to take a chance on these novellas and for giving me the opportunity to work with all of these talented people.

Thanks so much my agent, the tireless Tara Gelsomino. One day I promise I will read and watch everything you recommend. Baby fish mouth *is* sweeping the nation!

Many thanks to Brina Starler for her careful reading of this manuscript. And much love to Amber Belldene for always lending a willing eye.

To my daughter, your faith and enthusiasm mean everything. To my husband, thank you for always being kind, unflappable, and strong.

In a picture of me from when I was two or three, I'm surrounded by the uniform-clad altos and sopranos of the choir my father conducted for more than thirty years. In one way or another, I have always had music around me, and for that I'm very lucky.

Finally, to New York City, where I've lived for most of my adult life, no matter where I end up, this will always be the home of my heart.

About the Author

Ruby Lang is pint-sized, prim, and bespectacled. As Mindy Hung, she wrote about romance novels for *The Toast*. Her work has also appeared in *The New York Times*, *The Walrus*, *Bitch*, and other fine venues. She enjoys running (slowly), reading (quickly), and ice cream (at any speed). She lives in New York with a small child and a *medium-sized husband*.

Ruby is the author of the acclaimed Practice Perfect series. Find out more on her *website* (http://www. rubylangwrites.com). Follow her on *Twitter* (https:// twitter.com/RubeLang) and *Instagram* (https://www. instagram.com/ruby.lang/). Or sign up for Ruby's *newsletter* (http://bit.ly/Rubesletter).